Love, Lies
&
Sticky Toffee
Pudding

KARIN WALKER

POOLBEG

Published 2025 Poolbeg Press Ltd

123 Grange Hill, Baldoyle, Dublin 13, Ireland

E-mail: poolbeg@poolbeg.com. www.poolbeg.com

1

A catalogue record for this book is available from the British Library.

ISBN 978-178199-651-5

www.poolbeg.com

About the Author

Karin was born and raised in Northamptonshire, with a wanderlust burning inside her. With a law degree and a brief career in sales under her belt, she upped sticks and hoofed around the globe for a couple of years, before returning to work in London.

Two children later came a move to Cornwall, which is where she began to write, the one thing that competes with her top three loves – her boys, travel, and bacon sandwiches on white, real butter, naturally.

She now lives on the North Cornwall coast, the perfect home for a pluviophile (rain lover) like her, where she writes, walks, bakes and embarks on adventures of any kind. Anything to stave off the empty nest syndrome snapping at her muddy walking boots. She likes barbeques on the beach, skydiving (she's only done it twice, but it sounds good), and she makes the best chocolate brownies in the world (according to her children).

Acknowledgements

I've dreamed of writing this list of gratitudes for a long time now. It has come a little too late for my beautiful Gran, Marie Aldridge, to read it, but that doesn't lessen my thanks any. From the bottom of my heart, Gran, from somewhere in the middle of the Yellow Brick Road, I thank you, and I love you.

Thank you to my agents, Alison Lindsay and Fiona Lindsay, for being brilliant, for keeping the faith, and for putting up with my ridiculously long emails.

Thanks and appreciation to Paula Campbell, Gaye Shortland and everyone at Poolbeg Press, for everything. I have learned so much.

Thank you to everyone who played a part in helping me bring this book to life, for varying wonderful reasons: Mike Colgrave, Chris Pringle, Jackie Butler, Ginny Sealey, Charlie Hallings-Pott, Kyle Mulligan-Davies, Bruce McDonald, Claire Dean, Judy and Les Collister, Rachel Leigh, Sue Wilson, Julia Knight, Kevin Taz Tasker, and Emma Jane Lee.

Finally, the deepest gratitude to my mum, Jenny Colgrave, for believing in me, loving me, worrying about me, and supporting me, and without whom this book wouldn't have materialised. I love you, Mum. And of course, the hugest thanks to my children, for persistently ridiculing me, for making me laugh more than anyone can, and for being part of the formidable and unbreakable team of three we have created. I love you, my beautiful boys, I do.

Thanks in advance to everyone who reads this book. That alone is a gift to me. But most of all, I hope you find something within it, to take away for you.

Dedication

For Max and Spike.
'Nothing is impossible. My mum says so.'
It's all for you.

xxx

Prologue

Date: Monday, 12 Feb 08:35
Subject: Law Society Diary Dates

Jamie,

First of all, I want to say sorry for getting so cross with you for shagging me before you dumped me. In retrospect, I did start trying to molest you as soon as you stepped into the cottage, even though I could see you were desperate to say something.

While I'm at it, I'm sorry for shouting at you when you looked in my Filofax for the taxi number. You know what I'm like with my Filofax, and I had just been dumped ... but sorry anyway.

I also need to tell you this. When you delivered the fatal news, I felt like I'd been punched hard in the stomach and the sadness I felt made it hard to catch my breath. But something else happened, too – inside my head, that is.

Bells rang, fireworks erupted, ticker tape fell and champagne corks popped, and a big voice sounded out above the noise: *'Congratulations, Jamie Nathan, you are the hundredth person to dump me!'*

I know it sounds unbelievable, but I have a list of names dating back to 2003 to prove it – and no, before you ask, I did *not* sleep with all of them.

Well, you may be glad to hear that this accolade has won you a two-week holiday to Barbados, all expenses paid ... *with me*! There's always a catch, isn't there?

You can do whatever you want on the holiday, with whoever you want, apart from one hour a day. All I ask is that during this hour, you tell me why you, and everyone I've ever dated, has dumped me.

Jas always tells me I'm unlucky in love and that Mr Right just hasn't swung by yet. My wall and I think differently. I stopped off at Lincoln's Inn before work and sat on my wall to do some thinking. And I had a kind of epiphany, I suppose. We think 100 men can't be wrong. We think the problem might be me. Twelve days from now, I'll be thirty-eight – it's time I looked to myself for some answers.

There is no cash alternative. Do you accept your prize?

Charlie xx

PS: I apologise now for the knickers you'll get in the internal mail today. I whipped them off and posted them on Friday afternoon as a bit of fun, not realising you were going to dump me on Sunday. Sorry, but I'd be grateful if I could have them back because they're part of a matching set. Thanks.

PPS: I've cancelled the Lake District. They weren't that happy with only four days' notice, but they said they won't charge us – really good of them.

Chapter One

Charlotte Bloom

(Written the morning before the break-up)

To-do List: Monday, 12 February

- *Drink more water*

- *Put chocolate cake in bag*

- *Pelvic floors (on train)*

- *Tidy office for Robert coming*

- *Finish Montague contract – must do*

- *Do not go into Baby Gap – has to stop!*

- *Do not buy Bridal Magazine – must-must-must stop!*

- *Ring Mum*

- *Ironing (week's worth, including for Lake District – yippee!)*

- *Make salad for pack-up (choice: frolicking in jacuzzi or wallowing in jacuzzi – only four days to go)*

- *Put picture of Rebel Wilson (pre-diet) back on fridge*

- *Bleach moustache*

·······

Monday 12th February

'You can't change what life throws at you, but you can change how you react.'
Charlotte had read it somewhere and written it down in her Filofax (probably
not word for word), but on one of the dividers, for permanency. She liked it.
It empowered her. In fact, it had been the impetus behind her email to Jamie
that morning. It was the Dalai Lama who'd said it, and he was always laughing
whenever she saw him in pictures or on the TV, but she supposed it was easy to
laugh a lot when you were 'The Chosen One'.

Unfortunately for Charlotte, that was precisely the problem – no one had
chosen her, yet. She wasn't getting any younger and if she was going to have a
family, she needed to get a move on – her eggs were fast approaching their dotage.

She rubbed her tummy protectively and for the fifty-seventh time that
morning thought about what had happened yesterday. He really had ended it.
Jamie Nathan had dumped her. Had she been a gambler like her father, she'd
have laid all she owned on the fact he'd spent all week planning a romantic
marriage proposal in readiness for their trip to the Lakes on Friday. She'd seen him
whispering with Millie in the office on more than one occasion and was certain
they were discussing rings and the best jeweller's to get one from.

She massaged her temples to soothe the throbbing pain of the
drowning-her-sorrows hangover she was nursing. The adrenaline that had been
racing round her body was ebbing away now, being replaced by the much less
appealing feelings of humiliation, shame and sadness. She'd all but hired a town

crier to shout her impending betrothed status to the world, and Jamie was, well, he was simply everything she'd ever wanted.

She looked out of her office window, but she didn't see anything. She felt weak, sapped of all her passion and fervour, tiredness from no sleep steadily clawing its way in. Perhaps if she just laid her head on her desk for two minutes, just a small snooze ... it might all feel a bit better.

'Cheese on toast, on white, extra butter, and one can of fat Coke, just as the lady ordered!' Millie breezed in and wiggled her arms until the top triangular parcel nudged off and fell onto Charlotte's desk 'Coke's there.' Millie nodded towards her coat pocket for her boss to help herself.

Charlotte freed the can from Millie's jacket and breathed in the comforting smell of warm toast and melted cheese wafting up from the neat little breakfast package in front of her.

'Thanks, Mils. That should help.' She faked a yawn and quickly turned her attention to her monitor, continuing to hide her pink, puffy, crying-all-night eyes from Millie.

Thank God it was only Millie who knew about her relationship with Jamie, and thank God she could trust her, because she sure as hell wasn't ready for her failed love life to be discussed by all of London's legal profession just yet. Lawyers: nothing more than an unkindness of gossiping ravens most of the time.

'I thought you were making us choccy cake over the weekend? The girls and I were looking forward to it.' Millie mocked a sulky frown, her piercing eyes drilling suspiciously into Charlotte's profile, seemingly searching for clues.

'Oh, yeah, sorry, honey, I did promise a cake, didn't I? It's been a mad one.' Charlotte grabbed a handful of post from her in-tray, trying to act normal, except all memory of what was normal had left her.

'Have you been celebrating something, then?' Millie juggled the remaining bags of toast from her breakfast run into a more comfortable position, eager for the usual rundown on her boss's weekend.

'What? Oh, no, just too much to drink last night, that's all.' Charlotte flicked through the clutch of headed notepaper in her hand, desperate for Millie to leave so she could hole up in her little office all alone, where she could think and wait. 'Could you cancel my three o'clock, Millie, please? He won't mind.'

'Yeah, he will, you know he will. Every time he phones he says, "How's my favourite trainee today?" I've told him a million times you're a qualified lawyer now, but he –'

'He'll be fine!' Charlotte barked. 'Just pencil him in for Friday, will you?' She caught herself – it wasn't fair to project her ill fortune onto the unsuspecting, especially Millie, whose gatekeeping skills she was relying on today. 'Sorry, Mils, it's the Montague deadline, it's crept up on me. Can you make sure I'm not disturbed today, please?'

Relieved Millie had gone, Charlotte scanned her emails to see if it had arrived yet. No, still no reply. She sat slumped over her fat Coke (the only sure-fire hangover cure) and slowly unwrapped the waxy paper from her toast. She took a bite and tried to focus on the contract on her screen.

It was no good. She decided to indulge herself instead and fished her beige-leather Filofax out of her bag to thumb through her lists. She loved making lists and sometimes made lists of the lists she needed to make. She worshipped her personal organiser, so much so that she'd allow herself whole days to revamp it. These days only happened say twice a year but, when they did, she'd turn off her mobile, crouch down if the doorbell rang, and sit there all day with a bottle of Cabernet Sauvignon and an army-sized bag of honey roast cashews – just her and her Filofax.

Making lists and writing everything down had been Charlotte's crutch from an early age. It was her comfort blanket or snugly – she'd never had one as a child but knew loads of people who had, like her childhood friend, Jasmine, who called hers Stinker. A black-and-white teddy, which apparently she used to rub between her legs to get to sleep. Charlotte thought this hilarious and testament to the commonly held psychological belief that you develop your personality early on in life.

Writing in her Filofax cleared her head. There could be a million things swimming around in there but, as soon as she relinquished them to paper, she could throw them out, like a filing system, with her head being the in-tray, and everyone knows how satisfying it is to have an empty in-tray. Her Filofax was the most comfortable, familiar thing in her life and knew more about her than any living, breathing human being.

Although her existence was supported and underpinned by these lists, she'd learned to keep them a secret. She'd been misguided enough to let Jasmine read one once and subsequently endured three years of mickey-taking on the matter. It wasn't even one of the more obscure ones, either. Just:

Long-term To-dos

- *Qualify as a solicitor*

- *Lose weight*

- *Get married*

- *Have children (two boys, one girl, preferably)*

- *Learn Spanish*

- *Do some volunteer charity work (preferably in Africa)*

- *Set up orphanage or school in Africa*

- *Go on another travelly trip*

- *Give blood*

- *Learn to fly*

- *Take out pension*

- *Go on photography course*

- *Have moles removed*

- *Wardrobe overhaul*

- *Buy big farmhouse in middle of field*

- *Have psychic reading*

- *Find something I'm good at and get better at it – want to know what my 'thing' is*

- *Sleep with Chris Hemsworth*

Jasmine had rolled around in hysterics, wiping tears away, just managing to croak out bits of comments before the laughter took hold again. *'Learn to fly ... sounds ... like you're gonna ... take lessons from ... Superman! Who puts ... get ... hic! .... married ... on a list?'* and so on.

Charlotte took another bite of the cheese on toast that was helping to nurse her hangover and checked her emails again, almost involuntarily, as if her mouse were on a timer.

Still no luck.

She returned her attention to leafing through the ink-filled sheets of paper in front of her. Oh boy, what a lot of changes to be made, she thought as she flicked over to *'People to Invite to Our Wedding'* then turned the page to:

Children's names (must be more than one syllable to go with Nathan)

- *Florence Nathan*

- *Freddie Nathan*

- *Gabriel Nathan*

- *Eva Nathan*

- *Noah Nathan*

- *Verity Nathan*

The knot that had been revolving in her stomach tightened and wrung her pain out harder. Unable to bear it, she flicked quickly past '*Potential Dog Breeds That Would Be Good In A Family Environment*' and located her daily to-do lists, which she always wrote a week in advance and added to as she went along.

Yet another one of those awful things about being dumped. Not only do you have that horrible split-second moment as you wake, when you sleepily assess the status quo of your life, only to baulk at the realisation that it is in fact shit. But then, throughout the day, whichever way you turn, your life is peppered with little reminders about him: his smell on the bed linen, his toothbrush in the cup, your cream sofa looking like a small hairy dog has been to stay (Jamie's chest was particularly hirsute), photos everywhere and so on. In her experience, it lasted for about two weeks, after which she'd usually filtered them out, allowing for the healing process to start. No such luck this time, though, unless she found another job ...

Chapter Two

Charlotte

'Morning, Charlotte.' Robert, the senior partner of Ashling, Crowell and Walker, burst into her office with his usual gusto and deceptive smile, his joviality and trivial banter no doubt masking the real agenda for his visit. 'Good weekend?'

'Oh hi, Robert. Yes … great, thanks,' she lied. '*Erm*, I wasn't expecting you until later.'

She twiddled her pencil round in her fingers. Sweet Jesus, he always caught her red-handed – and red-eyed this time too. How did he know to walk in the minute she wasn't doing any work? There might be only sixty seconds in the day when she wasn't working, but that would be the moment he chose. He was a master.

Robert pulled up his pinstriped trouser leg and perched on the corner of her desk. 'Can't make it later, I'm afraid. Something's come up. Just wanted to have a quick word now, though, if that's all right?'

Of course it was all right. Robert had been known to fire someone on the strength of losing a game of golf to them. Although feared, and loathed a fair bit too, Charlotte couldn't help liking him, as unlikely as that was given his 'It doesn't count as unfaithful if you're in a different time zone' policy. His poor wife … especially as Robert flew to America most months.

Jesus, what's he going to say? Is this it? Have I finally been found out? She knew she wasn't the most committed lawyer in the world, so it was always going to be a matter of time before it was noticed. She promptly shut her Filofax and wheeled her chair back to create more space between the pair of them.

'I've been getting reports.' He put a casual hand through his thick grey hair and looked at her intently, his ever-present phoney smile firmly in situ, failing to betray one ounce of emotion.

'Oh yes?' She cocked her head and tried to smile, her swollen eyes finding it difficult to follow her mouth's example.

'Yes, from Bindleys.'

He's enjoying this. He's about to tell me the firm's biggest client is going to lodge a complaint against me and, consequently, my fledgling career is over, barely before it's begun – and he's bloody well stringing it out.

'Oh, right, yes. I'm hoping to finalise Project Montague today.'

'Well, you'll be interested to hear, I'm sure ...'— he leaned forwards like he had a secret to tell, maintaining his silence that bit too long, seemingly enjoying watching her squirm — 'they're so impressed with the way you've handled your caseload that they want you to take over the lion's share of their portfolio with us.' He sat back smugly, as if taking the credit.

'But what about my current caseload?' she asked, perhaps a little too quickly.

'Oh, we'll get a trainee on to it or something – don't you worry your pretty little head about that.' He stood up and peeled back his double cuff to check his watch. Although how he could see the hands among all those diamonds, Charlotte never knew. 'So, what do you say?' he asked rhetorically.

'*Erm*, yes ... fantastic! Great news!' she effused, gathering momentum. 'Thanks, Robert.' She nodded vigorously, albeit more for her own benefit than his.

She knew she should be pleased. Jamie would be wetting himself with delight had he been granted the same privilege, overjoyed that months of hard work, midnight shifts and crawling up the partners' arses had finally paid off. She found it difficult to watch when Jamie was with Robert – or any of the other big cheeses, come to that. It was sycophancy of the highest order, but he was fiercely ambitious.

Jamie was one of those lawyers who kept a spare coat in his office to leave on the back of his chair so wandering partners would think he was still there, busy beavering away in another part of the building or popped off to make a coffee. Charlotte knew if she wanted to get anywhere in this chosen career of hers she, too, would have to dance the merry dance at some point, but it didn't come easily.

'No, *thank you*, my dear. Good work. Oh, and while I think about it, there's news on the Law Society Seminar.'

'Oh yes?'

Charlotte's heart sank at the mention. The dreaded seminar had been weighing heavily for weeks now. She was struggling even writing her speech, let alone delivering it. Public speaking had never been her thing. She still had nightmares about opening her mouth and nothing coming out at college moots, even though that had never actually happened. She'd asked Jamie to help, but he was annoyed he hadn't been asked to talk, so refused to have any part in it, leaving her alone with her panic. She was sure he'd come round eventually, because that's what people who love each other do, they help one another in times of crisis, but it was only three weeks away now and his sulking was showing no signs of abating. Anyway, there was no chance now he'd dumped her.

'Casey Jones has double-booked, so I wondered if you'd take over his keynote speech. It's top of the bill, but he'll help you with the prep and I know you're up to it.' Robert flicked through a pile of paperwork on Charlotte's desk.

'Sorry? Did you say give Casey's speech?' Charlotte blurted out, subconsciously wheeling herself back in towards him.

Casey Jones was one of the most prestigious lawyers in town. His talk was anticipated weeks beforehand, discussed in Chambers, pontificated over in the waiting rooms of the High Court and covered by the press. How could she possibly replace him? How could she stand up in front of 300 of London's most notable solicitors and barristers and talk for forty-five minutes on 'Historical Jurisprudence: Rethinking the Separability Thesis'?

She wasn't sure she understood the title, let alone manage to cobble together a talk on it. Would she have to take questions at the end? What if she didn't understand them? And to open the day, to get up first and address the cold-off-the-streets crowd before they'd even had their first quadruple-strength espresso or whatever it was these top legal types drank to keep them working twenty-three hours a day ... She couldn't even rely on someone else to warm them up, and there would no time for any of them to have nodded off. She was first up. Sweet Jesus. Her life was rapidly descending into a Dante-esque hell.

'But what about my speech? I've just about finished putting it together. Millie's typing it up today.' Her eyes were wide and desperate.

'Perfect.' He smiled an immaculate, even smile and adjusted his tie before laying it back down on his pink shirt. 'That'll help your replacement at this late hour. Not sure who it's going to be yet, but that's my problem, not yours.' He tapped his forefinger on the desk. 'And while I remember – just seen your holiday form ... Bit short notice, but you may not see another for a while, so I've okayed it. Another thing, it might make sense to wave goodbye to your country retreat now, as well. Time to put your roots back here in town. All that commuting is valuable office time and you'll need it now you're the main girl.' He winked kindly, pleased with the gift he'd bestowed. 'Yep, make the most of this holiday, Charlotte, my dear.'

And off he chortled.

She needed a bloody holiday after all this.

'Oh, one more thing.' Robert's head popped back around her door.

She hated that Columbo thing he always did.

'I found this in the boardroom. It is yours, isn't it?'

Robert O'Keefe was the most observant man she'd ever met. His eye for detail bordered on the obsessive. What other man would have known who an ordinary beaded bracelet belonged to, in an office full of women mobbed with beaded bracelets?

'You must have dropped it on Friday. Didn't I see you go in there with Jamie Nathan?' He stepped back into the room and locked her gaze.

Charlotte's stomach lunged. Inter-office relationships were a sackable offence at most Magic Circle law firms and this one was no exception. But worse, far worse, was the thought he'd seen what they were doing.

But that little work moment had beaten today's freshly delivered promotion hands down. It had been fun. Jamie had been nervous and not entirely convinced of the idea, but he'd still enjoyed it – the look on his face had told her that. It was an uncharacteristically risky move for Jamie, considering the venue, but he was as sexually motivated as he was career driven. It must have been a tough call for the poor guy. Charlotte, however, had no such qualms.

The boardroom was her favourite place in the building, because at twelve-storeys high, it gave a magnificent view of the City and St Paul's. The cathedral had looked particularly stunning on Friday, surrounded by banks of large storm clouds threatening to collapse at any moment onto the grey and blustery streets of London. The sultry sky hinted at becoming a passionate and tempestuous one, whilst, hidden in the corner, behind the super-shiny boardroom table, she brought one of the profession's most promising young legal eagles to orgasm. He was in fact the hottest one this side of the City, who had everyone from circuit judges to office juniors fawning over him.

'Yes, it's mine. Thanks, Robert, I wondered where that had gone.'

Robert stood in front of a picture hanging on Charlotte's office wall, the one she'd taken in Nepal of a girl no more than ten with a baby strapped to her back in a sling made from rags.

'I do like that picture, Charlotte. You've captured her essence.'

'Thank you. I like it, too.'

It was one of Charlotte's favourites. She'd felt a rush of love and admiration for the scrawny, wide-eyed girl.

Robert surveyed the picture for a second longer. 'Yes, nice young man, that Jamie Nathan. Good litigator. Meticulous, loyal ... yes, loyal. Takes it all seriously. Only problem is he's a bit of a brown-nose. Cheerio.'

And with a cursory wave, he marched out once more, leaving Charlotte unable to curb a small chuckle.

Perhaps crawling didn't pay, after all. As today's promotion was testament to, it seemed. Robert had, however, left her with another of those annoying reminders of what she'd lost. Jamie was loyal and he did take everything seriously. Robert was bang on the mark, as usual.

Chapter Three

Charlotte

Charlotte slumped back into her chair after Robert's departure. The tremendous career news already forgotten, she set about hopefully checking her emails once more, trying not to see the pressing ones, eyes darting up and down searching for a reply. It wasn't there. Then, scrolling back, she saw that Sarah had emailed her late on Saturday.

Date: Saturday, 10 Feb 20:07
Subject: Send Help

Happy New Year! Belated, I know, I know. I went AWOL for a while there, sorry, but you know what my life is like. Although I did have a whole ten minutes the other day when I wasn't marshalling a sword fight, stopping Rudy from feeding the fire with the Sunday supplement so he could 'watch the different-coloured flames' or rescuing a neighbour's cat from one of Finn's squeezy hugs that make its lips go blue. I even managed a wee without an audience. We're turning a corner.

The return to school was tough. Christmas was welcome relief from the ongoing struggle to 'fit in'. Five months in and I'm starting to suss out the school gates crowd. There are two clearly defined camps. The up-their-own-middle-class-arse mums or Top Dog Mums as I like to call them, who huddle together looking like a page out of the latest Boden catalogue, all bright spotty prints and Bugaboo prams, mainly 'incomers' like me. And The Hippy Chic Mums – mainly Cornish but some from all the way across the border in Devon (about a mile away!). They're the arty ones, half of them wear caftans, floppy hats and bangles to their elbows, and the other half are just plain scruffy.

Then there's the odd few who stand out from the crowd: Big Lass From The North, the bossy one I've told you about who everyone seems to be scared of, who gives her son crisps for his school snack (the Devil's food). Bohemian Babe, who's younger than the rest and dresses like a Hippy Chic Mum with a penchant for peasant skirts and oversized sunglasses, but stands in the Top Dog Mums' scrum looking like the most useless spy in the world. And Ole Sunken Eyes, whose peepers you can't see for the giant sandbags she has stacked underneath them, like she's expecting the rains. To be fair, it does rain a lot here in Cornwall. Last but by no means least, there's Jinslet. So named by me cos she looks like the love child of Jude Law and Kate Winslet – strong jaw, roman nose, cherry-ripe oxbow lips, Hollywood smile and a small mole above her mouth. Not that I've been studying her or anything! She's all triple air-kisses, daaarling, but I can't tell what camp she belongs in cos she's always ten minutes behind the bell and, whatever the weather, she wears flip-flops – never seen her in anything else.

Not sure where I'm going to fit into that lot, really. Probably not at all, as I still don't have a single friend after five months of loitering lonely in the playground as the clock strikes three, but time will tell. Ironically, Cornwall seems exactly the place where those who have never fitted anywhere come. It's the land of the struggling souls: divorcees, widowers, eighty-year-old virgins, bankrupts, ex-cons and people who just want to get off the merry-go-round of life – all welcome.

What you up to, anyway? Is it next weekend you go to the Lakes? Ooo, exciting. Do you really think Jamie is going to pop the question? What will you say? Ha ha.

Now Christmas is over I can try and get some sort of routine back. The house has gone to the dogs. Didn't dust the skirtings for the entire holidays and we had the same sheets on our bed for six days at one point – yuk! Had a lovely time, though. Some fun family moments, and they're what make life special, aren't they – not the dusting. So that's my New Year's resolution: more fun, less dusting.

Can you believe the christening's only ten weeks away? Jesus, what a mad time I'm having. I'll be the one taking a little nap on the edge of the font while the vic does his stuff. I don't know why I do it to myself. And, on top of all the arrangements, I've got two weeks to write a bloody poem cos the printers need it for the order of service.

Grant keeps telling me I'm not prioritising right, my time management stinks and my standards are too high. Something has to give, he says, but what he really means is that I don't have the time or the inclination to greet him at the door with a blow job any more, although he rarely seems to be at the door these days.

I've got a treat lined up, though. Grant's going to babysit at some point, so I can go to the bright lights of Barnstaple to buy the biggest bucket of popcorn they have and go watch a movie, during the day, on my own! Is it freakish going to the cinema on your own?

Tatty-bye, then.

S xxx

PS: Made myself a premenstrual badge. Printed off a picture of a velociraptor, stuck it on to a circle of card and wrote 'Talk at Your Own Risk' underneath with one of Rudy's felt-tips. I'm going to wear it on the danger days so my delightful husband knows when to zip it from the off (not sure how it'll work on the phone yet – need to work on that).

PPS: Found a Power Ranger sticker in my hair today. Oh, how my life has changed!

Charlotte chuckled at the thought of Sarah with a sticker in her hair. Super-efficient Sarah was finding it hard to leave her old, perfectly groomed, successful City-worker self behind, even though she hadn't been that person for five years now – since she had Rudy. She liked to keep her marshmallow centre under guard with her uber-confident demeanour, and a Power Ranger sticker was definitely not part of the look.

Sarah was wired for success and had embraced motherhood as she did her career in fund management, with 100 per cent commitment and sheer determination. She was desperate to make her boys perfect. They were only ever allowed to eat home-cooked organic food and she had something scheduled for every minute of their time, right down to playing Beethoven and Brahms on car journeys. She loved the bones of those boys and wanted to give them the best chance life could offer, but Charlotte often wondered who she was really doing it all for – them or her?

Charlotte had met Sarah about eight years before at a book club in London. A friend of a friend had started it up and Charlotte had been badgered into going. Not feeling very literary, she'd been apprehensive – until Sarah arrived. She waltzed in wearing a very short raspberry-coloured power suit with a pair of Mary Jane shoes of identical colour. She had immaculately styled long hair with a razor-sharp fringe, the colour and shine of a chestnut racehorse, and just as S was for Sarah, it was for Sassy, Sexy and Self-assured too. It wasn't just Sarah's personality that made the outfit work – it had a lot to do with her disgustingly faultless body. With legs as long as a midsummer's day, she was one of those horrible people who looked great in a wet suit.

But the best thing about Sarah that evening was her quiet confidence and approachable manner. She walked around the rather grand living room, proffering a tin of home-made chocolate-chip cookies she'd baked that morning, instantly endearing herself to everyone. Never one to say no to a cookie, Charlotte and Sarah had been firm friends ever since. She was even going to be godmother to Sarah's beautiful boys in a few weeks' time. Luckily, the boys often had other ideas to Sarah and her quest for the 'perfect children', and were wonderfully mischievous, boisterous little things, especially Rudy. Charlotte was glad because Sarah needed something to lighten her up. She was sure that one day she'd be found face down in a bowl of chickpeas – death by homemade humous.

She closed Sarah's email and got out her mobile. Texting from the office was a crime worse than throwing a sickie – they sent a doctor round if you rang in ill. But she knew it cheered Sarah up getting texts, so she'd risk it for a quickie.

```
You're not freakish. It's good to enjoy your own
company. I do lots on my own - gives me time to
think. I do, however, worry about your habit of
doing housework at two in the morning. Grant's right
- something has to give, so I'm glad about your New
Year's resolution. Have fun, freaky cinema-dweller.
Cxxooxx
```

She put her phone away and checked her mail again. Still nothing. She looked at a few others that had come in. And noticed there was another from Sarah sent on Sunday. And one from Jasmine. Ah yes, from homemaker Sarah to home-wrecker Jas! She giggled fondly.

Date: Monday, 12 Feb 09:30
Subject: Slush Puppy

Hi, babe,

Just a quickie cos I'm on the road today, sans breakfast, because I feel sick. I hate feeling sick. Was glad you'd written. Laughed out loud several times. It's funny to be pitied for being an old spinster, but not surprising. Thing is, I wouldn't want to swap lives with anyone, even though you think all mistresses are despicable forms of human life not fit for the bottom of your stiletto. As I've said many times before, divorce is the future tense of marriage. Besides, there are blokes I *could* have married. I just didn't want to compromise. Plea-bargaining is more your thing.

Oh, and I do wish you'd warn me if you're going to go all slushy on me with talk of 'The One' and settling down and giving up your career, and ... *niños*? *Yeuch!* Jamie's a good catch, but it's only been eleven months. Not long enough for a good Stilton to mature, let alone embark on marriage, putting an end to casual sex for ever, Amen. (shiver)

Just a thought, but when you sit contemplating on this wall of yours, you don't do it out loud, do you? (freak)

Had a fun Saturday. Relaxed birthday dinner in Turkish restaurant with 12 women, then on to a Notting Hill club to strut our stuff. Sunday wasn't so good. Adrian the Married chose to go to the rugby, followed by dinner with wifey, instead of seeing me. Left me to go chandelier-hunting on my own. Found great repro though. I looked a sight walking down Balham High Road with it, but it looks divine in my living room. Come round and see it, and stay – the countryside can do without you for one night. You can do your pelvic floors on my sofa (promise not to watch). I'll cook Thai and we can see how quickly we can get fucked on three bottles of wine. I'll even do you cheese on toast for breakfast (weirdo).

Scary news just in! Don't tell *anyone*. Found a grey pubic hair this morning. Culled the bugger instantly, but not pleased.

So, Adrian 'I'm having a middle-aged Sunday' Barnes has some work to do to win me back. Some champagne and a rip-your-clothes-off shag tonight should do it. I'm feeling even more rampant than usual. Must mean I'm mid-cycle (too much information?). So I need to be careful, because I would rather press a hot iron to my forehead than have any *niños*.

I know a happy family is all you've ever wanted, babes, but please be careful of rushed decisions.

Adiós, my friend,

Jas xxx

Oh! Forgot to say – remember that new guy I told you about – Reuben, Machorn's latest bit of hot stuff. He's been dating Shelley in Buying, but I've wangled dinner with him, on a business pretext – watch this space. So next time you bump into an old school friend, can you tell them I may not be married, but instead I have three lovers!

Three? Who was the third? Unsure whether to laugh or cry, Charlotte clicked on 'reply' and contemplated how to break the news she'd been dumped, without looking a complete and utter fool. Still staring at the blank screen three minutes later, she decided to go and make a coffee. She closed Jas's email and opened Sarah's second one, sent the day before.

Date: Sunday, 11 Feb 15:32
Subject: Migraine

Hello, my lovely,

Me again. I don't email you for seven weeks then you get two in quick succession!

I made your mum's sticky toffee pudding today – scrum-diddly-umptious.

Bit of a bad time with Rudy again. He's always at his worst when we have guests. Typical, isn't it? It's the time you want your children to be best behaved and they end up behaving far worse than normal. It's the excitement. Nosey Nora, the next-door neighbour, popped round last night, and now thinks I'm the worst mother in the world. I'm worried there's something wrong with Rudy, Charlie. But any time I try to talk to Grant about it, he just brushes it off. Says it's normal five-year-old behaviour and maybe I should lower my expectations. I know I like everything to be perfect, but why can't I control him?

Grant's working up in London tomorrow now. I've got loads of cakes to bake and the boys are at home. Can't believe it. I really need to get these cakes right. My social life and my integrity are relying on them. None of the school mums like me, Charlie. Perhaps I should do a Jas and just start shagging all of their husbands and be done with it. Ha ha. Who needs friends, anyway?

How's work? Any more news on the dreaded seminar? Although knowing you, all you can think about at the moment is wedding dresses.

Well, that's me.

Hugs and kisses.

XXX

OOO (These are hugs – big fat ones like me, cos I've had six chocolate Hobnobs today. Shh, don't tell anyone. I've been hiding them at the back of the cupboard – isn't that what alcoholics do?)

Charlotte shook her head. Sarah was having a tough time with Rudy.

And then she saw it.

'Oh, God, it's here!'

It sat bold and unread in her inbox, goading her: his reply.

Chapter Four

Charlotte

Charlotte knew she should have opened the email there and then, but preferred instead to prolong the blissful ignorance. Which was exactly why she was now sitting in Costa Coffee, obscured from view at the table behind the stairs, otherwise known as Skivers' Corner, nursing a skinny cappuccino, with the email from Jamie intact in her inbox, patiently awaiting her return.

She'd pondered long and hard over the last twenty-four hours as to exactly why Jamie had dumped her. And although she kept justifying its irrelevance, she suspected the seven-year-old memory that kept popping up in her head had everything to do with the answer.

· · · · ● · ● · · · ·

She'd been going out with Pete for four and a bit months. They were redolent with the heady flush of new love, hanging on each other's every word and still happy to wake up and kiss each other with tongues before they'd brushed their teeth. Pete was as happy as a tramp with a house-sitting job, because he'd finally found her, the girl he'd spend the rest of his life with – at least that's what he'd told her, right before the balance of power shifted.

Charlotte stood waiting on the pavement outside the impressive glass-fronted block of offices that housed Trewells, the firm of accountants Pete worked for, scrutinising every inch of every female who left the building. She saw her Pete step into the revolving door and moved closer to greet him.

'Hi,' she said.

'Oh, hi,' he said, seemingly surprised to see her. 'Is everything OK?'

'Fine.' Charlotte kissed him on the lips. 'Just thought I'd come and meet you.'

'Oh, that's nice.'

A tall blonde with a sexy nose and hazel eyes detached herself from a group of people congregating on the path, presumably Pete's workmates, and walked up to them.

'You comin', Pete?'

'Yeah, go on without me. I'll catch up.'

The blonde rejoined the group.

'Who's that?' Charlotte asked.

'Gisela. She works in IT.' Pete nodded at another passing colleague. 'The thing is, babe, I'm off out for a drink with everyone tonight. Sorry, I thought I'd told you.'

'Well, I can come, can't I?' Charlotte linked arms with him like Dorothy about to skip down the Yellow Brick Road. 'I'm in the mood for a drink.'

'*Um*, yeah ... yeah, course you can. I don't see why not.'

Pete set off behind the others, arm in arm with Charlie, blissfully unaware his decision to let her join him that evening would mark the beginning of the end. The end of the relationship with the girl he loved.

Three years later

'Where have you been?' Charlotte asked as Pete walked into the kitchen of the small one-bed flat they shared in Archway, North London.

'Working.'

'You're late.'

'Barely.'

'You're forty minutes later than normal. Where have you been?'

'Nowhere.'

'So why are you late?'

'I don't know. I did a few minutes' overtime. I didn't bother ringing cos it was only about ten minutes, then I got the Tube home.'

'If you only worked ten minutes late, why are you forty minutes late home?'

'Look, Charlie, I don't know.'

'*Think.*' Charlotte's eyes narrowed dangerously.

'*Umm*, the Tube was packed, so I let one go and caught another. I bought a paper ... oh yeah, I stopped to look at the guitars in Wroes' window.'

'So that's ten minutes working late, say five minutes to buy a paper, tops, three minutes to look in the window, and five minutes to wait for another train. That makes twenty-three minutes. What were you doing for the other seventeen?'

Charlie's face was hard set, watching Pete's every blink, every expression. She scanned every inch of him like a laser beam, searching for body-language giveaways.

'*Jesus, Charlie, I'm so fucking sick of this. I don't know!*' he bellowed at the ceiling through gritted teeth, his eyes momentarily closing as he seemingly sucked strength from above.

'How can you not know? We're talking about the last forty minutes of your life. What are you, an amnesiac or something now?' Charlotte snarled. 'Have you spoken to her today? Or can you conveniently not remember that, either?'

'No, I haven't spoken to Gisela. I've told you – she works in IT, I rarely see her. Why are you so obsessed with her? She's just a work colleague.'

'Yeah, a pretty gorgeous one, too. Don't pretend you don't fancy her.'

'I don't!'

'Is that where you were? Were you with her? If you don't tell me, I'll find out. Lies always come out in the end.'

'*Aargh!*' Pete brushed his hand through his hair and grabbed a handful. 'Charlie, I can't cope with this anymore.'

'*Neither can I!*' Charlotte hurled the words at him, each one loud and precise, then her voice softened. 'Why can't you just tell me the truth?' she asked in a measured tone.

'OK, OK.' He put his hand up to signal surrender, to stop the familiar charade. 'Look, if you must know, I went for a drink with Bill. One drink. One really quick slam-it-down-my-throat pint, that's all.'

Charlie crumbled. '*I knew you were lying*,' she sobbed.

'He's my boss, Charlie, and he's been asking me to go for a drink for months. I keep putting him off, giving him excuses because I knew you didn't want me to go.' He shook his head. 'But it was getting embarrassing, and he's my boss, for fuck's sake! What could I do?'

'*Tell the truth, that's what. You're such a liar.*' She pulled out a chair but didn't sit. '*I knew you were lying. I knew it. You bastard!*'

'It's the first time I've ever lied to you, Charlie, I swear it, but you make it so difficult for me. I was between a rock and a hard place. If I'd told you, you'd have said I couldn't go, and Bill was getting annoyed. He could see I was making excuses. What could I do? Tell him my girlfriend won't let me go anywhere without her?'

'*No!*' she screeched between sobs. 'You could have talked to me, Pete. I'm thirty-four not fourteen. You don't have to lie to me. We should discuss things like adults.'

Pete shook his head dolefully, the image of a broken man.

'How do I know you went for a drink with Bill, anyway?' she continued, her voice revving up again, gathering momentum, the sobs abating now. 'You've already lied tonight, so who's to say you're not still lying?' She moved closer. 'All I want is for you to be honest. *Is that too much to ask?*' she hissed, like a swan with young, lunging at him with her words.

He flinched and moved back a couple of steps.

'*You went for a drink with her, didn't you? I know you did. You bastard!*' She slung the words at him. She scrunched up her fists tightly, trying to stop the anger, but it needed an outlet. '*I knew you'd cheat on me sooner or later. I knew I'd be right!*'

She looked around the room. She grabbed the Brabantia bin next to her, hauled it up and sent it flying across the kitchen, where it landed, upturned and dented, next to the washing machine.

Pete stood frozen.

Charlotte slid to the floor and curled into a tight ball, crying with great gulping sobs.

Eventually, Pete spoke, quietly. 'You know what ...' He straightened as if suddenly handed a baton of strength. 'I've had it with all of this, Charlie.' He walked over to where she was slumped, her whole body shuddering with tears. 'Look at me.' His tone was even, his manner cold. 'You check my phone, you go through my phone bills, you monitor my emails and you don't let me go out with my mates ... without you there. You spy on me and you turn up at my office unannounced ... and that's not the half of it. I can't breathe, Charlie. You're sucking the life out of me. You know how much I love you, but I've had years of this stuff, day in, day out. I can't take it anymore.' He shook his head angrily, seemingly furious with himself now. 'I should have walked out years ago. Stupidly, I thought things would get better. That's all I kept telling myself. But they're not, Charlie, they're just not.'

He walked out of the kitchen and into the hall.

Charlie raced after him. 'Don't you dare go out!'

'*I'm not going out, Charlie!*' he shouted back. '*I'm going!*' He grabbed his coat off the peg, stepped out of the front door and slammed it hard behind him.

· · · • · • · · ·

The memory was still hard to think about. She'd really loved Pete. And ironically, unlike previous boyfriends, who she'd caught red-handed on multiple occasions, she had a feeling Pete had been totally faithful. He'd loved her too. But that was then. She may have previous with the bin, but she'd never hurled one since, so it was possible to reform. She was different now ... wasn't she? She hadn't acted like that with Jamie, not so he'd have noticed, anyway. Yes, she concurred, she was different now.

Charlotte got up and made her way back to the office. She had an important contract to finalise and she'd be sacked if she didn't get it done.

She'd sent Jamie the email at 8.35 a.m., which meant it had taken him nearly two hours to reply. Was that a good thing or a bad thing? He hadn't dismissed the idea instantly, which was what she'd been afraid of. He'd taken time to think about it and surely that was a good thing? The nub of pain she'd carried in her stomach all morning turned into one of excitement and confirmed what she'd tried to ignore – that secretly she hoped he'd change his mind. She hoped that he:

1. had gone to bed last night feeling lonely and dejected and weeping uncontrollably into his pillow

2. thinks Barbados is a fantastic idea, but only if they can go as a couple; and

3. thinks maybe they should get married while they're there.

She also knew it was much more likely that he'd:

1. worked on the case he was handling, followed by a few beers in front of the TV with his flatmate

2. fallen into bed and had a wank, and

3. then dropped straight off to sleep.

She sneaked back into her office and sat at her desk. She straightened, took a deep breath ... and banged her finger on the mouse to open the email. There!

Date: Monday, 12 Feb 10:23
Subject: Law Society Diary Dates

Charlotte,
I'm coming round – I'll be there in an hour.
Jamie

What? Oh. An hour. Fuck, an hour! That meant he'd be here in ten minutes! Christ, she needed to sort herself out.

Chapter Five

Charlotte

Charlotte set about hurriedly plaiting her grubby-looking caramel-streaked hair, which she hadn't been bothered to wash this morning. Why did Jamie feel so different from all the others? Because she'd never felt so incredibly engulfed in love and happiness in all of her life, that's why.

It wasn't a particular trait he had or the way he looked, it was more about the feelings he evoked in her, the way she felt when she was with him. He criticised her quite often, but it was constructive criticism for her own good, always trying to help – he was good like that.

She cupped her hands over her eyes and pressed them tightly against her skin, trying to squeeze out all the exhaustion from the strain of trying all the time. The cold touch of her just-washed hands felt good against her tender skin. Why had he dumped her? He'd agreed not so long ago that they were perfect together, so why?

She assessed her image in the mirror, studying her eyes. The vivid blue of a child's paintbox, they usually glinted, but her swollen eyelids and gloomy mood had dulled them today. She breathed deep, pushed back her shoulders, and marched back to her desk.

'Hi, Millie. How are you?'

Charlotte's heart pumped against her chest Jessica Rabbit style as she recognised the full-bodied voice oozing confidence that she could hear outside her office. He was here.

'Good, thanks, Jamie, how 'bout yourself?' she heard Millie say.

She peeped through the small window in her door and watched Millie cock her head and look up at Jamie through her lashes, as was her usual flirty way, while coyly scrutinising his face for signs of trouble, the little minx. She'd tell her soon enough.

'Fine, thanks. Is Charlotte in?' He spoke with an authoritative tone and carried on moving, blatantly unwilling to take no for an answer. He knocked gently and opened the door.

'Hi.' His tone softened as he entered.

'Hi.' Charlotte tried to sound bright and breezy, but it manifested in some kind of pathetic bleat.

'God, Charlie, are you OK? You look dreadful.'

'Thanks.'

'You know what I mean. I don't mean –'

'Don't worry, I know what you meant. I didn't get much sleep.'

'Look, perhaps this wasn't a good idea here. Shall we meet for lunch instead?'

'No! No.' She needed to know. Plus, she couldn't possibly get her head around finalising Project Montague until she knew if he was coming or not. 'It's fine. Here, sit down. I've made you a coffee.' She nodded in the direction of the mug on her desk and pulled out a chair for him.

'Thanks,' he said, sitting down. 'Sorry it took me so long to get back to you. I've been in a meeting with the other side on the Jefferson case. They've assigned someone else to it.' He sipped his coffee and nodded appreciatively.

'Oh, right.'

'Yeah, so I had to get her up to speed.' He cupped his mug with both hands and relaxed into the leather chair, gently swinging it from left to right.

'Oh, who's managing the case now?' Charlotte asked, feeling the familiar flutter of panic pulsate in her chest as she sat up straight in her chair.

'Heidi Clarke. Have you had any dealings with her?'

'No – is she nice?' The vibrations in her chest quickened.

'Yeah, she's lovely. High achiever. Got a first at UCL, you know the type. She's keen to make her mark with this case, so she's right on it, which is great for me, of course.'

The pulsating turned into thumping and she fought a surge of nausea as the smell of her coffee wafted up to her nose. Wasn't Heidi that redhead who liked to party (*read: shag around*)?

'Is she pretty?' Charlotte enquired as casually as she could manage, trying to keep her voice even, her hands tightening around her cup.

'*Erm*, yeah, I suppose she is. I hadn't really thought about it.' Jamie's brow furrowed and his lips pursed.

'Is she blonde or ginger?' Charlotte's eyes dropped to the floor.

'What? Oh, *um* ... red, she has red hair. Charlotte, can w—'

'Do you fancy her?'

Shit! She didn't have the right to ask these questions any more, but the powerful force of her desire to know far outweighed that to remain dignified. It washed over her like a huge wave, enveloping her, rendering her usual rationalities drenched and immobile. Jamie was single now – it wouldn't be long before word got out that he was back on the market.

'Charlotte, I can't cope with you ques –' He stopped himself and stood up, adding dispassionately, 'I should go, I'm meeting someone in a minute.'

Bollocks! She shot out of her chair. 'No, no, sorry, that was stupid of me, sorry. Please stay.'

'Charlie, I'm truly sorry about what's happened. Really I am.' He moved towards her as if about to give her a hug, but stopped still, right on the perimeter of her personal space.

'You're not coming, then.' Charlotte played with one of her plaits, like a five-year-old trying to extract a pony from her father. Why the hell did she always let herself down?

'Actually, I was going to say I think it's a good idea.'

'You were?'

'Yeah.'

'Is that – you were, or you are?' She held her breath.

Jamie's arresting good looks became even more magnificent when he was troubled. His serene and hypnotising pale-green eyes became even paler, striking a bold contrast to his peat-coloured hair. At that precise moment, she wanted to nestle into his big, soft chest and forget about everything else.

'I am, but—'

'Oh, fantastic. *Yes!*' Shit. 'Did I say that *yes* out loud? Sorry.'

Jamie laughed fondly.

'Thanks, Jamie. You'll have a great time, I promise, and I'll ma—'

'*But,*' he interrupted and waited for her full attention, looking solemnly at her. 'Only if you understand that I'm not coming to get back with you. I'm coming because your email really moved me ... and shocked me. And because I care about you and want to help.' His gaze moved to the bare wall behind her, unable to meet her eyes.

Oh, God. Pity! She hadn't wanted to see pity. No, being on the receiving end of pity didn't make it up there on her list of favourite things, and she did have a list.

'Oh, and I won't let you pay for me.' His eyes quickly met hers once more. 'Anyway, I've gotta go, Charlie. Are we on, then?'

Charlotte eradicated the pity from her mind and concentrated on what had just happened. He'd accepted.

'Yeah, we're on, but only if you let me pay. You've got to let me have that, Jamie. That's the deal. That's the prize.'

He nodded, reluctantly, and left.

Now that she was alone once more, with an important deadline looming larger by the minute, she knew she had to get on, but she couldn't resist one last indulgence. She grabbed her mobile and quickly scrolled down the texts to her favourite Jamie message:

`I'm getting repetitive - another lovely night with you! I know you must have a bad side - I just wonder what it is!! I can't resist you - gorgeous, fantastic company and the best in bed! If you leave me, I'll`

go gay, cos you're the best female I'll ever meet!
Xx

He'd sent it in the first month they'd met and reading it made Charlotte's whole body smile, every part of her, inside and out. So what had gone wrong? She pulled herself together. One day at a time.

He's coming to Barbados – yippee!

Chapter Six

Jamie Nathan

Jamie sauntered down the eight flights of stairs to the ground floor and shouldered out of the double doors into the steel-cold February day. He reached into the inside pocket of his jacket for his Oakleys and strode up Fetter Lane.

'I knew it had to be you, only person with shades on in the middle of winter, you tosser!'

'Sensitive eyes, sensitive bloke, what can I say?' Jamie grabbed his friend's hand and slapped his back. 'Toby, mate, how you doing?'

'Good, good. Come on, it's bloody freezing out here. Thought we'd go to that Costa up there.' He pointed to the collection of silver tables on the pavement ahead. 'I've got some stuff for you to look at and, bloody hell, mate, that email you sent me must have taken you a while this morning. Slow day at the office, is it? I take it Charlotte hasn't seen it?'

'No, of course not,' Jamie said, as the two professionals marched off up the road, side by side.

'And you haven't told her about you know who?' Toby glanced sideways at his friend.

'What do you take me for?'

'You haven't changed since uni then. What was it they used to call you? "CasaNathan" wasn't it?'

Jamie laughed out loud. 'Once a bad boy, always a bad boy. What can I say? Girls love a bad boy.'

'Not sure this girl does.'

'You're right. Casanovas are definitely not Charlie's thing. But she'll never know she dated one, with any luck.' Jamie followed Toby into the warmth of the coffee shop.

They paid for their drinks and settled at the table behind the stairs.

'Is this for me then?' Jamie reached across and pulled the pile of paper towards him. 'Cheers for that, mate. Really good of you to look at it so fast. I know you're busy as fuck. The mental health business is booming, I do believe!'

'No problem, anything for an old mucker like yourself. All in a day's work.'

Jamie flicked through the printed sheets. 'Is it easy to understand? Not filled with too much of that mumbo-jumbo you psychologists like to peddle? Best to keep it simple and all that. I don't want her freaking out on me.'

'I try to keep my mumbo-jumbo-peddling to a minimum. I think you'll find that's perfect for the job.' Toby stirred a sugar into his mug. 'The thing I don't understand though, is why you're going on this holiday. You don't love her and you're not gonna get back with her, so what's the deal?' He shrugged and took a sip of his Americano.

'Well, I've gotta work with her for a start. She's highly thought of at Ashlings and I want partnership there. They're known for sacking people if they're found shagging, so I can't take the risk. What if Robert finds out? They love Charlie so who's to say they wouldn't keep her and sack me?' He looked straight at Toby. 'I'm the better lawyer, no doubt about it,' he added quickly, 'but Robert's got a soft spot for her – he likes the pretty girls. Yep!' he said, as if re-affirming it to himself. 'I need to keep this amicable, mate.' Jamie sipped at his coffee and opened his snack pack of Jaffa Cakes. 'Plus ...' He looked over at his friend with mirth all over his face. 'It *is* a free holiday after all, and who's to say I won't get the odd shag out of it? One thing you can say about Charlie, she is sexy and is definitely the BJQ.'

'BJQ?'

'Blow Job Queen – she's the best!'

Toby shook his head. 'Seriously, mate? Surely even CasaNathan isn't that heartless? Are you? And it's not like you're desperate for sex. Far from it. Are you sure you don't care for her a little bit? You're going to a lot of trouble for her. All this for a start.' He tapped his finger on the stack of printed information.

'The thing is, Charlie is a lovely girl – and at the beginning, when we first met, I did think she could be it, y'know, the one, the one to marry and sprog with. But then all this ...' It was Jamie's turn to tap the pile of paper on the table. 'It's not for me, mate.'

'Well, it does all point to one thing – she's got the full house of symptoms, that's for sure.'

Chapter Seven

Sarah-Jane Richardson

I hung back from the crowd at the gates as I always did, to avoid any contact, verbal or eye. I preferred instead to stand and dream of my perfect Mediterranean life and what it would look like. I was in the middle of meandering through my fruit orchard in my flowy white dress, basket over my arm, pondering the ripeness of a pomegranate, when Big Lass From The North burst into my world.

'You can't park there!' she boomed in her gruff voice, extraordinarily at odds with her glossy appearance. She pointed at my car in the loading bay next to the school.

I was later than normal today. Too late for a place in the school car park or any of the roadside spots. I couldn't be bothered to walk a tired Finn half a mile up the hill from the community centre, where there was ample parking, and then a tired Finn and Rudy back down again. So I'd parked in a loading bay I'd never seen used in all the time I'd been there.

'I'm sorry?' I said, rubbing my hands together, my fingertips aching from the cold February afternoon.

She stood square on in front of me and moved her burgeoning red face, not dissimilar to the ripening pomegranate in my thoughts only a moment ago, menacingly close to mine.

'I said, you can't park there. It's not complicated, pet.'

'It's not hurting anyone and it's only for a minute.' I huffed hot air onto my fingers to stop the pain.

Her eyes, the size and colour of raisins, narrowed momentarily and her nose, so flat and wide against her face as to be ambiguous in its role, twitched nervously, but her manner remained as severe as her sharp black bob.

'I will say it again, pet,' she laboured. 'You can't park there! It clearly says *No Parking* in big white letters on the tarmac.' She folded her arms across her generous frame and tilted her head to one side.

'Look, I'll tell you again. I'm only going to be a minute and I'm not hurting anyone. And don't call me "pet" – my name's Sarah.'

I heard the silence that had fallen around us and glanced briefly over her shoulder to survey the captivated horseshoe of an audience we were commanding.

Big Lass From The North shook her head and snarled, 'Bad manners obviously run in your family ...' She paused, for effect maybe but more likely to think what to say next. 'But I'm not sure who's more stupid – you or your bully of a son!'

I gasped then quickly gathered my composure. 'I'm not surprised.' I straightened my back and lifted my chin. 'Resorting to fabricated jibes of a personal nature in the absence of a decent argument highlights an acute lack of intellect and moral fibre.' I brushed past her then turned my head back to lay one last comment at her chubby feet. 'Oh, and it's not altogether sensible to slate the person you're expecting to bake nine cakes for you on Monday ... just a tip.' I walked away, striding purposefully to counteract my wobbling knees.

'*Probably best not to bother!*' she shouted after me. 'After all,'– she looked around to make sure everybody was ready for the punchline – 'if your cakes are anything like your integrity, we'd rather not risk them!' She said this as if she was spokeswoman for the crowd, arrogantly presupposing they were on her side.

I'd been really pleased when Big Lass From The North had asked me to bake cakes for the school. Bit of an honour, apparently, because the annual cake stall was renowned as being the best in Cornwall. People from more than twenty miles away had it in their calendars. Stupidly, and true to form for me, I'd volunteered to make three sponge cakes – one Victoria and two chocolate – a lime-and-ginger cheesecake, a batch of individual carrot cakes, macaroons, two sticky toffee puddings with sauce to pour over the top, and a date-and-walnut slice. All fully decorated and iced to a professional standard, of course. To make matters worse, they were all needed by 3 o'clock the afternoon before the event and I had strict instructions that all were to be made on that day, not before, to retain freshness and the upkeep of the cake stall's stupendous reputation.

It wasn't just their reputation at stake, it was mine too. This was the first 'task' (aka test) I'd been given. I'd been planning it for weeks, like some kind of bake-off. Each year the mums scrabbled for the newsletter to see whose name was mentioned in the same sentence as 'outstanding contribution'. And the reward for the mums who excelled? Well, you got to join the in-crowd, for a start (the Top Dog Mums). And word had it that your child got preferential treatment: leading role in the Nativity, chosen to take the hamster home, represent the school on trips, that sort of thing.

Like it or not, Rudy and I could do with the friends. It was five months since we'd moved to Cornwall and we still didn't have a single play date or coffee morning under our belts. I felt isolated and Rudy was desperately unhappy. But the goddamn woman who ran the cake stall had just publicly called my son a bully, so why on earth would I contemplate putting myself out for her now?

I collected Rudy from school, helping him on with his coat, while Finn hid among the coat pegs full of winter clobber, and decided there and then that I'd give Big Lass From The North a run for her money. How dare she call my child a bully! There was only one bully around here and it was her. I resolved to make these cakes the best I'd ever baked. I'd show her exactly how good my cakes and my integrity were.

·········

Grant got into bed beside me and let his hands wander freely up and down my warm body.

'Wanna play?' he whispered into my ear.

I'd been in bed a good fifteen minutes by now, so it was perfectly reasonable that I'd be asleep. I lay there, desperately trying not to swallow. But the more you try to stop something, the more ... *shit!* It sounded like a bomb blast in a library. Did he hear that? Or was it just that loud in my head?

'You asleep, Sar?'

I lay there, stock-still, trying to hush my thoughts and keep my eyelids from fluttering.

He rubbed my body some more, groaning with pleasure. 'Come on, Sar, why don't we have a little fuck?'

I steadied my breathing, labouring the odd breath here and there, sure that's what you did when you were asleep.

I felt the need to swallow again.

He rolled onto his back.

I waited ...

Almost immediately, he began emitting low, drunken snores.

I sighed with relief – home and dry.

I remember counting the minutes until Grant's hands would be wandering up and down my body, watching the oversized luminous digits change on the clock at work, until they reached the time I could finally race home to him. Now, his hands on my body make me feel slightly sick. How time changes things.

Chapter Eight

Sarah

'Never again!' I finished the drying-up from last night's dishes and slapped the sodden tea towel onto the kitchen worktop.

'All right, stop getting so worked up about it, babe. We won't have her back.'

'I mean, doesn't she have any family of her own to terrorise? I think she teaches torture tactics to SAS recruits. The woman's a walking interrogation room. I thought she was going to get a lamp out of her handbag at one point.'

Grant laughed. 'She's lonely, that's all. And that's what neighbours do round here. It's called "community spirit", Sar.' He fished the ground-coffee tin out of the cupboard. 'Anyway, we've been here five months and it's the first time she's turned up like that.'

'She had to observe us first, for her dossier.'

'Well, perhaps she won't want to come back. I don't think it was much of a secret that we didn't all hit it off.'

'Why do I have a feeling that's not going to stop her?'

At least Grant had been home when the neighbour had barged in bearing home-made pasties and truth serum, insisting on staying for four hours and thirty-two cups of tea, and dispensing invaluable child-rearing advice. Weekends were the only time I didn't feel like a single parent. Despite our big 'quality of life' move, we actually spent less time as a family now than before, with Grant still working in London because he couldn't find a comparable job in Cornwall.

It was our fault – we didn't do the research. Instead, we moved lock, stock and barrel on a romantic notion, not realising Cornwall was an employment wasteland. So Grant was only at home at weekends and Mondays, which was his 'work from home' day, although he rarely filled it with work, preferring instead to surf.

Despite him being away for most of the week, I'd still embraced the move. Thought that when we were together it would be much more fun – playing in the sea, mooching round rock pools, going on wild and woolly walks in the Cornish wilderness. I hoped it would be the marriage redemption we needed, but it was proving to be hard going.

It didn't help that we were so remote. There wasn't even a mobile signal in the village. You had to drive a mile to the neighbouring village of Shop (weirdest place name ever, but it does at least have a shop) to make a phone call. Landlines were still alive and kicking round here.

Grant knelt in front of me, easing his arms into the gap between me and the chair to put them around my waist.

'It's only some old woman who lives next door, babe. Try not to let her get to you.'

That was so typical of Grant – his answer to anything he didn't have to deal with.

'Try not to let her get to me!' I said, my voice on the rise, but I caught myself and reeled it back. A row was the last thing I needed. 'She told me she could hear Rudy "playing up" all the time and if I'd clipped him round the ear, like any decent mother would have done back in her day, he wouldn't be so spoiled.'

I could see Grant worrying about how riled I was getting. He hated rows more than I did, going to extraordinary lengths to avoid conflict, insisting all was well even when it was on the brink of disaster. We both knew we'd moved to Cornwall to try and be more of a family, to get our relationship back on track. But he'd never admit that was the reason, harping on instead about how he could teach the boys to surf.

Grant nodded soberly. 'She's a different generation, you know what they're like. You mustn't let her get under your skin. Now, would my lovely wife like a nice frothy coffee to make her feel better?'

I flinched. He was right. I had let her get under my skin. Because of the way she'd made me feel about myself as a parent. The way even her silence managed to be judgemental. All her judgemental thoughts unfurling and marching sternly across the floor to stare up at me with their arms crossed. She'd hit my weak spot, found my Achilles' heel.

Rudy didn't seem to respond to discipline like other children. I was a relatively new mum and had nothing to pitch it against but, it seemed to me, right from the early days, that Rudy was more spirited than other children his age. More stubborn. Health visitors, doctors, friends, family and shopkeepers, advice and criticism came at me like a round of machine-gun fire.

I could see people in the supermarket tutting at me, as I'd done to other mothers in the past before I'd had children, their whispered words ringing in my ears: 'Look at her, she can't even control her own kids. Disgraceful.' Of course me being me, I'd read all the books on discipline, sleep, routine, difficult children ... but nothing made a difference. I was normally so adept at things. This was new to me, to be so out of control.

'*Muuummmyyy!*'

Finn was awake, hollering from his bedroom. He never just got up. He loved his sleep, and his bed, and preferred me to take his morning 'milky' up and snuggle with him for a minute. Nestling in bed with my little angel every morning was my idea of heaven.

Rudy, on the other hand, was up with the lark. At 5 o'clock (earlier sometimes), he'd stumble into our room, rubbing his eyes, scratching his dishevelled blond hair, and climb into bed next to me. The wake-up call I'd always dreamed of.

Of course, the reality of my life wasn't quite so dreamlike and usually involved me running around like Roadrunner, barking out orders like 'get dressed', 'brush your teeth' and 'put the goldfish back'. All while conjuring up two nutritious packed lunches and cobbling together an eat-as-we-drive breakfast for three. But I wasn't complaining.

'Why don't we *all* go up.' Grant smiled warmly as I poured the last of the milk into Finn's cup. 'It's Sunday and it's raining. Let's have breakfast in bed. You get the boys and I'll follow with coffee and croissants.'

'We haven't got any milk left cos bloody Nosey Nora From No. 9 drank two gallons of tea last night.' I knew I was being petulant but had no inclination to shake it. I was wounded. Petulance stroked my ego.

Grant laughed. 'It's all right, I'll nip and get some from Shop.' He spun on his heel with an afterthought. 'And I can get the papers. *Ahhh*, those were the days, *eh*? Spending all morning in bed, having sex and reading the papers, then getting up to go to the pub for lunch.'

I shuddered and tightened my dressing-gown belt. Give me my current mundane existence over that one any day. Romantic sex, the type where you congratulate each other on your performance at the end, had long since gone off my list of favourite things to do ... with Grant anyway.

'See you in a minute, then!' I called, not wanting to reminisce.

Grant was a good husband, really. Most of the time, anyway. The type of husband wives dreamed of – always giving me compliments, saying how much he fancied me, doing the odd bit of housework here and there. Usually involving scrubbing some small orifice like a plughole or vent with a toothbrush – what is it with men and cleaning with toothbrushes? – generally making himself handy. The list was endless, but all I could do was wish he wasn't here.

In fact, in the week when he wasn't around, I loved the thought of him. I'd start thinking 'He's not that bad, I do love him'. Then the minute he arrived home, I wished for him to be gone again. I liked the help with the boys, the break I got, but that was about it. The worst bit, though, was that I loathed myself, because what kind of awful person dislikes someone who's kind and caring and a good father, too?

· · · • · • · · · ·

'*Boooys*, can you stop wriggling, please!'

'But, *Muuumyyy*, we're playing Harry Potter!' Rudy was indignant in that wonderful manner only a five-year-old can adopt and get away with.

I planted a kiss on top of his messy blond hair.

Grant had returned, with newspaper and milk, as promised. Breakfast in bed was underway, albeit very different from the old days.

'Put that down, Finn,' he said wearily.

'I'm not Finn, I'm Ron Weasley.'

'What?'

Grant didn't really get the role-play stuff. God knows what he did when he was a child. Probably practised his sales pitch in the mirror, ready for his role as Property Manager for Sandercocks, the international property service company he loved working for so much. He hadn't so much as sighed when they'd called him back early from his Christmas break unexpectedly.

'Can you put that knife down, please, before you hurt yourself!' Grant slammed shut his newspaper and grabbed the knife from Finn's podgy fingers.

Rudy grabbed his little brother's hand in solidarity. 'Come on, Finn. Let's get the dress-up out.'

'I'm not Finn, I'm Ron Weasley!' came the exasperated retort as they set off for the playroom downstairs.

Grant budged up to me under the duvet and slid his hand gently down my thigh. 'Sooo, now the boys have gone ...' He turned in to me so I could feel his growing erection on my leg.

'*Grraant!*' I pulled the duvet up around my chin. 'They could walk in any minute.'

He expelled a big puff of air and rolled back to his side of the bed. 'You're no fun anymore.'

'Thanks.'

'Well, we never do it anymore. There was a day when you'd have jumped at that chance.'

'Yes, Grant, and that was a day when we didn't have a re-enactment of the bloody *Philosopher's Stone* going on in the room below us.' I got out of bed and pulled my dressing gown off the back of the door.

'We've done it with other people in the room before. Remember when we stayed at your mate Lucy's, that time?' He smiled at me, eyes lit up like a naughty schoolboy with a wicked plan.

'That was different. Now the boys could come in at any time and—'

Right on cue, Rudy barged into the room. '*Mummy!* Finn's got my magic wand and he won't give it back.'

'Sort it out yourselves!' Grant snapped.

Rudy looked straight at me, not upset by his father's tone, just keen that I should sort it out.

Nosey Nora's omniscient judgment hung round my neck like a Hogwarts scarf, as I trotted off to the playroom.

Chapter Nine

Sarah

Sunday lunch was always a big roast affair, all the trimmings and a home-made pud. I liked to make the effort, especially because we rarely ate together as a family anymore. I'd made sticky toffee pudding today, Charlotte's mum's recipe. It was her new husband, Roger's, favourite and there was no denying its success.

She guarded it like it was the *Mona Lisa* but had finally let Charlie disclose it when I offered to trade my coveted bread-and-butter-pudding recipe (Roger's second favourite, apparently), handed down from my mum and her mum before that. Much to my chagrin, Hannah Bloom's sticky toffee pudding had knocked mine off the top spot in our house and was everybody's favourite. The only shred of pride I could hold on to came from the fact that I'd tweaked the recipe to make it my own, but I could never admit that.

'*Boooys!*' I shouted up the stairs. 'Can you wash your hands for lunch now, please!'

'*Owww, we're plaaaying!*'

'*Just do it!*' I ordered amicably.

A few minutes later Rudy ran into the room at full pelt with both hands in the air. 'Done it, Mummy!'

'Careful, darling, this is hot.' I held the tray full of roasties over my head, manoeuvring skilfully.

'But I've done it, Mummy, look!' He sprang onto tippy-toes in front of me and shoved his hands in my face, bouncing up and down, desperate for me to inspect them.

'Yes, I can see. That's great, darling. Move away now, please. This is hot. Can you set the table for me please, Rudy.'

'Where's Daddy?'

'He's nipped to Shop.'

'Again?'

'We've run out of cheese. Rudy, can you stop swinging on that chair, please, and set the table.' I began to carve the chicken. 'Where's your brother? *Fiiin!*'

'I'm not Finn. I'm Ron Weasley, Mummy.'

Finn wandered into the room wearing one of Grant's white work shirts, down to his ankles, and a black Dracula cape from Halloween.

'Have you washed your hands, Ron Weasley?'

'Yes.'

'Great, sit down then, chicken, and I'll dish up.'

'Can I have some chocolate after lunch, Mummy?' Rudy looked over at me and smiled cheesily, nodding in the hope I'd nod in unison.

'No.' I grinned at his incorrigibility. 'You know you're only allowed it once a week and you had a bag of chocolate buttons yesterday, didn't you, so that's it for this week. Good try, though.'

'*Owww*,' Rudy grumbled.

'*Owww* nothing. Now, get a move on with those place mats.'

'Where's Daddy?' Finn asked.

'He's—'

'I'm here. *Mmm*, smells good.' Grant walked in, peeled his fleece off and sat next to Finn.

He was empty-handed apart from his mobile.

'Where's the cheese?' I asked, trying hard not to get irritated.

'Oh, they didn't have any.'

'Great! I was making cauliflower cheese for tea.'

I grabbed a slotted spoon from the rack and noticed a cobweb. Shoddy. Must remember to get that later.

'Rudy, will you please stop swinging on your chair?' I said.

'Rudy, your mum has told you to stop.' Grant looked up from his mobile.

He was always playing with that thing lately, tapping away, oblivious to everything else. Suppose I was a fine one to talk, but at least I didn't do it at the table.

Rudy slid off the chair and squirmed on the floor under the table.

'Back on your chair, Rudy.' I placed four plates down, each piled high with a steaming roast. 'Back on your chair, Rudy, please.'

Rudy got up and sat one buttock on the chair, tipping his chair to the side.

'Sit on your chair properly, otherwise you'll have to go to your room.'

He hitched his other leg on, and swung his whole body, backwards and forwards, rocking the chair violently.

'Stop it, Rudy! You'll hurt yourself.'

He took hold of the gravy boat and chugged it round the table making train noises, gravy slopping everywhere. Finn giggled and grabbed the ramekin of bread sauce to follow suit.

'*Choo-choo. Choo-choo!*' Rudy sang loudly as gravy left the train at high speed, splattering across the tablecloth.

'Right. Up to your room!'

'*Nooo*, I'm not doing anything.' He continued to swing.

'*I said, up to your room!*'

He used his fingers to make patterns in the spilt gravy, while continuing to swing on the chair.

Starving hungry, I counted to ten and tried to not let the situation get to me. Roast was my favourite and, if I didn't eat, I was like an episode of *Eastenders*, a gloomy mix of anger and depression.

'*Look at the mess you've made!*' I yelled. '*And you are still swinging on your chair. It's dangerous! I've told you to stop and you haven't. Now go to your room!*'

Rudy continued to swing, his legs pushing off from the table, albeit a little less pronounced than before. But now his arms had joined in, shaking erratically, shooting out at random angles, punching the air, fingers jingling, continually moving, cooped-up energy forcing its way from his body.

'Now!'

'Can you cut my tato up, Mummy?' Finn asked.

I hastily chopped up Finn's roasties, the smell setting my stomach growling. 'Go to your room, Rudy. Now!'

'*No!*'

Rudy stepped up his swinging defiantly, making funny faces, expelling strange noises, smacking his lips together. I could see the energy bursting out from him, the lack of control over his mouth and limbs, yet still I expected him to stop. Because that's what children do when they're told off – they stop. Why couldn't Rudy do it?

'Right, I'm going to count to five. *One ... two ... three ...*'

'No, Mummy, don't count,' he whined, surveying me warily.

Grant stuffed another forkful of roast into his mouth, seemingly happy to let me deal with Rudy alone. Well, it wouldn't do to let his food go cold, would it?

'Look, Rudy, all I want you to do is sit still and eat, it's as simple as that.'

He continued to wriggle and squirm and chatter and swing.

'OK ... *four ... five!*'

There was no let-up. In fact, he had no intention of complying, that much was blatantly clear.

'Right! That's it.' I marched upstairs.

'*No, Mummy!*' Rudy shouted.

He knew what was coming and flew up the stairs behind me.

'I'm going to take a toy.'

'*No, Mummy, don't!*' He sped past me, screaming.

'I'm going to take a toy because you're not doing what I've asked.'

'*I am, I am! Don't!*'

He reached his bedroom before me and did a star-jump stance in the doorway, holding the frame.

'You're not going in.' His face was set hard with fury.

I picked up his arm to move it away. He was strong. He stood firm, glaring with fierce determination.

'I'm going in whether you like it or not, young man. All that's going to happen here is that I'm going to take two toys now. And the longer you make me wait, the more I'll take.'

Rudy's determined face crumpled, his bottom lip quivering, his eyes glazed with the onset of tears. He knew when he was beaten and reluctantly moved away from the door, stamping his foot.

'*Star Wars* toys today, I think.' I picked up the Tupperware box stuffed with small figures.

'*Nooo!*' He lunged for me, grabbed the box from my hands and threw it under his bed in one swift manoeuvre.

'*Right, that's it!*' I stormed over to the bed, bent down and slithered underneath to retrieve it.

Rudy jumped up and down, screaming loudly.

I dragged the box out and, as I tried to negotiate myself out from under it, I banged my head on the bed frame. *Ow!* My temper rose like a test-your-strength puck flying up to ring the bell and a red mist descended.

'Right! That's it. You'– I pointed at Rudy – 'stay here for five minutes. If you put so much as one foot out of this door, I'll be up with a black bin bag to put every single one of your toys in.'

I fled the room.

It would take considerably more than one bag to confiscate all of Rudy's toys, but he was five – he didn't know. I hated the anger. Before I'd even reached the kitchen I was mortified at my outburst. What would Nosey Nora say now? What would Supernanny say? She'd say Rudy had won and I had lost, miserably. I'd also lost my appetite.

I just wanted to sit and cry. I never used to be like this. Sarah-Jane Richardson didn't shout. Sarah-Jane Richardson was calm and assured, and always found a rational way to solve a problem. Before children, I blanched when I saw people screaming at their offspring in supermarkets. I felt sorry for the child, finding it incomprehensible that adults failed to act in an adult fashion, sometimes behaving worse than the child. I'd always felt smug, too. Smug in the knowledge that I'd never be that sort of mum. How premature I'd been ...

'What was that all about?'

Grant had finished his lunch and Finn was making a volcano out of cabbage, carrots and roast potatoes.

'Is that a joke, Grant?'

I walked to the timer on the fridge. It was on the swerve. I straightened it and set it for five minutes.

'Oh, by the way,' he said. 'I forgot to tell you earlier. Work rang when I was at the shop, I need to work tomorrow.'

'Grant, no! You can't ... not tomorrow. It's a teacher-training day, so the boys aren't at school and I've got a million cakes to bake.' I flopped onto my chair and gave a low moan.

'Oh, yeah, I forgot.'

He walked over and started massaging my shoulders.

I tensed at his touch.

'I'm sorry, darling, but apparently there's some big shot coming over from Hong Kong and I've got to meet him. It's an unexpected visit. No-one knew until yesterday.' He moved his hands down my back and up again. 'Crikey, you're stiff. You need to try and relax more, Sar.' He pummelled my shoulders. 'Anyway, we're talking about Sarah-Jane Businesswoman-of-the-Year Richardson here. You telling me a city high-flyer like you can't manage to look after two children and bake a few cakes? When I first met you, you fund-managed a portfolio of more than £5 billion with unnerving ease. I think you're going to be fine, Sar.'

Eventually the timer on the side of the fridge emitted a shrill beep.

'*Come down, Rudy!*' I shouted up the stairs.

I'd think about Grant's bombshell later, partly because I felt too let-down to speak, but mainly because right now my concern was Rudy. He bumbled into the kitchen with his head down and lurched into my open arms. I swept him up and sat him on my knee, hugging him tight.

He looked up at me with red eyes. 'Sorry, Mummy.'

'That's OK, baby.' I rubbed his back. 'Mummy's sorry for shouting, too. All I ask is that you do as you're told. I won't ever ask anything unreasonable of you, chicken.' He nuzzled into my chest. 'Now, sit down and have your lunch while it's still warm.'

I left Grant with the boys and disappeared while I could.

I sat with my mug of tea at the computer and thought about what Grant had said. He was right – I used to manage billions of pounds' worth of assets day in, day out, and still found time to file my nails at the office. I used to multitask in my sleep and wasn't happy unless I had at least three pressing matters to deal with. Now, I felt like I couldn't manage a couple of children while I baked some cakes.

I helped myself to another biscuit and thought back to the time when I beat seven finalists to win the coveted Emily Sharratt Busineswoman of the Year Award. The youngest person ever to win, at only twenty-nine years old. I was awarded it for my strong leadership, business acumen, inspirational qualities, innovation, style, tenacity and charisma. Did any of these apply to me now?

I was with Liam that night. The Irishman I'd met on my trip to Africa. Applause ringing in my ears, too overcome to move, he stood up first, to lever me from my seat. When I finally found my smile, it didn't leave me. He wrapped his arms around me. 'Well done, baby.' He breathed into my hair in his buttery soft Irish accent. 'You're amazing.'

We left early, walked to Green Park, and danced barefoot on the grass. Liam lifted me high into the air and twirled me around. 'Jeez, SJ, I love you so much!' He pushed me up against a tree where he kissed my lips, softly at first, then urgent and needy, his hand sliding under the chiffon of my dress.

And afterwards, as we lay on the dewy grass, pretending we were back watching the African stars, I wondered if this was my zenith. Was this as good as it got?

'Promise you'll come and meet me in Sri Lanka, SJ.'

'I promise,' I said.

That was the old me, and I wanted her back. She was much nicer to be around. Something had to change.

Chapter Ten

Sarah

'Right, boys, here's the deal. You show Mummy that you can be really good today and there may be something in it for you.'

'Presents?' Rudy enthused, jumping up and down.

'Maybe. Now, take your snack and off you go.'

I pulled my flowery Cath Kidston apron over my head. Grant's mother had bought it for me. Her exact words as I unwrapped it had been 'Now you've finally accepted your role in life, it would be good to look the part as well.' I wasn't the comfy housewife and mum type she'd hoped for her favourite son and she never let me forget it. Nice apron, though.

I pulled my hair into a ponytail and set about my task with the precision of a military attack. First job: cheesecake. Get the hardest job over first. Then on to the two chocolate sponges. Easy. Knew the recipe off by heart. Mustn't forget to marinade the chicken for tea tonight, though.

· · • • • • • · ·

Two sponges and one cheesecake later . . .

'*Muuummmyy, Rudy hit me!*' Finn shuffled into the kitchen with Rudy hot on his heels.

'Did you?' I asked.

'*No!*' Rudy said.

'*You did!*' Finn said.

I grabbed a spoon and smeared chocolate butter icing over the first chocolate sponge that had cooled on the rack, and placed the top layer on carefully.

Finn looked at me. '*He did, Mummy. Here.*' He pointed to his shoulder, nodding angelically.

'Did not!' Rudy huffed.

I iced the top of the assembled cake, smoothing the icing with the back of the spoon, carefully going round the edges, making sure the rim was perfect.

'I don't want fibs, Rudy. I want the truth or there will be consequences.' I stopped what I was doing and looked directly at him. Rudy knew I couldn't abide fibs. 'Did you or did you not hit Finn?'

Rudy traced his finger around the dinosaur motif on his top. 'Well, yes, but only because he hit me first.'

'*I never!*'

'*You did. He did, Mummy, he did!*'

Rudy was emphatic. He was just like me. He'd never fess up to something that wasn't true just for a quiet life. Conversely, he'd never stop going on about a miscarriage of justice until the truth had been outed.

'OK, OK. I think this is a case of six of one and half a dozen of the other. Now, I wouldn't normally do this, but Mummy's really busy, so how about, for a special treat ...'– I walked into the living room, one hand holding up the chocolatey spoon, the other grabbing the TV remote – 'you watch this ...'

I put *Finding Nemo* on, their favourite, and as I did I could see Nosey Nora From No. Nine's face rise up in front of me like an apparition. She was shaking her head and tutting, wagging her finger at me, silently condemning my substandard parenting skills.

'*Yaaayyyy!*' the boys chorused.

I escaped quickly back to the kitchen. Bloody Nosey Nora. What business was it of hers, anyway? I licked the spoon I was holding and dropped it into the washing-up water. *Oh. My. God. Garlic!* It tasted like garlic! *Shit!* I'd used the same spoon for my icing that I'd bruised the garlic with for tea ...

I slumped onto a chair and hung my head. Maybe it would catch on – garlic chocolate cake. All the rage in the Big Smoke, I could say. All the greats like Mary Berry and Rachel Allen swear by it.

I clicked the kettle on – *dink* – and set about scraping off the garlic-tainted icing. But there was no way of telling if the garlic taste had been transferred to the sponge. I couldn't eat a slice and I definitely wasn't going to hand it over and take the chance it hadn't permeated the cake, not with Big Lass From The North fervently waiting on my undoing at every turn. Oh, God, I could barely muster the courage to look at the clock but sneaked a glance despite myself: 11 already – four hours to go and only the cheesecake completed. Although it was rather a spectacular one, even if I did think so myself, decorated to perfection with home-made candied peel artistically sculpted to look like flower buds and piped cream rosettes around the edge. It was my *pièce de résistance* – and would surely be a hot contender for this year's best cake-stall cake.

What I needed was an energy boost, a raise in spirits to get me through this ordeal. Glass of wine, perhaps? It wasn't even lunchtime – ridiculous idea – although it was bound to be five o'clock somewhere.

I settled on a cup of tea, fished out the packet of chocolate biscuits I'd hidden in the bread maker and resorted to the next best thing: some reminiscing, just while the kettle boiled. I spooned sugar into my mug and set about transporting myself back to my African adventure.

I remembered the moment I set eyes on my Travelling IrishMan. It was in a hotel bar in the middle of the afternoon in Nairobi. He wasn't an obvious looker. I noticed him because of the laughter that seemed to follow him everywhere.

He was medium height with pale skin and long black hair pushed behind both ears, like Native American hair only wavier. He had the beginnings of a beard and a scruffy moustache with a hint of ginger running through it. Not one of those awful cultivated ones trimmed like topiary. It was simply the result of not shaving, as was the norm for most men backpacking around the wilds of the African continent on water rations. Drink it or shave with it – no contest.

I sipped gingerly on my hot tea and wondered what he was doing now.

That afternoon was just over ten years ago, but I could still remember everything about him, right down to his scuffed hobnail boots. He was kind and gentle and funny – really funny – and so sexy. When I was with him, life was a thrill. As far as we were concerned, we were the first people ever to discover love in the back of a dusty old overland truck.

I needed to get back to work, but first I needed some Charlie love. I hurriedly tapped out a text, speed-read it back and pressed Send:

Morning, Charlie. Been to the shop for baking supplies. I miss Waitrose so much. It's like the Land that Time Forgot down here. With sleight of hand and well-versed diversionary tactics, I managed to buy a couple of toys for bribery purposes. This goes against everything I stand for, as you know, but I've promised nine cakes to that hateful woman and nine perfect cakes she'll get.

Just heard a gorgeous Irish accent in the supermarket. Made me think of my African travels and my Travelling IrishMan (TIM whose name was really Liam, remember?). Can't stop thinking about our first kiss by the dying embers of a campfire, deep in the heart of Zanzibar. Does reliving moments like that count as being unfaithful?

Text me with news, and dates when you're coming to stay. I need something to cling on to.

Hey ho. S xxx

I got back to work. No time to waste. Rudy mooched in and shuffled around the kitchen floor. It was the ninth time he'd been in so far. Finn was the film buff. Rudy had never been one for watching them – he couldn't sit still for long enough.

'Rudy, darling, if you're not going to watch the film, can you go and do something else? I really do have to get this done.' I flitted across the kitchen with

.my floury hands in the air and turned on the taps with my elbows. 'Why don't you make something with your Lego?'

I flew over to the oven to check the date-and-walnut slice, rising nicely, perfect, then over to the table to finish off beating the carrot-cake mixture. The kitchen was filled with the aromatic fug of syrupy cakes baking in the oven. I moved the pastry I'd made for the macaroons to one side and cast a quick glance at the mixer, which was working on the Victoria sponge. All in order.

'But, Mummy, I don't want to do Lego.'

'Well, colouring-in, then.'

'Don't want to. Can I help you?'

'No, darling, not today.'

'But you normally let me.'

'I know, I do, but not today, OK. I'm really under pressure today. How about you get your pirate ship down?'

Rudy sat at the kitchen table and poked holes into the ball of pastry.

'Oh no!' I dived across the table, knocking bags of sugar and flour over as I went. 'Please don't do that.' I grabbed the pastry and moved it to a worktop. 'Please go and play, Rudy.'

He sat there, swinging on his chair. He jumped up and moved over to the mixer to watch it go round, his elbows in his T-shirt, baring his tummy.

I ladled the carrot-cake mix into individual cases.

'Out of the way, Rudy.'

I moved him out of the way and stopped the mixer. He slid up and down the kitchen floor, elbows in the air, then span round and round.

'Rudy, please, can you leave the kitchen, darling? It's dangerous – there's too much going on.'

I dumped the ladle and empty mixing bowl onto the Kilimanjaro-sized pile of empty pans and dishes by the sink.

'But, Mummy, I'm bored.' He moved to the fridge. 'Can I have some apple juice, please?'

'Yep. Go and watch the film with Finn and I'll bring you both a drink and maybe a biscuit.' I smiled and nodded to chivvy him on.

I cleared a small area on the table and sprinkled flour over the newly made space.

'I can get the drinks.'

He pushed a chair to the fridge, climbed up, and fished around for the apple juice.

'What's this?'

'What?' I said without looking.

I shoved the batch of carrot cakes into the oven to make more room..

'This.'

Damn, I forgot to set the timer for the date-and-walnut cake. When did it go in? I looked at the clock. No, how could it be one thirty already?

'Keep going, Sarah!' I told myself out loud.

'This, Mummy,' Rudy repeated.

'What, darling? Rudy, I really don't have time.'

I opened the oven door again and pulled out the date-and-walnut cake. It looked ready. I extracted it from the oven and straightened up.

'*Thiiiiss, Mummy.*'

I looked over at Rudy just as he grabbed the cheesecake in the fridge with both hands and pulled it forwards to show me what he was talking about.

PLOP!

My wonderful lime-and-ginger cheesecake belly-flopped onto the floor, creamy side down, with all the grace of a ballet-dancing hippo.

Silence.

I stood motionless, oven mitts on, cake in hand. '*Rudy!*'

He jumped down, raced over and launched himself at me, flinging his arms around my waist, gluing himself to me.

'*Rudy, get off, this is hot!*'

'It was the fridge,' he mumbled into my stomach.

'*Rudy, move!*'

'The fridge pushed it out, Mummy.'

The heat from the cake tin was burning through my oven mitts, causing me to wince. Rudy gripped my waist harder, refusing to release his hold.

'*I said move!*' I yelled, red mist falling around me like a poisonous gas.

I wiggled us both over to the vicinity of the sink and threw the hot cake tin onto the draining board, complete with perfectly cooked date-and-walnut cake. The cake ricocheted out of the tin and crumbled on its descent.

'*When I say move, I mean move!*'

I flicked my mitts onto the floor and grabbed hold of his arms that were firm around my middle. He was stuck to me like a limpet on a rock. I squeezed my fingers around his tender arms and pulled them away from me with all my might, anger fuelling my strength and determination, freeing myself from his grip.

It all happened so quickly.

Rudy managed to stop crying before I did.

'*Ow-ow-ow, Mummy, it really hurts!*' He stood forlornly among the chaos of the kitchen, holding his arms away from his sides like a gun-slinging cowboy about to draw.

I pulled him in to me again. 'I'm so sorry, baby, I'm so, so sorry,' I sobbed into his hair.

'*Ow!* Careful, Mummy.'

I peeled him from me and picked up his left arm to have a look at what I'd done. He yanked it back. 'Don't touch it!'

'I won't hurt you, darling. I won't touch it. I'm just looking.'

The bruise on his skinny white upper arm had become surprisingly angry, surprisingly quickly. A perfect circle – the precise size and shape of my thumb. His other arm sported an identical twin.

'Can I just put a bit of cream on them? Magic cream. It'll take the pain away.'

I knew before I asked he wouldn't agree. I'd have to wait until he was asleep. I paced around the kitchen then knelt down to his level, looking into his swollen red eyes.

'I am so sorry. I love you more than anything in the world and can't bear the thought of you being hurt.' These things shouldn't be happening, it wasn't normal. I had to get Rudy looked at. I stopped to catch my tears before they escaped. I needed to be strong now, for Rudy's sake. 'That was terrible of me, Rudy, and I am truly sorry. I got angry. The cake tin was burning my hand and

... well, never mind. The fact is that I was wrong to hurt you like that, but when I asked you to move, you should have done it. It was dangerous. You must do what I ask in future.' I cupped his innocent face in my hands and kissed his forehead tenderly. 'I love you to infinity and beyond, and I never want you to forget that. I love you no matter what, remember?'

He nodded, slightly cheered.

It was what I always said to him, and I meant it. *No Matter What* was one of Rudy's and my favourite books. It was about Large and Small, a mummy and son fox, and how Large would always love Small no matter what he did. Though there didn't seem to be a page to illustrate Small loving Large, no matter what she did.

Chapter Eleven

Sarah

I tried to ring Grant periodically throughout the day, ever since the fateful event, but his phone was off. I could have rung the office, but he didn't like me doing that in case he had a client with him. I felt bad about moaning at him for having to work today. It wasn't his fault and Grant always got nervous when the bigwigs were in town. I eventually got through about six o'clock.

'They're not just some little marks, Grant.' I paced up and down with the phone hard against my ear. 'What was that noise? Where are you?'

'At the B&B. Why?'

'No reason. I thought I heard a woman cough or something ...' I paced some more. 'It's child abuse, let's face it.'

'I think you're being a bit dramatic, babe. He's OK now, isn't he?'

'Yes, if you count having two sore arms as being OK, but the point is I abused him. I'm not being dramatic.' I brutally dead-headed the indoor rose on the sideboard as I cruised past. 'You can have your children taken away for this sort of thing, you know.'

'You're being too harsh on yourself, babe.'

'The school will definitely notice tomorrow. Teachers and doctors keep an eye out for damage to the soft bits. That's the indicator that it's abuse. They're the bits that can't get marked from boisterous play or falling over. What have I done, Grant? What if the school ask him where he got them from?'

I'd been conscious earlier of what Rudy might tell the school. After the initial shock, I wondered, for a split second, whether I should not have apologised. Whether I should have played it all down, but I couldn't do it. I felt so bad – I couldn't mess with his mind on top of everything else. And I couldn't not apologise for such despicable behaviour. I'd considered taking off for a week, going on holiday, just me and the boys, until the bruises had healed, but that was wrong, too. It would turn a regretful moment into something dubious. No, I'd committed the abominable act and now I had to live with the consequences.

'Calm down, Sarah, you're hysterical.'

'Calm down? Why do people say that? When are you going to realise I can't cope! And no, before you say it, that doesn't justify me abusing him, not for one second. But why can't I control him? Why won't he ever do what I ask him to do? I'm worried about him. I need you to help me on this, Grant. I can't do it on my own.'

I stopped pacing and looked out onto the back garden. It was dusk and the bats were filtering their way out of the roof tiles one by one, skitting around, and I could just make out the crows who'd roosted for the night in the wooded copse. It was beautiful here, and Grant's work was paying for it. That and the small amount of savings we were rapidly eating into. I turned my back on it all and slid down the patio door, where I sat slumped against the glass.

'Sorry. I'm just tired,' I murmured into the phone.

'I know. Don't worry. Listen, baby, I have to go. I'm out for dinner with the head honcho tonight. Stop beating yourself up. It'll be fine. We'll talk at the weekend, I promise. Now, go and make yourself a nice cup of tea and put the telly on. You need to relax. I love you.'

'*Put the telly on*,' I mimicked as I hammered the life out of a packet of ginger nuts with a rolling pin. 'Or maybe, just because I fancy it, I'll work through the night, baking cakes for that godforsaken school! Much more fun.'

I turned the freezer bag of biscuits over and battered them some more, enjoying the loud bang of the rolling pin hitting the table when I missed.

'*Thanks for asking how it was all going, though, Grant!*' I shouted into thin air. 'Thanks for enquiring whether I got all the cakes done! I mean, it's not like it was important to me or anything!'

I slammed the rolling pin down hard to annihilate a particularly stubborn chunk of biscuit.

'Well, just for your information, mister, I haven't delivered *one*' – *bang* went the rolling pin as I slammed it down – '*single*' – *bang* again – '*bloody*' – *bang-bang-bang* – '*cake!*'

I dropped the rolling pin onto the table, exhausted, and rubbed my wrist. I glanced at the clock. The morning was galloping towards me like a herd of stampeding buffalo and this time there was nowhere to go.

I'd rung Big Lass From The North, much to my displeasure, to say that due to the incredibly high standard required, it was only right the cakes were as fresh as possible for the cake stall tomorrow (marketing was always my strong point). For that reason I was going to bake my contributions this evening and would personally deliver them tomorrow morning to Ole Sunken Eyes' house, instead of taking them to her at the school gates this afternoon, which I'd been asked to do. Ole Sunken Eyes had been put in charge of 'cake transportation', which I thought funny because she could probably carry most of the cakes in the bags under her eyes. I sometimes felt bad about my harsh names for people, but I challenge anyone to say I'm exaggerating. The poor woman must never sleep.

Each of the Top Dog Mums had been given an additional job, on top of baking cakes. I, thank God, had not yet reached that level of privilege – the heady heights of dual jobs – and was simply asked to bake. I wondered if any of the Top Dog Mums struggled with motherhood. If so, they didn't show it.

By 4.17 a.m., every single cake was ready to go, all bar the cheesecake, Cheesecake Mark II, which still had to set. I cast my eye over the kitchen table which was nose-to-tail full of home-baked delights, and felt the balmy glow of satisfaction that comes with a job well done. I was particularly proud of my sticky toffee puddings, something a little different. I'd put the puddings on a foil platter, together with a small lidded container of toffee sauce, and wrapped it all in cellophane with gold spots, tied with a bright green ribbon. I rubbed my eyes and clicked on the kettle – *dink* (I loved that sound) – a quick cuppa before bed to unwind.

When I eventually climbed under the duvet, the tip-tap of Rudy's sleepy feet followed and he crawled in beside me. No sleep for me tonight – or today, as it was now. I snuggled up to his warm little body and sobbed gently into his hair.

·····•·•····

I delivered Rudy to school, and Finn to preschool complete with Power Rangers lunchbox, and finally … finally … delivered the cakes. I'd had to bite my tongue when Ole Sunken Eyes had casually enquired if that was the last of them as I'd handed over the cheesecake. But I was now bitterly regretting it, wishing instead I'd said something like 'Oh no, there are twenty-seven more to come. I simply didn't have room. I'll pop back in a minute with them.' But I didn't. And now I was yomping down to the beach in my wellies, a thirty-minute walk from the house.

I pulled my scarf over my mouth to stop the icy February wind from stinging my face. I turned onto the woodland track and the herbal smell of wet ferns hit my nose, catapulting instant stress relief along my nerve endings, like someone had flicked a switch. The beach was remote, and inaccessible by road, my favourite kind as it kept out the hordes. A wildflower meadow fell away from the track, down to a bubbling river, which merged with the sea, and right at the bottom, amongst the green-and-yellow gorse, sat the jewel in the crown: Duckpool Mill.

The mill house was several large buildings, arranged in a quadrangle and made from creamy magnolia-coloured stone. It had a huge waterwheel and seventeen windows (yes, my life was so sad that I'd resorted to counting windows). In the middle of the quadrangle was an enormous glass roof, filling the gap between the buildings. It looked like nice things happened there. Wild horses roamed the meadow. Ill-treated in a former life, they'd been rescued and brought to Duckpool to see out their final days in peace, and they seemed to have fostered a pheasant, who followed their every move.

I marched on and eventually hopped down the big stone steps, arriving on the beach. My eyes were watery from the cold and I breathed in a giant lungful of my surroundings, my shoulders visibly relaxing as I watched the rise and fall of the waves as they waltzed into the shore. As beaches go, it was exactly how I liked my men: raw, rugged and unpredictable. Just like TIM, I pondered.

I couldn't stop thinking about him lately. About the times we were in the back of the overland truck in 35 degree heat on dusty, bumpy tracks, when he'd gently stroke my arms and my head, and hug me to him, so I could get some sleep of sorts. He'd come up with games for everyone to play, to help pass the time, and even though he was on a four-week African safari, he never once took a photo, because he didn't want to miss anything looking through the eye of a lens. But the thing I loved most was when he got a certain look in his eye and I knew he was about to suggest something wild. The best sex I ever had was with TIM in the park at Victoria Falls, feeling the spray from the Falls on my body as we made love.

I cautiously picked my way across the pebbles to the sandier part of the beach. 'Hello.'

'*Crikey!*' I put my hand on my chest. 'You made me jump. I don't usually see anyone down here.'

The white-haired lady simply nodded towards the sea. 'Beautiful, isn't it? I saw a seal here yesterday.'

She stopped talking but I didn't feel like I could say anything. It was clear from her incumbent manner that she was still holding court.

'Occasionally they haul out – usually over there ...'

As she pointed, I caught a glimpse of a silver scar running down her elegant neck. She looked vulnerable. Breakable, almost, with her slight frame, translucent skin and thin grey hair pinned neatly up in a bun, like somebody's perfect grandma. But when she spoke, she spoke with authority and strength of character, her deep-brown eyes rich and intense like tea-soaked dates, giving away the fire in her belly. It was like looking at an old woman but talking to a young one.

'That's amazing, I never realised there were seals.'

'Oh yes – seals, peregrine falcons, the occasional dolphin, it's wildlife rich,'

She looked at me, taking in every detail of my appearance, no doubt trying to suss me out as I was her, her measured manner in contrast to her flashing, inquisitive eyes.

'I love the way it looks like a totally different beach every time I visit, even though I'm generally here the same time every day,' I said. 'The tide changes with the moon, doesn't it? I never realised that until I moved here. And the boulders and rocks shift, the sea is so powerful. I'm always amazed at what it's capable of moving.'

I was aware that the sea air was making me euphoric and a little bit rambly.

'Yes, the tide, like time, changes everything and takes what it wants along with it,' she said poignantly. 'Remember to take any rubbish away with you, won't you?' She eyed my rucksack, intimating it was awash with litter-wrapped goodies, and turned to go.

I sat down and unscrewed my flask, watching the lady pick her way across the pebbles, which was no mean feat. She stopped every now and then to sift through the flotsam and jetsam and bent down to dig something out of the shingle. Time clearly wasn't a consideration, in fact she seemed bored, looking to fill time, but she had something about her that kept me watching.

Oh, God, Rudy's arms ... I'd managed not to think about them for ten minutes. It was only a matter of time before the school rang. I slumped further into my rock armchair and fished around for my Flake. I unwrapped it and it dawned on me. No wonder! I was about to get my period, hence the chocolate craving. Grant called me The Velociraptor when I was about to come on. It was totally justified.

I bit into the chocolate and thought about Rudy. He was so difficult to deal with. Did he have a problem, like ADHD or something? The doctor didn't think so. I'd taken him there three times now. So if Rudy didn't have a problem, I must just be crap at motherhood. It was certainly the hardest thing I'd ever done.

I knew it would be hard – I thought I'd prepared myself for just how hard – but I didn't expect it to be like this. Poor Rudy. He needed a mum who could help him. I would be that mum from now on, with or without Grant's help. I raised my coffee cup to the sea to seal my resolution.

Chapter Twelve

Sarah

'So if I could just read that back to you, Mrs Richardson. That's the Jacobean Dining Room, seating 112 people, on Sunday, 21st April. Is that correct?' the Fawksley Hall receptionist enquired.

'Perfect. 'And – before I forget, you have got the bit about the windows down, haven't you?'

'Yes, Mrs Richardson, I've written it down, just like you asked. *Make sure all windows are cleaned the day before.*'

I could hear the contempt in her voice, but I was used to it. High standards and particular attention to detail carried that price.

'Brilliant. Just add whatever that costs to the bill. There's nothing worse than dirty windows, don't you agree?'

I finally ticked 'venue' off my list. At last I was making headway. Finding a reception space for the christening had been the hardest task so far, as April was the beginning of the wedding season, but Fawksley Hall was exactly the location I'd been looking for. I flicked my eyes down my list. Church booked, venue booked, florist organised. The whole event was turning into a rather grand affair. Not too dissimilar to a wedding, really. But it wasn't like we were ever going to have another child, and it was for both boys, so it warranted a big bash.

I ended the call and my phone rang instantly. Shit. The word 'school' flashed urgently on the caller display. Answer it or leave it? I knew what it was going to be about … but what if Rudy had had an accident?

'Hello, is that Mrs Richardson?'

'Yes, it is.'

'Oh, hello there, it's Mrs Davies from school.'

A cold streak of fear ran down my body. Even though I'd prepared myself for this moment, had run through the call in my head over and over, it wasn't any less scary now it had arrived. I'd expected a call yesterday. I imagine the teachers had been surreptitiously checking out his arms, one by one, getting a consensus before they took it further. It was the first thing I'd asked Rudy when I picked him up yesterday – did anyone mention your arms? But he said no and I felt like an abuser for asking.

'Oh, is Rudy OK?'

'Yes, yes, he's fine, nothing to worry about. I was just wondering if we could have a quick meeting after school today?'

For some reason, I hadn't expected to be summoned but, naturally, she couldn't have told me over the phone. She wanted to look into my frightened little rabbit eyes and watch my hands wring when she asked exactly how Rudy had acquired the bruises on his soft little arms.

'What about?' I asked, because that's what I'd ask if I hadn't abused my little boy.

'About Rudy. Don't worry, he's fine, but it's probably best we chat face to face.'

I put the phone down and checked the time. I needed to go for my walk now if I was going to make it back in time. I went to close the computer down and had thought about TIM for what was probably the fifteenth time that day when an idea trickled to the front of my mind:

Date: Wednesday, 14 Feb 10:00
Subject: African Thoughts

Hey there, gorgeous,

Not sure if you've still got this email account, but I've been reminiscing and I got to thinking about you. Was wondering if you ever did buy that motorbike and ride through Asia?

Best not go on in case you don't get this but, if you do, write back and let me know where you are. Bet you're still travelling, you jammy devil.

Much love,

SJ xxx

I knew it was risky sending an email like this from Grant's and my account, but TIM wouldn't reply, I'd lay money on it. Besides, Grant only ever checked this email account at weekends, or if I told him there was something he needed to see.

I'd always regretted that TIM and I had never really got it together as girlfriend and boyfriend, but he lived in Ireland and I in London, and our timing was consistently rubbish. Either he had a girlfriend and I was single (not that that stopped him in Africa), or he was single and I had a boyfriend. Sometimes it was simply that one of us was travelling, usually him. We joked that we were 'victims of unsynchronised passion' like Hemingway and Dietrich. TIM called me Marlene for months, and he often made restaurant bookings for us in their names.

Looking back, it seems strange we didn't ditch any partners and get it together from the beginning. But life's not like that, especially when you live in different countries and you're basing your whole attraction on a four-week holiday in Africa.

The closest we came to having a proper relationship was nine years ago. We finally found ourselves simultaneously footloose and fancy-free and spent two months flying over to see each other at weekends until he went off on a five-month trip around India he'd been planning for years.

This time was different, though, because we had plans. I was going to take two weeks' leave and meet him in Sri Lanka and, when he returned, he was going to spend a few months living with me in London, just to see what would happen.

If you added up the actual time we'd spent together, it amounted to nothing. It was weeks, not months, yet his kisses felt deeper and more familiar than any I'd ever known.

Five weeks after he left for Delhi, on the very morning I received a postcard from Udaipur saying how he was counting the days until I arrived, I met Grant.

··········

As usual, Duckpool looked completely different from the day before. The sea was far out and it was overcast, the low tide exposing more rocks than normal, grey and jagged against the smooth horizon, the waves high and white. I sat in my rock armchair, which was surprisingly comfortable. It was two large boulders, really, one on top of the other, forming a sort of chair. I would sit on one boulder, and rest my back on the other. It even had an adjacent boulder with a flat top – the perfect table for my flask.

I got my phone out. I'd heard it beep when I was jumping down the steps to the beach. It was Charlie, telling me to stop beating myself up because I'm a great mum. Swapping texts with Charlie was the highlight of my day. I typed out a reply.

Hello, my lovely. Stop worrying about work – they'll be fine without you for two weeks. I've been a naughty girl and emailed TIM. Doesn't matter, though, cos he won't still have that email address. It's been nine years.

Had another row with Grant on the phone last night, after I'd spoken to you – things not going well.

Got feedback from cake stall: am being hailed as new Mrs Beeton. Feel proud, except everyone seems to be asking me to bake cakes for them now. Not sure that was how I wanted it to turn out. Been asked to make puddings for a shoot dinner, of all things.

She's going to pay me! And Ole Sunken Eyes has asked me to do a load of baking for her son's party. All for free, out of the goodness of my heart! At least it's secured us a party invite at last - hooray! Rudy so excited.

Rudy's behaviour getting worse. We keep locking horns. Don't know if I can cope much longer - exhausted. Haven't been sleeping. Can't live with what I did. Got meeting with head at Rudy's school this afternoon - scared. You're a lawyer, can they take my children away? Wish me luck.

Hope you're getting excited. I have a good feeling about this holiday. Will email or text later. S xxx

'Hello again.'

'Oh, hello.'

I shoved my phone in my pocket. It felt wrong sending texts in such beautiful natural surrounds. Bet she thinks I'm such a heathen.

'Back again, then? Do you do this walk a lot?'

Bit rich, considering I'd been doing it for weeks now and she'd only just appeared a few days ago but had been appearing like Mr Benn ever since.

'I try to do it every day.' It was a lie, I'd only just started doing it every day, but what was the harm? 'Usually around this time, after I've dropped my boys off at school.'

'My name's Marion Glasgow, by the way.'

The old lady thrust her crinkly hand at me, liver spots and all, and I knew from the way her arm was positioned, like an iron rod, that it would take a braver woman than I to refuse it.

'Sarah-Jane Richardson. Pleased to meet you.'

The skin on her bony hands was paper-thin and felt cold, but her grip was strong.

'How old are your boys?'

'Oh, *um*, five and three. My youngest has just started preschool. Bit sad, really. I loved having them at home. It's hard letting go, isn't it?'

'Wouldn't know.' Her face was bland. She turned to go. 'Don't forget to take your litter with you!' she called back, raising her hand in a rather elaborate farewell gesture, before making her way down to the shoreline.

Isn't it funny how we assume everyone of a certain age has children, I thought. I watched her for a moment and saw her stop, almost mid-track, and just stand there watching for what seemed like ages. Watching for seals or dolphins, maybe. Perhaps that's how she sees them – she spends the time.

I sat for a while longer. Not sleeping was taking its toll. I shut everything out for a moment and tuned in to the constant din of the waves as they raced to the shore, tumbling inimitably forwards, propelled by the unstoppable force of the tide. The tide was a powerful dictator and Marion had been right to liken it to time. Time did indeed change everything. Time had changed the way I felt about Grant and about myself. It had taken the good bits of me and tossed them against the rocks, to break into pieces and dissolve into the surf.

I thought back to happier days, when my career was at its pinnacle. Grant and I had just got married and I laughed a lot, alive with achievement, success and love. What a shame time had taken those things from me. Not so much without asking, but slowly, without me realising.

Chapter Thirteen

Sarah

I waited for Rudy to come out of school and realised that today had been one of those horrible days when everything goes wrong. So far, I'd locked myself out, broken in through the downstairs toilet window, and pranged the car. It was only a small prang to the rear fog-light while reversing out of the car park, but Grant would notice it nevertheless and probably give me the silent treatment for the whole weekend.

And now, as I stood with Finn at the beloved 'school gates' (every expectant mother should be handed a leaflet about the phenomena that is the 'school gates' way before she gave birth, to give her time to prepare), I could see Big Lass From The North stomping over in my direction, like an angry bull snorting air out of its nostrils.

'I hear you've been asked by Mrs Peregrine-Jones to do the desserts for her shoot supper.'

I didn't answer.

Silence. Nothing but an icy-cool glare from her beady little rook eyes.

'That's right, why?' I wanted to say 'What of it?' but didn't.

Ah, the school gates ... As soon as the clock strikes three and the huddle starts gathering, intelligent, grown women – some who hold down responsible, high-powered jobs – revert to being eight year-old-girls in the playground all over again. If my hair was in plaits, I'd have been twiddling one of them, in rhythm with the gum I'd be chewing. And if Big Lass From The North had any proper mates, she'd have been arm in arm with one of them right now.

'I do the desserts for Mrs Peregrine-Jones' shoot dinners. You have to decline.' She puffed out her cheeks as if girding her loins.

'I've already promised I'll do it, actually.' I grabbed Finn's hand and pulled him to me, like she might kidnap him and hold him hostage or something.

She stared at me. I think I was supposed to be frightened and I was, but there was no way I was going to let her know that. She continued to say nothing, so I spoke.

'And just in case you're in any doubt, I never break a promise.'

'I've always done them. I always have and I always will.'

She put both hands in the pockets of her mac and stood up straight, her mind ticking over underneath her immaculately sleek treacle-coloured bob, no doubt deliberating where to go next with this dilemma. She hadn't expected a fight, that much was clear.

'Well, it's not looking that way this time, is it?' I replied.

I heard a rustle among the crowd and could have sworn there was a gasp in the rough vicinity of Ole Sunken Eyes. I stole a glance at the onlookers and noticed the gathered mums were unusually quiet and seemed to be inching nearer. What is the collective noun for a gathering of school mums? A gaggle? Maybe it's a scratch? Yep, that's the one. I wouldn't have been surprised if a circle had formed, with Big Lass From The North and me in the middle. Perhaps then they'd all start chanting '*Scrap! Scrap! Scrap!*'

I gave her a look that said 'Well?' It felt like I'd raised a singular eyebrow, but I knew from practising in the mirror as a child that I found that impossible.

Big Lass From The North was floundering, the audience reaction confirming what I'd suspected: she wasn't used to being challenged.

'We'll see about that, pet.' She turned to go, but not before her final word on the matter: 'I shall talk to Mrs Peregrine-Jones myself.'

'You do that.'

The bell rang, as if the person who rang it had been looking on, holding off for the end of the spectacle.

I walked over to meet Rudy, who was dragging his coat across the playground, and realised I was close to tears. I'd been known for playing hardball in my career and had been cruelly labelled Hairy Bollocks by my subordinates (they thought I didn't know, but all bosses know what they're called behind their backs). They were sure I had a pair underneath my pinstriped suit skirts, but this playground stuff was a whole different bag of marbles. It was like being a child again – it hurt.

'Be careful with that one. Don't take on more than you can handle,' someone whispered as I took Rudy's coat and book bag from him.

'Sorry?' I spun round to see Bohemian Babe looking sideways at me.

'Theresa.' She nodded curtly in the general direction of Big Lass From The North. 'She's not one to mess with.' She smiled nervously.

She was tall with pillar-box red hair and, unlike the rest of the crowd, she looked like she had some modicum of personality.

'Good for you, by the way,' she said. 'Good to see someone stand up to her at last.'

'Is she always that rude?' I asked warily, unsure if this was some kind of good cop, bad cop routine.

'That was nothing. She can be much worse.' She glanced round to check she wasn't being watched. 'In case you didn't already know, she's the Queen of Tarts around here, and you've come along and put a spatula in the mixing bowl. Everyone's raving about your cakes, especially your sticky toffee pudding, and she's not a happy monarch. But be warned – she won't let this lie and she won't play nice, either.'

'Oh, come on, women like her are all fur coat and no knickers.' I sniffed. 'What could she possibly do to me?' I wondered if this was all some childish ploy to make me back off.

'Plenty. Her husband's a powerful man in the area.' She glanced round again, like Michelle Dubois of the Resistance from 'Allo 'Allo!, perpetually worried she might be seen chatting to me for too long, sin of sins.

Apparently, round these parts you bake a few cakes and turn into Devil Woman, and anyone seen talking to you will no doubt be tarred with the same brush.

'Look, I don't want to get involved. I generally keep my nose clean and out of this kind of stuff, but you seem OK. I wanted you to know what you're up against. She's got it in for you. Forewarned is forearmed and all that.' She smiled, and walked away.

Anyone listening would have been excused for thinking it was about some top-secret governmental stuff, not about a school mum who was narked someone had baked a better cake than her. It was all subjective, anyway. One man's sticky-toffee-pudding heaven was another man's sticky-toffee-pudding hell. There was room for more than one Queen of Tarts, surely? We didn't even live in the same village. Big Lass From The North needed to get a life. It was ridiculous and I wasn't going to let it get to me.

I found Mrs Davies and she ushered the boys into the library, weariness from teaching her previous music lesson showing across her bunched-up forehead. While she sorted the boys, I utilised the time to have a mini-cry, wipe away my tears and gather myself together. Like a power nap but a power cry instead, it worked every time. I smoothed down my duffel coat, took a deep breath and put my hair behind my ears. I was ready for the firing line now. Bring it on, Mrs Davies!

·· · ●●●●●● · ··

I watched the boys kick their legs under and out on the swings, keeping themselves up high. Finn hadn't mastered it yet, but he was fiercely determined and under no circumstance would he accept help. I settled on the bench so I could watch them both and text Charlie at the same time. She was the only person who seemed to understand what I was going through with Rudy, and how difficult I was finding it all lately:

Hello again. At the park with the boys. Been a nightmare day, but one slight reprieve – headmistress chat wasn't about R's arms, was about his behaviour. He's really naughty in class. But

when they say 'really naughty', they mean talking
when he shouldn't and stuff like that. They thought
he might be bullying someone, but that's ridiculous.
Relieved no mention of the marks, but bruises have
turned yellow, so still time for them to be spotted.
Gonna head home now - I'm all in. Have you arrived
yet?

S xxx

Finn had moved to the slide and Rudy was on the roundabout, both playing happily. I pressed Send. *There.*

I looked up – a split second before Finn hurtled from the top of the slide, banging his head, hard, as he hit the ground with a thud.

Silence.

For what seemed like an age.

Then the loudest wailing I'd ever heard from my little boy.

I ran to him, my heart pounding, my mouth dry. I cradled him on the ground, worried about moving him. He was inconsolable, his eyes glazed, his pupils darting, crazy with pain. I could see the imprint of the rubber matting on his forehead and the beginnings of a bump. I scooped him up, blood pumping hot and loud in my ears.

'Rudy, grab the coats off the bench and follow me!' I yelled and jogged to the car. 'Don't worry, my baby, Mummy's got you, it's going to be OK,' I cooed as Finn writhed in my arms. 'Rudy, come on! Quicker, darling!'

'But, Mummy, my football's down there.' He pointed to the other side of the pitch next to the park.

'We'll come back for it later.'

'But, Mummy, my foot's hurting.'

'I'll look at it in a minute, Rudy. *Just get here, now!*'

I had to keep it together. I opened the car and gently eased Finn into his car seat.

The closest Minor Injuries was nine miles away in Bude. I'd never driven so fast or so dangerously.

I raced into the hospital, carrying Finn, and dragging Rudy behind me. The smell of disinfectant and sweaty waiting room hit my nostrils, triggering a ball of nausea in my throat. I was greeted by a tall male nurse, who wasn't showing nearly enough urgency for my liking. He took Finn's details and ushered us into a side room, where another nurse – a woman – was sitting at a desk.

'So, what do you think?' I asked the first one, staring deep into his eyes, scouring them for clues.

'It's hard to say. Everything seems OK, but his reactions are slow. How high did you say the slide was?'

'About nine feet.'

I inhaled deeply, ashamed I could have let this happen, and looked down at my curly-haired little angel sitting quietly now on my lap. I stroked his head and swallowed hard to keep down the nausea that was working its way up my throat again.

'OK, well, better to be safe with a head injury. I'm going to ask you to go to A&E in Barnstaple to get him checked over. They have all the necessary equipment there.'

Tears rolled down my cheeks in quick succession, maybe even two at a time. If only I hadn't gone to the park this afternoon. I knew it was a bad day. I should have just gone home. *If only* I hadn't been sending a text.

I had a load of questions burning inside me but couldn't make my mouth work. Eventually, I managed: 'He will be OK, won't he?'

'Don't worry, love.'

'But he'll be fine, yes?' I needed to hear it.

'Get yourself off to A&E and they'll check him over.'

The other nurse got up from the computer and handed me a tissue. The whole time we'd been there she'd sat watching me. It was probably the most fun bit of their job, deciding if the parents were good 'uns or bad 'uns. There was no doubt she'd decided on the latter. After all, I'd let my three-year-old fall from a nine-foot drop.

'It'll be fine, dear.' She patted my shoulder. 'It's just better to get these things checked out, that's all.'

'But Barnstaple's thirty-five miles from here. What if he falls asleep while I'm driving?'

'If he does, just let him sleep. Now, let's get you on your way. Have you got anyone to help? Husband? Partner?' she asked, more for her own information probably. Some juicy facts to add to the evolving picture of my life.

'At work,' I said.

'Do you want to ring him from here?' she persisted.

I shook my head, tears threatening again, and made for the car.

·····•·•····

'He's got to have a CAT scan,' I told Grant, trying to keep the shaking from my voice.

He needed to know I had it all under control, but we'd been at the hospital three hours now and I was finding it hard.

'Jesus, is it that bad?'

'They don't really know what's wrong, hence the scan. Everything about him seems fine, except he keeps falling over. Sort of stumbling and tripping. But there are no other symptoms. They want to be sure, though, so they want to observe him overnight, then scan him in the morning.'

As I spoke, things were occurring to me. The scan alone would be frightening for him. He was only three. I'd have to be there with him. What would I do with Rudy while he was having it? So far, Rudy had been acting up, jealous of all the attention Finn was receiving. It was understandable. Then it dawned on me it would be fine because, by then, Grant would be here. It would only take four hours from London to Barnstaple.

'I'm glad they're giving him a scan. At least we'll know for sure. Are you going to be OK, babes?' Grant asked.

'I'll be fine. Just get here as soon as you can.'

'Oh.' Silence. 'You want me to come *tonight*?'

I was in the corridor. People were coming and going from all directions and I was afraid that if I spoke, I would scream. I counted to ten in my head and attempted to talk.

'No, no, it'll be fine. Don't worry. I'll phone you in the morning.'

'OK, babes. Try to get some sleep and don't worry, he'll be fine.'

I buzzed to get back into the ward, got onto the bed and put an arm around each of the boys. I gently stroked their faces and they drifted off to sleep, Finn first, Rudy second.

What was happening to me?

I wasn't in any fit state to be looking after children and my marriage was in tatters. I knew it had been building, but it occurred to me that I didn't want to be married any more. I also realised I didn't have the luxury of that choice. I had two boys and all the responsibility that came with them. Who was I to take their daddy away from them? Who was I to make big choices like that on their behalf?

Suddenly, I understood all those parents who stayed together until their children reached eighteen. Suddenly, I realised that Grant and I were living separate lives, neither of us appreciating the trials and hardships in the other's life. Suddenly, I understood all the bitterness that accrued in a marriage over the years. I'd always said I'd never stay with someone for the sake of it, whatever 'it' might be, but it had become apparent, once again, that until you'd been to the top of the mountain, you couldn't comment on the view.

And suddenly I realised how selfish I was being trying to get in touch with TIM. How disloyal it was to my beautiful boys. I looked at Rudy, one springy tuft of golden hair sticking up from his double crown. Why couldn't Grant see what was happening? His inability to empathise with me over just how hard Rudy was to manage was the source of my bitterness towards him. I had to try harder, I had to make this family work.

Chapter Fourteen

Jasmine Rafferty

Jasmine knelt on the frosty grass and pulled out the lifeless flowers one by one, piling them up on the earth beside her.

'Why?' she whispered as she unwrapped the paper from the gangly lily stems she'd been clutching. 'Why did you have to go and leave me?'

She busied herself with the task in hand, snipping off the ends of the stalks, filling the pot with water from the empty Pepsi Max bottle she'd commandeered from her fridge, moving slowly and deliberately.

'I'll never let anyone else take your place in my heart, you know that, but you know I can never forgive you, don't you?' She jostled the blooms so they looked just so, leaned forwards and pressed her lips to the cold stone. 'Same time next week, then?' she said softly. 'But I'd be grateful if you could arrange for it to be a bit warmer, OK? Least you can do.' She stood up, pulled her coat tight around her and quickly wiped away her tears. 'In a while, crocodile.' She touched the stone one last time. 'Right,' she announced to the empty churchyard. 'Which sucker can I flog some paper to today, then?'

············

'What time is it?' Charlotte asked later that evening, at Jas's place. She checked her phone. 'Nothing.' Jamie had definitely said he'd let her know tonight. She sloshed the remains of her wine around the glass. 'I hope his gran's OK. I mean, even if he decides he can't come to Barbados now, I just hope she's OK. Must be scary having a heart attack.'

'Well, she's not dead, so that's a start, I suppose. Have you met her?' Jasmine reached for the wine bottle.

'No, never met any of his family. Didn't even know he had a gran in Oxford. In fact, come to think of it, I don't think he's ever mentioned any grandparents before. *Aw*, fuck, he's not lying, is he, Jas? P'rhaps he's met someone and doesn't want to come. He's made up a 'my gran has died' story, hasn't he, or a variation of it?' Charlotte nodded with certainty at the likelihood and stepped up her sloshing speed.

'OK, stop! Take a deep breath and let that wild fucking imagination of yours ebb away, back to whatever flock-wallpapered psychedelic place it hangs out when you're not using it. Right, do you want a top-up?' Jas dangled the half-empty bottle aloft.

'Go on, then.' Charlotte raised her glass for a refill. 'I'm so weak. I promised myself I'd only have one.'

'You haven't actually had that much. You've thrown most of it over my sofa. Will you stop with the sloshing now, babes. Besides, what's the harm?'

'I'll tell you what the harm is. I'm gonna look like a newborn rabbit tomorrow, all flat hair and fused eyelids. Not exactly the picture of dewy youth I had in mind.' Charlotte pretended to prise her eyes open. 'Mind you, it might be academic now. You'll come if not, won't you? I can't bear the thought of going on my own.'

Jas laughed. 'Two weeks in the hedonistic heaven that is Barbados, all expenses paid, with my best mate for company? *Hmm*, let me think now ... But Jamie's still going, I'd lay money on it. Just remember, though, he's not going to get back with you. You've gotta face it, Charlie.'

Jas stopped laughing and looked unusually serious. She reminded Charlotte of a secretary bird – long skinny legs, glamorous hair and a smooth face. Pretty but dangerous. Secretary birds caught their prey by stamping on it until it was stunned or unconscious enough for it to swallow. The printers Jasmine sold paper to probably wouldn't argue with that description. But she always flirted with her prey first. She had an undeniable sexual allure. Her dress sense told the story perfectly, always immaculately turned out in sleek little shift dresses or prim pussy-bow blouses, but with a short skirt or 4-inch heels. Sex meets sobriety, Miss Moneypenny with fishnets and an opinion.

'You're heading for a fall if you don't,' Jas concluded.

'Don't hold back, Jas, tell me what you really think.'

Charlotte's smile failed to reach her eyes. She should have come to terms with it by now, especially since she'd said Jamie spent all of last week avoiding her. Going to such lengths as taking the stairs instead of the lift and cancelling a meeting he had with a lawyer on her floor (Millie was all-knowing and all-seeing). Charlotte had tried everything to mastermind chance meetings but, on the rare occasion they'd happened, Jamie had been cold and unresponsive.

Despite all that, she found it hard to believe that Jamie coming to Barbados wasn't a sign of his love for her.

'Why would he agree to come if there wasn't a small chance he was going to get back with me?' she asked.

Jas just looked at her, not wishing to sanction such nonsense with a reply.

'I can't help it. I've been thinking of all different scenarios, reasons why we split and why he might be coming.'

'Bet you've listed them, too, haven't you? And they're in your freakofax, aren't they.'

'Of course they are.' She laughed sadly.

'Oh, baby, come 'ere.' Jas pulled Charlotte to her.

'I want you to tell me it's gonna be OK.' Charlotte sniffed. 'But I know you can't. I don't understand it. We were perfect together. He even said so himself. But he seems to have dealt with us splitting up like he's lost a tenner. Bit fed up but it's not the end of the world.'

'Well, men compartmentalise, don't they? You know that. Come on, Charlie, it's gonna be OK.' She gave Charlie a chivvying hug.

'Great Valentine's Day this is.'

'Talking of which, look what I got ...' Jas skipped into the bedroom and came out beaming, proudly exhibiting a pair of four-inch gold Prada heels. 'You like?'

'They're gorgeous Who bought you those?'

'Me. They're my Valentine's present to me.'

'Oh.'

'*Aw*, come on, babe. Life has a funny way of sorting stuff out.'

'You're right. *Ooh*, did you hear that? That was my phone.'

Charlotte grabbed her mobile while Jas topped up their drinks.

'False alarm, it was Sarah.' Charlotte settled back on the sofa. 'Now, tell me about these three lovers of yours.'

'How is Sarah? Are she and Grant still enjoying it in Cornwall?'

'Not sure, really. It's hard for Sarah with Grant in London every week – I think it might be taking its toll.'

'On their relationship?'

'A bit, perhaps, but they'll be fine. They're Sarah and Grant, they're couple goals. *Sooo*, back to these three lovers of yours you mentioned in your email. Adrian the Married, yeah? I presume number two is this Reuben you've got your eye on. Not quite number two yet, but soon no doubt if I know you. So who's the third?'

Jasmine went red. Really red. No half measures.

'No one. I haven't got a third. I was joking.' She pulled an 'as if' face.

'Come off it, Jas, you're scarlet. Stop fibbing.'

'I'm not!'

Charlotte narrowed her eyes.

'Oh, don't start!' Jas said.

'It upsets me, that's all. Can't you find a nice unattached man for once, Jas?'

'*Ooo*, now who's pulling the punches?'

'Yeah, well, I worry about you. It can't be good for your karmic energy, all this deceit.'

'Karmic energy?' Jas curled up with both hands cupped around her wine glass. 'How very Zen! How very bollocks! The thing is, I'm not the one being unfaithful, am I? It's the others. Anyway, life's too short. I don't want a proper grown-up relationship with proper grown-up things in it, like mortgages and kids.'

'Oh, don't start with all that again. What if you finally find someone you love, someone you think you could be with past your "threshold"?'

One year of anything or anyone was enough for Jasmine, who frequently reminded Charlotte that she was one of the few privileged people to have survived and made it under the bar.

'What if he was unfaithful?' Charlotte continued. 'How would you feel then? I'll tell you how, like shit.'

'You're wrong, actually. If it was only a one-night stand, I don't think I'd mind. And if it was a full-on affair? Well, that would mean there was something wrong with our relationship. Anyway, you're such a hypocrite.'

'What d'ya mean?'

'You've been unfaithful before.' Jasmine tucked a lock of carob-brown hair behind her ear.

'I haven't.'

'You have.'

'I'm telling you, I haven't.' Charlotte shook her head defiantly.

'Oh yes, you have. You snogged me at my cocktail party while you were going out with Pete.' Jas looked smugly at Charlotte, nodding triumphantly. 'Remember?'

'*Oww*, that doesn't count. We were completely off our faces and it was a bet ... And you're a girl. And Pete was there, anyway. He loved it. Besides, it was awful!' Charlotte wrinkled her nose and laughed.

'Oh, cheers!'

'Funny, though.'

'Yeah, worth it just to see the shock on everyone's faces.'

'It's a good job we don't like kissing each other anyway, cos we'd make a useless couple – we like all the same chocolates in a box for a start.' Charlotte laughed, enjoying the wine and Jas's easy company. 'Plus, you'd be unfaithful to me and I couldn't cope with that.'

'Yeah, and you'd suffocate me with your controlling ways, so I'd end up lying to you all the time ... you'd love that,' Jas said with a chuckle.

'What do you mean?' Charlotte had stopped laughing.

'Well, you hate lying, don't you?'

'I don't mean that – I mean the bit about my controlling ways.' Charlotte looked directly into Jasmine's green eyes and held her gaze.

'Well, you know you're a control freak, you've said so before.'

'I like to control my life in certain ways, yes. I'm controlling on occasion, but not without good reason. And I certainly haven't "suffocated" Jamie.'

Jas sighed. As ever, Charlie was in denial.

'What?' Charlie asked.

'Nothing. I was only joking.'

'No, Jas, this is important. What did you mean?'

'Look – we've talked about this before. You're just a bit possessive, that's all.'

'We all worry about what our men are getting up to, don't we?' Charlotte asked hopefully, then realised who she was asking. 'Well, not you, obviously.'

'No, you're right, it's normal to be a bit jealous, just not to the extreme that you go to. You know, like interrupting Pete at that conference, and getting him to change his physiotherapist to a male one.' Jas held a tortilla chip to her mouth. 'And let's not forget *the* birthday party!' She crunched on the crisp and looked pensively into the distance, just for a second – blink and you'd have missed it. 'I certainly won't,' she muttered into her glass.

'What?'

'Nothing.' Jas waved her hand in the air. 'Look, forget I said anything. I didn't mean to upset you.'

Silence.

'*Aw*, fuck, Charlie, you've gone all serious now. You're scaring me. I feel like I'm gonna get done. Come on, have another top-up!' Jas swiped the bottle of wine.

'I don't want any more.' Charlotte sat up straight and put her hand over the top of her glass. 'I was suspicious. He'd been acting strange that week.'

'What?'

'Pete. He was acting suspiciously.'

'You don't have to explain, Charlie. I wish I hadn't said anything now.'

'I just had to check he was doing what he said he was doing, that's all.'

'I know.'

'Well, what's bad about that?'

'Charlie, you rang the conference centre and got the speaker to announce to 200 delegates that there was an urgent telephone call for Pete Groves. Pete then had to stand up, and squeeze past everyone, to take a call from his girlfriend, who was "just checking" he was where he said he was. Then he had to go back into the conference to have his face scrutinised for clues of what the emergency was. Come on, it must have been dead embarrassing.' Jas took a glug of wine. 'I've been to these conferences, Charlie, and I know what it's like. I'm telling you, it would have been a nightmare. Even I would be embarrassed.'

'I suppose so. When you put it like that, it was a bit barmy. Pete was furious, I remember that much, but I didn't do it to be nasty.'

Jasmine remembered Charlotte telling her about that day. She'd said she'd paced up and down for hours before finally plucking up the courage to make the call. She knew Pete would be furious, but that never mattered. The only thing that ever mattered was satisfying the urge. Getting the information, making 100 per cent sure she wasn't being lied to, that she wasn't being cheated on, that no one was having a laugh at her expense. Nothing ever stood in Charlotte's way when she needed to know. But the conference wasn't the worst of it. In the three years they were together, Pete had been subjected to a continual smorgasbord of checks and restraints.

Jasmine glanced at her watch. 'Right, enough soul-searching.'

'*Uh-oh*, did you hear that?' Charlotte froze. 'A message ... He's not coming, I just know it.' She snatched her phone up and started pacing.

'Well? Put us both out of our misery, for fuck's sake.'

Charlotte read the message and looked sad.

'It's from Jamie all right, only it's unrecognisable as a Jamie text, all bar the number. It's addressed to Charlotte instead of Charlie, it's curt, non-emotive, and it has no kisses. But his gran is OK, apparently, and he'll meet me at the airport tomorrow.'

She put her phone down, tilted her head back and took a long, deep breath. Then stopped mid-lungful.

'What's that?' she asked.

Jas flushed red for the second time that evening. Charlie had spotted the pregnancy test she had carelessly left on the bookcase.

'I think you can see what it is.'

'Are you pregnant?'

'Don't be stupid.'

'Jasmine, be honest.'

'I don't know, OK!' She picked at her nails. 'I bought it cos I've been feeling off lately and I realised I'd missed a couple of periods. It's probably all the exercise I'm doing and the stress of bloody work. They keep upping my targets, the bastards.'

'So you haven't done a test yet?'

'No.'

Charlotte went and picked up the box. She held it out. 'Go and do it, Jas.'

'I'm watching this now.' She turned to the TV.

'If you're pregnant, Jas, you need to know.'

Jasmine got up reluctantly and traipsed across the living room like a belligerent child. 'Get the gin out the cupboard, then, and start running me a bath.'

···•••·····

She sat on the toilet lid, closed her eyes and counted the seconds in her head: one thousand, two thousand, three thousand ... it was a long five minutes. She opened her eyes one by one and peered into her upturned palms at the pregnancy stick balancing across them.

Two blue lines.

Two blue lines? That meant she was pregnant, didn't it?

She scrabbled around in the box to find the instructions.

'I'm pregnant!' She punched the air with her fist. '*Yesss!*' Then sat down on the side of the bath, floored by her own reaction.

24 January 1994

She dragged her teddy bear behind her, rubbing flakes of sleep from her eyes as she took the stairs one by one. At eight years old, she liked to think she was past the teddy-bear stage now – they were babyish – but being ill was no fun and Stinker had been keeping her company.

She got to the last step and jumped off, two feet together, onto the hall floor. The house was quiet so she knew her mum had gone to drop her brother off at school. She wouldn't be long, an hour tops, just long enough to drop him off and check on Paintbox the pony in the field down the road. Her mum had let her stay home from school this morning, because she was ill. Her dad was home today as well. Her mum had said not to wake him, because he was poorly too. Her dad didn't know she'd stayed home from school yet – it would be a nice surprise for him when he woke up. They could spend the day together.

She walked into the kitchen along the cracks of the cold brown ceramic tiles, counting them as she went, and stopped at the Aga to warm her toes, pressing the soles of her feet against the door. She sat her teddy on the kitchen table and toed the rest of the way along the tile cracks, one dainty foot in front of the other, to the fridge.

There was a note on the fridge, right at the top. It was pinned to the freezer section by the magnet with the wolf on that they'd got from Woburn Safari Park.

She reached up for the scrap of paper. It was addressed to Mummy. She read it anyway:

Jean,

Do not go into the garage. Call the police. Whatever you do, do not go into the garage. Promise me.

Love you,

Alec x

It was Daddy's handwriting. He usually left for work early, around seven, when he wasn't ill, so she rarely got to see him before he went. For that reason, she made sure she gave him a kiss and said 'have a nice day' before bed every night. He'd be watching TV from his favourite armchair. He'd ruffle her hair and say 'See you later, alligator,' and she would always reply 'In a while, crocodile,' then run up the stairs to bed.

Last night had been different. Daddy had read her and her brother a bedtime story, in each of their rooms, and snuggled with them in their beds for ages. He'd still said 'See you later, alligator,' though, her mum had told her so. He'd stood at her door and smiled at her as he said it, but she never gave her reply, because she was already asleep.

Was this a joke? Daddy was good at jokes. She raced from the kitchen into the utility room and down the steep steps to the door that led from the house to the garage. She turned the handle and pulled the door over the lip of ill-fitting carpet that Daddy still hadn't fixed.

The cold January air came rushing into the warmth of the house. She felt the rough concrete floor under her feet and sniffed the distinctive smell of white spirit. Then she saw him. Daddy. Hanging from the ceiling on the lunge rope that Mummy used for Paintbox.

His silver stepladder was lying on the floor underneath him and he was wearing his stripy jumper, the one Grandma knitted for him one Christmas. His arms and legs were hanging loosely, his feet pointing down like a ballet dancer, and his eyes … She didn't know it at the time, but it was his eyes that would haunt her for ever.

Chapter Fifteen

Sarah

'But I don't want to go, Mummy, I hate it.'

'What have I told you about using that word, Rudy? Hate is a very strong word and I will not tolerate it being used incorrectly.'

'Got my 'noculars, Mummy.' Finn toddled over dressed in a khaki shirt and a camouflage hat. He was an explorer today.

'But I do hate it,' Rudy whined.

'Listen, chicken.' I pulled Rudy to me. 'Daddy's back tonight, so you've just got one more day at school, then it's the weekend. That's good, isn't it?' I nuzzled my face in his hair.

'S'pose so.'

'Right, then, last one to the car is a monkey!'

I ran to the Jeep. I pretended to stumble and both boys raced past me. I watched them laugh and jump into their seats, Rudy helping Finn, working together to ensure that I'd be the monkey. No doubt the tears would start when we got to school, though, just as they did every day, but I was determined to make a swift exit today because I had so much on.

I definitely couldn't afford my usual habit of hanging around outside the classroom window, on hand to whisk Rudy away in the unlikely event he didn't stop crying after five minutes. Sunday was Mrs Peregrine-Jones' shoot dinner, so

I had to go shopping for ingredients, which was harder than it sounded when there was no supermarket within a thirty-mile radius.

I needed to prepare thirty-five portions of sticky toffee pudding tomorrow, as far as I could, and then Sunday evening I was going to the Peregrine-Jones residence to plate up and serve the desserts. It was nerve-wracking. I hadn't heard any more from Big Lass From The North on the matter, so I presumed she hadn't managed to dissuade Mrs P-J from employing me and I was feeling rather good about it. It was about time that bully met her match.

Also, today I had a meeting at Fawksley Hall to finalise the christening and check out the state of the windows. If I wanted to go for my walk, I had to get a wiggle on.

'OK, boys, we need to be nice and quick, so chop-chop!'

I pulled Finn away from the life-size robot in the school corridor made from cereal boxes and loo rolls.

'Here's your snack, Rudy. Go and put that in your tray.'

'But, Mummy, we've forgotten my book bag.' He looked hopeful.

'Oh.' I looked around on the floor. 'We have got it. I've seen it. It must still be in the car. Don't worry, I'll nip and get it. You wait here and I'll see you in a minute.'

So much for a quick getaway.

Pulling Finn by the hand, I jogged to the car. The book bag was suspiciously stuffed under the driver's seat. Poor love, he obviously thought that would secure him a day off. I locked the car and turned to jog back across the playground.

'Did you forget something?' Big Lass From The North was blocking my way, and my daylight, like a solar eclipse. 'I hope you don't forget anything on Sunday, pet.' A thin smile spread across her face (quite some journey).

'I'm sorry?' I asked, unable to refuse the bait.

'Sunday. Oh, hasn't Mrs Peregrine-Jones told you?'

'Look, if you've got something to say, can you spit it out, please, because I'm busy.'

I looked over her shoulder and could see Ole Sunken Eyes walking towards the car park and Bohemian Babe and a few others not far behind. No doubt they were hurrying over for Episode Two of the The Shoot Dinner Saga.

'Mrs Peregrine-Jones is offering her guests a choice of desserts on Sunday.' Big Lass From The North paused. 'Sticky toffee pudding, of course ...' She looked like she was chewing on a maggot as she uttered the words. 'Or a mouth-wateringly delicious frangipani tartlet topped with Armagnac-soaked prunes served with a dollop of home-made creamy Calvados ice cream.' She was smiling now.

If she was hoping for a reaction, I gave none. I had a million questions but firmly clamped my tongue between my teeth.

'I'll see you there, then,' she said with a saccharine smirk, her evil eyes simmering with ill-will. 'Oh, and enjoy being "busy" today, because I have a feeling you'll be positively redundant on Sunday.' She shuffled off to catch up with Ole Sunken Eyes, no doubt to spread the good news.

Bohemian Babe looked over at me and rolled her eyes.

I felt like I'd entered a parallel universe. I'd baked a few things for a cake stall and before I could say 'vanilla essence', I was in some kind of public cook-off, with a load of ex-colonels, High Court judges and their charity-working wives deciding my fate. I wondered if the local bookie was taking bets and was absolutely positive Ole Sunken Eyes would open a book on the event.

This cast a whole new light on things. Perhaps I should find out who the guests were and lobby them. Maybe I could offer a free gift with my pudding. What would it be? A springer spaniel? A flat cap? Most of them were judges, so maybe I should dress as a bunny girl and offer a free lap dance to anyone who ordered my dessert.

That might get the male votes, but what about the female ones? Should I lie and tell them that my sticky toffee pudding is a fat-free version and that it's like chewing on celery, because you actually burn calories while you eat it? The more you eat, the more you burn?

I nodded at Jinslet, who was running late as usual, unbelievably still wearing flip-flops, even though it was minus two with a ground frost. What would Big Lass From The North offer, I wondered. She was bound to go for the opposite approach – dead leg if you didn't choose the prune tart, good beating with a brace of pheasants if you left any on your plate, that sort of thing. Maybe I should just ring Mrs Peregrine-Jones and tell her I wasn't taking part in such a ridiculously humiliating bake-off under any circumstance, no matter how much she paid.

·········

I knew I was becoming obsessed with my daily walk down to the beach but, as obsessions go, it was a healthy one. I found myself fiercely protective of my walk but, in my defence, I was always a better person to know afterwards. The rolling mists that came in from the sea, the wild woodland and dramatic coastline made the walk one of a kind. It was a quiet, hidden place, where time seemed to stand still.

Marion, on the other hand, never stood still for very long, but she and her abrasive charm had become part of my walk now and I looked forward to seeing her.

I walked right to the end of the bay and back today. No sign of Marion yet. I settled on a large slab of slate instead of my usual rock armchair. It was a big, smooth platform jutting out from the cliff face, made from layers of different-coloured slate and tilting down towards the beach. It was cold to touch and not sheltered like my armchair, but it faced a different part of the sea and I fancied a change.

I got out my flask, book and mobile as usual. It was becoming a ritual: send Charlie a text, pour some coffee, read a couple of pages, chat to Marion – or at least listen to what Marion had to say – and head home. I flipped open my phone. Dead battery. Bugger. I'd been dying to tell Charlie about the bake-off and I needed to get Jas's mobile number from her.

I needed Jas's address for her christening invite. Jas was Charlie's friend, really. They'd known each other since childhood, but we all worked in London so with Charlie as a mutual friend Jas and I had got to know each other. Despite her questionable morals, I liked her. She was brash and funny and although I probably wouldn't want to cross her, she was always good value and a great cook too.

She invited Grant and me over for dinner at her flat just before we moved to Cornwall, to make up a six-some with Charlotte and Jamie. It was the first time Grant had met Jas and he found it odd that her boyfriend, Adrian the Married (as Charlotte called him), was there, celebrating his birthday with his mistress. Nevertheless Grant was clearly taken with the host and her green Bambi eyes and long, lithe limbs. It made me laugh. It was funny watching him get all tongue-tied, keen as a puppy dog.

Jas wasn't really one for children, but I decided to invite her to the christening anyway. Perhaps it might soften her up – there was bound to be a pussy cat under there somewhere.

I put my phone back in my pocket. Never mind, it would wait. I reached for my flask and unscrewed the top. The cup came off but the rest of the flask slipped out of my gloved hand and rolled down the slab of slate I was perched on. It was my V&A flask, the one with the beautiful blue flowers on that the boys had bought me for my birthday – they'd chosen it themselves.

I went running after it, but the slate was steep. I gathered momentum involuntarily. I tried to slow myself down, but the rock was wet from an earlier downpour, leaving it slippy like frost. I slipped and fell.

'*Bugger!*'

I thought I was fine. Bit dazed but unhurt, I prised myself up slowly and tried to move. It was then I felt the coldness on my leg. I looked down and couldn't make sense of what I saw at first. I focused more and saw a jagged piece of rock sticking out of my jeans just below my left knee.

Strangely, it was only when I noticed the wound that I felt the pain, but *ow-ow-ow*, now I felt it. Boy, did it hurt!

I gently lowered myself to the ground, keeping my leg as straight as I could.

'*Oooh, that hurts!*'

The stinging pain took my breath away. What now?

My mobile was dead and the beach was empty. Where was bloody Grant when I needed him? Unfair, really, considering that even if he'd been in Cornwall, he couldn't have been expected to know I'd injured myself on a remote beach. Even the best of marriages didn't boast ESP, but I was feeling bloody-minded.

I looked down at my wound. Should I take the shard of rock out or leave it? I didn't have a choice in the matter. If I'd taken it out, I would have been sick.

Despite being rugged up like a thoroughbred in January, I was cold and shaking. I zipped my coat up as far as it would go and wrapped my arms around myself tightly. I'd never seen anyone but Marion on the beach before – she was my only hope. So typical she'd chosen today not to be here. No doubt Fridays were her big trip into town to do her shopping or something. She was probably wandering up and down the frozen veg aisle right now while I quietly died, frozen and alone down here on the beach.

'*Marion!*' I shouted.

Nothing.

I took a really deep breath. '*Marion! Help!*' I yelled.

Fuck. This could be bad.

The pain intensified. I scratched at the sand with my fingers, the shingle getting stuck in my nails. I looked across at my flask, which had stopped halfway across the beach.

'*Oh no!*' I mewed.

The waves were nearly reaching it, the tide was on its way in. I couldn't lose my flask.

'*Help, Marion, help me!*'

Hot tears slid down my frozen cheeks. I tried to pull myself along on my hands. I moved a bit, but the pain was too bad. It was no use, the flask was miles away.

I tried to think of happy things. I leaned back on the slab of slate behind me and fantasised about TIM walking round the corner. I'd tried not to think about him since Finn's fall, but I needed him right now.

I felt his hands on my hair, gently soothing away the pain. I heard his Irish lilt murmur into my ear. '*It's gonna be OK, SJ. I've got it all under control. Yer man is coming with a stretcher any minute now.*' He cradled my head against him and held me tight. '*Don't worry, SJ. I'm here for ya now, baby.*'

I felt him hold my hand tightly and yank out the piece of rock from my leg. He stroked my head some more. I felt floaty and serene. I heard a rip of material. He was wrapping something round my leg now. Nice and tight.

'Right, then, let's get you out of here.'

I opened my eyes. 'Marion!'

'Don't talk, but you're going to have to help me here.'

'My flask.' I pointed feebly down the beach.

'Don't go worrying about that now. Right, then—'

'But the boys ...'

Her dark-brown eyes looked into my watery ones.

'OK, OK,' she tutted. 'Wait here.'

She trotted off down the shingle. She retrieved the flask, stuffed it into the oversized pocket of her shabby brown mac and jogged back again.

'Right, then, we're going to get you up. Just lean on me, OK?'

I nodded.

'*One. Two. Three – and up!*' she said as if raising a circus tent all on her own. 'Good girl. Now, we'll take it nice and slow. Doesn't matter how long it takes.'

'Where are we going?' I had visions of her marching me back along the three-mile uphill walk to my house, a walk that taxed me when both of my legs were good.

'To my house.'

A rush of panic-induced heat moved up from my chest and into my ears. The nearest house was two miles away, up the steepest, rockiest cliff I'd ever clapped eyes on.

'How far is that?'

'Just round the corner. Don't worry. We'll have a nice cup of tea when we get there.'

Cup of tea? I'll need an oxygen tent. Then it dawned.

'Duckpool Mill! You live in Duckpool Mill.' I smiled. I was pleased. Marion was exactly who I'd hoped would live there.

'Yes, yes, come on, now, put some effort in.'

· · · · • • • · · ·

I sipped my tea from a thick mustard-coloured mug with no handle. It was handcrafted and the perfect width to cup one's hands around. Like its owner, Duckpool Mill was exactly as I'd hoped it to be inside. Light, airy and ever so arty.

Art was everywhere. Shiny oak floorboards, white walls, no curtains, and lots and lots of art, books and photos. Pottery, paintings, wood carvings, sculptures and tapestry clamoured for attention. Even the functional stuff was art. All of the objects seemed to dance around the main attraction: the fireplace. It was like no other fireplace I'd ever seen, complete with four ornate dragon feet, taking up a large proportion of the floor space. The room was a veritable feast for the senses. An art emporium.

The smell of beeswax dominated the air, with the occasional waft of woodsmoke butting in every now and then from the magnificent fire dragon that presided over us. I lay, left foot raised on a tower of ethnic pillows, on a finely embroidered chaise longue, propped up by still more pillows, looking out to sea through an enormous window – an immaculately polished one, I was pleased to note.

'How you feeling now?' Marion asked.

'Much better, thank you.'

I looked up at her. She'd peeled off her usual walking attire of shabby brown waterproof jacket and trousers and was wearing a stripy red top and a pair of jeans. Very nautical. But given the creativity oozing out of every pore of the room, it was also rather staid. One almost expected her to float down the stairs in a hand-painted kimono with a cocktail-coloured cigarillo in one hand and a gin Martini in the other. Perhaps she only had enough creative energy to cope with the living space. She did, however, look softer somehow, against the backdrop of her beautiful home.

'That was the nicest cup of tea I've ever had,' I said.

She smiled and took the mug away from me. 'Good.'

'I was scared back there, you know.'

I watched her as she tended to the dragon, prodding around with a barley-twist poker. A pang of envy took me by surprise. Marion was at ease with herself and I envied her her independence. It was just her – no one else to make happy. Selfish? Perhaps. Appealing? Definitely.

'I don't know what would have happened if you hadn't been there to help me.' I closed my eyes to let the calm of the room engulf me.

'There's no point worrying about the what-ifs, darling. It's the here and now you need to focus on.' She pulled down the dragon's mouth and replaced the poker in its stand. 'That said, it's lucky for you, missy, that I'm expecting a delivery this afternoon, because Friday's normally my big day out in town.' She turned to look at me, her eyes teasing, her mouth turning up at the edges. 'I go to that fancy supermarket on Fridays and everything.'

Her sarcasm caught me unawares. Why, at thirty-eight years of age, did I still find myself judging someone on a ridiculously little amount of information, only to be surprised when I came to all the wrong conclusions?

'What? You go all the way to that Bude? That there place with all those *broight loites*?' I replied in my best Cornish accent.

She let out a chuckle but ended it abruptly as she turned away.

A horrible thought occurred. 'I'm really rather hoping at this point, Marion, that you're not Cornish.'

Nothing.

'Otherwise I'm going to be really embarrassed,' I pressed for an answer.

'No, you're OK. I'm definitely not from round these parts. Far from it.'

She glanced at one of the photos, the one that stood magnificent on top of the fire dragon, then quickly looked at the clock (no ordinary clock, of course, another *objet d'art*).

'The medics should be here in a minute. They'll know what to do.'

I suddenly remembered my appointment with Fawksley Hall. I wasn't going to make it now.

'I've got a meeting planned for one o'clock. Would you mind if I used your phone to cancel, please?'

She went to fetch her phone and while she was gone, I looked at the photos in the room. They were all of the same little boy, apart from two, that were of different men. I lingered on the most beautiful photo of all, in pride of place on the fire dragon, in a gilded frame, the one that Marion had looked at a moment ago. A glamorous, much younger Marion graced the frame, with dark-brown hair, wrapped in a fur coat, a chic fedora tipped to one side. She was cuddling the little boy who appeared in all the other photos. What made the photo so special was the way both were laughing. Open-mouthed, roaring-with-hilarity type laughter. The photo was natural, as if the subjects thought they were alone, unaware of anyone taking it. It was bursting with warmth and happiness.

A shiver ran across my neckline. I turned my head to see Marion standing there with the phone in her hand, staring across at the photo once more. She looked away quickly and held her arm out for me to take the phone. I looked at the photo and looked at her, and she told me with her eyes that it wasn't the time. I opened my mouth to speak and could see fear run across the lines in her face.

'I've got a quandary on my hands,' I said and smiled.

The fear departed, her face instantly relaxed. She perched at the end of my chaise longue.

'Oh yes?'

'Yes, and I was wondering what your thoughts might be.'

Marion found the whole bake-off debacle hilarious and surprised me by saying that she knew of Mrs P-J and found her to be a formidable but fair woman whom I shouldn't rush to judge. She also surprised (read: scared) me by how well she appeared to know me, considering how little we'd had to do with each other thus far. Marion was obviously a far better judge of character than I.

'You're a competitive woman who abhors bullies, and nothing on God's earth will stop you from doing this bake-off, but I think you already know that.' She patted the foot on my good leg. 'So it doesn't really matter what I think, now does it, my darling?'

I laughed. I liked how it felt to be her darling.

'I will say one thing, though.' She looked towards a noise coming from the kitchen and back to me. 'Do what you do for you, not to prove anything to others.' She got up to let the medics in. 'And tell me to mind my own business if you want to, but I think you're a troubled young lady.' She glanced at herself in the gold-leaf mirror on the wall and neatened her hair with her hands. 'I've learned a thing or two in my seventy-five years and would be more than happy to make a cup of tea for any troubled young ladies who wish to come and air their troubles.'

Chapter Sixteen

Sarah

'*Ow!* Watch my stitches! Don't press too hard!

There isn't a romantic, sexy way to tell someone to watch your leg while you're having sex. I could have said it in a breathy, *Happy Birthday, Mr President* way, but that would have just been ridiculous. It hadn't put him off.

I'd decided to try and be nice to Grant. I'd rung him from Marion's to tell him about my fall and he'd rushed back from London straight away. He got home just in time to pick Rudy and Finn up from school. He'd bought me flowers (white lilies, which he knows I don't like because they remind me of death, but he was pushed for time, so I let him off). But even if he hadn't done that, I'd still decided to try and be nicer to him. He was the boys' dad and he wasn't a bad man.

I didn't actually know where all this bitterness towards him had come from. It had kind of crept up on me over the years. And I couldn't work out if I didn't fancy him because of the bitterness or because that's just what happens when you've been in a relationship for nine years. I'd never been in a relationship for that long before, so it was impossible to know.

As Grant humped me from behind, I noticed a whole ridge of dust on the bed frame behind the mattress. Must get that later. Shoddy. I buried my face in the mattress, desperately trying not to think about what was actually happening for fear of wanting to cry.

I turned my mind to more appealing matters while Grant continued thrusting in and out of me. What dessert should I have for the christening? Perhaps sticky toffee pudding might be fun, considering everyone was raving about it so much. And I must take Marion a gift, to say thank you for today. What should I take her, I wondered. I'd make her some biscuits and package them beautifully, she'd like that.

God, it had been so long I'd forgotten what to do. I used to look forward to the bit where you made fake orgasm noises – I used to try and vary them every time. Grant never noticed. I could have howled like a monkey and he wouldn't have noticed.

I writhed around a bit and did a few particularly violent pelvic floors to authenticate my fake orgasm, leaving no room for any doubt that I had indeed come.

'Sticky toffee pudding biscuits!' I announced just as Grant was coming inside me, his body jerking frantically.

Whoops, did I say that aloud?

'What was that, babe?'

'Oh, nothing … that was nice, wasn't it?' I lied and got up muttering about needing the bathroom.

I felt the standard wave of post-sex satisfaction wash over me, just as it always did after Grant and I had sex. It wasn't the post-orgasmic glow I used to get. It was simply the lifting of guilt. I had a proper marriage again. I knew from experience that this feeling would only last for a couple of days, but for those few days I could feel happy that I was in a functioning marriage, that I was being a 'good' wife, doing all that could be expected to keep a relationship happy.

I didn't like being responsible for other people's happiness. I used to have just me to worry about, but now I felt responsible for the happiness of three others. It was a big undertaking, like I was lugging a hippopotamus around on my back, heavy and unmanageable, and it sometimes made me do things I didn't want to do.

I padded downstairs for water, trying not to put too much weight on my left leg, which hurt like crazy. Sticky toffee biscuits, what a great idea! Another post-sex ritual was me making a mental note that the thought of having sex with Grant was always worse than actually doing it and the satisfaction more than outweighed the discomfort. Therefore, I should do it more often. It was like going to the gym. Once you were there, it was fine and you felt really good with yourself afterwards. It was getting there that was the problem.

A whirr of ingredients raced around my head. It was late, but perhaps I could jot a few ideas down for the recipe. I could try them out tomorrow, while I was making the puddings for Mrs P-J.

I flicked the switch on the kettle – *dink* – and took my tea up to the office. An hour later, I had what I thought would be the perfect recipe for sticky toffee pudding biscuits. The computer was still on. I'd been thinking about ordering James Martin's new cookbook for a few weeks now and after the day I'd had, coupled with providing Grant with his conjugal rights and writing a new recipe, I felt vindicated in doing so.

I hobbled upstairs to check Grant was asleep.

Fast off.

I placed my order then quickly logged into Gmail so I could delete the confirmation email they always send. Money wasn't good right now and Grant was tired of me ordering cookbooks.

Oh, good, Charlie had emailed.

I settled down to read it, but just before I opened it, I spotted another email waving at me. I don't know if it was because I hadn't expected to see it or if it was the title that made me gasp, but gasp I did:

Date: Friday, 16 Feb 21:07
Subject: Sex Kitten

SJ, hun, So good to hear from you. You might have been reminiscing about me lately, but I've never stopped thinking about your good self. Thought about you only the other week, in fact, while I was in Barcelona. I was having sex with my girlfriend at the time. Is that bad? I don't think so. I take it from the email address and your new surname that you're happily spliced now?

As for travelling, naw, back in the old sod right now. Got plans for big trip through the Middle East soon though – bit of a dream of mine. Will probably be in the next six months. Leaving the girlfriend at home, so if you fancy joining me ...

Funny you should message, cos watched our Vic Falls bungee-jumping video last month. Jaysus. You're really funny in it. Reminded me how naughty and sexy you are! Reckon if I looked up 'sex kitten' in the dictionary, there would be a picture of yourself. No wonder I was so attracted to that English chick all those years ago. I really wanted to make love to you when I saw you again.

Where are you living, then?

I've missed you, my sex kitten.

L xx

A wave of euphoria flashed through my body and my mouth stretched into an impulsive smile the width of China. It was like I'd got on the scales to find I'd lost a stone – I was giddy with happiness. I looked at the message again. I wanted to read and reread it over and over, but that would have been foolish.

I pressed Delete and hurried, as fast as my leg would allow, up the stairs to check on Grant, as if he might have been woken by my pumping heart.

Still sleeping.

I hobbled back down and paced a bit. Fear and excitement tumbled around inside my head. My God, that was dangerous. What if I hadn't ordered James Martin's book and Grant had checked the email in the morning? He always checked them on Saturdays. How could I have been so stupid? What if Grant had come down just then, just as I was reading it?

I thought about Marion. 'Stop worrying about the what-ifs and focus on the here and now.' Right. Another cup of tea.

I hurried down to the kitchen once more and flicked on the kettle – *dink*. A few minutes later, with the office door firmly closed, I got to work. It was a long time since I'd set up a Hotmail address and it took me back to when I first went travelling.

I tapped away quietly and five minutes later, Africanadventure77 was up and running. I'd never felt so treacherous. This was taking it to a new level. Secret email accounts were for professional philanderers and other such morally depraved individuals, not respectable mums of two who lived in Cornwall and listed baking and walking as their two favourite pastimes. I composed my email.

Date: Saturday, 17 Feb 00:57
Subject: It's Me!

Hey there, gorgeous,

You're such a bad boy! Am shocked you replied – didn't expect it – but glad. Yeah, am spliced, although the jury's out on how happily.

You *are* still travelling – knew you would be. Too envious for words. Where are you living now? And why aren't you married? What have you been doing all this time?

Can think of nothing nicer than travelling with you again, but not sure you'd be best pleased when I turned up with a small boy karabinered to each side of my rucksack.

Can you believe that city-dwelling me is living in deepest, darkest Cornwall now? I have two beautiful boys, Rudy and Finn, and I don't work! Yes, you did read that right. I'm a housewife and mum. Typed that last bit with my eyes closed – still finding it hard to come to terms with.

I think there's a picture of you in the dictionary, too – next to the word *maverick*.

So good to hear from you and glad you're still my Travelling IrishMan (TIM).

SJ xxx

PS: Have been thinking about making love to you, too.

PS: Note new email address. Don't use the other.

I read it and reread it, then read it again to see whether some overwhelming moral fibre would wash over me and stop me from sending it. It didn't, so I pressed Send. I immediately logged out of the email account and brought up the computer history so I could delete all traces of the skulduggery I had engaged in.

I sat back and expelled a giant breath of air. I felt exhilarated and exhausted all at the same time. An old side to me that had been in hiding for a long time had emerged tonight – and now she was unshackled, she was raring to go. TIM had answered my email. TIM was still thinking about me, all these years on. TIM had been thinking about me while he was having sex with his girlfriend ...

I felt melancholy. Life could have gone in so many different directions. Was I happy with the one I chose? Not now, perhaps, but I was when I chose it, wasn't I? Or had I been blinded by desperation for a family? I was far from desperate when I met Grant, or so I thought, but thinking back now, maybe just a tiny bit of me thought him a good catch – and as good as I could hope for, so I shouldn't let him go.

Perhaps that kind of thinking goes on everywhere, I thought. The world is riddled with compromise and the law courts are riddled with divorce. Or is it that people change? How can a human being who's a changing entity pledge themselves to another changing entity for the rest of their lives? Marriage is a farce. We shouldn't try to quantify the future. It's like we're programmed to ring-fence a bit of security. But marrying someone doesn't guarantee anything. Surely we'd all be better off taking things day by day and making no promises to anyone, least of all our children, who are shaped by all they survey?

I logged in to my normal account again to read Charlie's email. It was nearly two in the morning, but there was no way I could sleep right now. I thought about how Grant could so easily have been TIM. If I were married to TIM now, would I be hankering after Grant? The surprise in all of this, I suppose, was that I'd overlooked Grant's infidelity. We'd only been seeing each other for a few months. Grant had already said he loved me and I was smitten. Then I found out he'd slept with his ex-girlfriend's best mate. His ex-girlfriend had rung me at work to let me know. She was clearly upset, even though she wasn't with Grant any more.

Your mate shagging your boyfriend, ex or not, is never good. It must have hurt, and I couldn't blame her for playing detective and tracking me down to tell me. It had happened at a party and someone had clearly felt the need to pass on the news to her, despite her and Grant having finished. Why do people love doing that so much?

She took a week to ring me – she'd obviously stewed on it – but I knew from her voice that she was telling the truth. I wasn't angry with her. In fact, I felt nothing but sympathy. I calmly thanked her for the tip-off, which I'm sure infuriated her even more, and put the phone down. I'd sat looking down and across at the City from my lofty position above London, twenty-four floors up, just a hop, skip and a jump from the Earth–Heaven border. And I decided there and then that I loved Grant. We all make mistakes. And his was a small one, considering the wide range of mistakes that were up for grabs in relationships.

I'd never felt so loved in all of my life. I didn't want a stupid mistake to end what we had. It was a reckless, brain-in-pants moment, not a premeditated, carefully orchestrated affair. I decided there and then that I'd make no mention of the phone call to Grant and would never give another thought to the matter.

I trooped upstairs to bed, tired and confused. I'd told myself all those years ago, that I would never give another thought to Grant's infidelity, but of course I had, subconsciously and consciously. Perhaps I'd been silly to build my life on a substandard foundation. I had no one to blame but myself.

Chapter Seventeen

Charlotte

To-do Thursday, 15 February:

- *Borrow Jas's Miss Masseuse outfit (just in case)*

- *Check Jas's Miss Masseuse outfit fits me*

- *Pluck eyebrows and hairs around nipples*

- *Fake tan (get Jas to apply before I leave)*

- *Check Filofax, passport, money and tickets in bag*

- *Buy new shagging underwear at airport (just in case)*

- *Buy magazine*

- *Buy cotton wool and flip-flops at airport*

- *Pelvic floors (on plane)*

- *Email Sarah*

- *Text Mum*

- *Email Millie to make sure everything OK with Project Montague*

- *Paint toenails (as soon as I get there)*

- *Bikini line (as soon as I get there)*

- *Be sassy, sexy and nonchalant! – must must must*

··••••••··

Charlotte caught her reflection in the sliding doors of Departures as she pushed her way through with her trolley and congratulated herself on getting her outfit just right. Wedge sandals, three-quarter jeans, shirt – showing just enough cleavage to whet an appetite but not enough to qualify as having one's tits out. And a cashmere jumper – despite flying off to sunny climes, Heathrow's version of February was bloody freezing. Sassy and sexy but without looking like she'd tried too hard, having tried on twenty-eight different combinations before settling on the look.

She glanced around to make sure he hadn't arrived yet then made a beeline for a hot skinny cap and a full-fat muffin (they really should start doing cheese on toast in these coffee shops, she thought) before texting her mum to tell her she was going on holiday. *Whoops!*

`Just to let you know am going to Barbados with Jamie today. Will text when I get there. Hope everything OK. Love you loads. Charlie xxooxx`

Bit mean, really, because her mum wouldn't rest now. She'd pace around her film-star house and her infinity pool (poor Mum) until she got that text confirming Charlotte's safety. Even then she'd have a problem sleeping for the next fourteen days because Charlotte was abroad. Ironic, really, considering she herself had emigrated to Greece two years ago.

Charlotte sat sipping her cappuccino, one eye on the time and the other watching passers-by, trying to guess what their lives were like and desperately resisting the urge to get her camera out. There were some lovely portrait opportunities.

'*Mmm*, and look at him over there,' she murmured into her cardboard coffee cup.

She had a penchant for public-schoolboy types and the way he wore his tailored blazer and stripy scarf over a pair of scruffy jeans positively screamed midnight pillow fights in dorms. Charlotte had never been out with a public schoolboy (surprising, really, given her wide-ranging and large number of conquests), but if she did, she'd definitely want it to be one like Mr Gorgeous over there with his curly blond hair and long, lean limbs.

She watched him put his passport in his inside pocket and stride over to the nearest bureau de change. Giraffe-like, he somehow looked both graceful and slightly awkward at the same time as he moved his long limbs almost in slow motion. It all added to his allure.

Bring-bring!

Uh-oh, that'll be Mum. No doubt I'm in for a roasting.

She peered at the incoming text:

Luvly, darling. Is that a new restarant? Let me now what you have. Going to have hare done now. Ring me on my mobille because Roger medeetating this afternoon and the phowne interupts him. Am sorting deetales for my visit - what was the date of your thing again? Luv loades Mum xxxx

Charlotte chuckled. She loved the way her mum couldn't spell. It made for very entertaining text messages, although it was often time-consuming to decipher them.

No, Mum, Barbados is not a restaurant. Jamie and I are going to the island of Barbados for a holiday. Just about to get on the plane now, so turning my phone off. Hope your hair goes well. Speak later. Seminar is Saturday, 2 March. Love you loads, Charlie xxooxx

'Hi, Charlie.'

She felt a hand on her shoulder and spun round, almost spilling her coffee, the familiar voice spurring on what felt like a line of mini-Maoris doing the haka inside her stomach.

'Oh, hi!'

Jamie took his rucksack off his shoulder and smiled, breathing life into his soft green eyes. Charlotte cursed that blessed smile she loved so much but quickly acknowledged four things in her head:

1. he was here

2. he was early

3. he'd called her Charlie, and

4. he'd touched her.

No sooner than the list was formulated the mini-Maoris slammed their hands on their knees harder and poked their tongues out further. *Stop it, stop it, stop it!* she chanted. *He's not going to get back with me! He's not going to get back with me!* She silently repeated the mantra inside her head, just as Jasmine had advised.

'How's your gran?' she asked.

'What? Oh, yeah, she's fine. Gave her a scare, but she's a tough old bird.'

'Oh, good, I'm glad she's OK.' Charlotte clumsily packed away her phone and searched for her passport and tickets. 'Shall we check in, then?'

'Yeah, the quicker we're on that plane, the better. I'm really hungover, so I'm looking forward to a Bloody Mary and a snooze.'

'Oh, were you out last night?' she warbled weakly. *Stop it, Charlotte*, she told herself again.

'Yeah, I was drinking Jack Daniels and you know what that does to me.' Jamie rubbed his sore temples.

'Crikey, so that was after visiting your gran, then?' *Stop it. It's none of your business!* He's seeing someone – I knew it. *Stop it!* Sassy, sexy and nonchalant ...

'Yeah, I went to a friend's. I needed a drink after all that business with my gran.'

Jamie stopped under the flight board and craned his neck to scrutinise it. The atmosphere had changed.

'That's nice. Anyone I know?'

You stupid cow! You've really gone and done it now. You're not even on the plane yet. There's still time for him to back out.

Charlotte attempted a casual smile to try to take the sting out of her inappropriate comment, but still she hoped for an answer.

Jamie ignored her and nodded abruptly in the direction of the check-in desks.

'There's our desk. Shall we?' He marched off with giant strides, leaving her scurrying to keep up.

She felt weak and nauseous. Who was he with and why wouldn't he tell her? She needed to know. She'd just come out with it. She'd ask if he was seeing someone. *No! Stop!* For once, she knew she had to listen to that other voice – the one that was always there, skulking in the shadows of her mind, half-heartedly making an appearance, tentatively trying to push itself forwards but never quite making it onto centre stage.

Chapter Eighteen

Charlotte

Charlotte skipped off into the air-conditioned main reception in search of an ice-cold drink. Considering the uber-cool atmosphere at the airport, the flight had gone well, apart from the tiny matter of her Filofax falling out of the overhead locker and nearly concussing a small child in its path. Followed by her David Seaman style dive to retrieve it before anyone, especially Jamie, could spy what was on any of the pages, when she nearly took out the shy, balding bloke in the window seat with her wedge heel in the process. Thinking about it, it was probably that same unfortunate incident that started the turnaround in mood. Jamie had found the whole debacle hilarious and seemed to lighten up after that.

When they arrived, tired, and in Charlotte's case sporting swollen ankles, as was usual when she travelled long-haul, they'd been buoyed instantly by the sights, sounds and smells of the Discovery Bay Hotel. After the *oohing* and *aahing* over the rooms and walking around the pool discussing various raucous and immature skinny-dipping experiences in years gone by (well, Charlotte's, because it transpired that Jamie had never been skinny-dipping), they went their separate ways. Jamie wanted to unpack and Charlotte was desperate to finish her to-do list for the day so she could concentrate on discovering Discovery Bay.

She sucked on the straw of her complimentary fruit punch, got out her laptop, and rattled off a couple of emails, one to Sarah and one to Jas.

Date: Thursday, 15 Feb 15:05
Subject: Paradise Found

Hi, honey,

Arrived in beautiful, beautiful Barbados. Because it's too stunning for words, and because I'll only make you jealous, I'll spare you the details, but let's just say that to call it Utopia would be decrying its merits. Anyway, enough of me and my winter sun Caribbean holiday (you hate me, don't you?). What's all this about Finn falling off a slide?

I don't think you should be worrying about the marks on Rudy's arms as much as you are – it was so out of character and it's not surprising considering what you've had to put up with. Rudy will be fine. You're only human and you're the best mum I know. Don't despair, everything will work out. And put Nosey Nora From No. Nine (I love this name) to the back of your mind! Cats are her companions. She knows nothing.

I stayed with Jas last night, and do you know what the little minx is up to now? She's only shagging three – well, almost the third – men! And yes, before you ask, none are single. Don't know how she does it. I know we laugh about it and everything, but it upsets me. Think of those wives and girlfriends ...

Wish me luck for tomorrow. It's my first hour of Jamie telling me why he dumped me, or my first 'Love Lesson' as I like to call it. I know it's not what this holiday is about, but I want Jamie back. Can't help it. Here's hoping ...

High fives and low fives for the boys. And I'm sending you huge hugs with wings attached! Watch out the window for them – they're winging their way over to you right now.

C xxooxx

PS: Am disappointed in you, Sarah – can't believe you emailed TIM. I hope for your sake he doesn't reply.

· · • • • • • • · ·

Date: Thursday, 15 Feb 15:25
Subject: Checking In

Hi Jas
Just wanted to check you're okay? Yesterday was a shock. I wish I could have stayed for a few days. I'm here for you, honey, always, whatever you decide.
C xxooxx

She still hadn't got her head round Jas being pregnant. She'd known her for twenty-nine years now and never thought she'd ever hear Jas utter those words. She was as likely as a cuckoo to embrace motherhood. From the first day they met, they had an understanding: Charlotte was the homemaker, Jas the joke-maker.

Jas had never owned a doll, nor liked playing house, preferring instead to put on magic shows and play practical jokes. Charlotte, on the other hand, had three Tiny Tears dolls, one Baby Annabel and six Barbies. Charlotte's parents didn't have much cash, yet they still somehow found it easier to bestow gifts over time. Considering Jas's apparent loathing of children, she'd taken the pregnancy well, although Charlotte suspected it hadn't sunk in yet and she resolved to keep an eye on her.

She sucked her glass dry and sent an email to Millie to check everything was on track at work. Millie had emailed already, wishing her a nice holiday. What a sweetie! She would buy her a nice present for being so loyal. Now, what first? The pool? Beach? Or find Jamie and drag him off to the bar? No contest.

·········

Charlotte sat upright on her sun lounger, one pink leg either side, and surveyed the beach through the lens of her camera. She still hadn't come to terms with her knock-back last night. Jamie had wanted an early night and had disappeared straight after dinner, but he did at least have dinner with her. And he did arrange a time and place for them to meet today for the first 'Love Lesson'.

With only two hours to go, she couldn't help but wonder what exactly he was going to say. Would he have a list of complaints and criticisms? Come to think of it, would her list-writing be on his list? She knew she wouldn't like it if her boyfriend constantly wrote in a Filofax and kept it hidden. That might be one of the problems. If so, that one was easily solved. She'd just let him read it – cover to cover, if necessary. She'd probably have to take some of the more embarrassing lists out. '*Men I've Slept With*' would definitely have to go, because she'd rated each man's sexual performance and Jamie had only scored 6 of out 10, whereas some had got a 9 and a gold star. That wouldn't sit well with Jamie's competitive nature.

Thinking about it, there were a lot of lists in there she wouldn't want him to see. And she'd forgotten about her diary entries, too, which were completely off limits. She thought back to the one she'd written that morning and shuddered.

Friday, 16 February 2024

If I dig deep, I know why I'm dumped all the time. It's like Jas said: I'm too suspicious and paranoid. I can't seem to stop it. It didn't help that my first love cheated on me. I will never forget waking up in that hotel room in Chipping Sodbury, at his sister's wedding, with him missing from our bed, only to find him shagging the bridesmaid in the rooftop jacuzzi. It turned out he'd been sleeping with said bridesmaid (his sister's best friend), for half of our relationship, and I'd been too naïve to realise. My prototype experience was a nasty one.

Given my suspicious nature, it must be my high sex drive that keeps men with me, but the problem with that is it's easily replaced.

I always believed Pete was too good for me – too physically beautiful, too intelligent, too witty, and so I couldn't understand why he wanted me. Jamie's the same. It's obvious that given half a chance, he will be off with a more successful, sexier female and that's why I do what I do.

I try to stop Jamie from having the opportunity, try and stop him from meeting gorgeous women who are better than me. I don't want to be controlling, I just want to keep hold of what I'm lucky to have.

Read a great article about electrolysis for nipple hairs today. Have booked an appointment for when I'm home. Now no one will ever know about my hairy nipples.

No, forget the idea of the Filofax open-door policy, it was never going to happen. She slid her bikini straps down her shoulders and pulled her arms out – nothing worse than tan lines.

'Coconut for yuh, pretty laydee?'

Charlotte opened her eyes and turned her head towards the beach vendor. He was standing too close and could probably see her bikini line still needed attention, despite it having been on her to-do list for three days now.

'No, thanks. I'm just relaxing at the moment.'

'Need a lil' sometin' to help yuh relax, pretty laydee?'

He smiled the widest, whitest smile and Charlotte found herself smiling back contagiously.

'I'm fine, honestly.'

Drugs were probably not a good idea right now. Although the cannabis she suspected the nice dreadlocked young man was offering was probably just what she could do with right now.

'All right, pretty laydee, but if yuh change yer mind, I is yer man. De name is Bannister.' He stretched out his smooth black arm, his muscle tone glinting in the sun, and offered her his hand.

Charlotte shook it, momentarily wishing he'd ensconce her in those strong, powerful arms and protect her for evermore.

'All right, you have yerself a good day now. Go easy on yerself.'

He took his sunglasses off, poking them into the wool of his red-and-yellow hat and padded off, over to the next 'pretty laydee'.

Charlotte looked at the sun lounger behind where he'd stood and there was Mr Public School from the airport. Mr Gorgeous Giraffe, no less. The empty bed next to him, complete with big floppy sunhat, confirmed what Charlotte had suspected when she'd first clapped eyes on him. Anyone that stunning didn't go on holiday alone.

She settled back on her lounger and wished she could run around the inside of her stomach with a net, catching all the butterflies she had fluttering around in there at the thought of seeing Jamie. Was it time yet? She sat up again and opened her beach bag to check. She switched on her mobile and a gratifying succession of beeps followed – such a lovely sound, like the thud of birthday cards on the mat. There was one from Jas and a giant one from Sarah:

The school mums all hate me, Charlie. Nobody will talk to me. Ole Sunken Eyes has told me not to bother baking for her son's party now. I think they're all petrified of Big Lass From The North. When I worked, I never used to care about having friends. Think I'm going soft in my old age.

Think I might have found one friend, though: Marion Glasgow. She rescued me when I slipped on rocks and hurt my leg – got carted off in an ambulance and had ten stitches.

TIM has emailed back. Yes, I know you're disappointed with me, and yes, I know I shouldn't have replied, but I have. I'm such a bad person. It's OK, though, because already the guilt is weighing too heavily and I've decided I'm definitely not going to do it again.

Rudy's getting worse. Had another run-in. Can't bear to see him this upset all the time. Grant asked if I was disciplining him enough. Lucky for Grant it wasn't a Velociraptor Badge Day.

Make the most of your time out there in that wonderfully healing Caribbean sun. It might not all happen as you've planned it in your head, but if you see the positives in everything, you'll be fine.

Much love, S xxx

PS: Grant keeps making excuses to go to Shop. I started to notice it, and then Nosey Nora From No. Nine popped by pretending she'd run out of eggs (she keeps chickens and has an egg basket in her window, which was full, I checked). She proceeded to mention that my 'husband', even though she knows his name, goes to the shop in Shop an awful lot, and could I please tell him she isn't ignoring him but, whenever she sees him there, she can't say hello because he's on a phone call. You've gotta hand it to her, the woman is the Dragon Warrior of passive aggression. Anyway, is that on your 'Signs He's Having an Affair' list? I know you've got one because you told me.

PPS: TIM still thinks about me.

PPPS: Just got Guinness World Record for longest text ever. xx

Charlotte quickly tapped out her reply. Texting on the beach felt wrong.

What? Stitches! You definitely have to stop doing so much now. You need a rest! School mums don't hate you - they're probs envious. Soon enough, they will love you as I do. I'm off for first Love Lesson from Jamie - wish me luck. Just been offered drugs by a Rastafarian Beach Vendor. May take him up on them later. xxooxx

There. Sent. And now the one from Jas.

So, how's it goin' then? Found anyone to shag yet? On way to conference. Reuben 'I'm the Hottest Bloke on the Block' Tate is going, too. Think he might need someone to show him the conference ropes!

Repeat after me: 'He is not going to get back with me. I am a goddess. I will meet my Adonis very soon.' Keep your chin up and your eyes peeled, babes. Keep lying on that beach - best place for finding new fishes. Ciao, J x

PS: Stop worrying about me, I'm fine.

Charlotte answered:

But I am worrying about you, Jas. Can't help it. You sure you're OK? A termination is a big decision to make all on your own. Am here for you. First Love Lesson in min. Will text with any major revelations. Thanks for wise words, but you need to keep your eyes peeled too - for a nice unattached fishy!

Keep looking. Have a good day, honey. C xxooxx

Chapter Nineteen

Charlotte

Oh. My. God. He's got his counsel's notepad with him.

Charlotte had caught sight of Jamie striding towards her and quickly twisted back round to concentrate on looking 'not bothered' and making swirly patterns in the water with her feet as they dangled off the end of the jetty.

Yep, true to form, he was taking this seriously. She took a deep breath, taking in the smell of the spicy 'grip you at the back of the throat and make you cough' Bajan cooking smells wafting from behind the jetty and braced herself. Hopefully, it would be an hour of criticism followed by a big, tearful reconciliation hug after she'd promised to change whatever it was that was bothering him. She stared down at the tatty wooden platform she was sitting on and began peeling off big splinters while she waited.

He arrived, clutching his pale-blue foolscap notepad, looking efficient and motivated. It was farcical, really. Was he going to ask how the defendant was pleading? She stifled a giggle.

'Hi, Charlie.' He smiled his familiar warm smile, but it was fleeting.

'Hi there.'

She budged over so Jamie could sit next to her. Eager to get this whole thing under way, she found herself staring at his notepad.

'Shall we get started?' she asked.

'Good idea. Well, I've jotted a few things down and—'

'So I see. I feel like I'm on trial or something.'

She peeled a few more splinters away, only faster now. He *did* have a list ... She could see it – numbered one to fourteen. My God, he'd apportioned something for every day. Are there fourteen things wrong with me? Maybe more ... Perhaps a two-week holiday wasn't long enough and he'd had to condense things to fit the schedule.

Sweet Jesus, I'm not sure I'm ready to hear all this.

Perhaps it'll work out brilliantly. Perhaps there's a film director holidaying here in Barbados right now and he'll overhear our 'Love Lessons' as he sips his rum on a nearby balcony. Perhaps he'll want to make a film about it – *Confessions of a Bad Girlfriend* – with Keira Knightley playing me.

She stopped and attempted to pull herself together. This was serious – 100 men had dumped her and Jamie was being kind enough to help.

'Charlie, this was your idea, and I'm only going to tell you this stuff to help you, not to criticise you. You do still want to do it, don't you?'

'Of course. That's why we're here, aren't we? I'm fine, let's just get on with it.'

She knew it wasn't his fault, but she couldn't help being mad – mad about him dumping her and mad about him helping her, too.

'Well, first, I just want to say that you're definitely the best person I've ever slept with. You're incredibly sexy and no one has ever made me feel like you do in bed.'

Oh my God, he was going for the spam-sandwich technique – a slice of spam criticism surrounded by two slices of Marks & Spencer's best ciabatta compliments, just to make the spam taste not so bad.

'Fine, whatever, now what about the bad stuff?' This wasn't going to work if he was going to patronise her.

'Well, you are quite controlling.'

'*How do you mean?*' she snapped. 'Give me an example.' There it was again, that word, the one Jasmine had used the other night.

'I suppose one example, off the top of my head, is the packed lunch thing. If I stay at yours or you at mine, you make me a pack-up for the next day, which is really nice of you, but then you go mad if I decide to go out for lunch instead. You don't even ask if I have anything planned. And I never ask you to make it, yet you expect me to eat it. It's controlling, really – don't you agree?' The colour had drained from his face.

He'd taken Charlotte straight back to her childhood. Her parents had been strict and short of money. If she didn't eat all of her tea, her dad demanded it was put in the fridge and brought out at the next meal so she could finish it. This would continue until that meal had completely gone or it had gone off, whichever came first. Only then would she be made a new meal.

She supposed the pack-up thing could be likened to that, in a way. It was a form of control, as stupid as it sounded. The real reason she wanted him to eat it was the onions. She always put raw onion in the sandwich so he'd have onion breath – sure to put off any potential admirers. Thinking about it, the onions were all about control, too.

'I don't really know what to say. Stupidly, I didn't realise my making you sandwiches had caused you such a problem.'

'Oh, God, I haven't used the right example. Talking about sandwiches makes it all sound so petty.'

'Just a bit!'

Charlotte knew she was being naughty. She knew exactly what he was getting at. But her ego didn't like it one bit and it occurred to her that it might be even harder to take these Love Lessons than she'd anticipated. Hearing criticism about yourself was difficult.

'OK, here's a better one for you. Remember that time you didn't want me to go to that party because my ex, Karla, was going to be there? I felt controlled then, stifled.'

He looked towards the horizon and Charlotte could see the stress etched onto his forehead. Poor Jamie – this was difficult for him, too. He definitely spent his life trying to sidestep trouble and this analytical confrontation didn't come easy.

'I think that's normal, Jamie. Most girlfriends are jealous of their boyfriend's exes.'

'Perhaps you're right, but they don't try to stop their boyfriend from going to the party, do they? And they don't turn up at the party, causing a scene and taking the boyfriend home. Anyway, it doesn't matter what other people do. The fact is,

I don't like having my freedom curbed to that extent. I couldn't care less about Karla anymore. You should have trusted me enough to let me go.'

And there was that other word – trust. Not one of my strong points, she thought.

She began to play her own little game of Poohsticks under the jetty with the splinters she'd collected. None of this was ground-breaking, though. So she was a bit controlling and didn't find it easy to trust. *Whoop-de-doo!* Same with most girls. Jasmine was clearly the exception – she encouraged her men to give her space and liked it if they shagged someone else because it made them less reliant on her. But Charlotte wasn't the only controlling female in the world and it was only because she loved Jamie so much.

'I don't think these "Love Lessons" are going to work, after all, Jamie,' she concluded.

'OK,' Jamie announced purposefully. 'I wasn't going to do this today. I wanted to build up to it but, what the hell, I'm just going to say it now.' He straightened his body and took another long breath. 'I hope you don't mind, but I've spoken to Toby.'

'What do you mean, you've spoken to Toby? What has Toby got to do with all this? Do you mean Toby, your uni mate?' Charlotte's voice rose.

'Yes. Please calm down, Charlotte. I really can't do this if you're going to shout and lose it again.'

Pressure built inside her, bubbling up from the tip of her pretty pink toenails and lingering around her solar plexus to gather momentum. If there was one thing she really couldn't stand, it was other people knowing her business, her innermost secrets, the real her. She hadn't given permission for him to tell anyone about their relationship. *About her.*

'What do you mean, *again*?' Charlotte spat, incensed by the words 'calm down' that Jamie had been foolish enough to utter.

'I mean *again* because we spent a large part of our relationship with you losing it for some reason or other and I don't want it anymore!' He looked out to sea, frustration and anger anchored into his face.

'All right. *OK*, I'm sorry.' Charlotte smoothed down a splinter with her fist, hammering it back into the plank of wood. If she wasn't careful, Jamie would get up and walk away, as he'd so often tried to do when they'd rowed.

Jamie straightened his T-shirt and took a deep breath. 'As you know, Toby is a clinical psychologist – a therapist.'

'A *shrink*.'

'Yes, if that's what you want to call it. He is in fact a very good *shrink*, and I trust him very much. I was worried about you. I've never experienced a relationship like ours before. I've had jealous girlfriends and suspicious ones and ones who checked my mobile as soon as my back was turned, but never anyone with behaviour as extreme as yours, Charlie. Then, when you told me you'd been dumped that many times, it all made sense. I'd suspected there was something wrong for a while, but I kept telling myself I was being stupid. After you told me about the other ninety-nine guys, I knew my instinct had been right. So I put together an email, a really long email, about us and the way you'd behaved and stuff like that, and sent it to Toby.'

Charlotte wasn't sure whether her tears were from humiliation, lack of control, sadness or anything else, come to that, but she did know that if she spoke now, they'd turn into big sobbing torrents.

Jamie shuffled his bum across the jetty until he was sitting as near as he could without them touching. 'He thought you were suffering with something called morbid jealousy. It's —'

'No! No, it's definitely not going to work.' Charlotte willed her arms and legs to move, to propel her up and out of this terrible, terrible place she'd found herself in, but they wouldn't budge.

'Oh, Charlie, give it a chance. No one wants to hear stuff like this, but I really think I can help. Look, he's printed you some stuff off on it.' He turned to the back of his notepad and pulled out a wad of paper neatly held together by a small butterfly clip. 'It's going to be OK.' He put his arm around her bare shoulders and gave her a buddy-buddy hug. 'Just think, this holiday could mean you end up marrying the next guy you meet. That would make it all worth it, wouldn't it?'

·····•··•····

Charlotte could barely see as she left the hotel gates and stumbled onto the cricket pitch, furiously wiping away torrential tears, desperately scouring left and right for the nearest wall.

'There must be a stupid wall around here somewhere!'

She almost overlooked it through her tear-soaked vision. It wasn't a pretty wall – it was made from concrete blocks with big lumps of render missing and the grass it once stood on was now bare patches of dry mud. But it was a good, solid wall that would let her sit there and cry. It would listen and not judge, and not tell anyone what it had heard. And it would maybe have a couple of big concrete arms that could come out and give her a big concretey hug. Any hug was better than no hug.

'*Fuck offf, everybody!*' she wailed at the top of her voice. '*Aaarghhh!*' She sobbed some more. 'Why can't I just accept stuff that happens to me?' She kicked her heels at the wall and her flip-flops fell off. 'Why do I always feel like I'm fighting?'

Saying stuff aloud always made things so much better and walls were always so good at listening. She knew it was a tad *Shirley Valentine*, but who cared? Someone obviously wrote that bit into the film where Shirley talked to the wall in her house for a reason, that reason probably being that walls were good at listening.

Her tears slowed and she managed a small laugh, albeit a demonic one. How could this holiday have turned so quickly to Jamie diagnosing me with a mental illness and promising to secure me a husband sometime soon, she wondered.

'Are you all right there?'

'Sweet Jesus, you made me jump!' Charlotte's head spun round and she saw Mr Public School from the airport standing there, or The Giraffe as he was no doubt affectionately known by his friends.

Fantastic! Goodbye 'drowning in humiliation and wallowing in self-pity' and hello 'public schoolboy banter and haw-hawing with a giraffe'.

'Fine, thanks,' she said, swinging at a mosquito and breathing in the feel-good smell of Mr Public School's sun oil. 'Just enjoying the *solitude*!'

'Mind if I join you, or is somebody sitting there?'

'Only Mr Invisible, but I'm sure he won't mind if you sit on his lap.'

He smiled and settled on the wall beside her, his leg briefly brushing hers as he made himself comfortable.

Charlotte sighed silently. The clue had been in the word solitude. Clearly, he wasn't that bright. Well, he couldn't have everything, could he?

'I'm going in a minute, so you can have it all to yourself then,' she said.

'Right, I'm Rich, by the way.' He held out his right hand.

Jesus, it was like a work party. Where you had to go round telling clients how wonderful they were and extract as much business from them as possible while keeping your perma-smile intact. Charlotte hated those parties.

'Hi, I'm Charlotte.' She shook his hand back and was surprised by a singular throb in her groin. Her cheeks burned red from the shock and she put her head down to concentrate on picking at the loose concrete on the wall.

'You're staying at Discovery Bay, aren't you?' he said.

'Yeah, just arrived. Well, yesterday.'

She looked up again and watched as he put a hand through his hair, extending one of his blond curls before it sprang back into place. Except it didn't actually spring back like you'd expect, it kind of just fell back softly.

'Me, too. Beautiful, isn't it? I come here every year.'

'It's the first time I've been. You must be rich, then, Rich. You know, coming here every year and everything.'

He laughed, his toffee-brown eyes sparkling with a hint of yellow, the colour lions have. 'No one's ever asked me that before. Well, yes, I suppose I am. Not excruciatingly rich, just a bit rich.'

'Not rich enough to stay at the Sandy Lane hotel or own your own house out here, but rich enough to holiday here every year, yeah? I'd be happy with that. Good for you.' Charlotte didn't really know what had come over her.

'Well, actually, I'm rich enough to do both of those things, but I choose not to. Having a house out here seems wasteful considering I only manage to get over once a year. And I don't like Sandy Lane – a bit too ostentatious for my taste.'

Charlotte checked herself. She couldn't let herself feel lifted, not today. Her life was too horrible. She'd found this wall so she could sit and feel sorry for herself, and fully assimilate the realisation that Jamie wasn't there to kiss and make up. She didn't have time to make idle chit-chat with rich Rich, who had his life completely sorted.

'Anyway, it's been lovely to meet you, Rich, but I really must get back now, and your girlfriend will be wondering where you've got to. See you around. Thanks for the chat.'

Charlotte catapulted herself down and distanced herself from Rich as quickly as possible, a flip-flop in each hand so she could feel the springy grass between her toes. She ambled across the pitch in the warm air, listening to the thwack and holler of an impromptu cricket match. How funny it was that people were rarely as you thought they were on first appearance.

Chapter Twenty

Charlotte

In the cool, safe surrounds of the hotel bar, Charlotte checked her phone and was glad to see that both Sarah and Jas had emailed. She needed to reassure herself that she was liked, that she was 'normal' enough to at least have friends, if not lovers. She clicked on the one from Jas first, knowing it would make her laugh:

Date: Saturday, 17 Feb 13:24
Subject: He's Not Going to Get Back With You

Hey, babe,
Conference broken for lunch. Managed to stay awake so far, just. I've escaped to send you an email. News just in: I've dumped Adrian the Married. Did it this morning in the tea break – by text. Yeah, yeah, I know, but it was easier that way. Be funny if that was the one text his wife read, wouldn't it? Imagine the irony – she finds out just as he's dumped. Poor guy. He's all right, really, but he was starting to get serious – wanting to see me more than twice a week and stuff, even making jokey hints about leaving his wife, so it had to be done.

Sooo, how's it going? What's your room like? How hot are the waiters? How hot's the weather? Stop enjoying yourself for a moment and email me back with a progress report.

Now, repeat after me: 'He is not going to get back with me. There are plenty more fish in the Caribbean Sea.'

Ciao, bella,

J xxx

Adrian was one of the lucky ones. He'd been told he'd been dumped, it was common for Jasmine to ghost her men. She hoped the fact Jasmine hadn't mentioned the pregnancy didn't mean she was in denial, although knowing Jas she was probably treating it like a faulty washing machine – get it fixed and carry on.

'Hi, there.'

Charlotte was engulfed by a powdery waft of expensive perfume and looked up to see a willowy girl in a short denim skirt. Judging by the fat black smudge under her eyes, she hadn't sharpened her eyeliner pencil in a while. Or, as became apparent, she was going for the sultry vamp look.

'Hi, I'm Rachel, the beautician here at Discovery Bay.' She stuck her hand out.

It was like some kind of hand-shaking fest round here. Charlotte shook the girl's slender, immaculately manicured hand, which felt cool given the searing heat that was causing Charlotte's own hands to resemble pre-milked udders.

'I hope you're enjoying your stay.' The girl checked her reflection in a windowpane over Charlotte's shoulder.

Charlotte smiled but didn't reply. She couldn't be bothered with polite chit-chat. She was trying to send an email and The Lovely Rachel, as the holiday rep had called her during his welcome talk, was irritatingly gorgeous (if not a tad slutty). She even managed to give her unmistakeable Essex accent a certain charm.

'I thought you might like to have a look at my price list. You name it, I do it.' She smiled.

I bet you do, thought Charlotte.

'I'm in the room next door, bang opposite reception, so if you feel like a bit of pampering, just pop in. I do waxing, as well, so if you want me to sort out those eyebrows' – The Lovely Rachel trained her eyes on Charlotte's bushy brows –

'that's not a problem.' She glanced down to Charlotte's hip and thigh area. 'And perhaps a seaweed wrap ...' And back up to her face.

She had an accommodating smile, but her eyes were keen and calculating, like a bird of prey about to swoop.

'Takes inches off you. You'd love it. Anyway, you know where I am.'

She sashayed out of the bar, into reception, where Charlotte could hear her discussing some poor bloke she had her eye on with the receptionist.

Feeling ten times worse about herself now than she had before she'd arrived, Charlotte took a swig of water from her bottle and clicked on the email from Sarah.

Date: Saturday, 17 Feb 14:05
Subject: Saturday Kitchen

Me again! Wondered if you'd do me a favour. Would you read the poem I've finally got round to writing for the christening, please? I'd appreciate some honest feedback. But promise you'll only read it if you've got time, because you are on holiday, after all.

I've been in the kitchen watching TV and baking sticky toffee puddings for tomorrow night. Please tell me I'm not the only person who cries watching *Saturday Kitchen*. I'm not even pregnant – at least I hope not.

It is a possibility, as Grant and I have finally had sex. The first time in Cornwall! My Rampant Rabbit has been holding the fort, but don't tell Grant – – he thinks I've spent the last five months too tired for sex. I can't quite bring myself to confess that I just don't want it with him. Poor Grant, I must try harder.

I actually think the reason I cried at *Saturday Kitchen* had more to do with the onset of my period. Oh joy and jubilation! Perfect timing for the P-J's shoot supper, then.

It's been such a bad week, Charlie. The slide that Finn fell from was really high – he had to have a CAT scan. He's fine now, but the thing is, and I haven't told this to another soul, I was texting you when he fell.

I don't think I should have had children. It's not me, I'm no good at it. I should have stuck with my career – I was good at that. Some people are natural mothers, I'm just not one of them.

Rudy's going from bad to worse and I don't know how to help him. I can't control him anymore. He won't respond to discipline and screams and shouts at me all the time. He won't sleep and he's getting into trouble at school. He cries every morning and begs me not to take him. Last night in the bath he said he couldn't go to a boy's party because the boy didn't like him. He said he calls him stupid and says he can't read, but the whole of his class were going and he wanted to go too. I could have cried, Charlie. It was like someone piercing my stomach with a large stake and turning it slowly.

But I think the boy might have hit the nail on the head. Rudy doesn't like school because he can't do the work. Must be awful feeling like you can't do things.

When you have children, you expect them to be the same as you. I didn't consider that the boys would be anything but grade A students. Feel so bad for him. I've tried to explain that he'll get better with time, but it doesn't help. I've tried to help him at home, but he won't concentrate, or can't.

I've decided I'm going to ground. I'm tired of people (apart from you).

Dying to hear how it's going there.

Keep smiling. S xxxx

PS: Here's the poem – and before you say it, yes, it is familiar. I've ever so slightly borrowed the style of Philip Larkin's poem 'This Be The Verse' but imitation is the best form of flattery and all that.

```
They mess you up, your kids.
They may not mean to, but they do.
They keep you awake most of the night
And shout embarrassing stuff that's true:
```

'Look at that fat man, Mummy.
Is it because he eats cake like Pooh Bear?
He's got a really big tummy.
And why hasn't he got any hair?'

They mess you up, your kids.
They change the person you thought you were.
That person who tutted at children on planes
And shunned practicality in favour of fur.

My children won't scream in restaurants
Or watch television all day.
My children won't wee in public places,
And bribery is just not OK.

Oh, how they change you, your kids,
And isn't it good that they do?
A love so deep, you didn't think it existed.
Infinite days with them still too few.

Our message to you, boys, is simple:
Don't judge, just follow your heart.
Believe in yourself, enjoy every moment.
And most important, love yourself from the start.

They teach you loads, your kids.
Far more than you might know.
So enjoy them as much as you can
And delight in watching them grow.
Remember - be honest.
S xxx

Charlotte cried. Softly – no noise, just tears. Self-indulgent and strangely satisfying. It was the bit about loving yourself that did it. She had trouble loving herself because of her behaviour, her controlling ways, the way she treated people. This and the fact she often felt like nobody had ever really loved her, even her mum and dad. No one had ever put her first.

Her childhood had been spent fighting hard to earn every single bit of attention she'd ever received. She'd become ingenious, even as a child, in the craft of being noticed. Once, when she was eight, she'd asked her mum if she could wear her wedge shoes to school to show her friends (why she had three-inch wedges aged eight, she had no idea). An hour or so into the school day, she'd feigned a fall and a sprained ankle. It worked – the teacher was really concerned and her mum was called in to take her home.

All of her life, she'd felt like an irritant, a burden. Even now, when she spent time with either of her parents, it felt like they were only there to do their duty. They checked their watches and stayed for as long as was polite. Her dad sometimes had one eye on the TV, not even fully committing himself in the short time he saw her. Her mum always had something to rush off for. She used to put her dad first and now it was Rog. Always dashing off to make his tea or iron his trousers or run his bath.

Charlotte crossed both of her arms tight to her chest and hugged herself hard. 'Go easy on yourself.' The words floated and bobbed around in her head, bouncing off each other, as if trapped in soapy bubbles. Who had said that to her today? Oh, yes, the beach vendor. What was his name? Banger? Bodger ... B-B-Bannister, that was it. What a wonderful piece of advice that had been!

She was weary but suspected Sarah was at a dangerously low ebb and could do with some love and reassurance:

Date: Saturday, 17 Feb 16:20
Subject: Birds of Paradise

What can I say, honey? I wish someone had written a poem like that for me. So beautiful, and so fitting, too. You've excelled again.

I want you to stop being so hard on yourself, sweetie. Accidents happen. You can't possibly watch a child every second of the day. And these things happen in the blink of an eye. Everything will work out with Rudy, I know it will, because he has you. And I know I've said it before, but you're the best mum I know. The boys will be fine so long as they have your love.

Had my first Love Lesson with Jamie. Not feeling too good about it right now, but I'll email you soon. Let's just say it doesn't look like J and I are getting back together. Saw him talking to a woman this morning. Turns out she's the hotel beautician. Don't think I need to worry, because she's not Jamie's type, but I still can't help thinking I've made a mistake bringing him to a paradise full of beauties.

Oh, and just to let you know – while I was reading that stuff you wrote about Grant, I felt like putting my fingers in my ears and saying 'La-la-la-la-la.' I aspire to your life – having a life like yours is the motivation behind almost everything I do. You and Grant are the perfect couple. I can't bring myself to believe any different. Please help me keep the faith and tell me you were joking. And please tell me you haven't replied to TIM.

Sending big hugs for you, because mums need hugs, too. And big, squelchy wet kisses for those delicious boys of yours.

Charlie xxxooxx

With her emailing done, Charlotte let her finger hover over the Google search box. She typed it in one letter at a time: M-O-R-B-I-D J-E-A-L-O-U-S-Y. *Bam.* There it goes.

She closed her eyes, unsure she could cope with the full truth. She didn't want Jamie to be right. It was easier to dislike him. She spent a few minutes looking but, as it became apparent that Toby was indeed spot on, she became less interested by the second. Now wasn't the time.

Chapter Twenty-One

Jasmine

Jas stood in her hotel room, square on in front of the full-length mirror, and admired her outfit. Sixties-inspired blue patent knee-length boots and a sheer silk tunic dress, embellished with a smattering of gold sequins, providing just the right amount of glamour for the evening ahead. It ought to look good, considering its four-figure price tag and the embarrassing financial shenanigans she'd endured to procure it. Namely asking the snooty man in the Bond Street shop to split the cost between four credit cards – funds were tight.

She swung from side to side, admiring the cut and feel of the dress, more mini than mummy, yet far more demure than her usual risqué conference attire. The dinner-jacketed members of Machorns Paper Merchants would be buzzing around her like a premium raffle prize, hoping they had the winning ticket this year, not caring if it was printed on A4, SRA2 or continuous business form, so long as the prize put out loose and dirty, just as conference folklore had it.

She sprayed a fine mist of Tresor into the air and walked into it. It was a black-tie do tonight and most of her female colleagues would opt for unflattering ball-gown type affairs. Jasmine had never been one for conformity. She twisted round and glanced over her shoulder at her bum, studying it intently. There was no hiding it – even with sheer navy-blue silk falling forgivingly over it, it had definitely got bigger. Not much bigger, not the six slabs of millionaire shortbread's worth that she'd eaten on the journey up to Blackpool, but bigger all the same. It was inevitable, she supposed. That's what happened when you got yourself up the duff, wasn't it? You got fat.

Should she ever be mad enough to keep the baby, slowly and surely she'd turn into one of her lovers' wives. She was only a waddle away from not being able to see to shave her own lady garden. She poured herself a hefty vodka and orange from the teak minibar and drank it down in two. Good job she wasn't, then – keeping it, that is.

She placed her hands over the gentle swell of her stomach and closed her eyes, imagining they were those of another, lovingly connecting with what they'd created. She kept her eyes closed, indulging in her inner self, the other 'her' that sat quiet and unassuming below the surface. Pretty yet scarred, as delicate as the lace wings of a dragonfly, too frail to be exposed to the sinister machine-gun fire of real life. The true her that she kept locked away, her little secret.

Although she'd never admitted it before, not to anyone, including herself, she now realised that being in love and pregnant – no, being *loved* and pregnant – was all she'd ever wanted in life.

'No such luck for this girl!'

She angrily swiped at runaway tears and unscrewed another miniature vodka. She put the bottle to her lips and drank it neat. There! That was better. What was wrong with her? It was conference time.

She grabbed her bag. She could hear the murmur of excited chatter and the click of hotel doors closing in the hallway outside as people congregated and made their way down to the main event. No, not the keynote speech by a respected captain of the industry – the piss-up.

In past years, Jasmine had stepped out of her room with lashings of painstakingly applied liquid eyeliner, a red-hot sexy outfit, and a treacherous look in her eye. Always, without fail, she'd teetered back several hours later with whosoever had taken her fancy, because that was what happened at the Machorns' conference. Everyone shagged. Plain and simple.

Whether you were married, single, a computer geek, gay or touched with the ugly stick at birth, you were guaranteed a shag – if you wanted one. A threesome here and a blow job in the ornamental garden there, it all happened at the conference. The team building, back-slapping and bonding all happened, too, only no one ever remembered that.

Nothing for Jasmine tonight, though. Tonight was different. She was different. She checked her reflection one last time. She did at least have a tantalising flash of tanned thigh on show, it wouldn't do to disappoint altogether.

She wandered towards the raucous pre-dinner drinks din, trailing her hand down the smooth oak banister of the red-carpeted staircase, feeling like a movie star making an entrance. It was the usual conference scene, loud, reckless and loose, with the odd roar of deep-bellied boardroom laughter. She wondered if her sleeved dress had been a good choice after all, as she felt the overwhelming heat of the room cloying around her, wafting up from the heaving mass of hot bodies, hope and hormones.

Despite the early hour, everyone was going for it. Smarm, alcohol, pendular bingo-wing activity, packs of men working the room, trowelled-on make-up and cheap perfume abounded. Tomorrow would paint a different picture – shabby décor exposed by harsh winter daylight, shifty eyes and embarrassed nods – but tonight was tonight. Jasmine had different plans: dinner and bed ... alone.

'Hey, gorgeous, what's a sophisticated broad like you doing in a place like this?' Reuben smiled lazily, his excitement betrayed only by his eyes, glimmering dangerously. 'Drink?'

It was more an order than a question and it sent a solitary shiver down Jasmine's silk-clad body, its journey ending abruptly in her knickers.

'Indeed, although I must say that a man of any calibre would know what it was I wanted and have it waiting for me.' She feigned indifference.

'What? Like this vodka and orange?' Reuben twisted his broad frame and plucked her drink from the bar. For the male of the species, he was unusually intuitive.

She accepted graciously, fighting the urge to conform to character, yet desperate to be flattered with more of this beautiful man's celestial attention. Momentarily, she caved.

'Not bad ... for a new boy. What else are you good at?'

She was doing exactly what she'd promised herself she wouldn't. It was going to take some serious effort to stop. Seduction was her default, her protection.

'Why don't you stick around and find out?'

Jasmine put a discreet hand on her belly. 'As enjoyable as I'm sure that would be, I'm having an early night. Need a clear head for the morning. Besides, what about Shelley?'

Jasmine tried to shake her sombre mood, suspecting it had everything to do with the text she'd received from Sarah earlier. She'd replied saying that of course she'd love to come to the christening and consequently she'd felt shit ever since. Sometimes – quite frequently, now she came to think about it – she really didn't like herself.

She glanced around the room for someone to talk to. The Leicester branch manager had told her earlier he was jet-lagged from his honeymoon, although not too tired to have his hand up Maria from Accounts' taffeta skirt now apparently, she noticed. Nobody so much as blinked an eye that someone was quietly being brought to orgasm in the corner, such was the joy of Machorns Annual Conference.

The red-waistcoated MC (oh yes, they had it all at these do's) announced that dinner was served. Jasmine found her name on the table plan and was grateful to see she'd been shoehorned between the managing director and head of European sales. A safe seat, and a premium seat indeed. Perhaps she was on track for that promotion, after all. She'd certainly worked her arse off for it, and that took some doing these days, she sighed, feeling her behind for the fifth time that night, unable to come to terms with its unauthorised growth spurt.

'The seating plan appears to be wrong. I believe your name's on a table over there ...' Reuben appeared by her side. 'Next to me.' He cocked an eyebrow and put a strong arm around her waist.

'How serendipitous.' She allowed herself to be led to his table.

They ate, they laughed, they flirted and, very occasionally, borne from good manners and a sense of duty, acknowledged others around the table, half-heartedly joining in and laughing on cue. Reuben's left hand frequently ducked under the starched white tablecloth to stroke her thigh and for one brief moment, she put her hand over his, meshing their fingers, making her groin jump mercilessly, electric pulses shooting up and down her body. There was a natural attraction between them, an intoxicating lust, but she felt removed somehow, with new insight. It was the caring gestures that got her heart pumping, not the carnal ones. This unfamiliar territory only served to deepen the navy mood she wore to match her dress, giving her mental indigestion.

'Thanks, Reuben, that was fun.'

Reuben just about held the puzzled look from his face.

'It's a shame for it to end,' he said. 'Fancy a nightcap? How about a walk? I hear Blackpool is particularly beautiful this time of year.' He held her gaze. 'We both know we're meant to happen, Jas. I felt it the first moment I clapped eyes on you. Don't tell me you didn't?'

'Yeah, I fancy you – I think that's obvious. I'm just not up for the conference shag anymore.'

'I was rather hoping it would be more than that, actually.'

He stepped close enough for her to smell his after-dinner mint and the thinly veiled aroma of alcohol on his warm breath. He reached for her hand and took it gently in his – a loose, tender connection. He looked at her with lust-soaked eyes, tinged with respect and admiration too. Reuben Tate was hot, sexy new blood and graced the top of every woman's wish list here tonight.

'What do you think?'

She, Jasmine Rafferty, had induced that look in his eyes. It was a powerful drug, the fact she could ignite such potent emotion in someone. It was good to be wanted. Needed, even.

'I think Shelley wouldn't be happy if she could hear you.'

He began to kiss her neck, slowly and sensually. He hooked a slither of hair behind her ear, momentarily adjusting his erection.

Perhaps Reuben was the answer. Maybe she could have her baby, after all, and they could fall in love and be a family. Reuben held her waist and brought his lips down over hers. Jasmine responded, luxuriating in his touch, tasting his sweet mouth.

He pulled away briefly. 'Don't worry about Shelley. She's not here.'

What the fuck was she doing?

How much longer was she going to do this?

'No!' Jasmine pulled away.

She liked Shelley. Shelley was nice, sort of, in an irritating kiss-arse sort of way. Shelley didn't deserve this. Sure, Jasmine had done it before, lots of times, to lots of women. But that was then. It felt wrong now.

'I'm sorry, Reuben. I can't, not tonight.'

He dredged her eyes with his, an air of menace and confusion about him.

'Look, I'm really sorry if I've led you on, but I'm just not ready for a relationship.'

•••••••••••

The corner where Maria from Accounts had been brought to public orgasm by the Leicester branch manager earlier, was really quite a nice place to be. Pleased with herself for doing the right thing for the first time in a long time, Jasmine felt chipper, not pandering to her own needs and insecurities for once. She nursed a hot chocolate on the squashy sofa at the far end of the bar, allowing for prime viewing of all conference antics. Angela from Swindon Branch was proving to be a particularly hysterical watch, as she lurched over, laddered tights, remnants of sick stuck to her hair.

'So I said to 'im, if you want me to marry you, you're gonna have to be more romantic than that!' she blurted out, carrying on a conversation she'd clearly started with someone else. 'Do you know what he got me for Valentine's Day? One of those George Foreman grills! It gets worse – I found out he got it half price at Argos. Oh my God!' Angela's hand flew up to her mouth as her attention fell to the floor.

'What?' Jasmine shot up straight – she hated spiders. 'Oh ... my bag.'

'Is that a *real* Prada bag? Angela stared down at her distraction, unable to take her eyes off the beautiful brown Prada Glace Calf Tote.

'Yeah, it is. Do you like it?'

'It's a proper beaut – can I stroke it?'

'Of course, put it on ... take it for a walk.'

Angela brushed her hands on the cerise polyester of her ball gown and tenderly plucked the bag from the floor. She closed her eyes and smelt it, sucking in a deep lungful of seductive calfskin leather, before carefully placing the strap over her bare shoulder. The transformation was instant. She stood tall, head up, chest out, and she was off, sashaying across the bar in a straight line (straightish anyway). She wiggled her hips and flung her head this way and that, working her inner catwalk model.

Jasmine was still laughing as she returned. Angela dropped a small kiss on the bag before gently placing it back on the floor, bidding it a sentimental farewell. 'Thanks for that, love, made my weekend it 'as.'

'You're welcome.' Jasmine smiled.

'Anyway,' Angela continued, as if no time had passed since their earlier conversation, 'so that's it, really, five years later and we're still not hitched. Mind you, every cloud has a silver lining. Means I'm free to shag Dean from Marketing tonight.'

'Technically, probably not, as you *are* still living with your man, but hey, who's looking at the technicalities?' Jas smiled at Angela who was looking confused. 'But yes ... Dean ... good choice ... he's very romantic, I'm sure of it.'

'Is he? Oh good. Well, love, it's been great having a chat but I'd best be off and find him.' Angela swung around in the direction of the dance floor.

'It was lovely to meet you, Angela.'

'You too, love. None of that stuff they say about you is true, is it? I didn't get one whiff of hard-nosed slapper who'd sell their own granny for promotion. You're a doll.'

Jasmine snorted with laughter and held out her hand to shake on her and Angela's new-found friendship.

Angela took it, a glazed smile spreading across her face. 'See you later, alligator ...' she said and paused, expecting the reply.

Splinters of light exploded in Jasmine's brain, a cloud of dust impaired her sight and when it cleared, she saw her dad, swinging by a rope, and those eyes.

Those eyes that had smiled when he told her he loved her. Told her he'd never let anything hurt her.

'Love? You alright?'

·········

'Fuck me!' Jasmine ordered, pressing her lips onto his, enjoying the debauched mix of alcohol and cigars that laced his adulterous breath.

'Oh Jasmine baby, you're even better than I imagined!'

She didn't need Reuben to tell her that. Home ground. She could do mindless fucks in hotel rooms – it was her gig. She closed her eyes, her head spinning from the five consecutive vodkas she'd downed, but her dad's face loomed. The flag of rejection. The giant badge of not being good enough. Mindless fucks were all she was worth. She was born to pleasure.

She opened her eyes briefly, but when they fell closed again, it was *his* face that taunted her from the darkness. Not Reuben's but the father of her unborn child. Forbidden fruit. But what if— she allowed herself to dream for a split second. Stop it! She chastised herself silently.

Reuben moaned. '*That's it, oh, God ... there she blows!*'

Jasmine laughed bitterly at the new addition to add to her list of bizarre things men say when they ejaculate.

How could she have been so stupid as to dream of being loved and cherished? This was what men loved and she'd never allow herself to be foolish enough to believe otherwise. She was fuckable, not loveable. A mistress, not a wife. There was just one little problem with that ... as unlikely as it was, she'd gone and fallen in love.

Chapter Twenty-Two

Sarah

I'd seen it coming, but that didn't make it any less annoying when I realised it was in fact a Velociraptor Badge Day, today of all days. I crunched over the gravel and opened the boot of the Jeep, carefully sliding out the first of my three industrial baking trays, bought especially for the occasion. I'd thought better of wearing my Badge – thought it best not to warn Big Lass From The North of my predisposition this evening. That way she'd feel free to bait me, to mock me, as was her wonderfully caustic way, while I'd be safe in the knowledge that at any moment, my inner Velociraptor could spring out and rip her head off.

Grant was in the doghouse. I'd been busy preparing for tonight and, instead of playing with the boys, he'd chosen to stick them in front of the TV and spent the entire day waxing his surfboard or whatever it is you do with surfboards. When he wasn't 'nipping to Shop' for milk we didn't need, that is.

Rudy was never captivated by a film for more than ten minutes, so he spent all day trying to help me. This hadn't done my bad mood any favours, which was clinging to me like the smell of a fry-up in a bedsit, refusing to budge.

'Mrs Peregrine-Jones, how are you?' I smiled sweetly and shook her hand.

Mrs P-J was a female hand-shaker like me. Whether a woman shook hands or not told you a lot about them. Mrs P-J's was firm and fast, her hand rough and calloused, like a labourer's, which probably explained the hole in her tights. I was itching to point it out but had enough social nous not to. Apart from the holey tights, she looked sophisticated and stylish and not at all how I'd imagined. She wore a black velvet cocktail dress and smelled like a bowl of rose petals, her manner equally fragrant.

I hobbled after her with my giant baking trays, her two terriers yapping at my heels, jumping up dangerously close to my stitches. Both were blissfully unaware that at any moment they were likely to receive a swift Velociraptor kick that would send them flying into the neighbouring estate's apple orchard, more than two miles away as the crow flies.

'Theresa's already here. Been here for a while, in fact.' She twisted her head to me so I could appreciate her raised eyebrows.

'Right,' I noted, trying not to baulk at the damp smell cloying around my nostrils as we sped through the great hall, with its buff-coloured stone walls, like the inside of a castle.

'I thought I'd let you set up, then perhaps we can all have a quick rundown on the order of play. The other caterers are sharing the kitchen with you, so it'll be cosy, but I'm sure it'll all go swimmingly.'

The kitchen was commodious, stainless-steel worktops running around the edge, three or four giant fridges and a large rectangular island slap bang in the middle. Rows of copper saucepans hung from the walls, the work surfaces an orderly clutter rather than haphazard. Bowls of chopped herbs, uncorked bottles of wine, bulbs of garlic and tasting spoons jostled for space. The air was warm, and awash with the smell of caramelised juices. Steam spiralled and people in chef's whites danced quickly around the room, tasting this and chopping that, shouting orders. It was loud and industrious.

Big Lass From The North was bent over a worktop, painstakingly placing Armagnac-soaked prunes onto beds of frangipani.

'Hello, Theresa.' I strained to keep the contempt from my voice.

'So glad you could make it,' she said as if somehow responsible for my being there.

She made a song and dance about peeling back the cuff of her cardigan without using her hands and glanced at her watch disapprovingly. I sensed a fatigue, her biting edge somewhat frayed.

'I hear you're having a christening over at Fawksley Hall,' Mrs P-J said.

I'd long since worked out that if you valued your privacy, you shouldn't live in a village, although I still wasn't used to everyone knowing the brand of shampoo I used or the exact week I was menstruating. Nosey Nora From No. Nine appeared to know both of those things about me. She'd seen my empty shampoo bottles in the recycling bag at our gate and I think it was the row of big pants on the washing line that gave away my menstrual cycle. I also had a nagging suspicion that she'd marked my date of menstruation on her calendar and continually monitored my cycle because, even though it was winter now and I didn't use the washing line, she seemed to be scarily aware of when I had my period. '*Time of the month?*' she'd holler across the fence. '*Never mind, my luverly, big bar of chocolate and a hot-water bottle will see you roight!*' A born-and-bred West London girl, where it was unusual to know what your neighbours looked like, I found it a considerable strain. The postman opened the front door the other day and just plain walked in. 'Only me,' he announced as I ran semi-naked upstairs.

'That's right, we are,' I answered Mrs P-J.

'Wonderful place for a christening. Princess of a pile, that one. I'm friends with the Dutsons who own it. They have a management company in to run the whole catering shebang, of course.'

'Of course.'

'But Hatty Dutson likes to keep a close eye on things. When I mentioned your name, she said you'd booked the Jacobean Dining Room. Quite something, that room, good choice. Great windows.'

'Oh, I didn't have a choice. That was the only room available. It was all booked up for a conference, but lucky for me they didn't need the Jacobean room.' I put my baking trays down and looked around for a clear work surface.

'Yes, shame about that. The conference, I mean. It's all been cancelled now apparently.' She lowered her voice as if about to out a dirty secret. 'Between you and me, I think the Dutsons are feeling the pinch of the recession. The rooms are generally booked out from here to eternity, but the restaurant's floundering. Don't suppose this latest cancellation will have helped. But I've no doubt they'll make it work. The Dutsons are from fighting stock.' She clenched her fist and pushed it forwards, the saggy skin on her upper arm swinging. 'Anyway, ladies. Onwards.' She strode off, legs wide like an old cowboy. There were some things a pretty dress and a pair of slingbacks couldn't disguise.

'I'd be grateful if you'd set up over there.' Big Lass From The North, who'd been listening intently while keeping up the charade of beavering away with her soggy prunes, waggled her pudgy finger in the general direction of the bins. 'I need space to plate up.'

What, like I don't? I thought petulantly. 'Fine.'

She wouldn't get any argument from me tonight – I was in no mood. The quicker this whole debacle was over, the better.

It took me precisely fifteen minutes to set up. I sliced my sticky toffee pudding loaves, baked yesterday and all the better for being a day old, and evenly spaced them onto baking trays. I turned out my sauce into two saucepans and put my ice cream in the freezer (bought, not home-made – Morrisons' best, though, no expense spared). I was particularly pleased with my miniature sticky toffee pudding biscuits – the perfect combination of crunch and crumble. Marion would hopefully love them.

Yesterday, I'd nibbled my way through eight full-sized ones. I bet Jinslet didn't eat eight biscuits in a row – you didn't get to look like her and eat eight biscuits in a row. Jinslet was the mum I most admired and wanted to be like, but the way I was going, I'd descend deeper into the dowdy housewife-and-mum stereotype I already was. I'd be fat, frumpy and vacuous with a penchant for *Judge Judy* before the year was out. I'd noticed I was pulling on the same old jeans and T-shirt every day instead of making an effort, because what was the point when all I ever did was the school run, my walk and the food shop? This let-yourself-go attitude was something I had always sworn I'd never entertain.

The starters hadn't even gone out yet and Mrs P-J was nowhere to be seen, so I jumped up onto a shiny work surface to read the message I'd heard ping on my phone:

```
Good luck for bake-off. Sticky toffee pudding
to win. Flock of winged hugs on their way over.
Watch out the tower for them. Make sure Mr P-J
```

`doesn't shoot the buggers. They're bringing special`
`good-luck dust to sprinkle over sticky toffee`
`puddings.`

`Been on an excursion - aaargh! Much to tell but`
`getting nicely pissed right now. C xxooxx`
`PS: Grant defo not having affair - he wouldn't!`
`PPS: Hope you haven't emailed TIM.`
`Night night. xx`

I loved Charlie's texts, they cheered me up. I sneaked a look at Big Lass From The North. She was still busy. What the fuck was she finding to do?

'*OK, girls, you're on!*' came the loud, crisp tones of the Lady of the Manor as she waltzed into the kitchen, bringing with her a waft of rose petal and Napoleonic brandy fumes. 'The guests are perusing the dessert menu, so it's guns at the ready! I'm afraid we've run over, so I've had to let the waiting staff go, but I'm sure you won't mind delivering your wonderful desserts yourselves, will you?' Clearly a rhetorical question. She turned to go. 'Oh, and girls,' she whinnied, 'I don't want to show any favouritism, but I'm afraid I will be having the sticky toffee pudding.' She made a sad face at Theresa. 'Can't help it. Absolute sucker for anything with treacle in. Sorry, old girl!'

'It's fine,' Big Lass From The North said. 'I'm confident there will be enough people wanting to eat my frangipani.'

She turned to shoot me a sneery grin, as I struggled to contain my mirth.

Mrs Peregrine-Jones walked past my table on her way out and swiped a mini biscuit. 'Good luck, ladies! Oh, and a word of warning ... watch out for old Judge Brathington. *Mmm*, they're *gooood!*' she mumbled through a mouthful of biscuit. '*Toodle-pip!*'

Big Lass From The North and I looked at each other. I wanted to laugh, but one look at her puffed-up, ruddy face told me we weren't about to pull together under the threat of a common enemy any day soon. It would take more than that. Battle lines had been drawn with edible ink. I moved back to my 'bit' of the kitchen and put my sauce on a low heat.

'Girls, I nearly forgot.' Mrs P-J was back. 'I'd like you to both plate up one portion of dessert and take it out to show the guests, so they can get an idea of what they're choosing between.' And she was gone.

Fucking hell, what had I let myself in for? This was way out of my comfort zone. Give me a multimillion-pound pension fund to manage for a client any day, over this malarkey.

We made a silent walk down a long corridor, which seemed to be operating a dual carriageway system, with a slow and a fast lane. It resembled rush hour on a Friday, with the comings and goings of the various 'staff' deployed in running this resplendent shoot supper.

Big Lass From The North walked into the banqueting hall first and I followed close behind. The heady mix of cigar smoke, candlewax and expensive brandy that greeted us made me wish I could pull up a chair and join in the general reverie. The hall was awash with white flowers, green glassware and pale-pink candles, creating a sultry hue, which flickered along the length of the inordinately long banqueting table. It wasn't at all how I'd imagined Mrs P-J's taste to be.

The sound of silver on glass cut through the room

'Quiet, please, ladies and gentlemen! I'd like to introduce our pudding fillies!' Mr Peregrine-Jones announced.

Much laughter filled the air, of the braying and hawing kind.

'This young filly'– he stood behind Big Lass From The North, putting a firm handhold on her upper arms. She giggled pathetically – 'has cooked for us this evening ...' He nodded for her to say her piece.

'Prune, Armagnac and Cinnamon Tart!' Big Lass From The North let out a tinkly little laugh, so out of character I had to steal a quick look, to check it was coming from her. 'Basically, they're frangipani tartlets topped with prunes soaked in Armagnac and served with a large dollop of home-made creamy Calvados ice cream,' she elaborated in an unusually subservient manner.

How, in God's name, had I arrived here?

There was a cacophony of silver on glass and knife-ends on tablemats and Big Lass From The North did some sort of mini-curtsy before stepping back a pace to make way for me.

'And this delicious filly ...' He stepped behind me and held my arms firmly, as he had Theresa's.

I stood frozen as the acoustics strung out the chorus of wolf whistles that filled the air.

'*Yes, thank you, thank you. Settle down now, please!*' Mr P-J quietened the noise with his hands, then replaced them on my arms. 'Is delighting us tonight with ...'

I wriggled free, completely ill at ease with being called a filly, let alone being manhandled like a chattel. I felt decidedly grubby, as if I'd been abused in some way.

'Sticky toffee pudding,' I said flatly.

I turned to go and for the first time let my eyes dance fleetingly along the row of seated guests. Jinslet! What was she doing here? There wasn't one person at the table not eligible for a bus pass, yet there, about three seats up from Mrs P-J, sat winsome Jinslet of St Joseph's school gates fame. I wondered if she had her flip-flops on. She looked up and smiled in recognition, mouthing 'Hello', even though I'd never actually spoken to her before.

Back in the kitchen, the catering staff were in buoyant mood, loading dishwashers, packing stuff into boxes and polishing surfaces so they could see their faces, all with a song and a laugh. Demob-happy, working fast to get away, they didn't need telling twice. The first of the much-anticipated dessert orders had arrived and it was for ... yep, you guessed it – prune tart!

Big Lass From The North nearly wet herself with glee as she sprang into action. Positioning her tartlet, daintily sprinkling icing sugar, carefully adding ice cream before powering her way through the double doors of the kitchen to deliver her first bit of pride retention to its wise recipient. Ten orders later, she tiptoed lightly around the work surface to place her tenth scoop of creamy Calvados ice cream onto her tenth plate. She'd never been happier, or more acerbic.

'Couldn't be a love and pass me the icing sugar drench, could you, Sarah, pet? While you've got nothing to do, that is.'

I turned my back on her, dark hormonal thoughts shimmying their way up from my toes to my fingertips.

'That's the round thing over there, in case you don't know. You're a bit of a novice, after all. Oh, and could you just pass me a couple of your plates, please? A few of the guests said they'd be wanting seconds and you won't be needing all of your plates, will you?' She shrugged merrily. 'If you'll need any at all ...'

I stomped (as best I could with my leg) over to my pile of plates, grabbed a couple and clattered them down next to where she was working. 'Anything else?'

'Not at the moment, thanks,' she tinkled, and I trudged back over to my sauce to turn off the heat once again.

That'll teach me to be all competitive then not put in any effort. Big Lass From The North had been all light and fluffy out there in the public gaze as they made their decision on which pud to pick. In contrast, my inner Velociraptor had been lurking, as had every feminist tendency I'd ever harboured, and had clearly subconsciously warned them off my wares.

'*Sticky toffee pudding!*' yelled the girl bringing the orders in. The one unfortunate member of the catering staff who hadn't been allowed to slope off, apparently.

'*Haha!*' I laughed wryly, as she smacked the order down and raced back out to pour a drink or assuage an upper-class ego.

Big Lass From The North shuffled over to add it to her collection but shrieked, '*It really is for you!*'

I set to work. There was still time to pull this back. Slice of pudding on the plate, hot sauce drizzled generously over the top, two scoops of ice cream, little stack of miniature sticky toffee pudding biscuits on the side, *et voilà*! I was off and running.

I arrived at the dining hall panting, having chosen the fast lane, not wanting the sauce to go cold, because that was part of the joy – the way the hot, sticky sauce merged with the frozen cool of the ice cream.

'Sticky toffee pudding?' I asked.

My shoulders slumped as I remembered Mrs P-J said she was going to have it. I looked to where she was sitting, but she wasn't there – AWOL. Probably throwing up in the loo if the last time I'd seen her was anything to go by. Typical.

'That's mine, sweetness,' came a genteel voice.

I looked around and saw Jinslet with her hand in the air, swaying it gently to grab my attention (she even did that sexily – no bingo-wing problem there).

She smiled. 'That's mine.'

I laid it carefully on the place mat in front of her.

'How's it going?' She smiled up at me.

'Oh, you know ... not so well, really, but never mind.' I smiled back. 'I hope you enjoy it.'

'It smells divine, darling. I'm certain I will. Thanks, sweetness.'

I felt close to tears as I turned to leave. Just another thing I'd failed at. I was becoming a great success at failure.

I closed the glass door to the dining room behind me and slumped against the wall of the hallway outside, not wanting to return to the kitchen and its poisonous inhabitant just yet. When I left Morgan Stanley, I was top of my game. I'd learnt my trade, worked hard and reaped the rewards. That's how you became successful – you had the ability and you worked hard, it was as simple as that. Or so I thought.

I hadn't fallen into motherhood, I'd planned it and embraced it. It was my new job and I was determined to be good at it, as was my way. But being a mum wasn't a black-and-white skill you could acquire, nor as simple as just working hard. I'd found that out.

Yet another spoon was banged against a glass. Who was making an announcement now? It was like a glass-banging competition in there. I sidled the few paces up to the door and peered in. It was Jinslet.

'*Excuse me for a moment, everyone!*' She waited for quiet. She had that wonderful lack of fear that good looks, money and no bingo wings afford you. 'Thank you. I just want to say that this sticky toffee pudding is possibly one of *the* scrummiest desserts I've ever tasted and I positively urge you to try some!'

Was I hearing right?

She grabbed hold of her plate with both hands and raised it like a sacrificial lamb. '*Do come and have a taste!*' she cried.

I watched, gob-smacked, as guests leant across the table and a couple even got up and went over to dig their spoons into the dessert.

'*Mmm ...*' '*Oh yes!*' '*Ra-ther!*' and '*Fucking lovely!*' came the responses.

Jinslet smiled smugly, as if it was in her interest to market the product in front of her.

'Who wants to lick the plate?' She held the empty Spode plate up triumphantly, like an Olympic gold.

I raced back to the kitchen just in time to see a flurry of orders being slammed down on the worktop.

Big Lass From The North lurched over to see what all the fuss was about and looked confused.

'*Sticky toffee pudding ... sticky toffee pudding ... sticky toffee pudding,*' I repeated over and over as I went through the slips of paper like a pack of cards.

Big Lass From The North narrowed her eyes at me, suspecting foul play.

'Nothing to do with me,' I said with upturned palms and trotted over to my ingredients, feeling a little bit sorry for her.

The rest of the evening went swimmingly. Every single person ordered sticky toffee pudding, even those who'd already had the prune tart, and some had seconds – and that was where it all went wrong.

I brought out the very last portion and delivered it to the sweet old lady wearing a bright orange corsage and red bra, which I could see because the weight of the corsage was dragging down her dress and showcasing her underwear. She was sitting diagonally opposite Jinslet.

I'd been desperate to know all evening if Jinslet had her flip-flops on, so after I'd given the sweet old lady her pudding, I dropped my white serving cloth on the floor. I bent down to retrieve it and shot a look straight at Jinslet's toes. *She was!* They were black satin flip-flops with gold sparkles, but they were flip-flops all the same! I was busy deliberating the merits of her 'flip-flops for all occasions' approach to life, when suddenly: *Thwack!* went a hand across my skyward bottom.

I straightened instantly and spun round to survey the culprit. Old Judge Brathington, of course, that Mrs.P-J had warned us about. A tall, thin, partially balding man, with the rolling grey eyes and pointy beak of a senile penguin. Could he have picked a worse day?

My eyes flitted to the table, where I made a snapshot decision on which wine glass to pick up. I raised it above his bald patch, gleaming in the candlelight, and tilted it just enough to let the red wine pour out steadily, a gear up from a trickle.

When the glass was empty, I said, 'I'll thank you not to assault me like that again, sir.'

My steely green eyes locked with his cataract-ridden grey ones. The room was silent. Surprisingly, so was Old Judge Brathington. Not so much as a *grrr* from him. Just quietly mopping his head with his napkin.

Jinslet broke the silence. 'That'll teach you, Daddy!'

I didn't know what happened next, because I fled. What I did know, however, was that life could be very unfair. If that scenario had happened when there wasn't a Grand Prix of nasty little premenstrual hormones rallying round my body at Formula One speeds, spreading hate and fury, I'd have dealt with it in a more sedate manner. As it was, my behaviour felt totally beyond my control. Lack of control had never sat comfortably with me and neither had dishing out abusive behaviour, of any kind.

And it had to be Jinslet's father!

············

Later that night, Grant popped his head into the office to say goodnight. I was sitting at the computer, attempting to relay the evening's events to Charlie.

'I'm off to bed. Don't be too late or you'll pay for it in the morning.' He got distracted by a pile of paperwork on the desk and stepped into the room.

'Oh, Grant, you should have seen Theresa's face when all those orders came in. I actually felt sorry for her.'

'Yeah?' He sifted through the papers.

'Yeah. She looked beaten, and tired. Maybe she's got other stuff going on. She's got a strong grip on her, though, I tell you.'

He didn't bother to ask how I knew that. 'Right.' He picked up a pen and scribbled something on the corner of a letter.

'How am I going to face Jinslet at the gates tomorrow, Grant?' My eyes widened with an idea. 'Perhaps you could do the school run in the morning.' I looked at him. 'Grant?'

'*Huh?*'

'The school run, in the morning?'

'Yeah, babe.' He put down the pile of letters and plodded towards the door.

'Oh, one good thing happened tonight, though,' I said just before he left the room. 'Jas texted me – she's coming to the christening.'

Grant spun on his heel like a dog on the scent of a fox. 'What's that?'

'Jas is coming to the christening. Not sure who she's bringing yet, but neither is she, probably.' I rolled my eyes and looked back to the screen.

'I didn't know you'd even invited her,' he growled. 'Why did you invite her?'

I looked back at him as he shot me a dark look and scratched his head.

'Because she's our friend, Grant.'

'Barely. When was the last time you saw her?'

'Oh, I don't know ... just before we left, at my leaving drinks?'

'Exactly. Months ago!'

'Grant! We live in Cornwall. We haven't seen *anyone* for months.'

'This christening is turning into a farce.' He turned away, massaging his forehead. 'We don't have the funds, Sarah. It's not a bloody wedding, you know.' And he marched out.

Chapter Twenty-Three

Charlotte

Charlotte pushed back the bed covers and rolled onto her back, accustoming her eyes to the light of the new day. She drank in the luxurious surroundings (albeit heavy on the wicker furniture – and the wicker rug was taking it just one wicker step too far). She welcomed the warm Caribbean sun streaming in through the open curtains. The bedroom window ran from ceiling to floor, to capitalize on the verdant island view, bringing the outside in. She closed her eyes briefly to tune into the raucous birdsong and the gentle lull of the morning ocean, which was practically rapping on her door.

And then the reality of her life came stumbling in – green around the gills, loud, drunk and disorderly. She knew she shouldn't have told Jamie she couldn't do the lesson thing anymore. He'd looked crestfallen and she felt bad raining on his altruistic parade, but even altruists should be sensible enough to carry umbrellas, she thought.

She needed to realise that Jamie truly was only here to help her. More importantly, she needed to absorb the stuff about morbid jealousy. Did Jamie really think he could casually mention he thought she had a mental illness followed by 'rum cocktail at the swim-in bar in five'?

She'd spent last night in her room revamping her Filofax, sorting through the pages, sifting through her mind, scribbling down a new life plan and relinquishing her thoughts to paper:

Saturday, 17 February

It's official and 100 per cent certain. Jamie has dumped me and he definitely isn't going to get back with me. My heart feels like a deflated balloon. Jamie was my hope. I know the love I felt for him was obsessional, just as my love always is, but it felt reciprocated. I thought he loved me the way I love him. Now, all I'm left with is a piece of paper telling me about a mental illness he thinks I've got and eleven days of seeing him every day but knowing I can't kiss him ever again.

I was ready to walk down the aisle with him. I've chosen my dress. I want children with him. The pram is on order. Nobody can ever know this, but I know, and it hurts.

Perhaps she wasn't meant to have a family. She'd spent her entire life being grateful if someone wanted to spend time with her. She always liked who she chose to go out with, but she liked that they liked her more, and hoped that one day someone would want to spend the rest of his life with her. The fact it hadn't happened yet was the reason she'd moved, to live a quiet, single life out in the pretty Warwickshire countryside, not harming anyone and eventually turning into a mad old woman with dogs. And then she met Jamie.

Plotting her life and her feelings on paper had been therapeutic, especially as she had the added delight of sipping a long, cool gin and tonic and listening to the waves outside. And it was true, she did feel slightly better this morning, despite almost not wanting to because it robbed her of her grief and grief could be a comforting companion. She felt so much better in fact, that she even felt slightly aroused. It must be the ambience of this place, she thought, as she closed her eyes, ready to conjure up some wonderful fantasy, inevitably involving Jamie.

Charlotte was contemplating getting out of bed, when a thought occurred. The man she'd been thinking about, who'd been going down on her so skilfully in her imagination just now, hadn't been Jamie at all. The man she'd been making love to was in fact ... The Giraffe, who annoyingly kept turning up whenever she wanted to be alone. How the hell did *he* end up helping her orgasm? The mind does funny things, she thought as she padded into the rest of the bungalow, to make a cup of tea.

What should she do today? She reached for her camera case like a smoker reaching for their first cigarette of the morning. Something, anything, to take her mind off Jamie and her apparent mental illness.

Something caught her eye – a piece of paper on the doormat. She shuffled over to pick up the note.

·•••••••••

Date: Sunday, 18 Feb 09:30
Subject: Excursion

My dearest, darling Jasmine (who's right far too often!)

Don't ask me how, but I've ended up waiting to go on my personal idea of hell: an excursion! Actually, do ask, because it's funny ...

A flyer was posted through my door this morning with a list of excursions, with one of them circled in Sharpie, and the words – "See you there? x" Don't know who posted it, but presuming, and hoping, and praying it was Jamie.

Anyway, sweetie, things are not going too well. Seems you were right – J only interested in helping. But fingers crossed it's him who posted the excursion note.

He thinks I'm suffering from something called morbid jealousy. It's a mental illness! He'd printed off information about it and everything, Jas. How humiliating!

I'm still determined to have a good time, especially as it's my birthday in a few days. Have met a wealthy giraffe who has a girlfriend, and a Rastafarian beach vendor called Bannister – both seem nice. Everyone's friendly out here.

Worried about Sarah. She's really down at the moment. You two get on well – thought perhaps you could give her a ring?

Unimpressed with how you dumped Adrian the Married but *ecstatic* you have. If only I could believe it was because you were going to start settling down now and going out with nice single boys. Do I sound like your mother?

Talking of not settling down, how was the conference? Did Reuben get lucky? And don't pretend it was a quiet night. I know what the Machorn conferences are like. Looking forward to this year's installment when I get back!

Have you made any decisions yet? Keep your pecker up.

C xxooxx

PS: How much do Brazilians hurt? If you say it doesn't hurt – and by your own admission you have pubic hair like Bob Marley doing a handstand in your pants – then I might give it a go.

There was something weird about spending time emailing one's friends while on a two-week holiday in Barbados. But then there was something weird about the whole holiday and emailing made her feel better. Bannister and his laid-back advice would think it fine, she was sure.

· · · • • • • • • · ·

She sat poised, trying not to look sad and unwanted in the most coupley place she'd ever been. Another of those awful things the newly dumped have to contend with: seeing couples everywhere. And why do they seem to quadruple as soon as you've been dumped? She watched the reception area carefully, desperate to discover who the mystery excursion man was. It had to be Jamie – excursions were right up his street.

'Hi.'

'Oh, hi. You made me jump,' she said.

'Sorry. You going on the trip to Harrison's Cave?'

'No, I thought I might sit in this crowded corridor on this beautiful sunny Caribbean day just for the crack.'

Charlotte smiled at Rich and wondered if he made a habit of turning up at the worst times and irritating the hell out of her on purpose. She craned her neck to see around him, to check out the latest people to arrive.

'Bit touchy, aren't you?' Rich parked himself next to her and fiddled with his rucksack. 'So, are you waiting for someone or is your neck set in that position after a particularly nasty water-skiing accident?'

'I'm not touchy! I'm probably the least *touchy* person you could meet. And yes, I am waiting for someone, and no, I haven't been water-skiing yet. Anyway, shouldn't you be with your girlfriend?'

'I don't mean to be rude, which obviously means I'm about to be, but you mention my girlfriend every time I see you and it's getting a tad annoying because, well, I don't have one.'

'But I saw her, on the sunbed next to you on the first day.'

Silence.

'Didn't I?'

Silence.

'No, now I come to think of it, I didn't actually see her, but you had an empty bed next to you.' Charlotte nodded as it all came back to her. 'And it had a big floppy sunhat on it.'

She noticed how Rich's face always looked one step away from breaking into laughter, imbuing a mixture of bemusement and intimidation in her.

'Probably because I sat on the first empty bed I could find and it happened to have another one next to it. And yes, there was a hat. Somebody must have left it there. Look, seriously, are you all right? You seem preoccupied.'

'I was OK, until you came over and started interrogating me.'

Charlotte's cheeks burned instantly at her petulant outburst. Accepting empathy was tantamount to admitting all was not well, something she avoided at all costs, but Rich seemed genuine.

'Oh, God, I'm sorry. What's happening to me? I'm turning into a really rude cow.'

'It's OK, it's hot and humid, and I don't think the air conditioning's working.' Rich fanned himself with the cowboy hat he was holding.

'It's not that. I'm in a bad mood. I'm waiting for someone who hasn't turned up yet.'

'Oh, who?'

'I'm not sure exactly.'

Rich threw back his taut giraffe neck and laughed. 'You're great! That's exactly why I hoped you'd come on this trip. You say the best things. Look, there's the bus now. As the person you're waiting for doesn't seem to have turned up, why don't you join me? See if we can't shake that bad mood of yours?'

He smiled one of those clean, wide smiles, the type you see on toothpaste ads, little creases forming around his eyes and the hollow of a dimple appearing on each cheek.

'OK, OK,' he said. 'I know it might be hard having a good time out in the Caribbean countryside among sugarcane fields and banana plantations, on this cloudless day, with the ocean as our constant companion, but hey, we can try!'

He locked his mischievous eyes with hers and awaited her reply.

'The cave *is* worth seeing,' he continued.

'It's him!' Charlotte jumped to her feet.

'Who? Where?' Rich looked around.

'Bannister. It was Bannister – he's driving the bus.' Her energy slinked away across the shiny marble floor tiles.

'What was Bannister?'

'Nothing, it's fine.'

Charlotte felt like a puppet dropped on the floor, all saggy strings and limp limbs that wouldn't move. It must have been Bannister who'd posted the note. Bannister, not Jamie.

Her instinct was to run back to her bungalow, lock the door, close the curtains and wallow in her misery. But she knew from experience that that didn't help anything. And apart from that, it was boring.

No, she'd go on this godforsaken excursion and try to have a nice day. But what about leaving Jamie here alone all day? With stunning twenty-somethings at every turn ... She didn't know if she was strong enough for that. But wasn't this holiday about change? What would Jasmine do? Apart from shag Bannister and be done with it? She'd take the go-out option. And Jasmine was proving to be right all the time lately.

'Are you coming, then?' Rich asked.

It'll be fine, she convinced herself and followed Rich outside to the bus.

·········

She hadn't broached the subject of the flyer with Bannister when she'd got on the bus. She thought it best just to say hello, and hope he didn't mention it, which he didn't.

It was only a short drive to the caves. As she disembarked, Bannister called after her. 'Don't sweat de small stuff, pretty laydee!'

'I won't, Bannister, I won't.'

She wondered if claustrophobia counted as 'small stuff'. It had only dawned on her as they pulled up that she was actually going into a cave. Her preoccupation with Jamie earlier had a lot to answer for. Even though her fear of enclosed spaces wasn't debilitating – she could manage a lift or an aeroplane, say – she recalled a previous cave incident that hadn't gone so well. She was glad to discover they didn't walk through the caves, but were taken underground by tram, a bit like one of those land trains that drive around the zoo. The caves were indeed astonishing. They smelt sweet and damp and the cool air that permeated the tropical heat as the tram descended felt like you were entering some kind of shadowy underworld. The space had a sexy, ethereal atmosphere, with stalagmites long enough to pole-dance around. She huddled closer to Rich and breathed in sharply as the tram traversed through what seemed like too thin a gap to get through, and he reciprocated by putting his arm around the back of their seat, affording a symmetry to their bodies. Every time the tram jerked or jolted or slowed, she could feel his fingers brush momentarily against her neck. She found herself anticipating the sensation, which routinely seemed to filter down her body to culminate in a groin twinge, and this diversion from the onset of mild panic she could feel building was welcome.

The tram slowed up to negotiate another slim gap before entering a large clearing where a 40-foot waterfall cascaded noisily into a turquoise lake in the deepest depths of the cave.

'Stunning, hey?' Rich pulled his gaze away from the glistening water and looked for Charlotte's response. 'Charlotte? Are you OK?'

'*Umm*, I think ... *ummm*, maybe?'

'What's wrong? Talk to me, Charlotte. Jeez, you don't look well.'

'I *um* ... I can't ... I can't breathe.' The words echoed around her, her heart raced, her mouth was dry and she was sweating profusely.

'It's alright, you're OK. Here, have a drink of this.' He pulled out a small bottle of water. 'OK, now breathe slowly, in and out ... that's it.' He mopped her brow with a tissue and held her hand. He leant forwards to whisper to the person in front, asking them to pass a message down the tram to the driver. 'It's OK,' he said, squeezing her hand gently. 'We're on our way out now, just keep breathing.'

They squinted to adjust their eyes as the tram pulled out into the bright sunshine, back at their starting point once more.

They'd left the cave behind, but Charlotte couldn't stop the tears, a mixture of fear, relief and humiliation all outing themselves at the same time.

Rich helped her from the tram, moved her to one side out of the way of prying eyes, and hugged her. He hugged her tightly and quietly while she sobbed into his chest. He said nothing and that was the best bit of all.

Chapter Twenty-Four

Charlotte

'Hi there, can I order some food, please?' Rich smiled at the receptionist.

'Hello, Mr Fisher, yes, of course. Has the doctor been? Is your lady OK?'

'He has, thanks for organising that. And yes, she's fine now, thank you.'

'That's good. It's bungalow twelve, isn't it? Here's the menu, just circle what you'd like.'

'I'm not sure what she likes actually, but I'll give these a go.' Rich pointed to a few options on the menu and turned to go.

'Cheese on toast,' said the man who was standing behind him.

'I'm sorry?'

'Cheese on toast, that's what Charlie would like to eat.'

'Sorry, should I know you?'

'Hi, I'm Jamie, Charlotte's boyfriend.' Jamie thrust his hand out and shook Rich's tentatively outstretched one vigorously. 'Is Charlotte OK?'

·········

Rich had popped out to get them some food. He'd insisted on going to reception to order, to give Charlotte time to gather herself together. He'd asked what she'd like to eat and she told him to surprise her. As soon as he left she freshened up quickly and took the opportunity to open her laptop and Google morbid jealousy again. It was time to face facts.

Morbid Jealousy: The delusion of infidelity of a spouse or partner. A state in which men and women become obsessively jealous, even when there is no basis for suspicion. Characterised by recurrent accusations of infidelity, searches for evidence, repeated interrogation, tests of fidelity and sometimes stalking. Has the potential to cause enormous distress to both partners.

Causes of Morbid Jealousy

Insecurity: Deep-seated feelings of insecurity about the relationship or oneself.

Past Experiences: Previous betrayals or infidelities in relationships.

Rich knocked and entered. 'All sorted. Should be here in 20 minutes. Wasn't sure what you liked, so I got a selection.' He sat on the bed next to Charlotte. 'Why didn't you tell me you had a boyfriend?'

'Because I don't.' Saying it out loud felt strangely liberating.

'Well, I've just met a guy at reception who says he's your boyfriend.' Rich locked eyes with her.

'Jamie?'

'Yes, Jamie. Why, how many other boyfriends do you have on the island? He said to say he hoped you were feeling better and he'd see you tomorrow.'

'He actually said that?' Charlotte sat up straight, eyes shining for the first time that day.

'*Yes*, he actually said that. Why? Weren't you expecting to see him tomorrow?'

'No, I mean the bit about him being my boyfriend. Did he actually say those words?' Charlotte watched Rich's face intently, picking up on every clue.

'Yes. I felt daft, actually, not knowing and everything.'

He looked cross, an emotion that didn't suit his kindly features.

'I'd never have posted the excursion flyer through your door if I'd realised,' he said.

'*What?* That was you? Oh my God!'

'Yes.' He was smiling now, little lights dancing in his eyes.

'Oh, God, I'm *sooo* embarrassed. It didn't occur to me that it might be you. Why didn't you tell me?'

'It was fun not to!' He threw back his head and laughed.

He was playful, with an air of unpredictability about him, something Jamie lacked.

'So let's get this right. Since we met, just one day ago, you've seen me cry uncontrollably on a wall, make an idiot of myself about a flyer and have a panic attack on a tram – and I don't even know your surname!'

'That's about the size of it. In fact, *Miss Bloom*, I feel like I know you rather well already.'

Charlotte clocked the word 'already' and liked how it made her feel. At the same time she felt a sadness. He wouldn't have said that if he did know her well, if he knew the truth about her.

'Ah, but you don't. How well do we ever really know anybody?' She rooted around in the fruit bowl for a lemon and tried to ignore her plummeting spirits.

Rich took the lemon from her hand and padded across the room to find a knife.

'That's deep, isn't it? You're supposed to be taking it easy. Sit there and let me make you the best gin and tonic you've ever tasted.'

'And how are you going to do that, exactly, given you have two miniature bottles of gin, two small tins of tonic water, a lemon and some ice cubes? Sorry to break it to you, but I'm not sure it's going to be that earth-shatteringly different from any other gin and tonic.' She'd thrown the gauntlet down.

'Now that's where you're wrong. What you've failed to mention there – is theatre.'

'Theatre?'

'Yep, theatre.' He picked up the knife, tossed it into the air, caught the handle perfectly and sliced the lemon as if it were a block of warm butter.

'Are you a chef?'

'Nope.' He threw a bottle of gin and a tin of tonic into the air, juggled with them, pirouetted, caught them, opened them and poured them simultaneously, shaken-up tonic and all. He popped a slice of lemon on the side, put the glass on his head and walked across the room to deliver it to an open-mouthed Charlotte.

'*Bravo, bravo!*' She clapped.

'Take it, then, before it lands in your lap.'

'*Mmm*, you're right – that truly is the best gin and tonic I've ever tasted.' She smiled up at him and noticed his long, sooty eyelashes. Why do men get all the best eyelashes? 'The theatre made all the difference.' She giggled. 'So, are you a cocktail waiter?'

'Nope.'

'So where did you learn that, then? It's pretty flash.'

'Uni days – that was my party piece,' he confessed, pouring himself the remaining gin and tonic.

'Why is it blokes always have a party piece? So what do you do then?' Charlotte watched the firmness of Rich's thigh muscles under his shorts as he sat on the sofa, mirroring her posture.

'Well, what I definitely *don't* do is talk about work while I'm on holiday. So' – he raised his glass – 'here's to a holiday full of laughter, fun and discovery here at Discovery Bay. *Cheers!*'

·· ···•·•···

Charlotte ambled along the beach to the jetty, the beige sand soft between her toes. It was late, her midnight stroll lit only by the moon and stars. They'd chatted for hours before Rich had gone back to his own bungalow, a mere three doors away. She needed fresh air, she needed to assimilate all that had happened on this crazy holiday so far.

Time was funny. It rumbled along at the same inimitable pace, yet it had the capacity to feel so different according to circumstance. In moments of panic, just ten seconds could feel like an hour. And in the lighter times, those you wanted to prolong, it shot by faster than an Olympic sprinter. She'd been in Barbados for only three days but already it felt like the full two weeks. If the last three days were anything to go by, a lot could happen in two weeks, she suspected, both emotionally and physically.

The jetty had become her 'constant', her new 'wall' and it was the most beautiful 'wall' she'd ever had the pleasure of sitting on. She'd managed to visit it about six times already and each time there had been something new to look at, to smell, to escape to. She loved the way one spot afforded so many different perspectives.

It was pitch-black right now, refreshingly free of light pollution, but in the day, if she sat with her back to the sea, she could watch colourful Bajan life. Washing lines bursting with primary colour, naked children running between gardens, a stream of never-ending reggae and exotic spices drifting from windowless houses, while scruffy dogs lounged listlessly away from the sweltering heat. If she sat facing the horizon, where pink-sailed catamarans clipped smoothly through the pale blue waters, she was transported to a faraway place, one that begins and ends with the sky. A place that lets you transcend all that is material and pressing and allows you to just be. At least before the mind orders the next thought or worry to march into your head, rectifying the vacuum it apparently abhors so much.

And last, and by far Charlotte's favourite perspective, was the downward one. If she looked down she could watch the translucent turquoise waters, rippling gently in the soft tropical breeze. The sun lit up the ripples, creating a fancy strobe-light show more characteristic of a glitzy Broadway production than the shallows of the ocean. But the best thing of all were the crab wars, where legions of crabs fought like jousting knights over dead bits of fish before making a sideways run for it. On occasion they would fight each other, raised claw to raised claw, lunging at one another like brave warriors. She liked to think of them as two dashing young suitors fighting over her hand in marriage – how nice that would be! How good to be able to give up the search.

It was hard hoping and thinking you'd found 'the one' all the time, only to be bowled over by hurt and deceit and have to get up once more, dust yourself down, relight the torch of hope and go searching again. It was soul-destroying. And the longer it went on, the more she was on her hands and knees, sifting through the debris that others had left behind, the probability of finding what she was looking for getting smaller and smaller.

But she could call off the search now. Not because she'd found the right man or even because she'd found a man to marry her. Simply because the search wasn't the issue any more.

Now she sat cross-legged at the end of the jetty, not risking a midnight foot-dangle. Who knows what goes on in that sea at night, she thought. She peered through the inky darkness, thinking of what she'd googled earlier. She knew the problem was with her. Her instinct had told her so. That was why they were on this holiday, after all. But she'd never imagined this – mental illness.

Jamie was right. It was like reading a description of every long-term relationship she'd ever had. So much of her life had been spent doing exactly the things listed in the definition. She wondered how many others bounced from relationship to relationship, blaming incompatibility or the behaviour of the other partner, without ever looking to themselves for the reason why all of their relationships were going awry. Was it ego that prevented this from happening, or the fact that people looked to lay blame elsewhere, never on their own doorstep? To shoulder the blame brings with it that hulking great unfriendly word: responsibility.

It was much easier to think life happened to you, to dismiss the possibility that we have choice. But we all choose more than we realise. When we're angry about something, it's because we choose to get angry. The event we're angry about may well be out of our control, but our anger is within it. But mental illness? The words conjure up straitjackets and rooms full of people sitting lifelessly in chairs. Dishevelled individuals talking loudly to anyone who'll listen. Not 38-year-old lawyers with a network of friends, gym membership, pension and a smart car.

Charlotte's thoughts were broken by the vibration of a large thud. She froze, unsure whether to dive into the water and make a swim for it or turn and see who was there.

'Sorry, pretty laydee. Didn't mean to frighten yuh. Just with the jetty being broken an' all, it's easier to make a leap for it.'

He was right, you did have to make a leap for it. That was another thing Charlotte loved about the jetty, the way it didn't connect properly with the beach because of the broken slats at the end – it was removed from real life.

'Oh, Bannister, it's you. Thank God. I panicked for a minute there.'

'Not surprising, missy. What yuh doin' out here all alone at dis hour?' Bannister sat cross-legged beside her.

'Oh, you know, just thinking.'

'It's pretty late to be doin' that. It might not be as safe around here as you tink.' He looked towards the houses behind the jetty.

'Oh, isn't it? Have things happened, then, muggings and stuff?'

'It's a holiday resort an' de locals don't have de money de tourists have. Sometimes they are tempted by de easy money.' He sucked his teeth.

'You talk about the locals as if you don't belong.'

Charlotte surveyed the man in front of her. He was a textbook Rastafarian with dreads and a single gold tooth. He had a calm, easy air about him, like he had healing qualities, and she felt like she knew him already.

'No, I'm a local all right, but yuh won't find me stealin' yer money. I have me some jobs and I is not that way inclined. If I was gonna steal, it would be wisdom, not money, pretty laydee. What is up wid you? I have been watchin' yuh and yuh is not a happy laydee.' He leaned back on his hands and looked out to sea.

'I'm not. You're very astute.' She sucked in the night air and listened to the waves gently lapping on top of one another. 'I've realised ... well, I've been told ... well, anyway, I've found out I've got issues. Ones that turn me into a bunny-boiling girlfriend who runs around stalking her boyfriends, sniffing their pants, checking their phones, trying to control every minute of their lives and making them eat raw onions.' She looked at Bannister. 'You don't think it's funny? You could at least laugh or sound shocked by my confession. You could give me that satisfaction.'

He stretched his legs out, resting his weight on one strong arm.

'Would dat make yuh feel better, if I was shocked?' he asked gently.

'Yes ... no ... I don't know. I'm so used to making light of things, pretending everything's OK, but it's not.' She sat on her fingers to stop herself from talking, her mouth and hands inextricably linked.

'Everybody battlin' wid sometin', pretty laydee.'

'Are they?' she asked, encouraged. 'Not like this, though, not mental illness.'

'You is one of de lucky ones. You got de self-awareness. Yuh's had de good grace to examine yerself. Now it's just a matter of stoppin' de suff'rin' an' startin' wid de sortin'.'

'You sound like Socrates. *"An unexamined life is not worth living."* Sorry, Socrates was a—'

'I know who Socrates was, Charlie.'

Charlie looked into Bannister's eyes and felt a surge of warmth and familiarity, a feeling of coming home. She had an overwhelming impulse to lay her head on his lap, and decided, really rather instinctively, not to resist.

'What we resist, persists,' she muttered as she lay her head gently on his outstretched legs.

Chapter Twenty-Five

Charlotte

Date: Monday, 19 Feb 9:45
Subject: Re: Update

How's it going, Charlie? All's well here. Mildred is on my desk so I remember to water her and I've lodged the Runcorn docs. Bobby slapped a new contract on your desk yesterday. It's a biggie, so get a good rest. I foresee a few all-nighters ahead.

Oh, and got a letter confirming your talk. There will be 382 people there. Yikes!

Have fun.

Love

Mils xx

PS: Say hi to the delicious Jamie for me. No one has mentioned you both being off, so I'd say you're clear. Just make sure your tans are different shades of brown.

Charlotte plonked herself on a sunbed in the one shady spot by the pool, positioning her mango smoothie and her camera within arm's reach, so she didn't have to move. She was excited about diving into her emails. She knew she'd been spending lots of time reading and replying to emails lately, but that was relaxing for her, and that was exactly what she should be doing on holiday. Especially after reading Millie's email, apparently.

Date: Monday, 19 Feb 10:30
Subject: Charlie Does Barbados

Hi, babes,

How goes it? I've been thinking about you, lying there in the sun as I slave away trying to flog printers a load of paper they don't want, although I have actually spent the last hour searching for last-minute flowers for the grave, cos I gave the lilies I bought to a friend (see, even I'm nice sometimes). And do you know who I bumped into? Lucy, Sarah's mate! Can't get away from the bloody woman, I'm always running into her. That much yoga can't be good for anyone.

Yes, ahem, well, I shagged Reuben at the conference – yes, I know, I know. And I'm still goddamn pregnant. I don't feel very good about myself, before you start. Also Reuben went and dumped Shelley last night. He's asked if we can start a proper relationship. Blimey, not sure I'm up for that!

Looking forward to the next instalment of Charlie Does Barbados. Don't think you should worry about the mental illness stuff, though. Technically, everyone suffers with some form of mental illness or other. Not everything has a name, but it's the same stuff whatever you call it. All boils down to our fucking parents in the end. That's why it's good not to have children, cos then there's no risk of fucking anyone else up.

Be kind to yourself, baby, you're one of the good ones.

Love you loads,

Jas xx

PS: Brazilians don't hurt – walk in the park. And all in a good cause.

PPS: If you ask me, you should give Jamie the elbow anyway and start working on The Giraffe. I like the sound of him. Don't giraffes have really long tongues?

·····•·•····

Date: Monday, 19 Feb 10:45
Subject: Off With Her Head

I've been barred from the Peregrine-Jones household. All because I threw a drink over Old Judge Brathington when he smacked my arse. He deserved it, the old pervert!

Also, had a scrap with Big Lass From The North in the kitchen. She was upset because my sticky toffee pudding kicked her prune tart's arse (it was an arse-slapping sort of night) and she made the mistake of calling Rudy a bully again. It was a Velociraptor Badge Day anyway and that was the final straw. I got right up close to her and hissed at her never to utter those words again. She slapped my face. I slapped hers back. Before you know it, we were grappling with one another like two big brown bears on hind legs.

The whole of the catering team cheered us on as we got down and dirty on the flagstone floor. Mr P-J stormed in and broke it up. Not best pleased with me anyway for anointing his mate with wine earlier, he ordered me off the premises. Big Lass From The North had the barefaced cheek to cry and I left her being consoled by a dramatically overconcerned Mrs P-J (who was totally bollocksed) and a large brandy.

What's more, I heard some of the guests talking about my new friend Marion. They said she hasn't got any family and one old codger said he wished 'the mad old bat would hurry up and die' because he'd had his eye on Duckpool Mill for years. Then they said stuff about her son being buried in the garden. Said she'd had him exhumed and put there years after his death. That must be the little boy whose picture she has everywhere. So sad.

But the worst news of all is that I got a call from Fawksley Hall an hour ago saying they've cancelled my booking for the christening. Some big business has booked the entire building for the day and they were most insistent the deal included the Jacobean Dining Room. They've given us a free meal in the restaurant to say sorry (like, thanks for nothing).

Was so depressed I went to the shop for crisps (don't keep them in the house – devil's food) and bumped into Bohemian Babe, who works at Fawksley part-time and told me it was a big haulage company from Bristol who'd booked the hall. Guess who owns it. Yep, Big Lass From The North's husband. Coincidence, hey? How callous can you get? So I've eaten six digestive biscuits, two Tunnock's teacakes and both bags of crisps I bought. That room was perfect, Charlie, and there's only nine weeks to go. What to do?

Glad you liked the poem. No one else has seen it, so you're to blame if I get laughed off the pulpit.

I know you don't like hearing about my marriage problems, cos you're a hopeless romantic and you've got some weird unrealistic view of married life, but I think something's afoot. Grant seems different these days. It's not like me to be suspicious, but I think he could be having an affair (I should be so lucky).

He bought some new underwear the other day, something he *never* does. Plus, he's constantly sending texts, apparently to do with work and stuff. Should I check his phone?

Anyway, I've got news for you: it's human nature to go off sex with your husband. Trust me, it's true, and if you hear anyone say any different, they're lying. One friend of mine bought a Rampant Rabbit without her husband knowing. She keeps it wrapped in a towel and stuffed at the back of her wardrobe to use when he's at work.

Well, I'm off to reduce the ironing pile from Everest to Mont Blanc. I'll leave you to your holiday.

Keep smiling

S xxx

PS: I promise not to email TIM again.

PPS: Feel bad about moaning about Grant. I do still love him and everything, just more as a flatmate, really.

Just time for a quick reply, thought Charlie.

Date: Monday, 19 Feb 11:00
Subject: Oh Dear!

Hi, girlies,

Sending you a joint email cos stuff has happened and I want to tell you both. Sorry, but you're my bestest people in the world and I value both of your opinions and I only have time for one email cos I've got an appointment with The Lovely Rachel (beautician) in fifteen minutes.

Am so embarrassed. Went on a day trip to a cave and ended up being rescued by The Giraffe. It wasn't pretty and involved me clutching my throat and gasping 'I think I'm going to die' a lot. He's the fittest, sexiest giraffe you've ever laid eyes on, and is so sweet – but not too sweet cos I've spotted a small tattoo on his arm. I don't fancy him or anything (that would be foolish, cos he's way too hot for me).

It gets worse. I ended up sitting in my room with him, eating supper, telling him my whole predicament. I told him everything. About being dumped by 100 men, wanting to get back with Jamie, about Jamie telling me I've got morbid jealousy and even all the weird stuff I've done – I did leave out the sniffing pants, thank God.

And now I've woken up this morning and I feel humiliated, violated somehow, like I've given too much of myself away. Gonna be embarrassed if I see him today. But the weirdest thing is that when I was telling him everything, I realised how bad it all sounded, how awful those things were. I do need help, Jamie's right.

I went to Jamie's bungalow to post a note through to say I'd like to start the Love Lessons up again, and he had someone in there.

Couldn't see who it was, cos all the curtains were drawn, but I could hear a girl laughing. I got close to barging in, but (and I'm really proud of myself for this) I didn't. I tried to listen to what they were saying at the door, but the noise of the bloody waves kept muffling the words, so I posted the letter, walked back to my bungalow and cried myself to sleep.

Off to forget my pain by putting myself through worse pain. Will keep you updated. Thanks for being great friends.

Ciao, bellas

C xxooxx

Chapter Twenty-Six

Jasmine

'What the hell do you think you're playing at, Jas?' Grant stood in her doorway with an uncharacteristically thunderous look on his face. 'Why didn't you just say no?'

He shouldered past her, loosening his tie. He put his jacket on the back of a chair and dropped his briefcase heavily on the floor.

'Great, I bail you out with lilies that were meant for my dad's grave and this is how you thank me.' Jas walked up behind him and kneaded his shoulders.

'I mean it, Jas. What the fuck are we gonna do? You can't come to the christening, you just can't.'

'What else could I do? I couldn't say no. Just a tad suspicious! You're rubbish at this, aren't you?' She turned him round to face her, her hands making light work of his shirt buttons.

'Bloody hell, Jas, I was determined to be cross with you.'

She raised her eyebrows and pulled open her shirt.

'Fucking hell, Jasmine Rafferty, you're so ridiculously sexy!'

'Same goes, sweetheart.'

She unzipped her pencil skirt and let it slip to the floor, grabbing at Grant's tie and pulling him over to the middle of the kitchen, before pushing him onto the cold floor tiles. She stepped out of her knickers, trying not to catch them on her heels, and straddled him.

············

'I will point out, however,' Jasmine said, 'that if you should so much as look at me that day, Mr Richardson, you're in trouble.'

She popped a long, tanned limb on top of the duvet to cool down, sinking her head into the downy pillow, after their second session of the evening. She wondered how many calories she'd burned and whether that meant she could now have the last slice of millionaire's shortbread.

'Thank you, oh wise infidelity expert! That should work. That'll avoid suspicion, I'm sure.'

'OK, OK, Mr Sarcastic. You know what I mean. You'll just have to avoid me, cos I'll find it difficult to be normal around you.' She studied his eyes. As changeable as an English summer. Golden, like honey, one moment, and the next they were a cool, pale green – hopelessly serene and hypnotizing.

'As we've already established, I'm not as good at the deceit thing as you. How is Adrian the Married, anyway?'

'Relax, I've dumped him. You're the only man in my life now.'

Grant smiled and Jas felt a warmth course through her veins, like swigging brandy from a hip flask on a frosty walk.

'Have you told anyone about me?' he asked.

'Well, I've kind of mentioned you ... in the abstract.'

'Like what?'

'Nothing much, really. Just that you like a lot of sex. But as you're fishing for compliments, if someone did ask me what you're like, I'd probably say ... *hot*!' Jas nodded. 'Yeah, hot, scurrilous, insatiable, and funny.'

'Scurrilous! I'm not scurrilous.'

Jesus, what did he think he was doing? Being the perfect partner? He was acting like taking a mistress was some sort of rite of passage – you're not a proper man until you have one. Was that how he avoided the guilt – told himself he wasn't doing anything wrong?

'I'm sorry to break this to you, babes, but what you're doing definitely counts as scurrilous. You're hardly a contender for Partner of the Year.' She traced her finger down the middle of his chest. 'But if it makes you feel better, I'd definitely call me scurrilous, too. Don't think I'm going to be Friend of the Year any day soon, either.'

Jasmine looked away and closed her eyes. How had this happened? It wasn't that she was ashamed of being a mistress. After all, it had been her only option in the past, the only way to have a sex life and remain unfettered by the constant threat of rejection. There was no chance of being hurt that way. They never finished with her – she always finished with them.

It was probably nearer the truth to say she was proud that, thirteen spine-tingling affairs down the road, she still hadn't had any of those awful moments they tell you about in magazines. The ones where the eight-month pregnant wife turns up at your doorstep demanding to know why you've been humping her husband over the photocopier, while she's been at home battling with heartburn, while batch-baking in readiness for their new arrival.

Jasmine thought every woman should be a mistress once in her life. It taught you so much and stood you on good ground for marriage should you ever be stupid enough to contemplate such a fate. You needed to know all the tricks to know what to look for.

She'd thought many times about what she'd do if faced with this sort of confrontation. She'd decided she'd tell wifey that if only she'd retained some sort of dignity during her pregnancy, like shaving her legs and painting her toenails (excuses about not being able to reach their toes were simply not good enough), and she hadn't turned into a sexless, pyjama-wearing baby encyclopedia, her husband might not have found the need to play away.

She didn't want the wives to find out, for their sake, but she didn't have much sympathy for these women. They denied their man any sex life to speak of, only to complain when he started 'getting it' elsewhere. It wasn't rocket science. It was common sense and common business practice that if you need something (and let's face it, men do need sex) and one source dries up, then you find another more reliable source. But everything had changed now. No, she wasn't ashamed of having been a mistress in the past. But ashamed of what she'd got herself into this time? Most definitely, yes.

Jas assumed her favourite spoons position, coiling herself inside Grant's muscular frame. She picked up his hand and casually placed it on her belly, closing her eyes to savour the moment.

'Is that your phone ringing?' she murmured.

He was out of bed like a shot.

Jasmine watched her once willing bedfellow turn from cool, confident, charming lover into someone altogether less attractive. Crouching naked on the floor he rummaged through his pile of crumpled clothes, seemingly desperate to find his mobile before it rang off.

'It's her,' he mouthed, gesticulating wildly for Jasmine to stay quiet.

After a few minutes of chat, he muttered 'I love you,' into his phone while facing the corner of the room like a two-year-old who thinks that if he can't see you, then you can't see him. He finished the call and turned round sheepishly.

'Sorry about that.'

He climbed back into bed and took hold of her body, spectacularly corroborating Jasmine's earlier thoughts: he was indeed scurrilous and insatiable and very, very hot. But, more than that, he was the man she'd fallen in love with.

Chapter Twenty-Seven

Charlotte

'*Ow! Fuck!* You wait till I see you, Jasmine Rafferty!' Charlotte unscrunched her fists and opened her eyes one at a time.

'I beg your pardon?'

'My friend … she said it wouldn't hurt, but it does, doesn't it?'

Charlotte wondered whether it would be too embarrassing to call a halt to the whole proceedings here and now, before any more of her bodily hair was exhumed in this way. There wasn't even anyone to see the end result to make it worthwhile.

'Perhaps if you relax. It would help me, too – there's quite some forest down here,' Rachel quipped from between Charlotte's legs.

Charlotte reminded herself not to tip The Lovely Rachel. How could one relax when someone was smearing molten wax over one's nether regions before yanking one's pubic hair out from the root?

'So, are you here alone?' The Lovely Rachel collected more wax on her oversized lollipop stick from what looked like a fondue set.

'Sort of.' Charlotte braced herself as another load of sticky goo was applied to the tender flesh of her inner thigh.

'Sort of?' Rachel placed her gloved hand on Charlotte's leg. 'I need you to be a big girl now. This might sting. Take a deep breath and—'

'*Aaargh!*' Charlotte didn't know what was worse, the waxing, the patronising cow who was doing it or the questions she was asking.

'There, that wasn't so bad. Of course the pain's worse on mature skin. Now, what were you saying. You're here alone?' Rachel smiled, all white teeth and deep tan, the picture of health.

'I came with a ... friend.'

'That's nice. Where is she today?'

'No, a boyfriend. Well, an ex, really, but he's still a friend.' There, she'd said it. It wasn't *that* hard to say, after all.

'Shame. Did he finish it?'

'*Uh huh.*' Charlotte wasn't sure whether The Lovely Rachel was completely crap at small talk or purposely trying to make her feel shit. Perhaps she was a sadomasochist who got off on inducing pain on multiple levels.

'My boyfriend finished with me recently. It's a bummer, isn't it?' Rachel made a sad face before getting back to the job of peering between Charlotte's thighs.

Charlotte hadn't seen that coming and felt sorry for The Lovely Rachel. No wonder she was fishing. It always made you feel better if someone was going through the same thing.

'I'm sorry, it's a nightmare.' Charlotte empathised. 'The worst bit for me is the thought of them with someone else. That they'll be intimate with another woman. Because I know we can't get back together once they've slept with someone else. I'd never be able to forget it. I'd always drag it up, in my mind, in rows ...'

'What, you mean if he was unfaithful?'

'Oh, I definitely couldn't be with him if he was unfaithful. That's one of my things – I can't abide cheating. But I mean if he slept with someone after we'd broken up. I don't think I could go back after that.'

'I agree. I'd feel the same.'

'How long had you and your boyfriend been together?' Charlotte asked quietly, smiling sympathetically.

'Oh, about two weeks. I've got a new boyfriend now. Well, I say boyfriend – it's very early days. Only met him two days ago. Well, it was yesterday, really, when we properly got it on. But he's to die for.' She simpered, her eyes rolling skyward. 'And the sex!' She yanked off another strip of wax. 'You'll be glad to hear that was the last one. You've been really brave. Are you sure you don't want a facial? I've got one that's really good for wrinkles.'

Charlotte decided to leave a tip, after all: 'Just a thought, but perhaps you might like to ditch the plastic bed sheet. It's more smear test than beauty treatment.' She flashed Rachel her cheesiest smile and hoofed it out of there before she punched her.

·········

Charlotte made a soapy heart on the glass shower door, just as she did at home. She carved out a C at the top of the heart, speared it with a big arrow – *whoosh* – and went to finish it off with a J at the bottom as usual. She stopped. When she finally found herself etching the letter into the soapy bubbles it wasn't a J at all. It was a big fat R, for Rich.

She knew why. It was her way to run from trouble. Run away and start again so she never had to face anything nasty or admit there was a problem. But this time was different – she couldn't run from Jamie because she loved him too much. It would be easy to start seeing someone else, whoever else came along, because someone always did, but that wouldn't stop what had been happening. It wouldn't change the fact there was something wrong with her that she needed to sort out.

She soaped her hair and almost squealed with excitement at the prospect of things getting back on track. Jamie had called her his girlfriend. She'd had time to digest the morbid jealousy stuff now and get her pride in order, and she was ready to take it on the chin. There was every chance they might get back together today.

She stepped out of the shower into the tropical heat of the bungalow and pondered the next big question of the day. The white crocheted bikini with multi-coloured tie-dye sarong or the silky brown bikini with animal-print sarong? Not tanned enough yet for white – brown it is, then.

It was all a bit *déjà vu*, sitting on the jetty, nervously awaiting Jamie's arrival. But this time, a bridge had been crossed. The only problem now was trying to control her urge to ask him who was in his room last night, but it was very important she didn't.

'Hi.'

Jamie bounded onto the jetty and marched along to the end. He bent and kissed her cheek, a tender, lingering connection.

'Hiya. You're in a good mood.' Excitement bubbled in Charlotte's stomach.

'Well, it's amazing here. How can you not be in a good mood?' He quickly sat down, and began leafing through his counsel's notepad.

'Jamie, before we start, I'd like to apologise. I shouldn't have railed at you. It's just ...' She watched a fish dart this way and that.

He smiled. 'Charlie, stop. You don't need to explain. It's not every day you discover there's something wrong like that.' He cupped his hand over the nape of her neck. 'If it's any consolation, I think you're brilliant. You're so brave to examine yourself and try to do something about the problem.'

He moved closer and gently placed his arm around her. She loved his smell. He smelt so familiar, like something that belonged to her.

'I don't think many people do that,' Jamie continued. 'They keep plodding along, bad behaviour recurring, blaming others.'

There was a quiet, mirrored closeness, a moment ... and then it was gone. He pulled her to him in a buddy-buddy hug, a 'well done, you' gesture, and that was it, hug over.

Charlotte looked out to the horizon, the sea glimmering in the sunlight like a mirage. 'Thanks, Jamie. Thanks for helping and for putting so much effort in. It means a lot.'

She turned to look into his eyes, scrutinizing the pale-green hue circling his pupils, trying to predict how he'd react if she were to ask for a proper hug, but she was a coward. As much as she desperately wanted to feel some love, she couldn't risk it.

'So, apparently there's quite a lot to talk about in these Love Lessons, then,' she said and started slapping suntan lotion on her arms. 'Can you tell me what Toby said? About morbid jealousy and what to do about it and stuff, because I can imagine what he said to you "Run, Jamie, run!" or "Lock away your rabbits!"' She attempted a laugh.

'He said it's more common in men, and that it probably stems from your childhood. I'm no psychologist, but basically he thinks you should have some therapy.'

Jamie pinched some suntan lotion from the dollop she'd squeezed into her hand and starting rubbing it into his face.

Therapy – there was a word. A great big hulk of a word made from iron.

'So he thinks it can be ... well, cured, then?' she asked, watching Jamie bat an insect from his knee and scratch the resulting itch, his toned legs already turning caramel from the sun. How she wished she could sit inside those powerful legs once more, watcher *Frasier* reruns, eating cheese on toast and Jaffa cakes, just like they used to.

'I guess so. I'm not sure how long it'll take or whether it'll get rid of it completely, but he said it could help.' Jamie leaned back on his hands. 'I'd never have left, you know, if it wasn't for ... well, you know, for the morbid jealousy and stuff.' He gathered her gaze. 'I've never met anyone like you, Charlie. The first few months were amazing, unlike any relationship I've ever had. You were the most perfect thing who'd ever walked, as far as I was concerned. Smart, funny, compassionate, full of energy. And positive, just so positive about everything. The small stuff didn't matter to you. You never got bogged down with the irritating minutia that everyone else seems so preoccupied with. And sexually, well, you were phenomenal ... Still are. Well, you know what I mean.'

Charlotte knew what he meant. She'd always tried to impress and snare with her sexual abandon. Sex was her currency. It was tried and tested and bought her attention 100 per cent of the time. The problem being it was short-lived – a quick fix, nothing more.

'Clever, really,' he said, as if reading her thoughts.

'Clever?'

'Yeah, you lured me in with this amazing relationship nirvana. Then when I was hooked and desperate for more, you turned into the complete antithesis of who I'd fallen for. Obsessive, controlling, a little bit mad. But it was too late. I wanted what I'd seen at the top of that mountain.'

Charlotte felt a spear of white hot metal burn through her stomach. Did Jamie know how it felt to be called those things?

I don't mean to be bad or mad, she whimpered inside her head, desperately holding on to her tears. I don't want to be that person.

'And you were always sorry. You know, once you'd calmed down and all your questions had been answered. You were desperate to make amends then, saying you'd change, that you wouldn't be like that again. I believed you because I wanted to. Because I kept hoping our relationship would return to those first three months. But it didn't and I was miserable a lot of the time. I felt abused, and that made me feel worse. What kind of bloke would allow himself to be abused? A sissy, that's what we'd have called him at school.'

He was over-effusive now, keen to show he understood, although she knew he didn't.

'I mean, the brain is a clever instrument. I know you don't plot or plan this behaviour, it's not premeditated.'

He didn't know – why would he?

'And I know you didn't make me stay. It was up to me to leave if I didn't like it. But I kept hoping things would revert, that the relationship I'd glimpsed would come back into focus. That's why I allowed myself to be controlled for so long. That and ...' He stopped abruptly.

'And what?'

'Nothing. I've gone on far too long. It can't be nice hearing all this. That was some monologue, wasn't it? Sorry if I've said too much.' He reached for her hand.

Charlotte gave it to him but decided against taking the look of pity he was also proffering. Pity and she had never got on.

'I was thinking ... well, wondering, actually ...' She knew she had no right to ask, and knew it was laughable, given what they were talking about, but she felt exposed now, powerless. Her comfort blanket was forbidden territory. She had no way of stopping it, it kept coming, again and again, like a horse on a merry-go-round. 'It's just that last night, when I posted that note through your door, I could hear a woman.' There. It was out.

Her eyes sought solace in the sea. She knew without looking he'd be angry.

'Yes, you could hear a woman. I did have a woman in there, just as you had a man in your room.' He looked up at her, happy with his response, challenging her for a reply.

She hadn't expected this. She'd forgotten about Rich in her room last night. He was jealous! Her relief spilled out in a smile, which she hurriedly gathered back in.

Jamie kept his silence, so Charlotte did as she always did and went running headlong into it like a bumbling fool, trampling all over it, making things loud and comfortable again.

'I'm not seeing him or anything. It's nothing like that, he's just a friend. Obviously I haven't known him long, but he's been nice to me. He's a nice guy and he's here on his own, but it's not like *that.*'

'So you're not an item?' Jamie narrowed his eyes at her.

'God, no! Not at all. So what about the girl in *your* room?' Her turn to be the inquisitor – second nature, her comfort zone.

'Fair's fair. Well, like your Rich, she's just a friend.'

'Oh, right, where did you meet her?'

She yawned and untied and tied her sarong. He'd tell her more if he thought she wasn't bothered. Being an inquisitor was bittersweet. She despised the role of interrogator she so readily entertained, yet it satisfied her innermost yearning, her quest for the truth, and there was something agreeable and warm about it. It was familiar, like slipping your arms into a favourite old coat. Cross-questioning was her game, but the defendant in this case was a formidable adversary.

'I met her in the restaurant, here at the hotel. We get on well. No, we didn't kiss. No, we didn't have sex. No, I don't intend to have sex with her. No, I don't fancy her. At all. And yes, I will meet her again … as a friend.' He knew the drill.

Charlotte felt the bile rise up her oesophagus. Just hearing that he liked someone hurt like hell.

'So do you thin—'

'*Jesus, Charlotte!*' He held his hand up like a traffic cop. 'No more questions. No more.' He stood up. 'Shall we call it a day today then?'

Like she had a choice.

'OK.'

'Same time, same place, tomorrow?' He started walking down the jetty.

She'd blown it. Unless ...

'I don't suppose you fancy dinner tonight, do you?' Hopeful, she knew, but that was the beauty of hope – it was ever-present and always worth calling for, just in case.

'Thanks anyway, but I've got plans.' He walked on and was gone.

Chapter Twenty-Eight

Sarah

Rumours continued to swirl around the school gates like autumnal leaves whipped on the breeze. There was much whispering and huddling going on, despite the news of Big Lass From The North's and my wrestling match being a day old now. They ought to be thanking me. I'd done good and brought a juicy morsel to the school gates table, to be dissected, shared and enjoyed.

I stood back from the throng. Despite having Finn with me, I cut a lonely figure, teetering over the gutter, not wanting to commit my full body to the pavement in case someone might engage me. My arrival had caused a stir, not least because of the thin scratch running down my right cheek left by one of Big Lass From The North's highly polished talons (why do big birds always have immaculate nails?). It had crusted over now, a scabby testament that a fight had indeed taken place.

I brightened as the playground filled with the rowdy noise of the day's end and Rudy came running at me, book bag in hand, coat hood on head like a superhero. I wrapped my arms around him and turned him with my hug, simultaneously manoeuvring him towards the car and dragging a reluctant Finn, who'd spotted a cat, picking up speed until we hit a jaunty pace.

'*Mrs Richardson!*'

It was Mrs Davies, the headmistress, semi-jogging to catch up, her furrowed brow deeper and more hard set than the frosted ground of a newly dug trench.

'Just a moment, if you would.'

I attempted to disguise my immense irritation with a half-baked smile but felt I'd failed dismally.

Rudy had apparently been caught bullying. She wouldn't actually say who it was he'd been bullying, but when I suggested his mum was called Theresa and his dad ran a large haulage company, her nervous smile was as subtle as a slamming door, confirming my suspicions. I agreed to talk to Rudy and meet with Mrs Davies in a day or two, but I was sceptical.

I strapped Rudy into the back of the Jeep and turned to see Jinslet standing there. I took a sly intake of breath to bolster myself and made an apologetic face.

'Hi there,' she said. 'We never actually met properly. I'm Lola.'

She offered me her hand and I shook it conciliatorily. It wasn't her fault her dad was an arsehole. Of course, this was all very grown-up, but when was she going to get to the bit where she told me that throwing booze over old men's heads wasn't the way it works around here?

Jinslet looked at me earnestly. 'What you did was brilliant.' She smiled at my surprise. 'I get so embarrassed by him. It's not the first time, as you can imagine.'

'I wasn't having the best of days.'

'Really, sweetness, you don't have to explain. He had it coming. The biggest shock of the evening was how he took it.' She laughed. 'He's used to being surrounded by yes-men, you see, and you took him by surprise. Someone finally stood up to the old bugger!'

'Thanks,' I said, genuinely grateful. 'Oh, and thanks for endorsing my pudding. I saw what you did.'

'I did it because it was gorgeous.' She looked over her shoulder. 'It was merely a bonus that it happened to upset Theresa to boot. She and my father make a good pair, don't you think?' She laughed some more.

I smiled but said nothing. I was in that awkward situation where people slag off a nearest and dearest but, if you do, they become all defensive.

'I was wondering actually ... please say if you can't,' she waved elegant jazz hands at me, 'but I'm having a coffee morning on Thursday and I'd love to give the girls some of those biscuits I tried on Sunday night.'

'Oh, the miniature ones. Did you like those?' Pride welled up inside me. 'They were my own recipe, actually.' A crowd of butterflies left my solar plexus, surfing the excitement that was washing through me.

'Oh, sweetness, they were *amaaazing* – just like eating a sticky toffee pudding but in biscuit form. Do you make cookie-sized ones?'

'I can do, yes.'

'Is Thursday too short notice, sweetness? Do say if it is.'

'Absolutely not. I'd love to.'

I was dying to say "But tell me, what's with the flip-flops in the middle of winter?" but didn't. Her toes must be freezing. The only possible answer was that she'd got a particularly nasty dose of fungal nail and needed to keep them aired.

'Thursday's no problem,' I said instead.

········· ···

Date: Tuesday, 20 Feb 07:40
Subject: Married!

Married with kids! Can't say it wasn't hard to hear, SJ. You and me, we were meant to be together. What happened to the kids we were having?

And SJ a housewife, eh, nah, it's not sitting right. There's something wrong about that.

I've never married, because the girl I was born to marry went and married some other lucky bloke! Been with the girlfriend about three years now, though. Good Irish girl with a heart of gold, so I can't complain.

Sorry to hear your marriage isn't going so well. We all go through a rough patch now and then. Hopefully things will work out for you two. If not, you know where I am.

TIM (I like that name) xx

PS: Can't stop thinking about our sessions in the good old days.

·· • • •• • • • ··

Date: Tuesday, 20 Feb 08:15
Subject: Re: Married!

My marriage is more of a rocky outcrop than a rough patch, but thanks for kind words. And your offer is tempting, but I come as a full set now and I'm not sure there's room on your welcome mat for three of us.

Your girlfriend sounds lovely. I couldn't help wishing it was me you were talking about. But our timing was all out and, who knows, maybe we were only ever meant to be a holiday shag.

Can't stop thinking about you, though.

Better get back to the washing-up now.

Much love,

SJ xxx

·· • • •• • • • ··

Date: Tuesday, 20 Feb, 09:00
Subject: Re: Married!

Oh, babe,

Life doesn't always turn out how we expect it to. You and your boys will always be welcome on my doorstep.

I've missed you so much, SJ. Not just the making love – I've missed seeing you, missed laughing about what we'd do if the world was going to end in four minutes. Do you remember? You said you'd buy the biggest cream cakes you could find and eat ten of them! I've missed planning where we'd go in the world if we won the lottery. I've missed you.

Can we meet up? I could fly to London. Book us a nice hotel. What do you say?

TIM xx

· · · • · • · · · ·

Date: Tuesday, 20 Feb 09:43
Subject: Rendezvous

Hey, gorgeous

Well, what can I say after that? Yes! I'd love you to book us a nice hotel. I really shouldn't ... but for old times' sake.

I can make the twenty-third or thirtieth of March. Will need to check with my friend to see if she's around first, cos will be in London visiting her as far as everyone is aware. Either of these dates good for you?

Much love and anticipation.

SJ xxx

Chapter Twenty-Nine

Sarah

I stood on the shoreline, listening to the crash and roar of the waves. I felt alive with that 'anything's possible' feeling that being close to the sea so often gave me. It was a spring tide – my favourite. It was so far in, it had left only a splinter of beach for me to stand on. I stood, watching the waves rear up at me, racing to my feet, foaming around my wellies.

'*I was hoping I'd find you here today!*' Marion called from the slate steps, using her hands as a megaphone as she walked over to me.

'My leg's fine now,' I said, and handed her the basket of biscuits I'd made for her.

She accepted them graciously. 'It's cold today – come in for a cuppa."

Duckpool Mill was warm and welcoming, with home-made bread and herby cooking smells billowing from the kitchen. We sat around the large oak table near the Aga, hands around mugs, nibbling on the biscuits I'd made.

'What is it they say in America?' Marion said.

I shrugged.

'What gives ... that's it. What gives, Sarah?'

Marion's usual abrupt manner shoved aside the niceties.

I spilled, told her the lot – my failure as a mother, my inability to control my children, my worries about Rudy, Grant's refusal to see it, my failing marriage and suspicions about Grant, my lack of motivation to get out of bed every morning and TIM. Well, what was the harm? She'd been good enough to ask.

'And the christening. I beat Big Lass From The North and she was annoyed.' I began to cry, unexpectedly, surprising myself, and Marion. 'We had a fight, and now she's booked the venue so I can't have it.' Tears rolled down my cheeks. 'I just wanted a really special day, for our family.' The torrent of sadness came gushing out of me like a burst pipe in the road. I fished in my rucksack for a tissue and put my hand on the order of service I'd drafted.

I thrust it at Marion, and walked to the window. Then I gasped.

The window looked directly out on to the sunken area of lawn that had the concentric circles mown into it, and there, at the centre, hovered a new addition. A huge bronze eagle with outstretched wings, each one at least two metres long, soared purposefully, a few inches off the ground like something you only expect to see in a dream. I thought back to what I'd heard at the Peregrine-Jones' dinner party.

'Christ, Marion, I'm crying about not having the perfect christening, for God's sake. I'm so sorry, I—'

She put up her hand to stop me. 'Don't.'

She poured thick black liquid from the cafetière into my mug, the rich coffee fumes soothing my emotions before I'd even taken a sip. She pulled out the chair next to me and sat, expressionless. Then she began.

'You're the first to hear what I'm about to tell you and I'd rather you were the last. Is that something you can promise me … and I mean *really* promise?'

I nodded. 'I promise. With all my heart.'

She told me about her little boy, Danny. She was thirty-one when she had him. She'd looked into his eyes when he was ten minutes' old and knew instantly that she'd never give birth again, because she never wanted to share the intensity of emotion she felt for Danny with anyone else.

Danny's dad was a writer and a drunk. He hadn't started off as a drunk – he'd been a hard-working journalist with a dream when she'd married him at the age of twenty-five. The drinking came later, along with the rejection slips.

Walter had written a good first novel, which went on to win a literary prize, but that was all he'd ever amount to. On the other hand, Marion's career as a sculptress went from strength to strength, causing a stir on the London art scene. Walter's increasing frustration and alcoholism left him prone to violent mood swings. Danny loved his daddy all the same and Marion worked hard to keep her five-year-old son from the grim reality of their relationship.

It was an Australian didgeridoo player who started the turnaround in Marion's life. He walked into her art studio in Fulham and fell in love, not only with a very expensive wooden sculpture, Marion's favourite, but with the sculptress herself. They started an affair. His tour ended and he was back in Australia by the year's end. They wrote, they talked on the phone and they decided theirs was a love that didn't come by too often. Marion would leave Walter as soon as the time was right, even if that time wasn't for years to come.

He came to England the following February. His first stop was a gig in Northampton. Marion found an excuse to be there, desperate to see him after months of being apart. They couldn't drag themselves away from one another and the train she eventually caught back to London was too late for the last Tube home.

Walter agreed to pick her up from the station and lifted Danny out of bed and into the car. They picked her up at Euston. She opened the back door of the car and kissed Danny's slumbering eyes, nose and lips, just as she always did when he was asleep, then got into the front.

She should have known better than to ask Walter to drive at this hour – she could smell alcohol on his breath. They argued, her wanting to drive, him not allowing it. They crashed head-on into a lorry somewhere on the North Circular. She could still remember the squeal of the tyres and the crack of breaking glass. Danny died immediately, Walter by the time he reached hospital. Marion was left with a scar on her neck where the door had perforated it and a heart that would never repair. She never spoke for two years afterwards, to anyone.

It was with a phone call to Kibells Estate Agents that she broke her silent tribute. Her London house was on the market for approximately forty-six minutes before it was snapped up. Fifteen minutes later Marion had put an offer in for Duckpool Mill, Cornwall. Somewhere she'd dreamed of living, for its superior quality of light. An artist's paradise. That was thirty-seven years ago now and she hadn't left Cornwall since.

She couldn't bear to leave Danny behind, so she had him brought to her and buried in the middle of the circular lawn, now fiercely protected by the golden eagle. Danny was in awe of the golden eagle and had asked his mummy to sculpt him one the week before he died.

Hot, silent tears trickled down my face from the moment Marion started telling her story. I couldn't remember the last time I'd cried for so long. My eyes felt tight, my lids heavy, my heart like a clod of wet earth, dense and black. Marion didn't shed a single tear.

'I've spent many years trying to live with the guilt. Years wondering where it all went wrong with Walter. With the benefit of years of harrowing hindsight, I've realised that all that guilt and worry got me nowhere, and solved nothing. None of us can predict the future, all we can do is listen to our hearts, and do what we think is best at the time, taking into account all of the circumstances. Whether we make the right decisions or not, well, only time can tell us that, but don't live under the shadow of worry, Sarah. Live in the light.'

She got up to stir the tomato and basil soup that was simmering gently and turned out a loaf.

'You'll stay for lunch, won't you?'

'I'd love to.'

I had to get to the printer's with the order of service, but being with Marion was addictive. Like the loaf of bread she'd baked, once you cut through her crispy outer crust, she had a soothing, malleable warmth about her.

We sipped soup from ornate silver spoons and listened to the wind howling outside the kitchen window. And after lunch, Marion surprised me, by kneeling in front of me, and taking both of my hands in hers.

'I can't live my life again, Sarah, but I can help you with yours. You're at exactly the point I was when it all went wrong.'

I nodded. I'd already made the connection.

'Usually people have to learn from their own mistakes, but why don't you buck the trend and learn from mine? Is it the right time to meet up with TIM again? Only you can answer that.'

She pumped my soft white hands in hers, each one housing at least two liver spots for each birthday since sixty. There was the hint of tears now, a watery glaze, threatening to turn into fat droplets of sadness but never quite making it.

She got up and walked into another room. When she came back she was holding my flask, my lovely blue V&A flask that I'd last seen rolling down the beach. I beamed. I knew she'd rescued it, but with everything going on I'd forgotten to ask for it back. It was stuffed full of wild flowers I recognised from the meadow. She handed it to me.

'It's broken, I'm afraid. The glass inside was smashed. But I like to give broken things an opportunity to fit into our lives in other ways. Sometimes that can serve to fix them and they just slide nicely into their new role.'

········•·•····

The boys were asleep. I used to read books in the evening, or prep for international business calls, but now I swap emails. Who needs Austen when you've got Charlie:

Date: Tuesday, 20 Feb 16:48
Subject: Les Dawson

Oh my God! Did I read that right? You poured a drink over Judge Brathington, *the* Judge Brathington, no less? Do you know who he is, honey? He was one of the top judges of his time. Fantastic! That and the thought of you fighting with a fat bird on a flagstone floor has made my day ... Only you.

Surprised to hear you suspect Grant – not like you. I can't imagine for one single teensy-weensy second that he'd do something like that. I think you're being paranoid. I know, I know, that's rich coming from me.

It's just that you and Grant are, well, you're you and Grant, and I can't imagine you ever being anything else.

That said, it did worry me when you said you love him like a flatmate. Jasmine's always harping on that men stray because they're not getting it at home. That's how she justifies being a serial mistress. If the wives won't put out, they can't expect their men to stay true. She sees herself as a service rather than a homewrecker, cos the man goes home happy and the marriage keeps working. But you had sex the other day, so I think this flatmate thing is an exaggeration. You two are going to be fine.

Have you managed to speak to Jas yet? I wasn't going to say anything, but I'm worried about her and I think she could do with a friend on the ground, as it were. She's pregnant. She's not sure what to do and I know this is harsh, but I don't think she'll keep it. Anyway, don't mention it – she hasn't told anyone, not even the father – let her tell you first.

Had a Brazilian today, so now I have a bright red, swollen, rash-covered pussy that resembles Les Dawson's gurning face. *Très* attractive. Too much information?

Had Love Lesson Two today! Went a lot better than One. He did have a girl in his room. Apparently, she's a friend ... I know I should believe him, but it's hard. Anyway, at least we parted on good(ish) terms. Can't stop thinking about the girl in his room, though.

Don't worry about Fawksley Hall. Something will turn up, honey, it always does.

How are the boys? I know I've said it a million times, but I'm going to say it again. You. Are. An. Amazing. Mum. Get Rudy checked out again if you're worried – don't give up. In the meantime, keep giving those boys huge great dollops of your unswerving love at frequent intervals. And don't forget to love yourself a little bit too, just like your poem says.

Big hugs coming your way.

Charlie XXXOOOXXX

PS: Have you emailed TIM again? The truth! Please don't, honey – think of the boys.

I knew I should call it a night, to slow our exchange down, but I simply had to reply:

Date: Tuesday, 20 Feb 21:10
Subject: Camel Train (Not Camel Toe)

I can't keep up. You send two emails to every one of mine. You're gonna come back as white as a duck egg.

Shocked to hear Jas is preggers. Last thing I thought you'd say. Give her my number so she can call me if she wants. Who's the father, do you know?

Think you're probably right about the Grant stuff. My underused brain is clawing at everything and anything to get its rotting teeth into. Not going to bother checking his phone. Was dreading it anyway.

Glad to hear you and Jamie are keeping it cordial. He wouldn't shag someone out there, Charlie, I'm sure of it. That would be a bad thing to do, especially as you paid for the holiday, for fuck's sake. Don't worry, I'm certain this woman is just a shoulder to cry on. She's probably sixty with pictures of her cats in her purse.

And as for morbid jealousy stuff, the preconceptions and stigmas that the words 'mental illness' carry around are mostly as accurate as your mum's spelling. We've all got some kind of mental illness or other. Are you telling me that I don't have OCD? I can't walk past a coaster or a pile of magazines without putting them straight. And I resort to cleaning at midnight because I'd rather die than live in a house that hasn't been hoovered every day and it's the only time I have to do it.

So stop being a drama queen and think about how good this is. If you know what's wrong, you're a step nearer to sorting it. Perhaps your next mission is to find out why you do what you do (perhaps that's a job for your next boyfriend). Promise me you'll laugh at this and try to see the funny side. I don't know what you're like as a lover, Charlie, but I do know you're the best friend anyone could have. That has to count for something.

Still no joy on the christening venue, been ringing round everywhere. God knows what I'm going to do. I may even have to cancel.

My friend Marion is amazing, Charlie. You're going to love her. She's seventy-five but the youngest person I know (no offence, she's just got such a great outlook).

She told me that life is like riding on a camel train through the desert. The scenery may not change for what seems like forever, but you'll reach the oasis soon enough. And when you get there, you may be wishing for the beautiful sunrises of the desert once more. Happiness isn't about getting what you want, it's about appreciating what you have.

Sorry. Realise this is a bit deep if you're reading it in a sunhat and sarong waiting for your club sandwich to be delivered. Just loved it and wanted to share it.

Much love,

S xxx

PS: Don't care who Old Judge Brathington is. The dirty old pervert got all he deserved.

PPS: Exercising my right to silence on the TIM question.

PPPS: The Giraffe sounds amazing. Shag him and have fun. You're on holiday!

Chapter Thirty

Jasmine

'What's all this about, then?' Jasmine asked, as they began to eat.

'Thought it might be nice to eat in town, instead of always skulking away in Balham after dark.' Grant smiled, his clear green gaze honest and direct.

Jasmine's heart skipped a beat. 'It is nice. Have you got the afternoon off or something?'

'No, I made up an appointment and said it wouldn't be finished until close of play. If that's all right with you, of course? Can you bear to spend this much time with me?' He inched his hand across the table, turning up his palm so she'd put her hand in his.

Jasmine didn't know if she could suppress the squeals of delight welling up inside her. She pursed her lips, concentrating on keeping her cool exterior. She needed sassy, not soppy. Grant would hate soppy.

'Not sure.' She employed every ounce of willpower to keep her features from crumbling into a love-struck teenager face. 'You were very cross with me yesterday.'

'Oh yeah, for about two minutes, until you seduced me into submission. Jesus, Jasmine, you were so sexy last night. Haven't been able to think about anything else all day. I think I'm in love.'

Everything around her disappeared, the restaurant back drop went fuzzy, catapulting Grant's face into sharp focus, as it erupted into a smile the width of a cruise liner. His sweet words rang in her ears, drowning out the chatter and chinks of people doing lunch. She'd never been happier.

'Anyway,' Grant added, between mouthfuls of thin crust Napolitana, 'you got cross with me as well. About that print in the living room.'

'I told you last night, it's not a print. It's an original. It's worth a lot of money.'

'What? You paid good money for that thing? It's the ugliest painting I've ever seen. The woman in it is hideous. She looks as miserable as sin.'

Jasmine's stomach tightened. 'It's a very beautiful painting and happens to be my favourite possession in the world.' Grant had no idea what the painting symbolised, so it was unfair to castigate him, but she couldn't help herself. 'It was my dad's. It was his favourite thing, too. It's all I've got left of him.'

'Oh, Jas, I'm so sorry —'

'Just leave it.' She felt bad she'd been so mean to him now she'd vented her emotion. 'You didn't know. Let's talk about something else.'

'OK, but I'm really sorry anyway.' He squeezed her hand. 'Sooo, how was it?'

'What?'

'The conference. I didn't get chance to ask last night.'

'It was OK. Usual stuff, really.' Jasmine focussed on her pizza, trying not to meet his eyes.

'What is the usual stuff? I've never been to a conference. Sandercocks don't do them, tight bastards,' he moaned, wiping cheese off his chin.

Jasmine's cheeks coloured. She thought quickly and peeled off her jacket, complaining about the heat of the busy restaurant. She'd been excited when he'd rung to invite her for lunch. She'd made hasty apologetic calls to her afternoon appointments and jumped on the first Tube, but all he wanted to do was quiz her on what she'd been up to. She wasn't used to being questioned – that was relationship stuff. Had it been anyone else, she'd have told them to mind their own business. What goes on tour, stays on tour. But this wasn't just another lover, this was her love. Ironically, it had taken the conference to realise that. He'd taken time off for her today, and now he wanted to know what she'd done this weekend. Proper relationship territory.

'Not much, really. Basically, you turn up, doze through a load of presentations given by promotion-obsessed egotists, fake-smile through a few team-building games, scoff loads of biscuits, and nod a lot. Then you get totally bollocksed, make a complete fool of yourself on the dance floor, and spend Sunday with a sore head avoiding eye contact with anything but the fried breakfast. It's like some kind of high-level arse-licking competition really, with a disco.'

'And the shagging?'

Jesus Christ, couldn't he just let it drop? She felt her cheeks sear as red as her bank account. She sipped on her glass of water to try and take the heat from them.

'Shagging?'

'Yeah, last week you told me it was a shag-fest. Couldn't hear for the sound of breaking wedding vows, you said.'

'Did I? Well yeah, it is a bit like that, but I don't go in for all that stuff. I've got two golden rules as far as work's concerned: never use the company franking machine for personal use and *never* take work home with you.' She lowered her chin and looked up at him through long, thick lashes. 'I'm a good girl.'

'Yeah, right!' His face broke into a salacious grin. 'I think I know different, Miss Rafferty.'

'Only think?' she said in mock indignation. 'We'd best get back to my place, then, so I can turn that "think" into a "know". She smiled provocatively, tilting her head. 'Sounds like it needs ramming home, to me.'

'Say no more! I'll get the bill.'

Grant took a wad full of notes from his inside pocket and got up to pay, leaving his wallet on the table. Jasmine sat looking at it, deliberating. She pulled it across the tablecloth towards her, pondering her intentions as she fingered the soft brown leather. She'd never done anything like this before, ever, but then she'd never been in love, either. She didn't really know what she was looking for. She was the mistress, after all.

Surely she didn't think he'd have two of them on the go? No, she wasn't looking for evidence of other women, she was looking for an endorsement of her own status in his life. Something subtle enough to avoid suspicion from his wife. Perhaps the four-leaf clover she'd given him on the picnic they'd had in Hyde Park last year. He was smitten with her, she was sure of it. He had just said so. He was bound to have something in there.

She flicked deftly through the contents while keeping a keen eye on the bar, which luckily was too far away for him to see what she was doing. Receipts, plastic, money-off vouchers, reward cards ... Oh, here we go, a photograph, him and the boys. Sweet. But wait a minute ...

She plucked a second photograph out of his wallet. Fizzy anticipation turned to unmitigated desolation in one tiny second. It was *her*. Sarah. She looked stunning, lounging back on the branch of a tree, hugging her knees and smiling sexily.

·····•·•·····

Grant kissed her goodbye after another night of clandestine love-making. A tender kiss, until he ruined it with a quick grope of her arse at the end, then he closed the door of her flat behind him. Jasmine picked up the brown envelopes that Grant had stepped over on his way out, and put them on the hall table, carefully adding them to the tower of other brown envelopes the postman insisted on delivering each day. More unpaid bills. They needed opening, but not today.

Jasmine thought back to the photograph of Sarah she had found in Grant's wallet. Guilt seared through her body. It was one thing shagging someone else's husband, but falling in love with your friend's husband was another thing altogether. But why should she feel guilty? She hadn't started the affair. It was Grant who'd rung her, Grant who'd made all the moves. And as Jasmine knew only too well, there had to be something wrong with the marriage for him to even contemplate doing what he was doing.

Jasmine loved and trusted Charlotte more than anyone, and Charlotte loved Sarah, constantly extolling her virtues and rambling on about what a beautiful person she was. But just because she was a beautiful person, it didn't mean she was necessarily right for Grant. It was no good if they didn't make each other happy.

Jasmine was disgusted with herself for doing what she was doing to Sarah, but it was too late now – she was in love. She didn't want it to be surreptitious any longer. She wanted it all above board. She wanted him to leave Sarah and be with her.

She smiled bitterly. She'd turned into a stereotypical mistress, wanting her man to leave his wife, analysing his every word, believing him if he said he was going to leave. She thought back to the photo. There didn't seem much chance of that. Sarah's legs were much longer than Jasmine's, her hair glossier, but worse than that she'd looked happy. And far, far worse than that, the photo was recent. Christmas 2023, it had said, scrawled across the back in Grant's handwriting, proving it wasn't even something Sarah had given him. He'd put it there himself. He carried it out of choice.

She peered surreptitiously from her living-room window, making sure Grant had definitely left for work, then picked up the phone and dialled.

'Good morning. Baytree Clinic. How can I help you?'

She placed a hand on her belly and closed her eyes.

'I'd like to make an appointment, please.'

Chapter Thirty-One

Charlotte

There was something invigorating about taking photos, removing yourself from reality by viewing people through the lens, appreciating the finer points of their faces, looking at the detail. Charlotte loved portrait photography. Studying people always reminded her that beauty was so much more than the overall picture of someone's face you got when you first looked at them. It was about the individual components that made it up. She saw the face as a portal for one's character to shine through, to colour in that person. She liked to capture more than just the look of someone – she liked to capture their essence.

It had been a strange few days. She'd had a couple of Love Lessons with Jamie, where they'd discussed her behaviour and what she should do about it, but each time he'd stopped them bang on the hour, like she was a paying client. He'd said he wanted some time on his own and she'd agreed. Despite everything, she still had an inkling he wanted to be with her and needed time to think.

Usually she'd bump into him on the beach or round the pool, but there were times when she didn't know where he was and that bothered her. On occasion she'd try to find him, creep round his bungalow, listening for voices, and casually enquire about his whereabouts at reception, but she'd never found him yet. She hoped this thinking period of his would end soon and they could try again. She knew it was a long shot, but she liked to hold on to something.

She'd taken herself off this afternoon, just her and her camera, tired of waiting for Jamie to turn up and declare his undying love for her, and she was glad she had. Glad she'd strayed away from the beaten track, away from the smell of suntan oil, and the buzz of jet skis, glad she'd found some of the real Barbados. She'd got some lovely shots for her trouble.

She breathed in slowly, tasting the salt air, smelling the rain-soaked palms as they dried in the tropical heat and listening to the cicadas resume their chorus after the downpour. She plucked her mobile from her pocket. It was out of place here, where time boundaries were fuzzy, but Sarah's texts kept her going, and her mum wouldn't rest until she'd made contact. Her mum worried about everything. A mere suggestion of high winds and she was busy texting stuff like: *Driving wind in your aria. Gail force in cuple of hours. Dont travel unless really nesesary.* She didn't seem to understand that turning up at work was necessary if one wanted to keep one's job.

Charlotte's head turned towards the laughter coming from the garden next to her – someone was having fun. She looked at her screen – six texts and nine missed calls. And yep, apart from one, they were all from her mum. She'd read them in a minute. She wanted to see what Sarah had to say first:

Shit! Have arranged meeting with TIM. Didn't want to tell you but can't help myself. Don't shout at me. It's something I need to do, Charlie. S xxx

Charlotte was surprised and annoyed. This was Jasmine territory, not somewhere she ever expected Sarah to go. She couldn't bear it if the one friend she admired for her morality had joined the merry band of polygamists who roamed the land. She angrily tapped out her reply:

Are you sure? What about Marion's advice? Think hard about this, Sarah. C xxooxx

She couldn't believe Sarah would go through with it. She had too much to lose. She was short on self-esteem right now and TIM was the only thing making her feel good. Hopefully she'd shake out of it before she did anything silly.

She opened the first of her mum's texts from 10 a.m. and her heart sank.

Hi darling. Havent heard from you. Hope everything okay? Mite have problum about your talk. Know how important it is so working on it. Leeve it with me. Gotta go. Need to get Rog his snac. Luv loads mum xxxx

12:45:

Hi darling. Still havent heard from you - u know how I worrie so would be gratefull if u could text. Luv loads mum xxxx

14:17:

Hi darling. Realy worried now. Ring or text asap. Roger has finals of bowls tornament the week of your talk but still working on it. Could Jas go with u if not? Will let you now. Luv loads mum xxxx

15:05:

It doesent matter what time it is just ring me. Have tryed ringing your mobille but turned of. Luv loads mum xxxx

16:00:

Charlotte ring me. I am out of my mined. Dont even know name of hottel u staying in. Mum xx

Charlotte didn't know whether to laugh or cry. Her mum's love was always so misplaced. She'd whip herself up into a hysterical frenzy if she didn't hear from her for two days, yet she couldn't make it to the most important event in her life that year, all because of Roger's bloody bowls tournament.

It was easy to dislike Roger for it, but she knew she shouldn't. It was the way her mum was, she couldn't help it. Charlotte didn't think she even realised she was doing it, so ingrained was her behaviour. Dad had reigned over her with an iron rule. A regime, not a marriage. They'd met when she was fifteen and he nineteen, and married two years later, and he had her dancing to his tune before the first year was out, whether he was there or not.

Family tales abounded of Mum being forbidden to wear miniskirts (it was the sixties), of Mum taking knitting to do in the school playground because he forbade her to talk to anyone, and of Mum being too frightened to wear make-up on her wedding day. Fact or fiction? Charlotte didn't know but suspected it to be true, because she'd seen him control her mother with her own eyes. In Charlotte's childhood she'd watched her dad control the purse-strings, the parenting decisions, what they watched on TV, and where they went on holiday. It was all non-negotiable. He made the rules. He also got to decide how much he gambled away each week, and how many times he drank himself silly at the pub. While Mum stayed at home, unable to drive (she wasn't allowed), looking after the children, the house, and working from home for 6 hours a day.

Dad came first, always, over everything and everyone. What Dad wanted, Dad got. Dad's word was always final. He wasn't a violent man, as far as Charlotte could remember. His particular strain of abuse was more of the mental variety. Charlotte had never understood why her mum had married him, and why her parents hadn't tried to intervene, but amongst other probable reasons, life was just different back then. Hannah Bloom had had her personality sucked from her just as Charlotte had taken Pete's. She could see this now, see the pattern.

There was the laughter again. It was familiar but out of context. Charlotte listened carefully and then it dawned on her. It was Jamie's laugh!

Her heart started thumping – big, echoey thumps. She turned slowly and stood stock-still, peering through the vegetation. She could just make out the shapes of two people, but they were too far away to see their faces. She slowly pushed the lens of her camera through the fronds of the palm blocking her view. She swallowed the panic rising up her throat and adjusted her lens to zoom in on the mystery woman.

'Charlie?'

'Bollocks!' She recognised that voice, too.

She jumped away from the garden wall, losing her balance, making her hop like a drunken kangaroo.

'Charlie, are you OK? What are you doing shoving your camera lens into someone's back garden like Inspector Clouseau?'

'Rich, hi. I'm just taking a few shots. Collecting a few authentic Barbados memories, you know.' She pleaded silently for him not to challenge her. 'Bougainvillea, local children, that sort of stuff.'

'You were spying!' He grinned back at her.

'I was not!' she spat back, a bit too quick and indignant. 'What are you doing down this way, anyway?'

'Oh, I love this stretch of beach. It's less touristy, and more rugged, more natural, you know.' He made patterns in the sand with his shoeless feet. 'Nature is a wondrous thing, isn't it? Evocative and uplifting. Puts everything in perspective.' His cheeks were red but his expression was benign, his thoughts elsewhere.

Charlotte knew where he was coming from. It was refreshing to hear in a world increasingly gripped by materialism.

'Perhaps because nature *is* perspective and everything else in life is superfluous,' she said.

'Exactly!' He beamed. All of sudden he was radiant. 'Come on.' He grabbed her hand and jogged down the beach. 'It's nearly six o'clock, what are we waiting for? Let's go to Oistins.'

The sun had set by the time they'd arrived, in its usual spectacular fashion, a ball of orange sinking into a serene and silvery sea. They walked together, close but not holding hands. Terry in accounts had told her about the Oistins Fish Fry, said it was all smiling happy faces and he was right. The place was alive, the night-time air stuffed full of the sights, sounds and smells of a street festival. Rich took her hand to guide her through the crowds and she liked how it made her feel – sort of looked after.

Red snapper and sword fish sizzled on grills and the seductive smell of Bajan spices – garlic, ginger, cinnamon and thyme – wafted over on the breeze coming in from the shoreline. It was only then she realised she hadn't actually eaten since breakfast, and she was starving.

Rich led her through the tables looking for a seat, his long brown fingers wrapped around hers. Reggae and calypso boomed out of temporary sound systems. Some people were dancing and others sat in clusters on white plastic chairs eating garlic potatoes and barbequed pork from food trays on their knees. What struck Charlotte was how casual it was, nothing more than a collection of wooden shacks selling fish and beer, yet its vibrant carnival atmosphere was contagious. Unsophisticated, but all fundamental human desires taken care of, nothing else needed.

Rich located two spaces at the end of a bench crammed with people. 'Do you want to sit here while I go and get us some food?'

Charlotte didn't know what was worse, sitting alone among a raucous gang of friends or the fact her bum seemed to be taking up the entire space that Rich had thought big enough for two.

'What would you like?' He was standing behind her, his hands on the bench, one arm either side of her protectively. His mouth was close enough for his breath to tickle her ears, starting a shiver running down her body. She could feel a pull between them, a magnetic force, as if it wasn't right unless they were touching in some way. Was this what people meant when they used the word 'magnetism'? She'd never felt it before, but she liked it. It was heady and addictive.

She sat surveying the scene while he was gone. The crowd was a mixed one, predominantly locals, with a few obvious tourist faces peppering the throng. She spotted Bannister and who she presumed were his brothers, swigging beer and laughing together.

She was experiencing some nerves being out for the night with Rich – it felt intimate. But she tried to ignore them, because if she was thinking about Rich in *that* way, that would mean Jamie and she were over. Besides, Rich was probably just feeling sorry for her. She hadn't been able to stop thinking about who Jamie was with today.

Rich appeared with bottles of beer and portions of breaded flying fish and squeezed onto the bench, his thigh firmly wedged against hers. He wriggled about, making himself comfortable, the warmth of his body permeating hers. There was a moment when their eyes met, but Charlotte pulled her gaze away, afraid of what might happen.

'Thanks for coming.' He nodded to acknowledge his gratitude, as if she'd done him a favour.

'No, thanks for bringing me, I love places like this.' She loaded up her fork, glad of the opportunity to silence her growling stomach at last.

'So, Miss Bloom, tell me about yourself.'

'What do you want to know?'

'*Umm?*' He held his fork midway to his mouth. 'Do you have any sibs?'

'You mean siblings?'

'Yeah, what's wrong with sibs?'

'Nothing, it's just so public schoolboy. It's funny.' She attempted a straight face. 'Sorry, I promise not to take the mickey out of the way you talk anymore.'

'Thanks, otherwise I might start on that piece of eighties memorabilia you carry around.' He grinned.

'What, my Filofax?' How dare he!

'*Yes*, your Filofax! You're on holiday with your Filofax, for fuck's sake! Who does that? Who even has a Filofax anymore?'

They crumbled with laughter. Charlotte knew it had been a mistake to tell him she kept it in her pillowcase to keep it safe in the event of a burglary. He gently touched her back and apologised for the teasing.

Something caught Charlotte's eye and she looked past him to see The Lovely Rachel in the background. She was chatting animatedly to some poor sucker she'd cornered but Charlotte couldn't see who. Her six-inch dominatrix heels and tight-fitting leather mini-dress wouldn't have been Charlotte's choice for an evening at a fish fry, but she wore them well on her Angelina Jolie frame.

As they were finishing their meal, Charlotte realised they'd spent the whole time talking about her again.

'So, Mr Fisher, what about you? I've known you for six whole days now and I don't know a single thing about you. Well, apart from you went to Cambridge University, and you make the best G & T in the world.'

'Come on, then, what do you want to know?'

'Let's start with your *sibs*.'

Rich laughed. 'All right, but we could be here for a while because I have six.'

'*Wow*. That's a lot of brothers and sisters. What was it like growing up with that lot?'

'Great, actually. I want a big family. Big families are fantastic, although I was robbed of my cuteness at a very early age as a consequence. I'm the eldest and by the age of one and a quarter, there was already someone cuter than me. Ghastly luck, isn't it? Whereas if you're an only child, I suppose you can stay cute until you're five or six or even older.'

'Simply *ghastly*.'

'Stop it. You promised.'

'Sorry. Well, if you want my opinion, I don't think you ever stopped being cute.'

Flirting with Rich came naturally and it occurred to her that she hadn't thought about Jamie for a whole hour.

'Besides, it doesn't seem like you suffered. I can tell you think nice thoughts about your childhood.'

'I suppose having so many brothers and sisters brought me lots of freedom. There were so many of us that I got to do my own thing. Case of having to, I suppose. It suited me perfectly.'

'Does sound pretty wonderful.'

Despondency ran through her, exterminating any flirty feelings she'd been foolish enough to foster a few minutes before. Everyone craved freedom. Supposing she *had* wanted it to be a date tonight. Freedom was the reason it would never amount to anything more than Number 101 on her list of failed relationships.

Eight months ago Jamie had announced he was going out for a few beers and a curry for his mate's birthday. She'd felt instantly sick. His mate was a particularly rowdy partygoer prone to a spot of philandering. The more Charlotte fell in love with Jamie, the more she felt threatened by evenings out like this. She didn't want to be like that, but didn't know what to do about it, either. So Charlotte had thought fast and told him they'd already agreed to dinner at Jas's that night. In the name of friendship, Jas had cooked a four-course meal for six as if she'd been planning it for weeks, carrying it off with great aplomb, right down to making up a birthday for Adrian to give the evening more authenticity. Adrian the Married had gone along with it – he didn't really have a case against lying, did he? She even made him a birthday cake. Sarah and Grant made up the six, and no one was any the wiser. Such elaborate measures, all to ensure Jamie didn't go out with his mate for a pint. It was unsustainable, it ignored the foundation that all relationships should be built upon – trust, and it was deceitful. Not the worst kind of deceit, the shagging your best friend's husband kind, but duplicity all the same. Charlotte knew this behaviour was inexcusable, but she also knew how the behaviour took hold – a compulsion so strong it felt impossible to restrain.

'Don't suppose you had your own bedroom, though, did you?' Charlotte asked Rich.

'Well, there's the thing, we lived in a crumbling old mansion, with fourteen bedrooms.'

'Oh wow! How did your mum cope? All those children, all those heirlooms to polish?'

'My mum's a bit of a hippy, so she was never worried about that stuff. We had a Chippendale table for our arts and crafts station. She was more concerned with spreading love and joy to her babies. We each had special time with her, to make up for there being so many of us. My day was Friday. She'd take me out of school every other week. We'd fly a kite, go to the woods, swim in the lake, that kind of stuff, just me and her.' He was smiling as he recounted stories from his childhood at the Manor, his toffee-coloured eyes dancing with merriment, turning deep cinnamon in the low light.

Charlotte's own childhood couldn't have been more different. Her mum only had her and her brother but still found it hard to make time for them. It wasn't her fault – it was down to a shortage of money and having to look after Dad. Her mother had spent most of Charlotte's childhood sitting at an industrial-sized sewing machine, filling the house with a dull rattle, as she churned out leather shoes and handbags. Swimming in lakes with her mum was the stuff Charlotte's dreams were made of.

'OK, so now that you've made me sick with envy, what about girlfriends?' She was eager to crack Rich the Enigma. 'Why are you here on your own? Patient girlfriend tucked away at home while you holiday in the Caribbean on a business pretext? Girlfriend in every port? Wife in every port, maybe?' She raised her eyebrows. 'Newly single and misogynistic after particularly acrimonious break-up? Gay? Swinger? Do you need more options?'

He laughed. 'Sorry to disappoint, but boringly single, actually.'

Charlotte felt a butterfly in her stomach. Just the one, but an energetic little blighter. 'How come? If you're single, there's no hope for the rest of us.'

He let his fork wander around his plate, reorganising what was left. Then he said it. It burst out like a greyhound from a trap.

'She's dead. My girlfriend died.'

Charlotte was dumbstruck for a few moments. She shook her head slowly and reached for his hand. 'Oh Rich, I'm so sorry.' She wanted to say more, but sensed that it wasn't up for discussion. Clearly, it had been hard for him to tell her that much. It was best to say nothing.

Rich broke the silence first. It was his call. Only he could determine how much quiet was needed.

And now they were dancing, his suggestion.

They shared the same dance rhythm, which was a relief. She was enjoying how good he was at twizzling her round, when she spotted The Lovely Rachel again. This time she could see who she was with. It took a moment for it to register. Charlotte looked away to make sense of what she'd seen. She stopped dancing and pulled free of Rich.

'You OK?' Rich followed her gaze.

She *was* right. It was Jamie. The Lovely Rachel was with Jamie. Rachel was whispering conspiratorially into his ear and he was smiling lasciviously. It was screamingly obvious they'd fucked. Charlotte elbowed her way off the dance floor and made a beeline for them. Such public humiliation. How dare he come on holiday with her and shag another woman? A smouldering, sex-mad, Lara Croft type woman to boot.

'*The bastard!*' she muttered to no one in particular.

'Charlotte! Come back!'

'*No, I need to do this.*'

She forged through the crowd, stepping on toes, barging past people, sheer determination set hard upon her face. *He wouldn't get away with this.*

Rich caught up with her and grabbed her arm. 'Come on, Charlotte. We can talk about it.'

'Talk about what? Let go of me!'

'Jamie isn't doing anything wrong, Charlotte.'

'I know, I'm ... I'm just going to say hello.' She shook herself free.

He grabbed her again but more forcefully this time.

'Take a look at yourself, Charlotte.' He dragged her over to one of the shacks and pointed to the window. 'Look!'

She stared at her reflection in the plastic windowpane. Her face was twisted, distorted, her eyes narrow and dangerous. Anger and defiance were embedded into her skin.

'Does that look like the face of someone who's popping over to say hello?' His grip had softened but his hold remained firm. *'Charlotte, look at me.'*

She looked at his face begrudgingly, such tenderness in those molten brown eyes.

'Let it pass. Breathe deeply and let the feeling wash over you. It will pass, I promise, Charlie.'

He'd never called her Charlie before.

She didn't want it to pass. She needed to know if it was true. She needed to know if he'd slept with her. If he hadn't, she still had time to stop him.

She yanked her arms from Rich's grip and made a dash for it. Then she tripped and was catapulted forwards, arms flailing. The world around her slowed and she vaguely heard a gasp as she nosedived onto the tarmac floor.

Chapter Thirty-Two

Charlotte

Charlotte stomped along the beach towards her haven. Bannister was at Oistins so she'd have it all to herself. She jumped onto the warm wooden boards and sat cross-legged, looking out to sea. She didn't know whether to be cross with Rich or love him for what he did. Although hitting the deck was a haze now, she couldn't remember the last time she'd felt so humiliated. Wait. Yes she could, just a few days ago, in a cave … with Rich.

He had a knack of being around at all the wrong times. He also had a knack of saying all the right things or, better still, knowing when to say nothing at all. The hug he'd given her after picking her up off the floor hadn't needed words. She'd got up fighting. Still determined to get where she was going. But he'd grabbed her and held her tenderly.

Her anger had dissolved. Instantly. It was a new experience and she could still remember how safe she'd felt as he cradled her in his arms, like a parent would nurture a child. But he wasn't just safe in a safe way, if that made sense. He was an edgy safe. An unknown quantity.

'You all right?'

'Bannister! You have got to stop doing that to me.' She peered through the darkness to see his lithe frame swaggering towards her.

He pulled off his trainers and sat next to her, peeling off his socks and rolling his trousers up to his knees, to dangle his feet over the edge of the jetty. He leaned back on outstretched arms, closed his eyes and took a long, controlled breath.

'Bannister, are you OK?'

'It's not me we should be worryin' 'bout now, pretty laydee, is it?'

Charlotte hung her head and pulled at the splinters again. It was times like this that she needed a supply of beer mats.

'I'm fine.'

'I used to be like you, yuh know, Charlie. Worried 'bout wat people think. Tryin' to control everytin'. But den I learned dat wasn't da way to happiness.'

Bannister was good. It was like he had some ridiculous sixth sense that tapped into how she was feeling.

'Did you see what happened?' she asked.

'I saw Jamie. I saw you fall. I put two and two together.'

'He was with Rachel. And it's obvious they're having sex. They were together today at some house, I saw them. He's lying to me, Bannister. So, I, well, I went to go and talk to him. I didn't know what else to do.'

'What would de man on de Clapham omnibus have done?'

'What? Oh, the reasonable man! How do you know about the reasonable man? You're so full of surprises, Bannister.' In law, the man on the Clapham omnibus was a hypothetical 'reasonable person'. He represented your average Joe and what he would do in any given situation helped the courts decide if someone's actions were reasonable.

'I'm not full of surprises, Charlie. I'm jus' not what you've judged me to be. Dat's de problem wid doin' stuff to please others. Nuttin' is wad it seems. All you can ever be sure of is pleasin' yerself.' He looked at her expectantly. 'So? What would de reasonable man do?'

'He'd very reasonably get back on the first bloody omnibus he could find and get the hell out of there.'

Bannister took his feet out of the water and lounged back on the still-warm wood, legs outstretched, to dry off.

'You know what yuh gotta do, Charlie? You gotta make life easy for yerself. There are many things we can't control in life. Can't do anything about. So you must accept it as if you'd chosen it.'

It was a familiar scene now. Bannister dispensed an invaluable nugget of wisdom and Charlotte curled up with her head on his lap and invariably had a gentle cry, all very innocent.

'I act like a spoiled child sometimes, but you're still so nice to me. Why?' she asked, as she lay across his legs.

He stroked her hair, picking up some strands, letting them fall gently from his fingers.

'"Love me when I least deserve it, cos dat is when I need it most" – dat is why, Charlie.'

•••••••••

Charlotte stood at the door of Jamie's bungalow and rubbed her eyes. Falling asleep on Bannister's lap hadn't been the plan and she had that groggy feeling you get when you're dragged out of a deep slumber – that and the itches from what felt like a thousand mosquito bites. Jamie was taking ages to answer the door, which she took as a bad sign. Probably shoving Rachel under the bed right now.

The strange truth was that half of her wanted Rachel to be there and the other half didn't. She'd felt like that before. Phone-bill checking was a good example – a practice she'd followed religiously when she lived with Pete. He had itemised bills, at her request. She scrutinised each number, ticking it off as she recognised it (she had a list of all of his phone numbers) and circling any queries. She'd ring the query numbers, and hang up when they answered, just to see if it was a woman on the other end of the line.

The feeling she had when she was checking those phone bills was similar to the one she had now. There was always some strange, twisted hankering to find the number of a mistress and catch him out, something that would prove she was right, that everyone did cheat on her, that she really wasn't worthy of loyal love. At the same time, she was petrified she might find something that would split them up, and always sighed a breath of relief when the checking was over for another month. Thinking back, she realised Pete must have loved her a lot to put up with that behaviour for as long as he did.

Charlotte heard a key turn and Jamie finally opened the door, wearing nothing but his white boxers, which set off the deepening brown of his tanned torso even more than usual.

'Charlotte. Do you know what time it is?' He scratched his tufty bed hair as she barged past him.

She winced at the neat alcohol fumes dominating the room, flicking her eyes around deftly, sucking in the scene, scouring for signs.

'There's no one here, Charlie.'

Her eyes shifted to the bathroom door.

'Nope, no one in the bathroom. I told you, there's nobody here. Now, what can I do for you? It's half one and I'm knackered.' He closed the door behind him and dragged a T-shirt over his head.

Gutted. She'd already earmarked that as evidence and was going to smell it for traces of perfume when Jamie went to the loo or something.

She knew it was no longer any business of hers whether he was seeing someone or not. He wasn't her boyfriend anymore and could do what he liked. But she needed to know.

She came clean – no point talking in riddles. She told him what Rachel had said about how good her new boyfriend was in bed, although she regretted that bit as soon as it had left her mouth. The last thing she wanted was to boost his greedy little ego, if indeed it was him. And let's face it, it was looking likely. Charlotte told him how she'd seen him with Rachel at the fish fry and how Rich had stopped her from coming over.

'Well, you know he does the same thing as Toby, don't you?' Jamie put the kettle on.

Charlotte took the opportunity of Jamie's back being turned to have another quick squint around the room. 'What do you mean?' She noticed the sofa had been pushed back against the window. To make room for shagging on the floor, maybe?

'Rich, or whatever his name is, he's a clinical psychologist. Rachel told me. Everyone knows him around here. Apparently, he comes every year.'

'I know that,' Charlotte snapped, no intention of letting on that was the first she'd heard about him being a psychologist.

'I was just surprised to hear you're hanging out with a "shrink", as you put it.' She peeled back a loose bit of wicker on the sofa. Why hadn't Rich told her?

Jamie made her a strong tea with a heavy-handed sugar, just how she liked it, and Charlotte felt instantly melancholy.

'I haven't slept with her, Charlie,' he said before she got a chance to ask. 'She's smitten with me, I think. That's probably why she told you what she did.'

Charlotte eyed him suspiciously. She wanted to believe him but it didn't sit right. He and Rachel hadn't actually been holding hands or kissing at the fish fry, though. Maybe he was telling the truth.

'Why would she lie to me? She doesn't even know who I am,' she persisted.

'Perhaps she wasn't. Maybe she has got a new boyfriend who's good at shagging.' He looked away for a moment. 'But I can tell you, it's not me. She does know who you are, though. I pointed you out the other day. You were with Rich. I don't think you saw us. To be honest, Charlie, she's been a good listener. This isn't easy for me either, you know.' He looked down at the floor. 'You've been spending a lot of time with Rich, I've noticed. Are you and him … you know?' He kept his eyes downwards.

'No, not at all. He's been really kind to me, that's all. He's not my type, in case you were wondering.'

'I was surprised, actually.' Jamie sat next to Charlotte. 'Surprised at how I felt when I saw you two together. I'm usually good at cutting off when something has come to an end, but I won't deny it – it hurt, seeing you with Rich.'

One of the Maoris who lived in Charlotte's stomach stretched awake and did a ginormous backwards flip.

'That's how I felt when I saw you with Rachel. That's why I came here tonight. I'm sorry.' She hung her head.

'Don't be.' Jamie put his hand under her chin and raised it. 'I'm glad.'

He kissed her tenderly. A slow kiss, as soft and plump as duck-down pillows. Charlotte closed her eyes and luxuriated in the moment, aching to melt into the contours of his body but holding back. Tonight was best left as a kiss.

Chapter Thirty-Three

Sarah

I watched for bobbing seal noses, but there were none. I had yet to see one, even though Marion swore there were loads around. A wave hit a rock in front of me and a fountain of spray shot heavenwards. I enjoyed the mew of a buzzard circling overhead, the winter sun warming my bones, gently nudging awake the serotonin in my brain. I knew my upbeat mood wasn't solely attributable to my beautiful surrounds. Some of it, most at a guess, definitely had something to do with my forthcoming tryst with TIM.

I'd been up most of the night baking sticky toffee pudding biscuits for Jinslet and had even invented a sticky toffee pudding cupcake – all while I'd had my meeting with TIM in the forefront of my mind. What will I wear? How will I hide my stretch marks? What will we say? Can I remember how to kiss? How will we fuck? Can I remember how to fuck? Have we got anything in common anymore? Our lives are so different now.

I thought back to the part of my life with TIM in it – I was young, vibrant and intoxicating. It was all about success. When I thought back to those days, the backdrop to my thoughts was a spring scene, lambs gambolling, cherry blossom and a field full of daffodils. How very different from now, where all I seem to do is dally daily with the deep blacks and navies of failure.

'*Have you seen any?*' came the familiar Marion Glasgow holler from the steps.

'No, I think you're having me on. You keep telling me there are seals so I bring you biscuits and cakes.'

I went and handed her the basket of sticky toffee cupcakes I'd made for her last night and she surprised me with a kiss on the cheek.

'Oh, how very civilised! How very London, *daaarling*!' I said with the longest vowels I could muster.

Marion laughed, thin wisps of grey hair that had escaped the clutches of her bun alive with movement from the wind, flicking at her lined face.

'Well, I's wouldn't want you to think I's weren't being proper now, wunce I?' she replied in a perfect Cornish accent. Then in distinctive Marion, quick and to-the-point clipped tones, she said, 'I've got something to put to you. Fancy a cuppa?'

'Oh Marion, I can't. I've got to deliver the biscuits to Jinslet and then I've got a meeting with the school. Maybe tomorrow?'

Marion's face fell. She scuffed one of her boots backwards and forwards over a big pebble.

'OK, tomorrow's fine.'

I'd never seen Marion disappointed before. She usually preferred to want for nothing, leaving no room for disappointment.

'Well, I can't come to the house, but I can spare you a minute now?'

I poured us a coffee from my new Thermos, and Marion unwrapped the cakes, releasing the syrupy sweet aroma of toffee.

'*Mmm*, Sarah, these are even better than the biscuits, and I didn't think that was possible.'

'Thank you, it's lovely to hear that. In our house they just get wolfed up.'

'Have you thought of setting up a business?'

'No, I hadn't, but the sticky toffee things do seem to be generating a bit of cash lately.' I helped myself to a cake, even though I'd promised myself I wouldn't – it was my third today. 'Where would I find the time, with the boys, and with Grant being away all week?'

'Well, I think it's a good idea.' Marion sucked each finger clean, rubbing her hands on her jeans. She took a slurp of coffee. 'Right, see what you think of this.'

I was intrigued. Marion seemed excited.

'How about you have your christening at the mill?'

'At Duckpool Mill? At your house?'

'Yes, yes, but—'

'Marion! Oh my God, you're amazing!'

I lunged at her, knocking my coffee flying down the goddamn slopey bit of slate that had caused all the trouble before and hugged her hard. I could feel that hot, prickly feeling I get behind my nose when I'm about to cry. It must have taken a lot for Marion to think about having people in her house, and Finn and Rudy, especially as Rudy was the same age as Danny when he died.

'*Sarah!*' Marion said sharply, pulling herself out of my hug and cutting through my elation. 'I haven't finished. There's a catch.'

'Oh, sorry.'

'In return, I want you to do something for me.' She looked out to sea. 'I'm having a memorial service, a private one ... just me and Danny. I want to read him a poem.'

I looked at my hands, embarrassed at my exhilaration a few moments ago, unable to comprehend this poor woman's loss.

'And I want you to write it.' She looked up at me, her deep-brown eyes diluted with the suggestion of tears. 'Will you do it?'

'Marion, I—'

'I'll help you, obviously. You know, tell you how I'm feeling and about Danny and what he was like. It's just I'm no good at writing and I want it to be right. That poem you've written for your boys, it's so ... honest, and that's what I want my poem to be. But I know you're really busy and—'

'It would be a privilege.' I took her hand and held it tight. 'Of course I'll do it, and you don't need to offer your house for the christening. I don't want anything in return.'

'No, I want you to have your christening here. I've thought about it a lot and I'd like it. I'm going to have the ceremony with Danny first, then I've resolved to carry on my life as normal as it can be. Celebrating the lives of your children in my house is a wonderful way to start that.'

·········

The meeting with Mrs Davies didn't go well. Big Lass From The North's son had complained that Rudy had been bullying him at break. I couldn't see it. I'd asked Rudy and he'd said it wasn't true. He was surprised I'd asked, saying he never really spoke to him. He wasn't even in his class. I'd pushed it, just to make sure he was telling the truth, and he'd got really upset. "No, Mummy, I'm not lying, please believe me, Mummy," he'd begged dolefully. I believed him. Rudy wasn't the bullying kind – naughty, yes, a bully, no. He didn't have the confidence.

Mrs Davies rubbed her corrugated brow and told me the boy was insistent. I asked if anyone had witnessed this supposed bullying and she said no.

Straight off the back of that, as if fuelled by the need to score a point, she mentioned the marks on Rudy's arms. Half of me was pleased the school was proficient enough to have noticed, reassuring me it was a safe place in which to entrust my children. The other half was filled with humiliation and reignited disgrace for myself.

'Rudy got himself into a dangerous situation and I had to stop him.'

Mrs Davies replied with contempt. 'You must have held his arms *very* hard to have produced marks like that.'

It was all downhill from there, really. She said she'd be punishing Rudy for bullying the next time the boy complained. I told her she'd do well not to, unless she had proof. Otherwise the school would be acting akin to some kind of vigilante group, upholding the premise that its children were guilty until proven innocent, which I explained might not look good in the local rag.

She tutted and shook her head violently, causing her brow to ripple, and said, 'I've taught many children in my day and I know when I see bad behaviour resulting from a lack of discipline at home.'

I looked directly into her eyes, trying not to be distracted by the ridge and furrow across her brow, which got more pronounced every time I saw her. 'Well, until you can prove such, forgive me if I don't take your subjective view as conclusive.'

I picked Finn up from preschool and we waited in the car for Rudy, instead of standing at the school gates, unable to bring myself to be near Big Lass From The North in case I thumped her and her lying little toe-rag of a son. The unmistakeable beep-beep of my phone signalled a text – nectar for my ears. It was from Charlie:

```
I love your emails. You always make me laugh and
cry. I had a freak-out at a fish fry. Rushing now,
so details later. Just wanted to say this, though:
'Love me when I least deserve it, cos that is when
I need it most.' When Rudy's being vile, just hug
him, no matter what he's saying or doing. It works,
honey. I wouldn't have believed it myself until the
other day, but it does, I promise. Millions of hugs,
Charlie xxoooxx
```

Not for the first time that day, I felt the onset of tears. Charlie was so good at understanding, and so honest, too.

Rudy came out and I beeped the horn so he'd see me. I got out to meet him.

'Mummy, Mummy, can I take Sniffy home one day, please?' He was hopping from foot to foot with excitement.

'Who?'

'Sniffy. The school hamster.'

'*Umm*, we'll see.'

I'd never been one for pets, especially not rodent ones.

'They let you take him home. Look! There he is.' Rudy pointed down the road to where a small child was grappling with a big cage. 'Ben's taking him home tonight. Come and see, Mummy.' Rudy raced off in hot pursuit of Sniffy.

'Rudy, wait!'

Ben carried Sniffy across the road with the help of his mum. Rudy looked set to follow.

'*Rudy! Do not cross that road. Wait!*' I yelled at the top of my voice. I told Finn to stay in his seat, locked the car and chased after Rudy. 'Stop right this minute, young man!'

He hesitated.

'*Rudy!*' I shrieked. '*Stop!*'

Too late. He ran out from behind a parked car ...

The sound of screeching brakes resonated through the air, ricocheting off nearby cars and houses.

'*Nooo!*' I yelled and ran towards the noise.

The smell of burning rubber wafted up in a cloud of dust, then silence. It was eerily quiet apart from the scrabble of hamster feet on the bottom of a cage as Sniffy dived for cover. That and the systematic pounding of blood thumping fast and loud in my ears, raw terror banging hard against my skull.

I couldn't see what had happened – the car was in my way. I raced around it and found Rudy standing next to Ben and Sniffy, oblivious to what was going on. A relieved Jinslet sat at the wheel of her car, parked diagonally across the road. I ran to Rudy and pulled him to me, squeezing the life out of his beautiful bones.

'Oh, Rudy!' I breathed deeply and hugged him tight, not wanting to let him go. I took hold of his arms and held him out in front of me.

'Don't you ever do that to me again, Rudy. Why don't you ever listen to me?' I asked him softly.

'I don't know, Mummy.'

I hugged him to me again. 'I can't have you in that amount of danger, Rudy. You're too precious.' I closed my eyes tight and scrunched away the encroaching tears. 'You're going straight to your room when we get home and I'm going to take a toy, too. You've got to learn, Rudy, for your safety, if nothing else.'

'*No!*' he screamed and cried all the way back to the car.

'Everything all right?'

Ole Sunken Eyes pecked around nosily, desperate to be thrown a scrap of information.

'Everything's fine,' I replied firmly as Rudy and I marched on by.

'*I saw what happened!*' Big Lass From The North shouted over to her. '*Very dangerous ... could have been nasty!*'

'Wasn't, though, was it?' Bohemian Babe chipped in on a positive note, but piped down when Big Lass From The North eyeballed her.

Mrs Davies strummed her brow like a guitar as she took in the scene, throwing me a cautionary look. A loud car alarm filled the air. Finn had got out of his chair and was in the driving seat. He had put his hand on the horn and kept it there, laughing at us through the window as we approached.

'No discipline at all!' Big Lass From The North snapped to no one in particular as she shook her head and corralled her son into their huge four-wheel-drive with blacked-out windows, which looked more like a luxury tank.

'You OK?'

It was Jinslet.

I nodded, unable to speak.

She rubbed my shoulder tenderly. 'That happened to me once, it's frightening.'

I got Rudy into the car, still protesting about the toy I was going to take, begging me to change my mind. I fastened Finn back into his seat with shaking arms and closed the car door. I took a deep breath and turned to Jinslet.

'I'm fine,' I lied. 'But what about you? I'm so sorry, Lola.'

'Sweetness' – she held her hand up to silence me – 'stop right there. I'm splendid, it's you we need to worry about.'

I tried to speak. I moved my lips to form the words but a torrent of sobs tumbled out.

'I can't control him, Lola!' I blubbered. 'He just won't listen.'

Jinslet hugged me and turned us both round so I was facing away from the gates and any lingering souls waiting for a story.

I pulled myself together, embarrassed by my public meltdown.

'Thanks, Lola. I needed that hug.'

'Anytime, sweetness.' She winked a perfect almond-shaped eye at me. 'Do you fancy meeting up for a cuppa? Mums moaning together and all that?'

'That's really kind, thank you.' I put a hand through my hair. 'Is it OK if I see how I feel in the morning?'

'Of course it is.' She smiled. 'Oh, and before I forget, your biscuits and cakes blew everyone away. A friend of mine runs a couple of coffee shops and wants to buy some. I used to be in the catering business, before I became the legendary marketing guru I am today. So I know loads of people with cafés and restaurants.' She winked at me again.

Jinslet's wink was balm for my heart, warm and soothing, like a drop of unexpected honey.

I got into the car feeling marginally better. Life was looking up. I was going to be busy, what with poems to write and cakes to bake. I even appeared to be making a couple of friends. Genuine friends, too, it seemed. I looked in my rear-view mirror. But life would never be OK as long as Rudy wasn't happy, and as long as I couldn't control my children.

He'd stopped crying and was sitting forlornly in his car seat. I needed to help him badly. I resolved to email TIM tonight and cancel. Plotting illicit liaisons wasn't helping anyone and would only end in tears. Simply texting Charlie to tell her had made me feel bad about myself. There was no justification to be found.

We drew up at the house.

'Go straight to your room, Rudy, please,' I told him sternly.

He flew up the stairs and slammed his door, barricading himself in. I could hear various pieces of furniture being manoeuvred across the floor.

I hurried upstairs.

'Rudy.' I pushed his door, which opened a bit before jamming against his bedside cabinet. 'Rudy, move this now and let me in.'

'*No!*' He banged the door closed again.

'Rudy.' I opened it once more, so I could talk through the two-inch gap. 'What you did was incredibly dangerous. I worry about your safety, that's all. Now let me in.'

'*No!*' he said again and pushed the door against my hand with all his might.

I pushed back and opened it enough to wiggle the cabinet out of the way and let myself in. I walked over to his drawers and lifted down his Cyberman.

'I'm going to take this for what you did but, if you can show me you can be good, you can have it back tomorrow.'

'*No!*' He jumped up at me, trying to snare his Cyberman out of my possession, hitting me, banging his fists against my stomach. '*I hate you!*' he yelled. '*I hate you, I hate you, I hate you!*'

I winced, trying to ignore the anger welling up inside me.

I attempted to leave his room, but he grabbed hold of my leg and attached his full body weight to it, stopping me from moving. He continued to shout and then the crying started. He hit me again, a huge great wallop into my stomach. Anger surged through me now. How dare he hit me? I yanked my leg from his grip.

I sat on the bottom stair, listening to his sobs, hearing his sadness. It was about more than just taking his toys away, I knew it was, but I didn't know what. I thought of Charlie's text: *'Love me when I least deserve it, because that is when I need it most.'* I went back up to his room, where he sat, wracked with tears, on the floor next to his space rocket. I crouched down beside him and opened my arms. He looked worried at first, not recognising my behaviour from any previous situations of this nature.

'Can I have a hug?' I asked.

He was confused, desperate to say yes but unable to, as if a loss of pride was involved. I took the decision away from him and swept him into my arms. I sat with him on the floor, rocking him back and forth..

'I love you, my baby,' I whispered into his sandy locks. 'I love you so much.' I stroked his face. 'I love you no matter what, and I'm going to make everything OK.'

I felt him melt into my arms as I stroked his hair gently. He quietened. His relentless sobbing abated. He curled into me and hugged me tight, and five minutes later he was asleep.

Chapter Thirty-Four

Charlotte

After a fitful night's sleep, Charlotte opened her eyes, one at a time, and looked first at the empty expanse of bed next to her and then over at the doormat. Some birthday, she thought. No man in her bed, no cards on the mat. But something felt good. Ah yes, Jamie had kissed her. Not only that, but if she wasn't mistaken, it had been a tender kiss, stuffed full of love. It hadn't led to anything – it hadn't needed to – the kiss alone had said it all.

The kiss had been a day ago now, but it wasn't any less significant. Jamie had suggested they didn't see each other yesterday, said he had some things to do. Charlotte hadn't complained because she'd hoped he was taking the day to plan her birthday, especially as he knew how much she loved birthdays. They were meeting at the jetty this morning, for another Love Lesson, so she'd find out then.

Charlie's phone vibrated on the bedside table. She flipped it open expectantly. Maybe it was Jamie texting her happy birthday before he saw her, now that would be romantic. No, never mind, it was from Mum:

`Happy birthday darling. Heres hopping you have a lovelly day. Bet its gorgous out their. Love u loades and loades mum xx ps definatly cant come over for speech my darling sorry but Rog cant get out of bowlling tornament. Will come over soon I promiss. Xx`

Charlie snapped shut her phone, feeling her bright, shiny birthday balloon deflate like one of her soufflés. Her mum hadn't even waited until it wasn't her birthday to tell her the bad news. She'd seen it as a show of love that her mum had agreed to come over for her speech. Not surprising she'd pulled out, then.

She hit the button on the shower and closed her eyes to try and shut out the day.

Having put the final touches to her birthday bikini outfit with a necklace she'd strung together from shells collected over the last few days, she had an hour before she was due to meet Jamie – just enough time to see if she had any birthday emails.

Date: Saturday, 24 Feb 09:14
Subject: Happy Birthday

Happy birthday to you, happy birthday to you. Hip, hip, hooray! For she's a jolly good fellow ... Think you get the idea. You do, however, need to picture the scene – I'm singing these while wearing my best Cath Kidston pyjamas, which have a large orange juice stain down the front of the left leg. I have greasy hair with a full head of roots and eyebrows akin to Poirot's moustache, which still have mashed banana in them from Finn helping me to make the porridge this morning. Aaah, motherhood – it's a glamorous affair.

The boys have made you cards and we've got you a present. Don't get too excited – remember it's devoid of shops down this way. Although I promise it's not clotted cream.

I have good news. Marion's letting me have the christening at Duckpool Mill! I'm so excited. You're going to love it there. Can't wait. Can I take it you'll be bringing Jamie again then? After the kiss and everything?

Had coffee with Jinslet yesterday in Big Bad Bude. She's great, Charlie, and she doesn't have athlete's foot, after all. She works in town three days a week so I should introduce you. I think you two would get on.

She stays with a friend in Balham, in a flat over her restaurant, The Mockingbird or something. Apparently, they might want some of my sticky toffee puddings. Jinslet's already got me a gig this weekend, baking for her café-owning friend. The woman's a marvel. Not all superheroes wear capes, some wear flip-flops. Get me, eh? Baking for the commercial market. Who'd have thought ... I've turned into Fanny bloody Cradock.

Of course Grant won't like it, cos he'll have to look after the boys all weekend while I bake. Grant and I not getting on any better. Every time he phones, we row. Every time he comes home, we row. He avoids my calls now, and I've even thought about leaving him ... seriously. We're falling apart. The move to Cornwall hasn't been a success.

You'll be glad to hear I'm going to cancel TIM today, though. Meant to last night but too tired.

Anyway, I'd better be off and organise an activity for my two mountaineering boys, who are currently scaling Mount Sofa. Do you know how much that sofa cost? Hugging Rudy while he was being naughty worked by the way. You're the best.

Have a fantastic day. No worrying about anything. What are you up to? Has Jamie got plans for you? I bet he has – ooo, err, missus. Anyway, my lovely, have a rum punch for me.

Oh, and I think this is going to be your year. I have a feeling.

S xxx

·····•·•····

Date: Saturday, 24 Feb 08:36
Subject: Appointment

Hi, babes,

I know you're on holiday and everything, so you don't really want to read doom and gloom, but thought I'd better keep you updated. Going to clinic on Tuesday for termination. Think it's the best thing all round.

Thanks for text the other night. Was shocked you and Jamie might be getting it on again, but glad, if only because it makes you happy.

Have fun, babes.

J xxx

·········

Date: Saturday, 24 Feb 09:39
Subject: *Feliz cumpleaños!*

HAPPY BIRTHDAY!

Shit, fuck, sorry! Don't read my other email if you haven't already. So sorry, babes, had a momentary lapse and forgot it was your birthday for a miniscule second there. Wouldn't have sent other email if had remembered.

Happy birthday, baby. Hope you have a great one. Big kiss from me.

All my love, Jas x

Charlotte felt deflated for the second time that day. First her mum's news and now Jasmine's, and Sarah and Grant ... she hated it when people were unhappy. She composed a new email and tried to think of some inspirational words to cheer Sarah up.

Date: Saturday, 24 Feb 10:10
Subject: The Greatest Cook In The Land

Just a quickie because it's my birthday and I'm well aware I should be whooping it up somewhere – hooray! Thanks for lovely birthday message, sweetie. Look forward to present and cards and, for future reference, I love clotted cream.

Thrilled the hug worked for Rudy. Those boys are the best thing that's ever happened to you, honey. You're so incredibly blessed and I want you to think about that when you're rowing with Grant. I know things aren't good right now, but it will get better. Things change, they always do, just like Marion said.

So even though you're thinking about it, promise me you won't leave him. Not yet, anyway. At least wait until I get home so we can talk about it.

Amazing news about the cakes. At this rate you'll be Businesswoman Of The Year again before you know it. The Mockingbird rings a bell. I've got a feeling Jas goes there a lot. Not sure I'd fancy staying away three nights every week at a restaurant in Balham when I had a little kiddie at home in Cornwall. Your poor friend.

Right, then, off for some birthday fun. Can't wait to see what Jamie has got planned for me. It would be nice if it was today that we finally got back together. My kind of birthday present.

Charlie xxooxx

PS: Mum not coming to my talk.

PPS: So glad you're cancelling TIM. Make sure you definitely do, because I don't want you to turn into a philanderer. You're too nice for that.

She pressed Send, then opened the email in her sent box to reread it, as always. It read differently somehow when it was in the sent box.

Shit!

She looked at the address at the top of the email. She'd sent it to Jas instead of Sarah. She instantly deleted Jas's address as if by being fast she could change what had happened and tapped in Sarah's address, double-checking it this time, and pressed Send again, then quickly composed an email to Jas:

Date: Saturday, 24 Feb 10:38
Subject: Sorry

Jas, honey,

Now it's my turn for sorry. Sent you an email meant for Sarah by mistake. And it's got stuff in about the boys you probably don't want to hear right now. I'm so sorry, Jas. So typical it should happen today of all days, with your decision and everything. It was a genuine mistake. I really am sorry.

Wasn't surprised to hear you'd decided to have a termination. I don't think anyone can advise you. Only you know what's right. All I can say is that I'll support you 100 per cent in whatever you do. I'm here for you, honey. Have you got anyone going with you on Tuesday? If not, you could reschedule for when I'm back. I'd be happy to go with you. It won't be easy, no matter how sure you think you are, but I'm here to help.

Much love,

C xxooxx

Not the best start to a birthday. She made her way into reception and glanced at the clock. Her birthday was about to get a whole lot better. Jamie had said to be there about eleven, so she'd be bang on time if she set off now.

'Beautiful morning!' she called to the lady from the gift shop as she breezed past.

'Happy birthday, Charlie!' came a Caribbean voice she recognised.

'Bannister. How do you know it's my birthday?' She gave him a kiss on the cheek.

'I saw Rich dis mornin'. He's plannin' a big surprise.'

'How does Rich know?'

'Don't know. Thought yuh must be after tellin' him.'

He handed her a small package wrapped scruffily in tissue paper and secured with a long piece of sticky tape wound round and round.

'You got me a present? Oh, Bannister, that's so gorgeous of you!'

'Don't tink nuttin' of it. Just a little sometin' I thought might help. Anyway, I won't be keepin' yuh, Charlie. Rich is waitin'. Hope to see yuh later, pretty laydee. Have fun and don't ignore wat's right in front of yer nose.'

She smiled. She was used to Bannister's pearls of wisdom, but he'd said 'Rich is waiting'. He must have meant Jamie.

Chapter Thirty-Five

Charlotte

Charlotte took her sequined flip-flops off and padded lightly over the already hot sand to the jetty, a slave to the smile plastered indelibly across her face and widening by the minute. She got within sight of the wooden platform she knew and loved so well and could see a figure dangling his feet off the end. She could vaguely make out bottles and glasses and other things glinting in the sun. Her heart did a quick spin and sat dizzily thumping in her ribcage. He really had gone to town.

As she neared the jetty, she noticed that the man dipping his toes in the water wasn't Jamie at all. He was tall and lithe, with a mop of blonde hair, and was stretched out lazily on the sun-drenched wood. It was Rich.

Her dizzy heart stopped spinning. This was going to be awkward. He obviously didn't realise she was here to meet Jamie. But how had he known she'd be here at all? Surely he wouldn't go to all this effort without inviting her? Perhaps the picnic he was guarding languorously was for someone else entirely? That would be annoying, because it was on her jetty.

Reaching the jetty, she tentatively made her way towards Rich, feeling the familiar roughness of the warm wood under her toes.

He got up to greet her. 'Happy Birthday, Charlie,' he said and gave her a kiss on the cheek.

'Thank you,' she replied, not sure what to say or do next.

'I know what you're thinking, but don't worry. I've got a note from Jamie.' He handed her a small envelope. 'He asked me to give it to you if I saw you. He told me he was supposed to meet you at eleven – that's how come I'm here. He also told me it was your birthday.'

Her dizzy heart was now as heavy as a brick. How could Jamie do this to her? She smiled up at Rich, unable to vocalise her thanks or indeed anything. She looked at the brown envelope in her hands and slit it open with her finger.

Charlie,

I'm so sorry. I forgot I'd promised Rachel I'd take her up the island and you know how I don't like to break a promise.

Have a great birthday and I'll see you later.

Love, Jamie xx

Torn between putting a face on things for Rich's benefit, wallowing in her true feelings, and laughing out loud at Jamie's inadvertent euphemism, Charlie stood silent and motionless, unable to put any of them into action.

'Can I give you a hug?' Rich asked calmly.

'You most certainly can.'

She faltered and moved towards him. He hugged her hard and gave her time to cry into his T-shirt. She took a deep breath and did the mental equivalent of dusting herself down and putting her chin in the air. She looked at the multi-coloured picnic rug, choc full of edible delights and two champagne flutes sparkling in the sun.

'You've done all this for my birthday?'

'I love birthdays. I don't like to see them sneak by uncelebrated. That would never do.' He pulled a bottle of champagne from a silver bucket overflowing with ice and popped the cork.

'But you didn't find out till this morning – how have you managed all of this?'

'With a lot of help from the hotel staff, and Bannister.' He handed her a flute of fizz.

She held her face over the glass to feel the cold bubbles jump out onto her nose, as if to surreptitiously soothe her disappointment.

'It's amazing. Nobody's ever done anything like this for me before. Thank you.'

'It's my pleasure. I only hope I'm around to do something even better for your next one.' Not giving her a moment to digest, let alone reply to his comment, he raised his glass. 'Happy birthday, Charlie! Cheers!'

They lay on the rug and picked at the delicious feast. King fish, cou-cou, asparagus, baked plantain wrapped in bacon, and more ... a Bajan banquet laid out in pretty hand-painted plates and bowls.

'Bannister did well. He's fond of you, you know. Oh, I nearly forgot.' Rich fished around in the picnic bag. '*Ta-da!* Cheese on toast for the birthday girl!'

Charlotte laughed. 'I could get used to this. Tell me ... you don't have a compulsion to do the ironing, an obsessive cleaning habit and a degree in foot-tickling, do you, by any chance? Cos if so, I think I'd like to take you home with me.' She laughed and took a bite of cold, but none the worse for it, cheese on toast. 'How do you know Bannister so well then? Is it because you come here every year?'

'No, it's the other way round. I met him in England, at Cambridge. He studied law. He was quite the scholar, actually. He got a double first and stayed on to do a masters in juris ... legal philosophy.'

'Jurisprudence – are you joking? *What?* I feel bad ... I just assumed—'

'Don't worry, Bannister's used to people stereotyping him. He plays on it, if anything.'

'Jurisprudence, that's what I'm giving my talk on, the Law Society one I told you about, when I get back. 380 people and all that jazz. Perhaps he could help me?'

'I'm sure he'd love to. He was passionate about it.'

'So what happened?'

'His mum died suddenly, leaving him and his three younger brothers without a parent, so he flew home to look after them and he's been here ever since. I visited him, fell in love with the place, and haven't stopped coming.'

'That's an amazing story.'

'I feel for Bannister actually. He's been through a lot and he's such a decent bloke. He's got a good heart.'

'Oh, I forgot, he gave me a present.'

Charlotte plucked the parcel from her beach bag and tore through the green tissue paper to find a set of brightly painted Russian dolls. She twisted the head off the first doll, then each in turn, until five little wooden Matryoshka dolls stood in a row along the jetty.

'They're beautiful.'

Rich nodded. 'They are ... they were traditionally given as a gift of friendship and love, you know. And I think Bannister's trying to tell you something ... they're a clever analogy.'

'What do you mean?' Charlotte asked, picking at the coconut bread Rich had laid on for dessert.

'Well, I haven't told you yet, but I'm a—'

'Psychologist, I know. Jamie told me – Rachel told him.'

'I didn't intend to keep it from you. It's just that, well, after that night, when you sat and told me everything, I missed my chance.'

'I know. And then it was too late because I started blabbing about my life. I'm still embarrassed about that, by the way.'

'Don't be.' He took her hand. 'I felt honoured. I just wish I'd told you that night.'

'So, do you think I've got this morbid jealousy thing, then?'

He smiled gently. 'I think Jamie's friend is right, but I also think you're one step ahead of the rest, because you knew there was a problem and you went looking for it. Admitting there's a problem is the first—'

'Step to recovery, I know all that, but what if I feel like I can't recover? What if I can't change?'

Rich picked up the smallest doll in his long fingers. 'You have a bad experience, say, when you're five years old. You deal with it in your five-year-old way and then you carry it around inside you for the rest of your life.' He popped it inside the next doll in the row. 'So even when you're forty-five, you'll be carrying it around. And you'll still be acting according to that five-year-old's experience in the same way you dealt with it then. Of course, we all deal with things differently. That's what shapes us as individuals.' Rich picked up the next doll in the line-up. 'Give me an example from your childhood, a bad experience that's stuck in your mind.'

Charlie gave a Gallic shrug. 'I don't know ...' There were loads of bad memories from her childhood, but she didn't want to get too personal at this stage. 'OK, I've got one. I was about twelve. I was doing PE. There were three classes doing PE together so the teacher went round giving everyone a number from one to three, to split us into groups. I was given the number two. Stormtrooper Sullivan – that's what everyone called him, cos he was ex-army and horrible – told each number group where they should go. We all ran off to our designated spot. He took one look at the group sizes and yelled that someone had got it wrong. He looked around at the huddle of faces and spotted me. "*You!*" He screamed, pointing at me. "*I didn't give you the number two, you're in the wrong group!*" Everyone turned to look at me. I felt like a prefect at a rave. I was quiet at school, academic. Suddenly being the centre of attention, with everyone craning to see who the felon was, was my idea of hell. If you had to bet on anyone getting their number right that day, it would be me. He told me to stand in the middle of the tennis courts. I shuffled over there, burning with embarrassment. "*I want you to shout 'I am stupid!'*" he hollered. I couldn't believe it. I wanted to run but I was too scared. "*Do it!*" he thundered. "I am stupid," I squeaked, desperately trying not to cry. "*I didn't hear you. Shout it louder!*" he yelled. "*I am stupid!*" I said. "*Louder, I still can't hear you!*" he bellowed at the top of his voice. "*I AM STUPID!*" I shouted, as loud as I could manage as ninety faces stood there silently peering at my humiliation. Sullivan put me in group three, like it made all the difference to the obviously unbalanced group sizes, and we did PE.'

'That's horrible, Charlie.'

'It wasn't nice, but the worst bit was when I went home and told my mum. I sobbed the whole story to her as soon as I got there and she didn't stop making tea for one minute. Didn't hug me, didn't kiss me. Barely even looked at me while I was telling her. She kept saying "I must get this stew on, Charlie. You know how your dad likes his tea bang on six." Eventually she did say "That must have been awful, darling" and squeezed my arm on her way past to the sink. I heard her telling Dad about it just after I'd gone to bed, and he said "Oh, right," and that was the end of it. It was never mentioned again.'

Rich shuffled up next to her and put his arms around her. They sat in silence for a moment, Rich's strong arms squeezing her tightly in a healing hug, just like the one she should have had as a child. She embraced his hug, feeling the pain of that day wash away into the Caribbean Sea.

'Memories like that are painful, Charlie, and they live like Russian dolls inside us. You don't even have to remember the experience for it to live inside you.' He looked out to sea, the blue of a robin egg, silent and still. 'I bet you've been cheated on too, haven't you? That's a common one.'

She raised her eyebrows, then nodded quietly, confirming what he already knew. 'I've been cheated on a lot.'

'You'll have loads of experiences like this, including lots you don't even know about. You're living your life now through all of your past experiences, including those bad Russian dolls. But this present from Bannister shows you how you can get better, too. You need to try and replace a few of the old dolls with new ones, with good ones. There's no limit to the amount we can have inside us. You need some good experiences. With a little love and a lot of determination, you can do it.'

Charlotte sat pensively, enjoying the small sapling of hope that was tugging at her brain.

'I know it's a lot to take in.' he said. 'It's hard trying to live with behaviour you're not comfortable with. I know you didn't enjoy being that person at the fish fry the other night, hell-bent on finding out.'

Charlotte looked at him, at odds with the realisation that possibly he really did understand how she felt.

'You might not like the idea, but mindfulness might help. It's a way of increasing your calm and anchoring you in the present. You just pick something you do – anything, like the washing-up or eating a meal – and do it mindfully. Take showering, for instance. You could step into the shower and draw your attention to the task. Listen to the noise of the water, feel the movement of your arm while you wash, the warmth of the water on your body, smell the shower gel, that sort of thing. Focus on being in the moment. And if a thought pops into your head, don't throw it out, just let another one in.'

They pushed the picnic to one side and stretched out on the blanket, chatting and laughing. It was only when the sun began to set, a rich apricot blaze sliding down an acre of cerulean sky into the horizon, that they realised how long they'd been there. Charlotte took a long look at Rich. Eyes the colour of maple syrup, dirty blonde curls and those dimples. She was a sucker for dimples. He was so at ease with himself. He didn't have the usual arrogance that accompanied a good looks and great body combo like his. She'd felt good about herself while she'd been with him today, rather than just feeling good about being with someone. He was way too good for her. It was a shame not to end her birthday on an up-note, though.

'Isn't this the bit where we're supposed to kiss?' Charlotte asked, at the ready with "It was a joke" as her fall-back.

Rich looked at her and smiled, little lights dancing in his eyes, betraying both his surprise and excitement. 'You know what? I think it is.'

Charlotte felt his lips brush hers as he held her waist firmly but gently, and kissed her slowly. They explored one another's mouths, tentatively at first, the passion mounting, Charlotte's body yielding to his as she breathed in his musky masculinity. Just like their dancing, the rhythm of their kiss was a perfect pairing. She ached for him. Never before had a mere kiss evoked such a heightened physiological reaction, nor left her in such a daze.

·· · • · • · · · ·

Charlotte giggled from the safety of Rich's arms as he carried her over the sand with the champagne bucket dangling from his elbow and the picnic rucksack on his back.

'Only you could manage to burn the soles of your feet while lying next to a tube of suntan lotion, Charlotte,' Rich moaned as he struggled with his load.

As they reached Charlotte's bungalow, they could see Jamie at the door. He was dressed in a white linen dinner suit and he turned to look at them as they approached. He was holding an enormous bunch of pink lilies, which he proffered to Charlie with a blank expression.

Rich let Charlie's legs drop to the floor and they stood there like tittering teenagers who'd just been caught by their parents.

'Jamie, hi.' Charlotte tried to swallow her giggles, which were building at the ridiculousness of the situation, and the look on Jamie's face.

Jamie remained silent.

'Are they for me? They're gorgeous.' She took the lilies and sniffed them, her stifled laughter evaporating as she felt Jamie's embarrassment. 'Are you coming in for a drink?'

Rich looked away.

Jamie held out a brown envelope, the same type as from that morning.

'I came to apologise ... for today ... and to take you out for dinner to celebrate your birthday.'

'Oh ...' Charlotte looked down at her burned legs and feet. Her whole body covered in sand from being dunked in a dune by Rich.

'We've had a picnic,' Rich explained tersely.

'So I hear.'

Jamie looked sulky and hurt. He handed Charlotte the envelope.

'I've booked us a table, at a restaurant where you can watch Stingrays swimming in the sea while you eat. I'll be there all evening if you want to join me. If you don't, I'll understand,' he said graciously, his face awash with contempt. 'It's fine dining.' He scanned her sand-encrusted limbs.

Then he left.

Charlotte turned to Rich. 'If it's all right with you, I think I'd better –'

'Don't say anything, it's fine.' Rich hoiked his rucksack onto his back, unable to hide his disappointment. 'I hope you've had a nice birthday so far. Enjoy tonight.'

He walked down the path, head hung, in the same direction as Jamie.

···········

Charlotte walked gingerly down the beach, her burned soles still sore, despite multiple coatings of freshly sourced aloe vera. She looked through the dark to see if Bannister was there. He wasn't, but she knew he'd come. She hadn't felt like coming tonight but wanted to thank him for his beautiful birthday present.

As she walked to the end of the jetty, a show reel played in her head. Snatched moments from the day. What a beautiful birthday! Rich had made all that happen. The kiss had been the biggest surprise. It was pure, not needy as they so often were. It was a kiss laced with feeling and not just sexual desire – an altogether novel experience for Charlotte. But surely it was easy to create a kiss like that in such magical surrounds? The sunset had been spectacular.

She turned her mind to Jamie and how deflated she'd felt this morning, utterly devastated he'd chosen Rachel over her on her birthday. Then his crestfallen face this evening when he saw her with Rich. Robert O'Keefe had said Jamie was loyal and he was right. Jamie couldn't have let Rachel down because he'd promised her and that was Jamie's way. But he'd tried hard to put things right this evening. He'd booked one of the most expensive restaurants in town, dressed all dapper for the occasion and got her some beautiful flowers. And his note had been sincere, really apologetic. What more could a girl want?

She'd chosen not to meet him this evening. She needed time to think. She'd rung to let him know and had been proud of her conviction. But, in retrospect, perhaps she'd made the wrong decision.

'Hey, pretty laydee, am I glad to see you!' Bannister bounded onto the jetty, his voice deeper than the black of the Caribbean night.

'Hey, Bannister, I'm so glad you came. I want to say thank you. I adore my dolls, they're beautiful. And the food ... it was divine.'

'You're welcome, Charlie.'

'I've brought beer.' Charlotte held a cold bottle aloft for Bannister, who was busy removing his socks to dangle his feet into the ocean.

They talked about Jamie and Rich, and she told him about the jurisprudence talk she had to give when she got home. Bannister spoke about his passion for legal philosophy and the book he'd been penning secretly when his brothers were asleep. Charlotte watched his face come alive, his expressions exaggerated, his gesticulations sharp and precise. His speech got faster and she noticed how his patois gradually slipped away, revealing the Oxford English he presumably used to speak before his mum had died and he was forced to make a living in the tourist industry.

Bannister had been privately educated in England from the age of eleven. He'd won a much sought-after scholarship for a place at Eton, Rich had told her. It was a different Bannister to the one she'd come to know, but the soft, wise glow that seemed to dance around him thankfully remained intact.

They counted the stars and fought over which was which, and which was really a satellite, the discussion more argumentative than usual because it was such a clear night. The Milky Way draped itself across the sky like a great swag of white organza. Charlie lay her head in his lap, as usual, and, as usual, he had a golden coin of invaluable advice from his treasure trove of wisdom.

'Trust yer gut instinct, Charlie. Yuh never look back if yuh trust de gut.'

Chapter Thirty-Six

Jasmine

Jasmine re-read the email mistakenly sent to her by Charlie for the seventh time that morning. There was no other way to interpret those words. Sarah was thinking of leaving Grant and, by the looks of it, was thinking of cheating with someone called TIM. Who apparently was so hot he deserved capital letters. She sat cross-legged on her bed. She never wanted this to happen. Didn't even know how it had happened, it just sort of did. Isn't that what all mistresses say?

Jas had never said it before. She always knew exactly how it happened and always knew the right time to end it. She didn't do the devious mistress thing, plotting to get her man, surreptitiously leaving an earring in the footwell of his car, dousing herself in a heavy perfume that would cling to his shirt. None of that was her style, but then she'd never fallen in love before.

The first time Jas saw Grant, he was holding a bottle of champagne in one hand, a bunch of wilting carnations in the other, and wearing a cheeky smile as an apology for being thirty minutes late. Jas hadn't given it another thought. Sarah, however, who was already there, wasn't so easily mollified and proceeded to berate him in the bathroom, where she thought no one could hear.

Charlie had hijacked Jas's big night out in town that night with Adrian the Married, who'd been treating her to a slap-up meal in a flash restaurant of her choice, simply for being such a good shag. Charlie begged for a last-minute favour, so dinner for six and a false birthday had been whipped up at a minute's notice.

Charlotte had suggested inviting Sarah and Grant, to make up the numbers for added authenticity. Sarah was Charlie's friend, really. Jas had got to know her a bit over the years and found her nice enough, but she was way too uptight for her liking. The evening was a success and as it bandied along with peals of laughter hard on the heels of each bout of heckling, no one noticed the inadvertent footsie going on underneath the table or the smouldering eye contact across the breadsticks.

A month later Grant, Sarah and the boys moved to Cornwall, leaving Grant working in the Big Smoke on his own for most of the week and in need of a dinner companion. When Jas heard his voice on her answerphone six weeks after they'd met, she wasn't surprised at all.

Jasmine sat pondering. The email had said that Sarah's mate spent three nights a week at The Mockingbird. It didn't say which nights, but it was guaranteed she'd be there on a Wednesday if the nights were consecutive. Considering she lived in Cornwall, they had to be, surely.

Jas picked up the phone and dialled the number for the restaurant. She knew it off by heart because, as Charlie had rightly said she ate there all the time. She'd been there with Grant a few times, because he loved it, too. He loved the intimacy and the way some of the tables were tucked into a dark corner, like a cosy cave à deux. It wouldn't be hard to persuade him to meet her there. The whole idea was a long shot, but anything was worth a try.

Grant was the first person she'd ever loved – a love that came close to that for her dad. Grant was the first person she was prepared to commit to, at the risk of him leaving her again, like her dad did. That was monumental.

She knew her dad hadn't known she was in the house that morning, the morning he decided to take his own life. He didn't know her mum had said she was too ill to go to school that day. But it didn't make it any easier. It didn't take away the pain that her dad could leave her like that, or the pain that came with knowing her love wasn't good enough to stop him from wanting to die. From that day, she believed her love wasn't good enough for anyone but, maybe, if her and Grant were given a chance, she could change that.

Chapter Thirty-Seven

Jamie

Jamie read the email again:

Date: Friday, 23 Feb 11:09
Subject: Hello

How's it going out there, Jamie? I know I'm not supposed to email you, but I've got some information you might be interested in.

There's stuff going down back here at the ranch. Word on the grapevine is that you and Charlie are a serious item (nothing to do with me, I swear – I haven't said a thing). Robert knows. I overheard him talking on the phone and he's not happy with Charlie. Says he expected more of her. He's annoyed she's been lying, but she's the most promising lawyer he's got and he doesn't want to lose her, blah, blah, blah.

He said that firm's policy says he should sack one or both of you and he's been considering sacking you (sorry, know that won't be easy to hear). Under the circumstances, he's not going to, just in case Charlie follows you. He's not happy, so I'd keep a low profile when you get back if I were you. Think your dream of making partner might just have gone belly-up, though. You'd have to pull something serious out the bag for that to happen now.

No one knows about us – can you imagine what Robert would do if he found out you were sleeping with two members of staff?! Well, Fiona in accounts knows, but she's my bezzie mate and would never tell a soul, so you're safe.

Hope you're having fun.

Bet you've got some great white bits!

Mils xx

He'd first read it yesterday afternoon, on Charlotte's birthday, when he'd got back from his day out with Rachel. The trip had been his idea. A chance to get away from prying eyes and fuck the life out of the delicious Rachel on a remote beach, and in the jeep, and in the sea. Anywhere he could think of, in fact, without the fear of Charlotte turning up.

The email had come as a blow. Just as he was starting to have fun. Within an hour of reading the email, he'd managed to book a flash restaurant, acquire an impressively large bunch of flowers and don his best linen suit. Perfect. What girl could turn him down? Only she had, which had taken him by surprise. It was time to up the ante.

Chapter Thirty-Eight

Charlotte

'So I was wondering ...' Jamie said.

Charlotte's whole world slowed down, every fibre of her being holding its breath, straining its ears. He was about to say something cataclysmic.

'Yes?'

'Well, if you wanted to get back together?'

A loud, colourful carnival struck up inside her, batons twirling, drums rolling, feathers shimmying, huge headdresses swaying.

'Do you mean it?'

'Look, you know how much I love you, Charlie. You've always known. It's just, well, I'm not good with being controlled, that's all.'

'I know.' She nodded soberly as every member of the carnival procession inside her broke into the samba to the shouts of '*Arriba!*'

'Perhaps if you had some therapy or something ... you know, when we get back. Then maybe we could make it work.'

The carnival ground to a halt. She looked down, her pulse banging loudly in her ears like a sped-up death march. It was bittersweet. He wanted her, but not as she was. Who could blame him? She knew he was right, it was just hard to hear.

'I really want to make it work, Charlie.' Jamie picked up both of her hands in his and gazed into her eyes. 'I can't bear the thought of my future without you in it.' He squeezed her hands. 'What do you say?'

They all but broke into a trot as they headed for Charlotte's bungalow. She fumbled with the key and they burst into the room.

They threw themselves onto the bed, undressing frenziedly. She baulked slightly at the stale alcohol and coffee rancid on his breath as he pressed his lips to hers, but no doubt her breath smelt the same. They were back together, and that was all that mattered.

········•·•····

Charlotte zipped around the hotel grounds before scouring the beach, scrutinising every sun lounger under every stripy umbrella, searching frantically for Rich. She needed to explain she couldn't go on the trip they'd planned tomorrow. It sounded fun, coasting round a Caribbean island in a beach buggy with someone who looked like Chris Hemsworth's younger, fitter, curlier brother, that had the capacity to make her laugh until she cried, but it wouldn't be fair now. Now she and Jamie were together again. Shame really. But she couldn't wait to tell everyone. It occurred at this moment that she was often preoccupied with what others thought of her, but perhaps never quite worried enough about what she thought. A bit like why she became a solicitor – to be admired.

She made her way back along the beach towards the hotel, keeping an eye out, the smell of sea and suntan oil cajoling her feel-good hormones out to play. They didn't need a lot of cajoling today. Sex with Jamie had been just how she remembered it, all thrust and grind and high energy. He wasn't the most attentive lover she'd ever had, but he was passionate. She wondered if she'd ever actually 'made love'. She knew it was her fault. She liked to please. Sex was her way of gaining affection. It occurred that she might also avoid making love because she wasn't at ease with the emotion.

Surely someone needed to love you in order to make love, and she'd never felt very loveable. It was best all round to ignore the whole loving side to sex and get on with the job of having good orgasms.

That was probably all she'd ever wanted, really – someone to love her. Perhaps she should suggest to Jamie that they try making love one day. She was sure he'd be up for it. But she was happy enough for now.

She checked her watch: 6 o'clock. She didn't want to go round to Rich's bungalow to tell him in case Jamie saw her – it wouldn't look good. Jamie had decided it best if they slept in their separate bungalows and take things slowly, as if they were dating again. Charlotte had been upset at first. Was it a sign he didn't think she'd change? But she could understand why. And it was nice, because it meant she could carry on meeting with Rich and Bannister. She didn't like to think of life completely devoid of those two – not yet, anyway.

She walked into the cool marble reception area of the hotel, welcoming the breeze from the overhead fans. Still no sign. He wasn't in any of his usual haunts – she admitted defeat and turned to go.

'Charlotte, how nice to see you. Is the rash still stinging?' The Lovely Rachel pulled the door of the beauty salon to, circling her finger in the direction of Charlie's crotch. 'There was rather a jungle down there, wasn't there?' She grimaced.

'Hello, Rachel,' Charlie said cordially.

'I hear you're back with lover boy, then.' Rachel's sweet smile failed to mask the layer of vitriol sitting behind it. 'He told me today.'

Rachel had taken her by surprise. When had Jamie told her?

'Congrats. The best woman won and all that. Shame, though, cos he really was a great fuck!' And she left.

Charlotte thought about chasing after her. Swinging her beach bag at her, snaring her like a hunted wildebeest, bringing her down, putting a flip-flopped foot on her back and demanding to know what she meant.

Instead, she thought of something Bannister had said: '*Accept it as if you'd chosen it.*' Jamie swore he hadn't slept with her and if this relationship was going to work, she needed to believe him. Especially today – their first day back together. And what was the use in questioning Rachel? She was bound to lie. She wanted nothing more than for Charlotte and Jamie to split up again.

Charlotte retired to her bungalow and settled down to her favourite thing, writing in her trusty Filofax. Writing stuff down made it real somehow and she was always surprised by what she learned from the process. The equivalent of confiding in a friend over a cuppa, only better because she didn't really like people knowing how much of a failure she was, not to the full extent, not even Jas or Sarah. Only her Filofax had that honour.

She poured herself a gin and tonic, which she could never again do without thinking of Rich. She smiled to herself and ignored the fluttery feeling in her stomach. She opened the door of her bungalow for the balmy evening air to join her, welcoming the soothing regularity of the sea as her background music. She made herself comfortable and began. She'd let her diary slip in the last few days, so she found the page for her birthday and made a start:

Saturday, 24 February 2024

Gold Star Day!

As birthdays go, it was a good one. Started off dodgy. Jamie stood me up to take The Lovely Rachel around the island (she's so stunning – how can anyone deserve legs that good?). But he'd promised her and he's nothing if not loyal. Still pissed off about it, cos I don't understand what allegiance he has to her after knowing her for one week. The morbid jealousy side of me is suspicious, but I need to move on and not dwell, like Rich said.

Am proud of myself that I spent the day with Rich instead of stalking Jamie, which is what I would have done before I came to Barbados. Rich and Bannister are rubbing off on me, oo-er!

Mum can't make it to my speech now. Really fed up. She used to put Dad first and now it's Roger. Talked to Rich about it. He asked me what she was like when I was growing up. I told him I couldn't remember her hugging or kissing me as a child. Couldn't remember her reading me a bedtime story, either. She was always too busy running round after Dad. She tells me she loves me all the time, but she rarely shows her love and it's the showing, not the telling that counts.

Rich said Mum was in an abusive relationship which she was bound tighter to when I arrived, which maybe made her resent me ... And there's the possibility she was scared not to put my dad first. She probably didn't like it any more than I did.

She may have projected her anger and inadequacy onto me and, me being a child, I wasn't able to see this. I presumed it was because I was bad or had done something wrong. And there was Dad and his abusive behaviour, which I'd have watched and learned from, too. His behaviour would have had a big impact on our family.

Rich said I'd learned gradually that my wishes, opinions and emotions were unimportant, so I didn't develop good ways to soothe myself when I felt sad or angry or scared. I developed core beliefs like 'I'm not good enough', 'No one wants to spend time with me' and 'No one wants my love' and found evidence to support these. Meanwhile, the emotions kept coming, because we can't stop them.

I developed a host of mechanisms to control my emotions or gain control over my environment, or to get the attention and affection I deserve and need. These included morbid jealousy and using sex to gain attention and affection. Neither of which are optimal methods and need to be replaced with better, more adult strategies.

Although my parents are the root of my problems, Rich said it's futile to blame them. After all, they didn't fuck me up on purpose, 'But they were fucked up in their turn.' That Philip Larkin poem 'This Be The Verse' says it all.

And I'm lucky, because I can see I'm fucked up. I'm not sure my parents realised they were. They did the best they could for me, and they didn't act maliciously. I need to take responsibility for myself. Rich suggested talking to Mum and being honest about how I feel. I think it's a good idea.

Rich laid on a birthday picnic for me, complete with champagne. No one's ever done anything like that for me before. We had fun, and we kissed! It still feels like the kiss never happened – it was so perfect. But Rich is like a class A drug, addictive but forbidden because he'll never stay in one relationship for long. There will always be a prettier, more intelligent, classier girl around the corner for Rich. He may dabble with the likes of me, but he'd never settle for the likes of me. I'm surprised he's still hanging around ... Probably because I haven't slept with him. Shame, really, cos he is very addictive indeed.

Bannister gave me some beautiful Russian dolls and I found out he has a law degree. I love Bannister.

Charlotte always learned something about herself when she wrote in her diary. She looked back at the page and saw it was smattered with the word Rich.

It was just about dark when she reached the jetty and she could already hear the tinny cicada chorus rhythmically bringing in the evening. She skipped through the fringe of palms onto the soft manicured beach and made a bee line for the shore, so the warm waves could roll gently over her toes. Bannister was already there. The moon was full tonight and illuminated his profile against the soot-black sky, as he sat dangling his feet, as usual.

'*Hey, Bannister, it's me!*' she called.

'Who else would it be at this time, pretty laydee?'

'How are you doing?'

'Not as good as you, by de sounds of tings.'

'How very astute. Yes, I'm in a particularly good mood this fine evening. Jamie and I are back together.'

'I know.'

'Jeeez, are there no secrets in this place? Doesn't take long, does it ... how come? Rachel!'

'She made it her business to tell me earlier. She's not a happy laydee. Metinks she was smitten wid Jamie.'

'Oh God, I bet Rich knows too then.'

'He's not a happy gentleman. You 'as been causing quite a stir since yer arrival, pretty laydee.'

'I really wanted to tell him myself. I tried to find him earlier but he wasn't anywhere.'

'I tink he found out for himself ... came to yer bungalow.'

'Shit! Me and Jamie ... the curtains were open.'

'Yeah, baby.'

'*Shit-shit-shit!* Do you know where he is now?'

'Don't tink he's wantin' to see yer right now, Charlie. He took himself off today, got some space. Tink he's smitten, too, yuh know.'

'Who, Rich? No, he's not smitten with me. It's not like that. I mean, I think he likes me but, well, he's a bit of a bad boy, isn't he? Just look at him. He's gorgeous. I don't think he's going to lose any sleep over me. I don't think he does feelings.'

Bannister chuckled. 'Yuh really do tink yuh know it all, Charlie, don't yuh?'

He circled his feet in the water, sending ripples through the moonlit ocean. There was a sadness about him tonight.

'So, tell me about Jamie. Is yuh happy now yuh got what yuh wanted?'

'I am, Bannister, I am,' she gushed, realising for the first time there was a tiny doubt, up on tip-toes, pulling ever so gently at the far reaches of her mind.

It was ridiculous. Probably just nerves. She always got them when things were going too well. Always thinking she couldn't be this lucky, always looking for the catch, for the rug to be pulled from under her, but it wasn't going to be this time.

She got the sense that Bannister didn't think it was good news that she was back with Jamie, which didn't help with her questionable conviction.

'Why? Don't you think I should have got back with Jamie?' she asked.

'I'm not saying nuttin', Charlie. It's not my life.'

Charlotte felt dejected. It mattered to her what Bannister thought.

'Jamie's got his faults, but I know him so well and he knows me, and that's important given my problems ... isn't it?'

'It is, Charlie. There is a saying in Barbados. *"De new broom does sweep cleaner, but de old broom know de corners."*' He said it kindly, handing her the exoneration she craved. 'Just remember, though. Stop tinkin' dat your love isn't good enough. Your love doesn't need to be anyting. Yuh don't need to do stuff to make yuh worthy of love. Someone can love yuh just for being you.'

Bannister's *Jerry Springer* moments were the highlight of Charlie's day. His voice was buttery soft, his Caribbean lilt deep and spiritual, and his perceptive understanding of her wise and mysterious. He was the perfect nurturer.

Charlie leaned back against him, dangling her own feet in the water. They swirled their feet, their toes touching every now and then. She looked up at him. His dreadlocks fell to his jawline, his woollen hat still firmly in place, despite the heat. He blinked lazily, a raft of differing emotions no doubt hiding behind his devil-may-care attitude.

She touched his beard and pulled his mouth to hers. He didn't resist, and they kissed.

Chapter Thirty-Nine

Sarah

Checking my secret email account was risky when Grant was in bed, but since he'd been home – the sum total of four hours – he'd wound me up big time. I'd been talking about my week and my apparent lack of control over our children and how unhappy Rudy seemed to be. How I didn't know what to do anymore and that I needed extra help from him with the boys, and he went off-the-scale ballistic.

'The only problem with this family is your ridiculously high standards. We can't all be superhuman, you know, Sarah!' he'd hissed and stormed off up to bed.

All rather dramatic, really, which wasn't Grant's style. I think the commute is getting to him.

Since then, I'd spent the whole evening trying to stop myself from checking my email account, resulting in one empty bottle of Shiraz, two mint Club wrappers, a half-empty bowl of peanuts (or half-full, depending on your disposition) and one cafetière of cold coffee. But it had finally got the better of me, 'it' being the desire to read the ego-boosting goodies that were possibly waiting for me in my inbox from TIM. Besides, regardless of what he had to say, I needed to tell him I was cancelling. It wasn't fair to string him along.

Date: Tuesday, 20 Feb 10:12
Subject: Rendezvous

The twenty-third is good for me, baby – try stopping me.

Give me a ring and let me know when you've confirmed it with your friend. That way I can hear your sexy voice.

Jeez I've missed you, SJ.

TIM xx

· · · · ● ● · ● · · ·

Date: Wednesday, 21 Feb 08:35
Subject: Rendezvous

Where are you, babe? Everything OK?

Am gagging for news. Can't get you out of my head.

Ring me.

TIM xx

· · · · ● ● · ● · · ·

Date: Thursday, 22 Feb 03:56
Subject: Call Me

You still alive, babe? It's four in the morning and I can't sleep for thinking about you. Desperate to know if we're on or not.

I want you, SJ.

Ring me.

PS: Send me your address. I want to send you something – I'll post it on a Monday so hubby won't be around when you get it.

PPS: Remember when we made love in Green Park?

TIM xx

Each email tugged at my heart, but it was the mention of Green Park that was the clincher. I wanted some of that night back. The night I won Business Woman of the Year, with TIM by my side. It was as clear in my mind as if it had happened yesterday. I'd known at the time that no other night was ever going to top the way I felt then as I lay on the damp grass watching the stars in the middle of London – and I was right, no night had.

There were other times that were up there, of course, but I couldn't compare those times, like the birth of my boys, because they were different. The love you feel for a child is different to the love you feel for yourself, and that was what it had been about that night. I loved myself so much that evening.

If I were on one of those reality TV shows right now and I'd said that aloud, my votes would have plummeted like the wake of a bad Jenga move. People would loathe the self-congratulatory female who thought she was the bollocks and was arrogant enough to say as much. But there's nothing wrong with loving yourself, so why are we all so ashamed to admit it?

I think that's where I've been going wrong lately – not loving myself. I can't even bear to be with me most of the time. But why? What is it that made me feel good about me back then? What am I missing right now? What makes me sparkle like the polish on a seventeen-year-old's car?

Ah yes, loud and resounding came the answer. Popped into my head in a puff of smoke. Success. Being the best at something, succeeding, that's what ices my cake, plain and simple. Good old-fashioned success.

·····•·•····

I sat at the kitchen table holding my phone in one hand, making arrangements with my London friend, Luce, for next weekend, and trying to gouge out crispy playdoh that had been ground into the grains of wood with the other.

I told her I wanted to spend a bit of time shopping and mooching around on Saturday during the day, sucking up the hustle and bustle of London again, moseying around my old loves – Bond Street, Liberty, John Lewis. I explained I wanted some time on my own, to relax for a few hours, and then I'd meet her that evening and stay the night, and we could spend Sunday together too. I wanted to spend the night with TIM, but if I did that I'd have to tell Luce what I was doing for her to give me an alibi, and that was a big no-no.

Luce said she had a yoga class at eight on Saturday evening but would skip it. I tried to dissuade her but she was adamant. She then mentioned meeting Jasmine on her way to yoga the week before and remarked that Jas had put on a lot of weight. This was awkward. I wasn't about to tell her Jas was pregnant. I just laughed and said 'Yes, she has put on weight but she can afford to' and quickly wound up the call.

Grant had just come into the kitchen. I looked over at him as he made a mug of coffee at the counter, and felt suddenly sad.

'Thanks, baby, by the way,' I said.

'What for?'

'For letting me go to London for the weekend. I know you work hard and it can't be easy for you doing all this commuting. Then to have the boys on your own for a weekend just so I can go on a jolly –'

'You deserve it, babe.'

Our eyes met, something that hadn't happened for a while. He held my gaze, a wistful look on his face, like he was yearning for what we used to have. It was unsaid, but we both knew it had all gone wrong.

How had it happened? Was it me? Had I been projecting my unhappiness onto him? I didn't know the answer.

Grant was the first to speak, predictably moving the situation away from the truth that probably neither of us wanted to face. 'Was that Charlie you and Lucy were talking about? Putting on weight? Is she up the duff? Hope so, cos then we can hear the end of the egg monologues. "My eggs will all be in rocking chairs knitting gaudy sweaters if I don't get a move on … My eggs will all be drawing their pension soon …" She nearly put me off my beer last time. If she doesn't stop going on about her bloody eggs, I'll personally strangle each and every last one of them.'

I laughed, enjoying the fun that used to skip around Grant and me when we were together. 'You're such a git!'

He seemed different today, melancholy, yet like a burden had lifted too, which was surprising given yesterday's outburst. It seemed I'd been forgiven.

'No, Luce was talking about Jas. She keeps bumping into her.'

Grant was stirring sugar into his coffee. 'Oh? Where?'

'Luce goes to a yoga class in Balham, close to Jas's house.' I resumed my table inspection and ran my nail over a bit of dried Weetabix. Shoddy! Sets like concrete that stuff. Must scrub that later.

'Oh right,' Grant said. 'Do you want a coffee?'

'No thanks, let's take the boys for a walk, it's a lovely morning. Anyway,' I continued, 'I couldn't tell Luce Jas is putting weight on because she's pregnant, could I?'

Grant swung around. *'Jasmine's pregnant?'*

'Oh, didn't I tell you? Charlie told me. She's the last person you'd expect to be pregnant, isn't she? Poor Jas, it's her worst nightmare come true. God knows who the father is. She probably doesn't even know.'

'Yeah ... that's a surprise,' Grant said. 'Well, I've got some work stuff to do. You take the boys for a walk, and I'll make dinner later.'

Chapter Forty

Jasmine

'*Why the fuck didn't you tell me?*' Grant yelled down the phone.

'Oh, hi. Yeah, nice to talk to you, too.'

'What the hell, Jasmine? How far gone are you? Is it mine?'

'Don't you worry, I'm fine, but thanks for asking.'

There was a long silence.

'I'm sorry, Jas, I'm just—'

'I know, I was shocked, too. And to answer your questions: because I knew you'd react like this, four months gone, and yes, it's yours.'

'How can you be sure? Aren't you shagging someone else?'

Jasmine swallowed hard. It hurt that he could be so blasé about her sleeping with other men, that he expected her to be, even. He'd been merrily fucking her three nights a week, all the while thinking she was shagging other people. And he was perfectly happy about it, it seemed.

She laughed to herself. How the tide had turned. Normally, she was the one trying to wriggle out of commitment.

'No. Well, I was ... I was seeing Adrian the Married, as you know, but he's had the snip, so I'm afraid it has to be yours.'

Grant groaned. 'Shit, Jas, what a mess!'

Jasmine flinched. 'You don't need to worry,' she snapped. 'I've got an appointment booked at the clinic for Tuesday. I'm having a termination.'

She could hear the relief in Grant's silence.

'Grant?'

'Yeah, I'm still here. Sorry, babe. *Um*, do you have someone to go with you?'

'No, I'll be fine. I'd rather do it on my own.'

'But what about getting home? You won't be able to drive. Shall I pick you up?'

'Honestly, I'll be fine.'

'Are you sure it's what you want?'

She shuddered. She couldn't bear the falsity.

'Just leave it, will you, Grant? It's like you've got some cheesy script in front of you on what to say when your mistress announces she's having an abortion.'

'Sorry, don't really know what else to say.'

'Say yes.'

'*Huh?*

'Say yes to dinner with me at The Mockingbird on Wednesday night.'

'The day after? Will you be up to it?'

'Well, I probably won't be up to "it" –'

'I didn't mean that.'

'Yeah, I'm sure I'll be up for dinner. Meet me there at seven.'

'OK, see you then. *Um* ... Good luck? Is that the wrong thing to say?'

Jas attempted a laugh. 'See you Wednesday, Grant,' she managed, desperately corralling the tears until the end of the call.

Chapter Forty-One

Sarah

Saturday had come and gone as quick as an English summer and now it was Sunday. Time to bake some more cakes – for The Mockingbird restaurant in Balham this time. I couldn't get my head around the logistics of selling puddings to someone in London. It was a bit crazy, but Jinslet was a marvel. The woman was a flip-flop-wearing social butterfly with a little black book the size of Russia. I'd tweaked the recipe slightly and was interested to see if it had worked. Good to try it out on the least viable outlet.

Grant took the boys outside to kick a ball around so, while the cakes were in the oven, I raced upstairs to do what I'd been itching to do ever since I'd booked my train tickets yesterday – email TIM. I punched in my secret email address, my head nervously twitching towards the door every other second. I could do this stuff on my phone, but that felt more duplicitous somehow, like I would be welcoming it into my normal life. Like I had accepted it, and I hadn't yet. Who was I kidding?

The computer was slow. I hated it when it was like that. I had visions of it getting stuck, freeze-frame on an email from TIM. That would be the moment Grant walked in. I ran through the scenario in my head loads of times and my emergency plan was to hit the on/off button on both the console and the monitor.

I put in my password and waited.

Part of the euphoric Green Park experience that night was down to the fact that I'd been in love with TIM. It hadn't all been about me being happy with myself. But I wondered if those two were linked. Can you love someone else if you don't love yourself? And even if I could answer that, was I certain I really had loved him? Other emotions can so easily be mistaken for love. I think I loved him, but love is annoyingly eco-friendly like that. It has a habit of disappearing without a trace, so you're not sure whether it ever existed or not.

I typed in a quick message and fired it off without rereading it – most unusual but necessary. Asking him to meet me this weekend instead of in three weeks was asking a lot, but I also felt sure he'd get there somehow. If I didn't get on with it and do it soon, I'd get cold feet, and I didn't want to get cold feet. I wanted to see him.

I went through the usual pantomime after sending TIM an email, namely deleting all traceable history of the debauchery I'd just engaged in, and ran back downstairs to take my cakes out of the oven.

·········

I reversed into the last empty space in the school car park and heard the *beep-beep* of my phone. *Yippee!* A text from Charlie.

But it wasn't from Charlie at all.

`Morning, sexy,`

`And what a particularly beautiful morning it is, because in just four short days from now, you and I will be together again. Hotel booked. I'm arriving on the Friday night, so we have the hotel for the whole of Saturday. I've sent you an email. Off to book flights now.`

`Love ya. TIM xx`

'Love ya!' Damn, he really was taking it seriously.

I looked in my rear-view mirror at Rudy, worried he'd somehow read my text, and saw my own reflection and the crinkles around my eyes from the smile I'd been unable to keep from spreading across my face. I went to delete TIM's text but thought I might save it to read when I had a coffee later – a little treat to brighten the morning. A circle of primary colour in a landscape of black and grey.

I was becoming poetically morbid lately and knew I had to snap out of it before I started adding Leonard Cohen tracks onto my Spotify playlist. I saved the message. I'd delete it later.

My phone pinged a few more times. Charlie this time. I quickly read her first message while ushering Rudy out of the car. We were late, as usual.

`Oh my God, Jamie and I are back together! C xxooxx`

'Yay!' I shouted, then quickly looked around to see who'd heard.

'If you're happy, Mummy, does that mean you'll let me have the day off school?'

I laughed and bent down to give him a squeezy hug. 'No, darling, I'm afraid it doesn't.'

I waved him off. He stopped at the threshold and turned and waved at me. He looked serious and sad but resolved and brave, all at the same time. His expression looked wrong on a child so young.

I did my usual waiting around and peering through the window and despite his forlorn farewell, Rudy looked fairly settled. Bohemian Babe was waiting for me at the car. She was clutching something in her hand and regarded me nervously as I approached, seemingly unsure of what she was about to do.

'Hi, I thought you might like to see this.' Her eyes darted left and right. She was doing that French Resistance thing again. She thrust a piece of paper at me.

It had been ripped out of an exercise book with something written on it in big misspelt words – by a child, for sure:

GET HIM TOLD OF £5

GET HIM DEETENSHUN £10

GET HIS MUM CALLD INTO SKOOL £15

'I don't understand.' I shook my head, scouring my mind, trying desperately to make a connection.

'I looked after Theresa's son at the weekend and found that in his pocket.'

She pointed at the piece of paper I was holding and watched me carefully, seemingly waiting for the penny to drop.

'I asked him about it and he said it was a secret. Then later, at tea, he told me proudly how his mum gave him money for bullying Rudy Richardson.'

I gasped, my mouth staying open long after the gasp had dissipated. '*That. Is. Low,*' I said and re-opened my mouth, in awe. 'Even for her. I've known politicians who wouldn't do that.'

Every inch of me tightened, my adrenaline working overtime, racing round, shouting for back-up.

'Apparently, he pinched himself really hard on the arm the other day, so he could say Rudy did it. And he said he was pleased he had because the mark had nearly gone now, and he got £20 for that one.'

Bohemian Babe looked at me and no doubt saw the hatred I felt mounting up inside me.

'You can't blame him, Sarah. It's a lucrative business. He's only seven.'

She was right, it was the mother I needed to find.

Bohemian Babe held her hand out for the piece of paper. The uncomfortable look on her face and the way she stepped back gave away the fact she felt she'd maybe miscalculated the situation and would have been better off keeping schtum.

'I'd better have that back now. He doesn't know I've got it,' she said.

'No.' I was categorical. 'I need it.' I took her unawares by moving forwards and employing all of my redundant adrenaline in a big hug. 'Thank you. I really do appreciate it.'

'It's OK, but please, please promise you won't say it came from me.'

She looked suddenly frightened, her hippy cool upstaged by a vulnerability that didn't match the look.

'Looking after Theresa's son is my main source of income. I'd be stuck without it,' she said, explaining her fear. She was a single parent struggling to get by. It had taken a lot for her to tell me.

······

I didn't drive straight to Big Lass From The North's house. I needed to calm down. Take the emotion out of the situation. If I was going to get anywhere, I had to think smart.

When I eventually pinpointed exactly which house she lived in, I found it to be big and uninviting, a bit like her. I drove up the tree-lined drive and parked in front of the imposing building, next to Big Lass From The North's decommissioned tank. It was a good start – she was in at least. I rang the bell and busied myself counting the rubber boots neatly upturned on the wellie spike while I waited.

Big Lass From The North opened the door and visibly baulked. She was out of breath, her usual sleek bob dishevelled, unflatteringly tucked behind her ears. And she had no make-up on for a change, revealing a sallow complexion.

She regained her composure and barked, '*What do you want?*'

'Can I come in?'

'No, you can't.'

'I'm worried about Rudy. He's a sensitive boy and he's being picked on at school.'

I launched into it. I had to keep her attention or the crack in the door she'd afforded me would be closed in my face.

She looked confused, like she wanted to pinch herself to see if she was awake. The soft edge to my voice had seemingly taken her by surprise and made her curious.

'And what's that got to do with me?' she asked, her own manner tempered slightly.

'Do you know what it's like to be bullied?'

I didn't know whether she did or not, but the statistics for being bullied were high, and I felt like I was on safe ground. Her public displays of bravado and exaggerated sangfroid had all the hallmarks of someone who'd been bullied in their youth. Emotion flickered across her face just long enough for me to register it, but she didn't reply.

'I do,' I said. 'I was bullied at school. The usual stuff. You know, I had sticky-out ears' – I lifted my hair so she could see for herself – 'and I was a swot with a pair of NHS glasses, who sucked up to the teacher and got all of her homework in on time. I suffered the odd bog wash, being pelted with chips one day, a few Chinese burns, nothing too serious. But Grunter Groby here hasn't forgotten any of it. It shaped who I am today. It made me insecure and needy and has probably made a few of my decisions for me in my adult life. Oh, I know what you're thinking – I don't look insecure or needy. But that's always the way, isn't it? The more unstable the person, the bigger the show they put on.'

I watched as what I'd said seemed to resonate, her frame tensing and standing tall, desperately attempting to showcase her own purported security.

'What's all this got to do with me?'

'I struggle to get Rudy to school every morning. It tears me apart to watch how miserable it makes him there.'

Big Lass From The North went to say something.

I put my hand up and continued, 'I know your son is lying to the teachers about Rudy bullying him.'

'Rudy *is* bullying him. *My son wouldn't lie!*' she protested fiercely, the hatred back in her eyes, tinged with a smidgeon of fear.

'We both know your son is bullying Rudy. It's a clever type of bullying, I'll give him that. Indirect bullying – genius! But I don't want my son to be bullied, in any way, shape or form.'

'You're a liar. He'd never do such a thing. How dare you come here, to my house, accusing my son of such a despicable act.'

'What's more, you've been bribing him to do it.'

She blanched, her face startled.

'That's enough now.' She took hold of the door, ready to slam it. 'You've gone mad. Get off my prop—'

'*And I've got proof.*' I held up the piece of paper, close enough for her to read but too far away for her to swipe.

She stopped mid-slam and looked at it carefully. Then she clung to the door silently, visibly shaking.

'I don't want to hear any more reports of your son bullying mine. *OK, pet?*' I said.

I nodded in a conspiratorial manner and walked back to my car, my knees wobbling so much I thought I might not make it.

I drove off and pulled over as soon as I could. I was in no fit state to continue.

I was pleased with how it had gone. Contrary to most people's opinion of me, I found conflict hard. I pulled out my phone to read the rest of Charlie's messages. I was dying to know what she'd been up to:

I kissed Bannister. Fuck! C xxooxx

Followed by:

Please don't tell anyone. C xxooxx

I wasn't sure whether aliens had stolen Charlie's phone, but the texts sure as hell weren't reading right. They implied that Charlie had been unfaithful – that was a contradiction in terms and about as likely as Victoria Beckham having Rebecca Loos round for pre-theatre drinks.

Grant was asleep on the sofa when I got back. I was buzzing and needed to tell someone what had happened. I considered rousing him, but he was Mr Grumpy Bear if he was yanked out of his sleep.

I emailed Charlie instead:

Date: Monday, 26 Feb 11:45
Subject: Who The Fuck Is Bannister?

All roight, my luverly. Just back from confrontation with Big Lass From The North. Found out she's been bribing her son to pretend Rudy's bullying him. They got caught out, though, because he wrote it down. So you see, that's what happens if you write stuff down. I've told you that loads of times and I know you don't believe me, but let this story be a lesson to you and that blessed Filofax of yours.

Going to Marion's tomorrow, to start work on a poem she's asked me to write. Looking forward to it, actually. How my life has changed.

Anyway, anyway, anyway, pray tell ... who the fuck is Bannister and why have you been kissing him? Was Jamie there when it happened? Was that his birthday present to you? I was excited when I heard about you and Jamie, but now I'm just confused. Tell all! And don't leave out the details. I want all the gory glory of the make-up sex. You know I live my life through you.

Lots of love, S xx

PS: Toying with idea of starting SJ's Sticky Toffee Pudding Company. What say you?

PPS: Am meeting TIM, after all.

Grant was snoring now, so I grabbed the opportunity to check for any TIM messages.

Date: Monday, 26 Feb 08:00
Subject: Saturday

Hi, babe,

It's all systems go, then!

Have booked into The Landmark. I'm arriving Friday night, what with flights and everything. I'll be in the bar from 11am on Saturday, waiting for you.

Can't wait, SJ – I really can't fucking wait.

Lots of love, lust and longing,

TIM x

PS: I've changed a bit since the last time we saw each other, so I'm attaching a recent photo. (This will mean I don't have to get the carnation out.) Don't laugh.

Till Saturday.

I felt nervous while the photo was downloading. What if he wasn't how I remembered him? What if I'd built him up in my mind and put him on a pedestal along with all my other travel memories, which got sweeter with every year that passed.

I needn't have worried. He was still the same sexy TIM I remembered. Leaner, even, with less of a beer belly. But apart from that and the hair, he was the same. His long tresses had been one of the things I fancied most about him when I first met him. It set him apart and epitomised his character, and I felt a pang when I saw the conformity of his current shortish mop of jet-black hair. But it was still him, John Travolta cleft and all.

I found myself wondering about the person behind the camera. Had his girlfriend taken the photo? What was she like? Would he leave her for me? Was I contemplating leaving Grant? I knew I'd been toying with the idea, but was it all hot air, or did I mean it? What would life be like without Grant? What would life be like with TIM? How did I feel about TIM really? I'd know on Saturday.

Chapter Forty-Two

Jasmine

It was only eleven o'clock and already Jasmine had received an email from Charlie that had made her jump for joy, followed by the pregnancy call from Grant that had made her cry. Not to mention the spot of evil plan-hatching she'd done this morning. All that and she hadn't even brushed her teeth. But she still wasn't convinced she'd done the right thing booking a table at The Mockingbird. Just another crazy day on the rollercoaster of emotions that was her life.

She chomped on a piece of heavily buttered toast and flicked through last week's Sunday supplement. Heightened awareness meant that every other page showed a picture of a baby or a happy family or very smiley pregnant lady, resplendent in her forthcoming joy, which would of course 'make her life complete'. She threw the magazine on the floor, dabbed at the toast crumbs with her finger and glugged back her cold tea.

She rubbed her tummy in a stereotypical pregnant-lady way, which she found surprisingly comforting. Only three more days of carrying her baby around. She hadn't imagined how she'd feel, hadn't imagined she'd be thinking of the foetus as a child. Had named it, in fact. But she now understood every anti-abortion argument that had ever been put forward. Quite a turnaround for someone who'd once given a convincing pro-abortion presentation in her ethics class at uni.

She got up to do the dishes in an attempt to ignore the nagging sadness at the back of her mind. She knew she should have told Grant, especially since he'd gone and found out now, from someone else. His wife, ironically. But hindsight wasn't on prescription yet.

Women dreamed about the moment they told the man they loved they were pregnant with his child, waiting for the emotion to twinkle in his eye, to be swept up in a giant rush of love and pride. But Jasmine had known full well how Grant would react. She hadn't needed to see him to know that it was fear that was twinkling in his eyes. That's why she hadn't told him. Her baby deserved better than that.

'Who's that now?' She dried her sudsy hands on a tea towel and answered the phone.

A little voice inside her desperately hoped it was Grant ringing to say he loved her and was leaving Sarah. Moving back to town so they could have their baby and live happily ever after in a North London suburb in a middle-class life full of Mini Boden and Sunday morning strolls on Hampstead Heath.

'Hello?' she said.

'Hello, Jasmine, it's your mother.'

Jasmine's shoulders slumped. She prayed her mother wasn't going to moan about some petty family issue or other. Going toe to toe with her mum would just about top today off.

'How are you?' her mother enquired.

'Good, thanks,' Jasmine lied, suddenly sad her mother knew absolutely nothing about her, or her life any more.

Probably a good thing. She'd be inconsolable if she knew Jasmine was a mistress. And as for the abortion ...

'I have some news,' her mother said.

Jasmine's stomach flipped. She might have guessed there was something up, her mother never rang for a chit-chat.

Jasmine was eight years old when she found her dad hanging from a rope, but somehow her mum and she had managed to grow apart since that day. Her mother hated her husband for what he did. She made no secret of the fact she could never forgive him for ruining her life. She grew cold and defensive, turning against her and her brother, rather than helping them through their grief. She moved them from the family home, warned her children never to tell people the truth about their father's death and proceeded to carve a new life out for herself in a new town. She'd never once visited her husband's grave since his funeral and never spoke of him. Jasmine was desperate to reminisce, to remember the good times, to find out more about him, but she was encouraged not to speak of him because it 'just upsets everybody'.

'Good or bad?' Jasmine asked, lodging her phone between shoulder and ear so she could carry on with the dishes. Her mother didn't warrant her full attention.

'Good. Very, very good,' Jean Rafferty tinkled, a rare soft edge to her voice. 'Christopher and I are moving ... to America.'

Jasmine nearly dropped the phone in the washing-up water.

'Oh, wow, that's fantastic, Mum. Are you pleased?'

'Of course I'm pleased. I wouldn't be going if I wasn't, would I?'

'No, you wouldn't. Why America?'

'Christopher's had an amazing job offer out there. He's not getting any younger. He'd be mad to refuse.'

Jasmine wasn't sure she'd even miss her mum, she rarely saw her.

'That's not all ... Christopher and I are getting married.'

Jasmine stopped what she was doing, her hands motionless in the hot soapy water, the clock suddenly very loud.

She wanted to cry, to slump down on the kitchen floor and sob. She knew she was being ridiculous. Her dad had died thirty years ago and her mum had been going out with Chris for fifteen of those, but that didn't stop her heart from freezing, the sharp cold stinging her chest, forcing her to fight for her next breath. Her mother couldn't marry someone else. She was her dad's wife. He'd be waiting for her.

Everyone else had got over her dad dying, had moved on, learned to love again. So why had she made such a mess of things? Why couldn't she forget?

'Congratulations,' she said, slamming a mug onto the drainer, plunging her hands back into the water to scrub the next one. 'I'm really pleased for you.'

'Don't lie.'

Jasmine dried her hands.

'You're right. Mum. I'm not pleased. I know everyone else has moved on, but ...' She trailed off.

What was the point? It was too little, too late. It wouldn't change her mother's actions all those years ago. It wouldn't transport them back to the months after her dad had died and make her mum hug her this time round.

'Don't worry, Mum. It's my problem, not yours. I'll be fine when I've had some time to get my head around it.'

'Good, but don't take too long – the wedding's two weeks today.'

· · · · ● · ● · ● · · ·

As she marched down Marylebone High Street, Jas pondered for the ten millionth time whether it would be so terribly wrong to go ahead and have her baby, who she had now named Elvis, despite not knowing if she was carrying a boy or a girl. Elvis and her, they'd be a team. Just the two of them, there for each other, through thick and thin. But Jasmine knew that having a baby to procure unconditional love wasn't the right reason. Besides, babies grow up and there's nothing to say they'll still love you when they do.

Straight after her mother's call, she had hopped on the Tube and was now proudly swinging a bag from Prada and a bag from Chanel on this crisp blue-skied winter's day.

Shopping had been a good idea. She was feeling better already. Never mind that she'd spent half the limit on her new credit card – shopping filled a hole in her soul. She slowed and stopped beside a window.

'There it is, Elvis! I might not be able to buy you a pram or a cuddly teddy bear, but I'm going to buy you that. I'm going to put it over my bed and every morning when I wake up, I'll open my eyes and think of you.'

She stared at the classic yet sublimely contemporary Gino Sarfatti chandelier, presiding over the window display with stylish superiority. She pressed her face against the cold glass, trying to make out the price.

'One thousand pounds, Elvis, and you're worth every penny.'

Chapter Forty-Three

Charlotte

It was no use. Charlotte got up and threw on a T-shirt. It wasn't that she hadn't enjoyed kissing Bannister out there on the jetty tonight, because she had. It was the fact it was morally wrong and that she wasn't sure how to reconcile it with her scruples that was bothering her.

She pulled her Filofax out from her pillowcase and began to write:

Sunday, 25 February 2024

A strange thing happened today. First, I got back with Jamie, and then I kissed Bannister. Anyone who knows me would say that Charlotte Bloom being unfaithful was as likely as spotting Stella McCartney on a fox hunt, but it's true, I was.

And what's more, I'm glad! I think. Well, I'm not glad I was unfaithful, but I am glad I kissed Bannister, because it was tender and loving. And, it was the first time I wasn't doing it to gain something. Bannister already likes me, and I didn't feel like I had to prove anything. I did it because I wanted to, for me.

What to do now? Own up? Or not?

Still unable to sleep, Charlotte took the insomnia-laden opportunity to put a few dates in the diary in an email to Millie. The dreaded return to work was looming, so it would be good to get organised.

She looked down her inbox and saw mostly junk, apart from one from Millie and one from Jennifer Newcross who worked in personnel. It wasn't like Jennifer to email her. It must be news on the speech.

Charlotte laughed at the ridiculousness of her life. Jennifer sending her an email to Barbados on a Sunday. As was common at Ashlings, she had clearly found the need to work during her weekend. What was happening to the world?

Charlie opened the one from Jennifer first, keen to see what was so pressing.

Date: Sunday, 25 Feb 14:03
Subject: Private and Confidential

Charlotte,
It's with much regret that I write to inform you that Millicent Gamble no longer works for you in her capacity as legal secretary. She was found to have had dealings of a sexual nature with Jamie Nathan and so consequently we've terminated her employ.

The vacancy Millicent has created has been advertised and until such time as we appoint her replacement, you shall have the use of Margaret Hall, the in-house temp.

I trust you're having a good holiday and I'm sorry to have broken this unfortunate news to you in this impersonal manner.

Kind regards,

Jennifer Newcross

Unable to comprehend fully what she'd just read, Charlotte opened the email from Millie in the vain hope she'd explain it all away.

Date: Sunday, 25 Feb 19:28
Subject: Sorry

No doubt you'll have heard by now. I'm sorry, Charlie. I never meant it to happen. It was only once, the night of the summer ball. We were both pissed and you left early to get back to Warwickshire. Me and Jamie shared a cab home and, well, I'm just really, really sorry. I feel like a right cow. Hope it all works out.

Mils xx

The air conditioning was no longer having an effect. Charlotte burned from head to toe, white-hot heat scorching her skin, decimating her insides. She felt woozy, like she'd stood up far too quickly, as her reactions swung between anger, shame and pure heartbreak. Her ego stalked in the background, woken and bruised. How could she come back from this? She didn't have any fight left.

She got up and rushed for the bathroom but didn't make it further than the potted palm.

She sat on her bed, dazed, not sure what to do next. She picked her Filofax up and clutched it tightly to her chest. How ironic – not five minutes ago she had been confiding her earlier infidelity, albeit more of a minor indiscretion really, to her diary, and wondering whether she should confess it to Jamie. While all the time, he was hiding this bombshell. She felt the anger welling up inside her as she played images of Millie and Jamie in her head. She got up, raced out of the door, and ran to Jamie's bungalow.

'*Jamie!*' She battered her fists on his door. '*Open up!*'

No reply.

She kicked the door violently.

'*Jamie ... Wake Up!*'

She saw a light coming towards her. It was the security man.

'Everytin' all right?'

'No, everything's not all right!' Charlotte spat. 'Does everything look fucking all right?'

'OK, laydee, I tink we need to be getting yuh outta here.' He grabbed her arm gently but firmly just as Jamie opened the door.

'What the hell's going on?'

'*I. Want. A. Word,*' she snarled.

The security guard looked at Jamie for direction.

'It's fine. I can deal with this now.'

The guard stepped back but didn't leave. Jamie tried to usher Charlie into his bungalow, but she wasn't having any of it.

'*I'm not going in there!*' she thundered.

The guard raised his eyebrows, but Jamie reassured him with a shake of his head and some mouthed words, heightening Charlotte's paranoia, fuelling her anger.

'*Stop talking about me like that!*'

'Stop shouting, Charlie! Come on, then, let's walk. Where do you want to go?'

They walked along the beach in silence, Charlotte placated by the fact that Jamie was there, that she'd get her answers. A gentle sea breeze touched her skin warmly and smelled of the ocean. It was always the normal stuff that got to her at these times, the rain, a sneeze, perhaps, or a yawn. All reminders of normal times gone before, of a time she wasn't knee-deep in anguish or pain, of a time she wanted back.

She sat down on the beach, hugging her knees, and buried her toes into the soft sand. Jamie sat opposite, their body language predicting a fight.

'You're gonna have to give me a clue here, Charlie,' Jamie said.

'*I know!*'

'What?'

'*I. Know.*'

'You know what?'

'Oh yes, very clever. You think I'm gonna fall for that one? Give you your answer so you don't give away any other stuff you've been up to?' She picked up a handful of sand and threw it towards the sea.

'OK, all right, let's sort this out. Is it Rachel?'

'You tell me?'

'Charlie, I can't do this. I haven't done anything. I need you to help me.'

'*Millie. I know about Millie.*'

She watched him carefully, hoping desperately it had all been a lie, that personnel had got it wrong, and Millie was messing around. But the story was corroborated by the shock on Jamie's face. He said nothing.

'How many times?' Charlotte asked quietly.

'What?'

'How many times did you fuck her that night?'

'Just once. I was so drunk, I ca—'

'What positions?' Charlotte studied the sand, repeatedly snatching up fistfuls and letting it fall through her fingers.

'I can't remember.'

Charlotte looked at him, venom in her eyes, silently warning him not to lie.

'I want to know. Tell me!'

'I'd had a lot to drink, and it's a long time ago.'

'Where? Your flat or hers?'

'Hers.'

'Did you stay the night?'

'No.'

'Did you cuddle up after sex?' She stood up and paced around, kicking the sand hard, sending big puffs of it into the air with her toe.

'No, Charlie, I was bladdered.'

'Did you have oral sex?'

Charlotte knew the problem with questioning someone over and over was that they might get fed up and start saying anything, just so it would stop.

Jamie shook his head and put it in his hands.

'Is there a chance we can come back from this, Charlie?'

She didn't answer.

'I'll do anything to make it up to you, to show you how much I love you. We can't throw this away. We're too good together.'

Charlotte still couldn't register what had happened, especially that it had happened with Millie, the one person she'd trusted at the office. How expert people can be at lying How cleverly they look into your eyes and smile and be your best friend, while lying all the time

Her mind tried to reprocess her life since the night she'd left Jamie at that ball with Millie. Everything that had happened in the last six months had been a lie. Different things could be read into those times now, like Jamie and Millie whispering together in the office. She'd stupidly thought they were plotting an engagement surprise for her. How wrong she'd been!

Suddenly she turned and fled, all the way back to her bungalow, without looking back. She flung herself on the bed, face down, and sobbed.

There was something nice about hitting rock bottom. It took her back to the basics. If no one else would love her, she'd do the job. When she felt this low, it was as if a basic primeval urge was triggered. Even the crying felt good – soothing and reparative. The energy used to cry snatched away the energy needed to feel pain somehow.

She pushed herself up on her arms and felt in her pillowcase for her Filofax. The next best thing to crying it out was writing it out.

It wasn't there ...

She tried the other pillowcase.

Not there, either.

She cast her mind back to the last time she had it ...

Shit! In all the panic, she'd run out of her bungalow holding it. She remembered putting it down on Jamie's step while she battered on the door.

She got up and jogged back there.

It was gone. Of course it was. She raced to reception. She pushed through the door and there, smiling her Pan Am smile behind the desk, was Rachel.

'Rachel. What are you doing here?'

'Charlotte ... Oof, you look a state.' She eyed Charlotte up and down, shaking her head and tutting. 'Not that it's any of your business, but I'm doing a shift here for one of the staff, repaying a favour ... can I help you with anything?'

'Has anyone handed in a Filofax?'

'Filofax? When did you leave it –1980?'

Charlotte refused to dignify Rachel's snide comment with a reply.

'It's about this big, beige leather, fastens with a press stud, and it's really fat, almost too crammed to close.'

'Really fat, you say?' Rachel's eyes flitted up and down Charlotte's body. 'I'll check, hold on.' She bent to look under the reception desk and rummaged around loudly. 'Nothing there, which is where they usually put the lost property.' She glanced around, picking a folder up here and a pile of post there. 'No, nothing, I'm afraid,' she said, shooting Charlotte a saccharine smile.

Charlotte left reception with as much composure as she could muster, holding it all in, fully aware that Rachel was loving every minute of her obvious panic. Outside, she crumbled, her shoulders heaving as the tears came.

Her Filofax wasn't just a material possession, it was her life. She didn't carry things around in her head, she carried them in her Filofax. If that was gone, so was everything she'd ever thought and felt, and her lists ... She'd had some of those for over twenty years. She'd never be able to remember them all again.

She wanted to grab some paper and start scribbling. Write down everything she could remember from the inside of that leather life wallet. But even though her brain wanted her to, her body wasn't letting her.

She cried harder at the shame of someone reading her Filofax, her innermost core exposed for anyone to see. It would be like someone walking around with her soul on a plate.

She traipsed back to her bungalow. She didn't have the energy to look anywhere else. It occurred to her that Jamie might have it, but he wouldn't have even noticed it in all the chaos when he'd opened his door to her, and they'd walked straight to the beach. Though he might have seen it afterwards, when he went back. But no way could she face another confrontation with him now. If the security guard had it, he would have handed it in to lost property. Looking for it now would be a fruitless task. Instead, she lay on the top of her bed, and cried herself to sleep.

Chapter Forty-Four

Charlotte

Charlotte woke to a loud banging noise. She forced open her eyes, fused together with sleep and dried tears from the night before, and recalled yesterday's events. The warmth of the new Caribbean day flooded through the flimsy curtains, only to be stamped on by the steel-capped boots of her wrathful mind as it stretched and yawned itself awake. Her Filofax was missing. Life was not good.

'*Charlie!*' Rich shouted from outside.

Charlotte sat up, a smile tugging at her mouth, and then she remembered.

Oh no! She hadn't told him she wasn't coming today. What time was it? She grabbed her mobile and tried to focus. It was ten o'clock already.

'*Comiiing . . .*' she croaked.

She tugged at the bedspread, pulling it behind her as she walked across the room, wrapping it round her like a cloak. She opened the door and flinched at the sunlight bouncing off the sand behind Rich.

'Hi,' she said.

'Well, I can see you're not ready.' He nudged past her and walked straight to the kitchenette to put the kettle on.

'Rich, I'm not coming. I tried to find you yesterday to tell you. I ...'

So much had happened in the last twenty-four hours that everything had come full circle. She'd been looking for him last night to tell him that Jamie and she were back together and that she couldn't come on the trip and already, just the following morning, the news had changed.

'Don't say that. You go home in three days and you haven't seen any of the island. Come on, get dressed. I'll make you a cuppa.'

'But last night I found out that Jamie slept with my secretary and ...' Her tears came quickly, their threshold weak. 'I've lost my Filofax.'

Rich took a giant stride in her direction and wrapped his arms around her.

'Why don't you get dressed and meet me outside in ten minutes. It'll do you good. You need to get out of here and you can tell me everything while we drive.' He dipped his head to meet her gaze. 'I'll wait for you,' he said, not giving her an option. 'Take your time.' He planted a soft kiss on the top of her head and a frisson of excitement hurtled its way down her body. 'I'll be the one in the blue beach buggy, by the way. Wait till you see it. Oh, and I've got everything we need. Just bring yourself.'

· · · · ● · ● · · ·

They drove through acres of sugar cane fields, the flimsy leaves billowing like hair ruffled in the wind. The roads were fringed with coconut-studded palms, and bananas hung from trees like edible chandeliers. Charlotte closed her eyes, heightening her other senses, allowing her to taste and smell the saltiness of the ocean as they drove alongside it and feel the warm wind on her skin, like balm on her sore eyelids. Neither of them had spoken a word. There was so much she wanted to say, but she was enjoying the tranquillity and the magnificent surroundings, and the comfortable silence to which Rich and she were privy. The journey had given her time to think, to bring semblance to her thoughts and feelings.

'You OK?' Rich eventually asked.

'I am, actually. Thanks to you ... again. What are you? My Guardian Angel?'

'I'll take that as a compliment.' He scratched his arm as he drove, moving his sleeve up so Charlotte could see his tattoo properly for the first time. Two fish swimming in a circle.

They found a shady spot on the edge of a secluded beach and Rich laid out a picnic. Charlotte felt ready to talk and Rich listened patiently, hearing her version of yesterday's events. She told him about her and Bannister's nightly rendezvous on the jetty, and how loved he made her feel.

'I'd be fine if I could just have Bannister with me all the time. Not in that way. I don't fancy him or anything. He's my nurturer. He looks after me and makes everything OK.'

It seemed odd now, given they'd kissed. But she didn't fancy him. Yesterday hadn't been about physical attraction, it had been about connection. It was a moment in time that felt right.

She knew if Rich found out she'd kissed Bannister, he'd think she fancied him. It felt deceitful not mentioning it. But Rich would never know. Only Bannister and she knew about last night and she trusted him implicitly. He wouldn't tell a soul.

'You're right, Charlie. That's exactly what you need – a perfect nurturer like Bannister. But that nurturer can also be you. You can look after yourself and love yourself. You were born with that love – it's there inside you – you just need to find it again. Happiness from within.'

They packed up the picnic and drove on, leaving behind the tranquil stretches of powdery beach of the south-west coast, where the blue-green sea was as smooth as glass. They drove past orange, green and yellow-painted wooden shacks selling fresh fruit and vegetables, dotted like marzipan fruits along the roadside, as they made their way up the east coast. It was like entering an entirely different world, where white-peaked Atlantic breakers crashed ceaselessly onto giant rocks and jagged inlets.

Charlotte sighed, holding on to her cap, protecting it from the grip of the trade winds. '*Wow!* It's desolate, almost.'

'I really wanted you to see it. You can't come to Barbados and only see the touristy side.' Rich pulled over. 'It's surfers' paradise.'

He looked away from the view and watched Charlie drinking in the panorama. 'You know how I feel about you, Charlie, don't you?' he said suddenly.

She turned to meet his gaze, surprised at the turn in events, not quite sure what to say. Her heart started to pound, but she said nothing.

'I like you,' he said. 'I'd like to see you ... you know, a dating sort of thing.' His usual eloquent confidence had faded away, leaving behind a self-effacing awkwardness which Charlotte found sexy. 'I know it's not a good time for you, but I just wanted to tell you how I feel, especially because you fly home soon.' He looked at her, waiting for a reaction.

'Thank you,' Charlotte said. 'But it's all a bit academic. It wouldn't work after we get back.'

'Because I live in Scotland? That's easily solved. It would be a shame to let a physical barrier stand in our way. We could work something out.'

'No, I don't mean that. I mean me, the way I am. I know you're a psychologist and everything, but you don't know what I'm like. What I'm really like.' She looked away, breathing in the sweet sea air riding over on the wind. 'I'm always nice at the beginning, but it's a trap, and you'll fall into it, just like everyone else I've managed to snare. And before you know it, you'll have a psychopath on your hands who won't let you go to the toilet without her escorting you.' She attempted a laugh.

'I know what you can be like, Charlie. I've had loads of experience of morbid jealousy through my job. And I saw you last night, with Jamie. I've seen the other side to you.'

'You saw me with Jamie?'

'Yeah, the shouting woke me. I followed you to the beach. I was worried. I don't know Jamie. I didn't know what might happen. You were really upset.'

'So now I can add "seen me turn psychotic with boyfriend" to my list of embarrassing moments that Rich Fisher has witnessed. And no, before you ask, I don't actually have that list.' She felt a jolt of pain. 'I don't have any lists now.'

'It'll turn up, Charlie. There's nothing valuable in it, is there?'

'No.'

'It'll turn up, then.'

'I hope you're right.'

Rich spotted something and jumped out of the beach buggy.

Charlotte joined him and watched as he pushed back some foliage to expose a singular bright red flower.

'A Hibiscus flower, I adore them,' he said. 'Smell it.'

Charlotte bent down and inhaled its scent. 'It's beautiful. It's delicate and fruity, but deep somehow ... like a three-dimensional smell that reaches down inside you.'

'Just like you then,' Rich said, smiling.

Charlotte smiled back, allowing herself to enjoy the light and zingy energy pinging around her body from his compliment, adding to the mixed emotions of the day, both sweet and sharp, like citrus.

They climbed back into the buggy and Rich turned to look at her. 'I'm coming to London in April, on the twentieth. It's a weekend. Perhaps we can do something?' He looked at her hopefully. 'I won't give up easily.'

'Oh, I would've loved that, but it's my friend's boys' christening that weekend, in Cornwall.'

'You don't have to make stuff up, you know, you can just say no.'

Charlotte laughed. 'It's true. I'm godmother and everything. It's at a place called Duckpool Mill – sounds gorgeous, doesn't it?'

'I believe you. If anything changes, let me know.'

·········

The sun began to set, the golden light casting elongated coloured shadows over their drive home, signalling the end of their adventure. It started to rain, fat droplets glowing like fireflies in the final honeyed rays of the day. Charlotte looked for a rainbow, and turned her mind to the end of the holiday. She thought about never seeing Rich again and her world went black. Then she thought about not seeing Jamie anymore and she felt nothing, not even a flicker of negative emotion. What was it Bannister had said? *'Don't ignore what's right under your nose.'*

·········

Rich reversed the buggy into the hotel car park and cut the engine, bringing silence, exposing the palpable sexual tension, the air thick with emotion. A kiss was inevitable, but Charlotte jumped out, conscious of the public arena. It had been a veritable kissing-fest of late – she would start to get a name for herself if she wasn't careful. And besides, she was happy in the knowledge they had dinner plans tonight.

·········

Charlotte stepped into her floaty, vintage crepe dress that she'd saved for a special occasion. It made her look elegant and stylish, yet undeniably sexy, a combination she hoped Rich would approve of. She took a long look at her reflection in the mirror. Thin red lines snaked through her eyes, a souvenir from the past twenty-four hours. But there was something else there, too. It was self-respect. She was cultivating it at last. It was time for her to start behaving with dignity. She sat on the bed and sent Sarah a quick text:

`I've dumped Jamie - he shagged Millie! I've lost my Filofax. I'm in love! Want you to think hard about what you're doing meeting TIM. Please, please reconsider. C xxooxx`

She squeezed her warm feet into her sling-backs, turned off the lights, and opened the door.

'*Argh!*' she screamed. 'God, Jamie, you made me jump!'

'Wow, you look stunning!' Jamie's eyes flitted over her body. 'Were you coming to see me, dressed like that?'

'No, actually. Funnily enough, you weren't at the top of my list.'

'Look, Charlie, I'm sorry, I truly am.'

Charlotte watched as he acted out his apology with overcooked sincerity and hammy theatricals. It's a funny quirk of life that when the balance of power finally shifts it's usually when it doesn't matter anymore.

'I believe you. Thanks.'

'I want to prove to you how sorry I am, Charlie. I can't bear to lose you.' He fumbled in his pocket and got down on one knee on the doorstep. 'Charlie, will you marry me?'

Shock stopped her in her tracks, silencing her mouth and her mind. She hadn't expected this. It was exactly what she'd dreamed of since she was a teenager: the soft sound of the Caribbean ocean lapping at the shore, the sun setting, a ring, a marriage proposal and a handsome, eligible man down on one knee.

But that was then.

She closed her eyes, sad at the turn of events but glad, too. Two days ago, she would have accepted his proposal. And then where would she have been in a few months or years' time? Pregnant with the wrong man's child, probably. Instead, she suspected ulterior motive, and could see only pitiful desperation as she looked at him now.

'Jamie, I—'

'I know, you don't have to say anything. I forgive you.'

'*What?*'

'We're quits now. We can put it all behind us.'

'What do you mean, we're quits? You slept with Millie!'

'Yeah, and you kissed Bannister. OK, not quite as sinful, but infidelity all the same, and I know how you feel about that.'

Charlotte reeled. How could he possibly know that? She hadn't told a soul. Her stomach tightened. Had Bannister betrayed her? They'd both agreed it best not to tell anyone. She'd trusted him more than she'd ever trusted anyone in her entire life, including her own mother. He'd started to restore her faith in humankind. He'd let her glimpse hope, allowed her to start mentally shredding her cynicism. He was the beginning of a new Russian doll.

'Charlie, are you OK? What's wrong? I'll get you some water.'

'Who told you?'

'Haven't you seen them?'

'Seen what?'

'I thought you knew. Everyone's talking about them. I can't believe you haven't seen them. They're everywhere! I thought you'd taken it well.'

'*Seen what, Jamie?*' she cried, suddenly very scared.

··········

Charlotte sprinted towards reception clutching a sling-back in each hand, the chain of her evening bag banging painfully across her chest as she ran, the sound of happy tourists burning her ears. She spotted the first one taped to the trunk of a large palm. As she got closer she recognised her writing. Closer still, she could make out a montage of diary entries neatly photocopied on an A4 piece of paper, then another next to it, full of lists. She skidded to a halt, her feet stinging from the rough concrete path. They were diary entries from her Filofax.

She snatched both sheets off the tree. Her 'Long-term To-do List' was there, as was her '*List of Men I've Shagged*'. Words and phrases jumped out at her, but it was the diary entries that stung the most:

I suppose, if I dig deep, I know why I'm dumped all the time. It's like Jas said: I'm too suspicious and paranoid.

Read a great article about electrolysis for nipple hairs today. Have booked an appointment for when I'm home. Now no one will ever know about my hairy nipples.

Jamie has dumped me and he definitely isn't going to get back with me. My heart feels like a deflated balloon ... All I'm left with is a piece of paper telling me about a mental illness he thinks I've got and eleven days of seeing him every day but knowing I can't kiss him ever again ... I was ready to walk down the aisle with him. I've chosen my dress. I want his children. The pram is on order. Nobody can ever know this, but I know, and it hurts.

Jamie stood me up to take the Lovely Rachel (she's so stunning, how can anyone deserve legs that good?) around the island.

A strange thing happened today. First, I got back with Jamie, and then I kissed Bannister.

Charlotte raced off, too angry to cry, stopping at every sheet she came across to rip it down. She hurtled into reception and rattled the door to the beauty salon hard, banging it loudly with her tightly clenched fist. She ran over to the desk.

'Where's Rachel?' she demanded, then stopped herself and softened her tone. 'Sorry. Is she here?'

'No. But she asked me to give you this.' The pretty young Bajan girl put her hands under the desk and brought out Charlotte's shiny, leather Filofax.

Charlotte grabbed it from her and hugged it, caressing it like a baby. She looked up at the clock behind reception. *Shit!* It was half past eight. Where was Rich?

Chapter Forty-Five

Charlotte

'Y'OK?' Bannister asked.

'Fine ... I think.' Charlotte settled on the jetty and peered through the darkness at the slothful navy-blue sea. 'I take it you saw the whole of my life plastered around the hotel grounds this afternoon, along with the rest of the world and his Chihuahua?'

'*Uh-huh.*'

'Thought so. I'm so sorry, Bannister. Obviously when I wrote it, I didn't intend anyone to read it. I—'

'When we kissed, Charlie, I was flattered, yuh know. It took me by surprise, but I always knew it was nuttin' more than a moment. It was a beautiful ting, Charlie, and metinks we should remember it like dat and make no more of it.'

Charlotte was silent for a while, then she shoved up next to him so their thighs touched. She took one of his strong hands in both of hers and looked deep into his eyes, surveying his face, which was wise but tortured, with an ever-present tinge of regret.

'You're so special to me, Bannister. I really love you.'

Bannister kissed her forehead and hugged her to him. A big, hot tear dropped onto her head.

'I love yuh, too, Charlie.'

The usual argument over the stars ensued and Charlotte happily relinquished the name of one constellation if he'd concede she was right about the other.

'You never talk much about your family. Tell me about them,' she said.

He shrugged a little too quickly. 'Nuttin' much to say.'

'I bet your brothers keep you busy.' She batted away an annoying mozzie that was doing an aerial recce of her knee.

'*Aah,* they do that all right.' He gave way to a small smile. 'They can be trouble, but they is good 'uns at heart.' He thumped the middle of his chest with his fist and nodded.

'What about your mum? Do you miss her?'

He shot a look at her.

'Rich told me she died.'

'It makes me sad when I tink of my ma. She was a special laydee. I find it hard dat I wasn't there for her when she died. I should have been there, Charlie, y'know.'

'No, Bannister, I don't. You couldn't have known what was going to happen. Nothing makes a mother happier than their child's happiness, and you were passionate about law. I can just imagine how proud she was. I bet your happiness and your life in England was one of the best things about her life. You should stop feeling guilty.'

'Meybe. I just feel like I didn't get chance to say goodbye. I miss her, yuh know.'

'I don't think anyone can know until they've been through it. But I do know that you're the best son in the world. You gave up your life to step into her shoes and that's the best goodbye you could ever say.' Charlotte leaned over to hold both of his hands. 'But your brothers are grown men now. Living with your grief makes your mum real still and living without it will make you feel like you're bailing on her, but it's time to make your mum happy again, Bannister, by doing something for you.'

He was silent, his hands still in hers. Charlotte could see tears running down his face. She wondered if she'd gone too far, said too much.

'Look at yuh, givin' de advice. I have taught yuh well, my little *protégé*. I tink yuh is ready for de world now, Charlie.'

Charlotte laughed and flicked bits of peeled-off jetty at him. 'And so are you, my dear Bannister, so are you.'

Some reggae started up from behind the canopy of trees fringing the beach. Bannister had brought a hip flask with him – said he was thinking she would need it after the diary fiasco. They swigged rum and discussed everything from jurisprudence to why cuttlefish change colour and what crabs eat. Bannister was an authority on them all. She was dying to ask about Rich, but the moment wasn't right. She'd sat at The Mango Tree restaurant for two hours, nursing a gin and tonic and a basket of bread, waiting for Rich to turn up, but he never did.

She guessed he'd seen her Filofax entries like the rest of the island. Word had spread fast, it had threatened to become a tourist attraction. She supposed he'd read the bit about her kissing Bannister and she knew it would have felt like a betrayal. In his eyes, it had probably cheapened the kiss they shared. How was he to know she didn't go round kissing any old Tom, Dick or Bajan Beach Vendor? And how was he to know that the kiss they'd shared was more powerful than any kiss she'd ever had before? She never told him. And Bannister was his friend, to boot. Double jeopardy.

As usual, Bannister picked up on her thoughts.

'I is feelin' bad about Rich.'

'You knew how he felt about me, didn't you?'

'*Uh-huh.*'

'And you tried to tell me, didn't you? And I couldn't see it, because I was so preoccupied with Mr Infidelity, wasn't I?'

'*Uh-huh.*'

'That's one of the really irritating things about life, Bannister. You can never just heed advice, get it the easy way, you have to live it to know. Irritating, don't you think?'

'*Uh-huh.*'

'Just like you bloody saying *uh-huh* every two seconds. Listen here, Confucius,' she swiped him playfully, 'if you don't stop saying *uh-huh*, I may just have to push you in.' She pointed down at the inky night-time ocean.

'*Uh-huh.*'

The dark water drew her back to her thoughts.

'Do you think he'll be mad with you?'

'Yeah, he's mad all right.'

'I'll tell him it was me, that I instigated it.'

'We all need to take responsibility, Charlie. You didn't force me. Anyhow, yuh can't tell him cos he's gone.'

'*Gone?* What do you mean, gone? Gone where?'

'He checked out this evenin'. Didn't even say goodbye. Not like Rich.'

Charlotte closed her eyes, her heart pumping fast, bright lights and a loud screeching noise crowding in on her head space. She'd finally got close to finding what she'd been looking for her entire adult life, for it to slip out of her hands at the last moment. It was typical of her life. She was like a spider climbing up the side of the bath, always trying but never quite making it. She was weak now. It was time to surrender and accept her lot. It was time to just be. She lay her head in Bannister's lap.

'We have a sayin' in Barbados. Cou-cou never done till de pot turn down,' Bannister said, his voice as soft as silk. 'It's not over until it's definitely over, Charlie, and it definitely ain't over yet.'

···•••••···

'Bridgetown, please,' Charlotte said to the taxi driver as she slipped off her Hermès scarf and oversized sunglasses and stuffed them in her bag.

Being in disguise was fun, but being holed up was the pits, even in paradise. But the sheer embarrassment of what had happened didn't leave her any choice as far as she was concerned. FilofaxGate was out and out the worst thing that had ever happened to her. She'd spent the last two days hanging out at her bungalow with only the wicker furniture, the geckos and the sound of the sea for company, trying not to think about it, attempting, but failing dismally, to write her upcoming speech. Distraction was key. Accepting it was too painful yet. Her inner self, that she had spent years ingeniously hiding, had been exposed, spectacularly.

She had at least managed to swot up for her talk a bit, and for the Q&A session, which she was dreading more than her own death. Bannister had explained a few things to her, but if anything it had only served to panic her more, making her realise exactly how much she didn't know and how much work she had to do.

She'd crept out each evening after dark to see Bannister. Life just wouldn't be the same without him. He was an unadulterated delight to be with and also kept her up to date with the gossip, like how Jamie had been seen sneaking Rachel into his bungalow. It hadn't even hurt to hear it. She found it hard to trust her own judgement, but that little gem of information had proved she was sometimes right.

There was no word from Rich, but she wasn't really sure how there would be. He didn't have her mobile number or her email address, so it wasn't likely. He could, of course, get in touch with the hotel or Bannister, but he hadn't. She knew Bannister would have Rich's number and probably his address in Scotland, too, but she didn't think it fair to put him in a difficult position by asking him for them. It was killing her not being able to talk to Rich, to explain why she kissed Bannister, to apologise for not telling him, and to let him know how she felt about him.

Tomorrow, she was flying home. Today, she was shopping. Bridgetown was a colourful capital, a sunny mix of modern and colonial, with an eclectic assortment of people bustling along, but everyone had time for a smile. Charlotte knew what she was looking for.

She spotted the shabby exterior of Raymond's, the shop she'd been told about. She stepped inside, setting the bell ringing as she opened the door. The place had a cerebral feel to it, with that musty old paper smell that pervaded old bookshops. It was small and dusty and Dickensian, almost, crammed with row upon row of books of every genre.

She sifted through a pile of second-hand books and it was there that she happened upon her treasure, like a butterfly collector stumbling upon a Queen Alexandra's Birdwing, one of the rarest in the world. A first edition of John Stuart Mill's *On Liberty* blinked blithely back at her. She wondered if she dared touch it. In her college days she'd have given up her free periods for a year if she could have owned this book. Jamie would go celibate even now at the thought of being able to spend just a day with it.

The book Charlotte gingerly held in her hands was Mill's most controversial piece of writing. No jurisprudence student's bookshelf was complete without a copy. Charlotte had the 2016 edition on her bookshelf, but here was the 1859 original. You needed only to touch and smell it to know. It wasn't in pristine condition – it had been well thumbed, pored over and argued with over the decades, annotations scribbled in the margins, words underlined, dates circled, every sentence analysed, and it felt all the better for it, like a well-seasoned wok with years of flavour indelibly ingrained.

She wondered about its origins. Had it belonged to a Bajan scholar who sold it to buy his ticket to Harvard, or been left on a bench by a travelling Oxbridge grad? Whoever owned it, she was eternally grateful they'd relinquished it.

The man in the shop wrapped the book like it was a piece of wet fish. She couldn't watch. It cost her only £20 which the bookseller seemed jubilantly surprised Charlotte was willing to pay – and Charlotte couldn't believe there wasn't a nought missing, so it was win-win.

·· · • · • · · · ·

Charlotte sat in her bungalow with her case packed ready to go. She was looking forward to it now, getting back home to her own bed and her quiet corner of the countryside, where she could retreat and lick her wounds. She wondered if that's why she'd moved to the countryside? Subconsciously seeking isolation to shield herself from pain. You can't control nature, so to be among it is freedom. You have no choice but to surrender. An enforced rest.

She unwrapped the precious first edition and cast her eyes down her list of Bannister's Jerry Springer moments to find the quote she was looking for. She wrote a message for Bannister, and slipped it inside the cover.

Bannister,

'The one thing you can control is your happiness. You have the power. Take your dream and make it happen.' Quote by a well-known Rastafarian Jerry Springer and my new best friend, Bannister Bates.

Thank you for being my perfect nurturer, Bannister. I owe you a lot. I wish you all the love and happiness in the world.

Love you.

Charlie xxx

·· • •·•• • ··

Bannister drove the bus to the airport and Charlie sat in the seat behind him, which served a dual purpose: she could avoid sitting next to Jamie and she could chat to Bannister on the way, making the most of every last minute. Bannister was the only reason she was sad to be leaving. They'd swapped details and she'd made him promise to message her soon.

She'd spoken to Jamie briefly after his proposal, just once. She'd told him categorically that it was over between them but that she was happy to be cordial for the sake of work.

Charlotte couldn't believe how much had happened during her time in Barbados. It was like a whole year's worth of events had been stuffed into two tiny weeks, like how she'd tried to cram her entire summer wardrobe into her meagre suitcase. Of course she hadn't worn more than five favourite items, but that was beside the point.

She stood up reluctantly. She couldn't bear goodbyes and this was a particularly sad one. Bannister had taught her so much in their short time together and he felt like a part of her now.

He hauled her case out of the luggage hold under the bus and pulled something from his back pocket.

'I wrote this ...' He handed her a scroll of papers tied with a floppy yellow ribbon. 'Yuh don't have to use it. I jus' thought it might help.'

Charlotte undid the ribbon, unfurled the papers and saw the heading of the Jurisprudence talk she had to make on Saturday. Written in longhand was line upon line of a prepared speech. She scanned down it, marvelling at the content, pace and prose of it all. It was a masterpiece.

'Yuh's gonna have to check a few tings. I did as much as I could on de internet, but there were a few tings I couldn't find. No doubt yuh's got a big fancy library back at dat firm of yours.'

Charlotte couldn't hold her tears. They spilled out fast and silent. It was the most gigantic act of love she'd ever received. It was personal and thoughtful and completely without motive. She reached up and hugged him.

'What am I going to do without you, Bannister? I can't bear it.'

'Same goes, pretty laydee.'

'Promise me you'll visit.'

He hugged her hard but didn't speak. She didn't know why until she felt his tears splash onto her bare back.

Charlotte pulled away and composed herself. She opened her hand luggage and reached for the book, also tied with a yellow bow.

'This is for you. Don't open it now. Wait until I've gone. I hope you cherish it like I've cherished our time together.'

'Yuh is a good girl, Charlie. A smart laydee wid a good heart. Yuh is gonna be all right, Charlie.'

She hugged him again then pulled back. 'I know it's a long shot, but if Rich gets in touch ... well, I'd be grateful if you could pass on my number. I mean I know he probably won't and—'

Bannister put a finger to her lips. '*Shhh*. We have a saying in Barbados. "If greedy wait, hot will cool." If yuh wait patiently, Charlie, yuh will get what yuh want, yuh'll see. Take care, pretty laydee, and remember, don't sweat de small stuff.'

··•••·••··

Charlotte sat on the plane two rows behind Jamie, after negotiating a clever seat swap with a wealthy American widow by assuring her that Jamie was a significant member of the legal team assigned to the king. And he knew all the corgis' names.

She poured a miniature bottle of Merlot into her plastic cup, ripped open her honey-roast cashews, and opened her beloved Filofax. It was time to update her *Long-Term To-Dos* list.

- *Find a great therapist*

- *Freeze my eggs before they buy a Harley-Davidson and leave for Route 66*

- *Tell Mum I love her every day*

- *Tell Robert O'Keefe I am leaving to become a photographer*

- *Learn to be a photographer*

- *Travel the world in search of the best cheese on toast, and publish a photo-journal of the trip*

- *Write to Millie and say 'Thank You, you did me the best favour'*

- *Accept everything as if I have chosen it*

- *Don't sweat the small stuff*

- *Only agree to a second date with someone if I like them, not because of how it feels for them to like me*

- *Never have a Brazilian, ever again*

- *Visit Bannister every year*

- *Stop looking for The One – let him find me*

- *Start collecting 'good' Russian Dolls – tangible ones and ones to live inside me*

- *Keep on top of nipple hair electrolysis*

- *Write fewer lists. Less planning, more doing.*

- *Get a Filofax padlock*

- *Sleep with Chris Hemsworth's younger, fitter, curlier doppelganger – Rich Fisher*

Chapter Forty-Six

Jasmine

Jas pushed open the door of the private clinic and stepped outside, putting her bag down on the gravel drive. She pulled a deep breath in, welcoming in the fresh, wet air of the foggy February afternoon, the little hairs on the inside of her nose tingling with the cold. She wasn't sure how she felt, really. Had she made the right decision? Who knows, but it was done, so there was no point worrying now.

She waited for her taxi. The woman in the clinic had suggested she wait inside in the warm, but she needed to get out of that place. Her phone beeped. It was Charlie, worried about her. Asking her to think long and hard about what she was doing, and telling her that she'd support her whatever. Charlie had always been like that, like a mother hen clucking around, keeping her chicks in order.

Jas remembered when they first met. After her dad's funeral, her mum had put the house on the market immediately and shipped them all out of Berkshire to Surrey. Her first day at school had been inconceivable. Not only had she just lost her father and all of her friends, but her memories, too. Memories that had all been left behind in the home they'd shared with him.

Jas closed her eyes to stem the tears. Charlie had been the only redeeming feature of her first day at St Mary's Primary School. She'd been the one smile in a classroom besieged with frowns and doubts as they peered up at her from their miniature milk bottles as she entered the room. Charlie came bounding over with her white-blonde plaits and kind eyes. She'd held her hand and led her to where she was sitting, so that Jas could sit there, too. That moment of kindness set the tone for the rest of their friendship. Thirty years on, Charlie was still there for her, but she doubted she would be when she found out about her and Grant. Surely even Charlie couldn't find the good in that situation, or the heart to forgive?

The taxi was winding its way up the driveway, just visible under the low mist. Jasmine stamped her feet to keep warm. Even though Charlie didn't know it, she was the one who'd got Jasmine through the death of her father, had moved along the mourning process, shone over the grief, helped to put the guilt in perspective and given her hugs to replace the absent ones from her dad. Charlie didn't know the truth about Jasmine's dad's death even now. She still thought he'd died from cancer. Jasmine hated her mother for making her lie about that.

'Egham, please. To the graveyard there.'

·····•·•····

Jasmine sat twirling the plastic cocktail stick around her drink, piercing it through the slice of lemon every now and then, keeping an intermittent eye on the door and salivating at the thick smell of garlic wafting out of the kitchen. Grant was late, but she wasn't worried. He was too much of a gentleman to stand her up, especially today.

Her stomach was churning at the monstrosity of what she'd masterminded. A scene set for a crime. A crime of passion, yes, but a heinous felony no less. It frightened her how the power of raw emotions could negate moral fibre and rationality so goddamn easily, without so much as a 'put 'em up' from the latter. She knew that no matter how long she sat here telling herself what she was doing was wrong, nothing would make her stop now.

The door opened and a woman with a briefcase walked in. She was alone and dressed smartly, like she'd just come from work. She smiled at Kate, the owner of The Mockingbird, as she entered. *Bingo!* It had to be her. She was pretty and had that innate grace and poise that seemed to go hand in hand with wealth. And, Jas noticed, she was wearing flip-flops. How bizarre!

Next in was Grant, hurrying across the room. He kissed her hard on the lips, making his excuses. He peeled off his coat and Kate came straight over to take it from him.

'Can I get you a drink?'

He looked over at the bar. The lady who'd just arrived smiled at him, not realising he was trying to look at the beer pumps behind her. Grant smiled back.

'A pint of London Pride, please.'

Kate nodded. 'I'll bring some menus over. Would you like a wine list?'

Grant looked at Jas for the go-ahead. She nodded.

'Yes, please.'

He scraped his chair out. 'How are you?' He squeezed her hands, looking deep into her eyes, burrowing for the truth.

'I'm fine, honestly,' she said. 'I'd rather we didn't talk about it. I just want to forget it now. Just give me a kiss and we won't say another word about it.'

Grant seemed surprised but pleased. She guessed discussing your child being aborted while enjoying a cosy meal for two with your mistress – who was actually a friend of your wife's – had never been up there on his wish list. He leant over and kissed her.

'So, what sort of a day have you had?' she asked, warmly engaging him in a conversation about the ins and outs of his working day, listening to scenarios involving people she'd never met and jargon she didn't understand.

He chatted animatedly, full of theories as to why so and so hadn't made promotion, why what's-his-name had flunked his target last month and how the flagging economy was putting a strain on them all. Jasmine kept half an eye on the woman she suspected was Sarah's friend as Grant continued to gambol through his day.

'Jas ...' he said suddenly.

Jasmine took one look at his face and swallowed hard. She took a mental deep breath and prepared herself for what she'd hoped wouldn't happen.

'I can't do this anymore, Jas.'

She levelled her gaze at him, a million different questions and protestations swirling round in her head, but she knew it was no use. That was why she hadn't wanted him to know she was pregnant. She'd known all along it would spook him, give him a taste of what could happen. She was pissed off with Charlie for telling Sarah. If she hadn't, none of this would have happened.

His stormy eyes were soaked with regret and apology, the hazelnut flecks jumping out and goading her.

As if he hadn't hurt her enough, Grant continued, 'I love Sarah, Jas. I've loved being with you, but I can't do it to Sarah anymore.'

Jas thought about the email she'd been sent by mistake, about Sarah's feelings for Grant, about the possibility Sarah might be seeing someone else and the fact she might even be about to leave him. Her mind worked quickly, looking two or three steps ahead, nimbly sorting through the different strategies she could adopt like it were a game of chess.

But as much as she loved Grant, she couldn't take it any further than she had. She'd done enough. You couldn't force someone to love you, she knew that only too well.

·····•·•····

Jasmine sat hugging her knees on the living-room carpet, slumped against the wall opposite her dad's picture, her nightie stretched over her legs, her dainty toes peeping out underneath, rocking herself to and fro, crying desolately.

'It's gonna be OK,' she repeated over and over, focusing hard on the tortured young woman in the frame, comforted by their joint misery, her forlorn expression bringing Jasmine some kind of twisted relief as she cried herself to sleep on the floor.

Chapter Forty-Seven

Sarah

Jinslet crossed my path as she sprinted into school, dragging her little girl behind her. '*Hi, SJ!*' she called, blowing me a kiss as she ran past.

She'd taken to calling me SJ since I'd told her my name was Sarah-Jane. That's what rich people do, don't they, call people by their initials? I liked it, especially because that's what TIM called me too.

'*Oh, buggery! Nearly forgot!*' she shouted back at me, not remotely concerned she'd loudly alluded to the pastime that was anal sex in the primary school playground. 'Can you wait, sweetness? We really must talk.'

'I'll wait at the car. Quick, quick, run like the wind!' I shooed her off.

I took Finn's hand and hummed on our way to the car. Rudy had gone in without a fight for the second day in a row. No tears, no indirect naughtiness. I didn't even have to pin him down on the sofa to force him into his uniform.

As I neared the Jeep, I saw something on the bonnet, lodged between the windscreen wipers. It was probably a home-made bomb, crafted out of cake tins and tied together with cooking twine, placed there by Big Lass From The North in a last-ditch attempt to eradicate me from her life. I sniffed the air for the smell of marzipan – apparently that's what Semtex smells like – but there was no sign.

I walked to the front of the car and saw that it wasn't a bomb at all but a pretty square basket stuffed full of muffins and pastries, home-made ones, tied with a big raffia bow, with a small brown envelope taped to the cellophane.

I ripped it open. It simply said '*I'm sorry.*'

I spun round to see if the benevolent baker was anywhere to be seen and I spotted the unfortunately large rear of Big Lass From The North bouncing up and down as she jogged down the road to her tank.

'*Theresa!*' I yelled and ran after her, as fast as one can with a basket of biscuits in one's hand and a three-year-old glued to one's side.

Big Lass From The North stopped running, possibly because she couldn't run anymore but probably because she knew it was no use. She waited at the bottom of the road, hands in her pockets, looking down at the path.

'Damn these Cornish hills,' I mumbled as I puffed down the road, the gradient making me run faster than I could cope with.

I reached her and stood, trying to catch my breath.

I put the basket down and put my hands, one still clutching Finn's, on my hips in that classic out-of-breath pose. 'Thank you,' I panted.

'You're welcome, pet.' Big Lass From The North smiled.

Yes, smiled! She *did* know how to do it.

I resisted the urge look over my shoulder to see who she was smiling at and simply smiled back instead.

She hung her head. 'I know I didn't exactly welcome you when you first arrived. Had it in for you, in fact. But I was jealous.'

It was my turn to be astounded. Were those words really coming out of her mouth?

She continued, seemingly not wanting to stop now she'd started.

'We all knew you'd been Businesswoman of the Year because Susan' – (Ole Sunken Eyes) – 'used to work in finance, too. Said you were a bit of celebrity in the city. Youngest woman to achieve what you did, headhunted three times a day, your photo in all the business magazines, that kind of thing. And you're so ... well, glamorous.'

I looked down at my scuzzy jeans and mud-splattered walking coat and back up at Big Lass From The North and raised my eyebrows in comic fashion.

She laughed. 'OK, so you were glamorous when you first arrived. But as if all that wasn't bad enough, then you turned out to be good at baking, too. Baking's my thing, and you came along and poached the only plaudit I'd ever had.' She got a hankie out of her pocket and wiped her nose. 'I love baking. I'm good at it. And it makes me happy inside when I watch someone enjoying something I've baked. Anyway, I'm really sorry and I'd like it if we could be friends.'

I went to say something, but she cut in.

'I know all those things I did were despicable, but I really want to make amends and I promise I'll never do anything like that again. If it's any consolation, my husband's furious with me. He's even stopped my allowance and says there's to be no rumpy-pumpy for a month!' She blushed.

I fought back the urge to laugh out loud and gave her a big hug with Finn clutching my leg.

Then I chased a giggling Finn back up the hill to find Jinslet waiting.

'Oh, God, Lola, I'm so sorry. Big Lass From Th ... I mean Theresa left me these on the car and so I ran after her and—'

'SJ, please!' She put up a French-manicured hand to stop me. 'All that ranting is doing my hangover no favours, sweetness.'

I smiled. 'Well, I'm not sorry, because if you're lucky enough and mad enough to have been out drinking on a school night, you deserve all you get.'

'Lucky? Oh, no ... husband's work do. Only sane thing one can do is get fucked.' She grinned mischievously. 'I've got great news.'

I strapped Finn into his seat. 'I'm all ears.'

'Well, my darling friend, the sticky toffee puddings at The Mockingbird went like smoke in the wind. A raving success!'

I clapped my hands in glee but managed to stop myself from doing a little jump as well.

'Kate wants more, lots more, but that's not the really good news. This news is gonna blow your mind.'

•••••••••

I ran into the house to change for my walk. I couldn't wait to tell Marion. I dressed like a ninja prepped for bad weather. Bandana around my ears, woolly hat, walking boots, gaiters, rucksack and walking coat, which I'd bought a size too big so I could fit warm jumpers underneath. Although it appeared to be snug without the jumpers now.

I stepped outside.

'All roight, my luverly?'

It was Nosey Nora From Number Nine. I prickled, PTSD from her judgment of my child-rearing skills creeping around my body like bony fingers.

'This came while you were away.'

She had a knack of making the school run sound like an odyssey, which it probably was for her.

'It's from up cuntree. Well, from over the water, actually.'

Damn, it was from TIM. The goddam woman had clocked the Irish postmark and no doubt already logged it in the diary she keeps on me and my menstrual cycle. I could see the entry now. *'Small rectangular parcel arrived from Ireland addressed just to her. Not heavy and doesn't rattle. Scruffy handwriting, probably a man!'* she'd write, raising an eyebrow to the semicircle of cats sitting along her windowsill.

'Oh, thanks. That's kind of you to take it in.' I said, imagining her running to the postman before he could leave it on my doorstep.

'No bother. I like to help where I can, dunce I?' She stood expectantly. 'What d'ya suppose it is, then?'

I chose to pretend I hadn't heard, which given my headgear could easily have been the truth. I needed to get going on my walk, and if I opened the door again she would be in before you could say "PG Tips, milk and one sugar, homemade biscuit, don't mind if I do", so I took my rucksack off my back and stuffed the parcel in, creating further suspicion and no doubt a double diary entry.

'Thanks, then.' I walked with her to the gate.

I only hoped bloody Nosey Nora didn't mention it to Grant.

I waited until she was out of sight then took my rucksack off again, and ripped the parcel open. It was a DVD of me and TIM bungee-jumping in Africa. I sent him a quick text:

LOVE, LIES & STICKY TOFFEE PUDDING

Hey, gorgeous, thanks so much for present. Will
dust down the old DVD player and watch later.
Can't wait till tomorrow. Until then, my Travelling
IrishMan. SJ xxx

And one to Charlie because I was bursting to tell someone:

Breaking news! Lunch at Larry's (yes, I do mean the
major sandwich chain, the biggest in London) want to
sample my sticky toffee pudding cakes and biscuits!
Fuck-fuck-fuckety-fuck! Wish me luck! That rhymes!
I'm so made for this poem-writing business. Sxxx

···········

'What are you taking that for?' Grant pointed into my weekend bag, which he'd unzipped, poised to slide some surprise chocolate in for my journey.

I stood stock-still, unable to contemplate his findings. It could be one of many things. My brand-new silk basque that had good tit-lift, my fuck-me shoes with heels the length of my arms or the bottle of champagne, which he'd never believe I was taking to Lucy's as it was far too extravagant. Or was it my intimate wipes for a quick freshen up when I got there, which I'd only just discovered existed and had never used in my life before?

As it turned out, it was none of the above.

Grant pulled my small hand mirror out of the bag. 'You won't be needing this if you're going to Luce's. There's probably a mirror on every vertical surface, and on the floor, for when she's doing her downward dogs. You know how vain she is.'

Grant was in the best mood I'd seen him in for a long time. He was fun and carefree and seemed unshackled, somehow. I was wary of this new, rejuvenated Grant, because there was every chance he'd be hankering for sex as soon as I got back from London, which might leave me with some explaining to do.

I'd shaved off every pubic hair I possessed last night while Grant watched the football. I hadn't wanted to do it because of the suspicion it might arouse but it was a choice between not arousing suspicion and TIM being greeted with Grandma's pussy, as I'd acquired more than the odd grey hair since we last met. This subterfuge business was really quite exhausting, both mentally and physically.

'What are you doing, Sar?' Grant asked. 'We've got to get to Exeter yet and if you miss this train you'll have to catch the slow one and mark my words, your muffins will have gone off by the time you get there.'

Grant still hadn't come to terms with living so far out.

'Don't worry, I'm just making sure the house is tidy for you and the boys.' I pushed the vacuum nozzle behind the sofa cushions. '*Anyway*,' I shouted over the noise, '*it doesn't matter if I'm late! I'm only gonna be bumbling around town on my own!*'

I had a feeling it was the tenth time I'd said that in the last twenty-four hours. I was beginning to think I wasn't cut out for infidelity.

'That's the tenth time you've said that. Are you sure you're not meeting your secret lover?'

'*Doh*, Grant, you're so funny today.' My cheeks flushed hotter than the eternal flame. I hung my head and busied myself violently plumping sofa cushions.

'We really don't care about the sofa, Sar. We're lads. We're gonna be yomping across fields, eating our tea by torchlight and spending the night downstairs in our sleeping bags like we're on exercise. I can honestly say we won't spend one single minute bothering about whether there are crumbs down the arm of the sofa.'

My heart sank at the chaos I had to look forward to on my return.

'I know, Grant, but you know what I'm like. I'm obsessional, an extremist. I'm either full on or not the tiniest bit interested. Not a good trait really.' I was wittering, buzzing with nervous energy. 'I'm like it with people, too, come to think of it. I either love 'em or hate 'em. There's no halfway house with me, is there?'

'I'm well aware of that.'

'What do you mean?'

'Nothing.'

'Grant, what did you mean?'

'Well, that's how you are with me.'

'What do you mean?' I pressed.

'Well, you started off madly in love with me, couldn't get enough of me, and now you can't stand me. Haven't been able to for a long time. I'd go so far as to say you despise me, even.'

I was stricken – I felt a stab to my heart. He was right, but not for one moment had I imagined he'd realised it. How naïve of me, how arrogant!

'That's not true,' I said.

'It is. I know it is, Sar. You don't have to pretend. But I love you and I think we can work it out, if we give it time.'

Chapter Forty-Eight

Sarah

I arranged my frothy coffee, magazine and mini-muffins on the table in front of the seat next to me, as a deterrent, praying I could enjoy the solitude of the train journey without a potentially germ-ridden, elbow-wielding stranger as a companion.

I flipped open my mobile and settled back. First job was to text Charlie. I was worried about her. She hadn't sent me an email for days but instead just a load of texts with one-liners giving me snapshots of information I didn't really understand. I'd managed to glean that she was no longer with Jamie, despite the brief reconciliation. It was her speech today and she'd been worrying about it for weeks, so I wanted to say good luck. The last text she'd sent had been begging me not to meet TIM. I'd replied, telling her it was something I had to do, and I wondered if that was why I hadn't heard back from her since.

All roight, my luverly. I'm on my way up cuntree. Back to civilisation - yippee! Rudy and Finn were sad when I left, but Grant smoothed the way with the promise of a new Hot Wheels track and a McDonald's! I'm going to let it go this once.

Tried to pack light but bag is a brick. I'm excited although riddled with guilt already. Please don't

hate me, Charlie, I need you. Sending you a flock
of winged hugs to land on your shoulders while you
do your speech. You'll be brilliant. Just remember,
speak slowly. It's like looking at things through
water - they're always bigger than they really are.
When you talk, it's always faster than you think
it is, so really concentrate on keeping it slow and
steady. You'll smash it! Go, girl!

S xxx

I knew Charlie was right, I shouldn't meet TIM, and the nearer it got, the harder it became. Seeing the boys' faces crumple as the train pulled away this morning had been the worst bit so far. I couldn't find any justification for what I was doing that would still allow me to think of myself as a nice person, and that was hard. It's not a good feeling to know that you've purposely engineered something you know is wrong.

Grant had made everything worse this morning. He was being so caring lately and he looked crestfallen when he told me he knew I didn't love him. I felt like an ogre.

I sipped my coffee and thought back to the last few months and how I'd gradually slipped deeper into a depression, becoming increasingly bitter with Grant by the day. It wasn't his fault he was working away – he was doing it for us. But it still bothered me that he didn't see how hard I was finding everything, how he didn't realise or seem to care that I was crying out for help.

My phone beeped:

It's hard to stay angry with you, but I'm urging
you not to meet him, Sarah. Waiting to go on and
bricking it. Keep everything crossed for me. C xxooxx

My phone beeped again:

Forgot to say - guess who turned up on my doorstep
yesterday. My mum! I was thrilled. Will tell all
when we speak.

Don't do it!

`C xxooxx`

And again:

`Is the country mouse on her way into town? Hope`
`so, cos this city mouse is gagging for her.`

`TIM xx`

It was all too much. I flipped my phone closed and put it away.

······•·•···

I lugged my bag across London on the Tube. I'd be glad to relinquish the bubbly. My heart was banging inside my chest. What was I hoping to get from this? Was I putting myself through all this torture just for a shag? Or was I hoping for a more permanent fixture?

The guilt pangs were coming thick and fast. I wondered whether or not to turn around and run back down the station steps, but the idea of never seeing TIM again was as painful as the bloody guilt pangs. Plus, I couldn't bear the thought of carting my bag back across London without having a drink first. Fuck it, life is for living. My phone vibrated in my pocket:

`You arrived yet, babe? The room's great, good bed,`
`I had a very comfy sleep last night. It will be`
`better with you in it though. I'm waiting in the`
`central lounge. It's got palm trees and everything.`

`TIM xx`

I walked into the huge central lounge, which did indeed have palm trees and a glass roof which let the winter sun flood in. The restaurant and lounge areas were overlooked by the rooms and suites. I knew it wasn't TIM's fault, because he hadn't been here before, but it didn't strike me as the best choice for an illicit liaison. It was all a bit on public view for my liking. I ducked around the corner towards the loos and hoped TIM didn't see me.

I made it. I checked my face, added some sparkle from my bronzer and popped a mint in my mouth. I'd got my intimate wipes with me and now was the time I'd planned on using them but didn't bother because I'd made a decision.

·········

'SJ, babes!' TIM pulled me to him and gave me a great big kiss on my cheek.

'Hi.'

I was embarrassed and I think he was too. It was an odd situation. It was contrived. We sat next to each other on a deep-red corduroy sofa with zebra-print cushions and a waiter arrived to take our order.

'Campari and orange, please,' I said.

'Haven't changed your drink, then.' TIM beamed.

'I haven't had it for about eight years, actually. I'd forgotten I even used to drink it but, being here with you, it came back to me.'

I didn't know what to with my hands. It was all a bit awkward, not at all like the swooping up in arms and undressing urgently in the lift that I'd imagined it would be. On the one hand I felt like a coquettish girl being wooed and on the other I felt like a high-class prostitute about to make a month's rent in one seedy afternoon. On no account did I feel like I was reunited with a man I once loved after nine long, hard years of being apart.

'How ya feelin', so?' TIM asked, intuitively picking up on my nerves.

'Bit odd, actually.' I seemed to have lost the skill of speech. I'd clearly spent too long away from town and life generally.

He smiled and took a long look at me. 'You haven't changed one bit.'

'You neither.'

'I've thought about this moment for years, seeing you again.'

I smiled nervously, apparently unable to articulate anything else, until the waiter returned with our drinks, placing them on the table with theatrical movements as if choreographed.

We had lunch and chatted over old times. We laughed and occasionally TIM put a hand through my hair and looked dreamily into my eyes. I'd fantasised about this moment, seeing TIM, smelling him, touching him, falling under the spell of his witty Irish banter. But I realised as we sat together that some of his attraction had been his unavailability. He'd been an enigma back then, a challenge, something for me to strive towards. The book lover's signed first edition, the shoe lover's jewelled Louboutins, I was never happier than when I was striving.

We declined pudding in favour of coffee, and I knew it was time to tell him.

'Liam ... I don't think I can do —'

'You don't have to say it, SJ. I know.

'I've wasted your time, I'm sorry.'

'You haven't wasted it at all. I've loved seeing you again. Let's just say 'never say never', and keep in touch, eh? Who knows what the future holds?'

·••••••••··

I closed my eyes on the train back to Cornwall, after a much needed relaxed Saturday night with Lucy, and Sunday spent schlepping round London, pavement-café hopping together. I realised that despite not going to the hotel room with TIM, the weekend hadn't been a waste of time at all. It had been relaxing and revolutionary. It had helped me solve the riddle of me. The right person alone wouldn't make me happy. Trying to resurrect a past life had not been the answer. I needed to sort my current life out.

Since having children, and used to being a successful, driven, person, I had turned my children into my job. I tried to make them perfect specimens of childhood. I tried to turn them into bilingual, organic-food eating, perfectly behaved child geniuses. I thought turning them into textbook children would make them happy, and me too. I was wrong. It turns out it's impossible to be a textbook mum and rear textbook children, and trying to didn't make them, or me, happy.

I needed to focus on getting Rudy help. Despite what several doctors had told me to the contrary, he had a problem. I needed to help my children become happy, not perfect. I needed to work on my marriage to Grant, and repair our family unit. And I needed to find out what made me tick. What was fizzing and popping inside me right now? It wasn't TIM.

I couldn't wait to tell Charlie.

·····••·····

I didn't do it, Charlie! How did it go? Tell all.
Sxxx

I flipped closed my phone. And then it beeped. Jinslet.

I've postponed going into town until Tuesday
morning cos Larry from Larry's is on my case for
your wares. Get baking, SJ. I'll be round Monday
night for the goods. Get the Aga lit, Fanny, we're
on! Yee-hah! Lola x

That was exactly what had been fizzing and popping inside me in the past few
days. That was the source of my renewed vigour for life: Sticky Toffee Pudding!

Chapter Forty-Nine

Sarah

I greased a baking tray with one hand and gesticulated with the other.

'So, what do you think? I thought I might ask Marion to help me – she'd love it. I know it's going to mean a few changes, but Finn starts big school in September, so I'll have more time then.'

'Sar, I think it's a fantastic idea.' Grant licked golden syrup off a spoon and dropped it in a bowl of water.

'Really? Because I won't do it if you think it's a pants idea.' I hummed over to the hob, making the third batch of toffee sauce in as many hours.

'Sar, anything that puts a smile on your face like the one you've had lately is a great idea.' He planted a sticky kiss on my forehead.

I shuddered internally and realised that just because I'd resolved to make my marriage work didn't mean it would miraculously mend straight away. There was a lot of work to do and it would probably be a while before I found Grant attractive again, but I was sure I'd read somewhere that you could re-fancy someone, given time. Perhaps, like Juliet, my sexual attraction to Grant was comatose, not dead. I just had to make sure it came back to life before Romeo thought it was gone forever and took himself off to somebody else's balcony.

'I was thinking of calling it SJ's Sticky Toffee Pudding Company. Is that a bit long-winded?'

'Shouldn't it be Hannah Bloom's Sticky Toffee Pudding Company?'

He grinned wickedly and slapped me on the arse, which caused me alarm. Arse-slapping had been known to constitute foreplay in Grant's book. Rudy was at school and Finn at preschool, which meant an invitation for a shag could be imminent. And if it came, I'd have to accept. I'd promised myself I would. But I'd rather spend the afternoon cleaning the oven, the fridge and the toasted-sandwich maker. And there was still the little matter of the undisclosed shaving. I worked faster to keep a steady flow of baking in the oven.

'No! I'll have you know I've changed Charlotte's mum's recipe about six times now and the cupcakes and biscuits I invented myself ... from scratch!'

'Tad defensive, aren't we?'

'Sorry. I do feel bad about it. Hannah guards that recipe with her life, but I have changed it, that's true.'

'I believe you, Sar. I'm sure Hannah will be thrilled to know what you're doing. Why don't you just call it The Sticky Toffee Pudding Company?' He was stalking up and down the kitchen looking for things to scavenge, sniffing at the toffee and treacle fug that filled the air.

'Hey, hands off, fatty!' I slapped him away as he tried to extract a biscuit from the box I'd packaged ready to go. 'You've already had three.' I poured cream into my saucepan like an over-ebullient sommelier. 'There's already a company in America with that name.'

'That's America, though ... or ...' – he rolled his eyes in realisation – 'have you got plans for world domination?' He put his hand up to silence me. 'No need, stupid question. Yeah, I think SJ's is fine.' He crept up behind me, encircling my waist with his hands and kissing the side of my neck while I stirred the hot sauce on the hob.

'*Graaant!* I can't concentrate.' I shrugged to shield my neck. '*Ooo*, is that the post?' I was saved by the sound of letters slapping onto the doormat. 'I'm waiting for the proof for the new invites. How exciting! Can you check, please?'

Grant schlepped off dutifully, readjusting a fledgling erection in his trousers as he went.

'No, nothing from the printers. There's one from Plymouth hospital, though. It's about Rudy. Is everything OK?'

'It's from the consultant. Pass it to me.' I took my sauce off the heat. 'It's an appointment, to see a paediatrician.' I glanced at Grant as he sat down at the table, worried how he might take it. 'I finally found a doctor who agrees with me that Rudy might have ADHD, or similar. And she's referred him to a specialist. It's a really good thing, Grant.' I hurried back over to my sauce, as if it might deflect an argument.

'I'm sorry, Sar, for not listening.' He dragged his finger through the spilt flour on the table. 'And for not helping. There's so much I could have done. Even small things, like giving you support over the phone, talking to you about how you were feeling. I've been so wrapped up in my own life in London that I've forgotten what's important – my life down here.'

I walked around the table and sat on his knee, draping my arms around his neck. 'It's OK, baby. I understand, I do.' And I did. All of a sudden, I did.

'But you've had so much to put up with. Looking after the pair of them is exhausting and you've had to do it all on your own most of the time. And I've been jealous, too. Of you spending so much time with the boys and me not spending enough. So I distanced myself, to make it easier.'

'It's OK, Grant.'

'It's not OK. I feel like a shit.'

I quietened him with a kiss, slid off his knee and led him upstairs to bed.

· · · · ● · ● · · ·

'*Graaant*, can you get that, please?' I called up the stairs, holding my floury hands up.

'*Can't, babes. Just wiping Finn's bottom.*'

'Oh, OK.' I rubbed my hands on a tea towel and went to answer the door. It was Lola.

'Hi, Lola! Come on in.'

'Hi, sweetness. Are they ready for the off?'

'They are, actually. I was just rolling out one last batch of biscuits, but they were extras, in case of any transit disasters.' The one and only time Jinslet had ever been on time for anything, I was running behind.

Grant came trotting down the stairs. 'Who is it, babe?'

'It's Lola. You two haven't met, have you?'

'Ah, you're the lady keeping my wife so busy these days, then.' Grant held out his hand, but Lola didn't move. 'Nice to meet you at last. I've heard lots about you ... all good, although you probably can't say the same about me.'

Lola's hand wasn't forthcoming. He looked embarrassed as he let his arm fall back to his side.

Lola was uncharacteristically silent, transfixed even. Suddenly she jolted back to life. 'Sorry, how rude of me!' She offered her hand to Grant, who shook it warmly. 'Got an awful lot whirring round the old grey matter today, not quite myself. Lovely to meet you.'

Puzzled, I led her into the kitchen. 'OK, here it is,' I said. 'Is that enough?'

'God, yeah, that's ample. Lenny tried the pudding on Wednesday night, and raved about it. Think this is a done deal.'

We carried the stuff outside to her car.

'Keep everything crossed. I'll let you know as soon as I can, but you know what these people are like. He might have to consult everyone from the chairman to the cleaner before he can make a decision, for all I know.'

Jinslet pulled down the boot of her Range Rover and dusted herself down as if the job had been a particularly dirty one.

'But Lenny's a good egg. We summered together as kiddies. Tuscany. Same place every year, incredibly tedious, but we've shared a funny story or two.' She gave me a big hug. 'We're in with a chance, sweetness.'

'Obviously you and I'll have to talk sometime, Lola,' I said. 'You know, about your cut in all of this.'

'Oh no, wouldn't hear of it, darling! Doing it for my new friend.' She winked at me. 'That's you. *Ciao, bella!*'

I waved her off, chuckling at her warm eccentricity but still puzzled by her reaction to Grant. It was like she knew him.

'She seemed nice,' Grant said. 'Bit barking, but nice.'

'She's not barking, she's just filthy, stinking rich. You can't hold that against her.'

'I know her from somewhere,' he said. 'Can't put my finger on it though. Maybe I've just seen her around.'

'Well, barking or not, I love her, she's the best.'

· · · · · ● · ● · · · ·

I picked up the phone. A London number was flashing on the caller display.

'SJ? It's Lola. Are you sitting down?'

'I am now.'

'Good, because I bring news.'

'Oh no, I can't bear it. Tell me quickly – don't do that suspense thing.'

'The man from Lunch at Larry's ... he say *yesss!*'

Chapter Fifty

Jasmine

Despite a good eight hours' sleep, Jasmine was exhausted and in desperate need of more caffeine. It was a cold and frosty March morning and the smell of fresh coffee wafting from the pot challenged her resolve. She was sorely tempted to pour another and wake up a bit more, but there was no time today.

She raced into the bedroom in search of her jacket and shoes. So much for a promotion. If she carried on being this late for work, she'd be sacked. She could get away with it when she was making calls on her South London patch, but not when she was due in the office, like this morning. The MD was down from HQ today, as well.

Now, where were her keys? She just couldn't get it together lately.

A stern rapping noise resonated down the hall. Who was here at this hour? She didn't have time for this.

She opened the door to find an ugly wedge of a man with a shaved head and large hairy shovel hands standing in the hall. He was wearing a black leather jacket and no expression to speak of, a bit how you'd imagine a bailiff to look.

'Jasmine Rafferty?' he asked in a gravelly drawl that could only be explained by a forty-a-day habit.

The whiff of cigarettes emanating from his person confirmed Jasmine's initial thoughts. She took a step back.

'Yes, that's me. Who wants to know?'

'I'm from Bristow & Cross Debt Recovery. Got a warrant of execution for monies owed under a county court judgement.' He handed her the paperwork.

Oh, fuck, he *was* a bailiff.

'Unless you can stump up £12,372.91 right now, darlin', I've come to remove goods to that value.' He plunged his eyes into her ample cleavage.

Jasmine was startled. A judgement? When had this happened? She thought quickly, trying not to become flustered. She'd read about bailiffs somewhere. You didn't have to let them in but, once they were in, they could take what they wanted.

She stepped forwards and then further still, edging into the communal hall. She pulled her shoulders back to tighten her shirt across her chest and breathed a dainty sigh of dismay.

'I can't believe I've overlooked this.' She giggled and traced a finger round one of her shirt buttons. 'Well, I obviously haven't got that kind of cash lying around the house, so why don't you give me a week so I can get the money together?'

'OK. You've got till Friday. I'll be back then, darlin'.' He grinned lecherously and left.

Jasmine slid down the closed door, slumping to the floor. That would teach her to not open her post. She hadn't been able to meet her outgoings for a long time, but rather than face it she'd ignored it, even lying about her income and duplicitously acquiring more credit cards to keep her finances afloat. She'd known her mortgage was in arrears, but she didn't know by how much.

What had she thought was going to happen? Had she thought it was all going to be fixed by a finance fairy with a magic wand crafted from rolled-up tenners? She didn't know. Her head was a mess. Fat tears came quick and silent down her cheeks. Her head might be a mess, but her life was fast becoming an anarchic apocalypse she wanted out of.

She got up and made herself the obligatory cup of tea that all English people are compelled to make in such circumstances. Then she rang work and pulled a sickie, which would appear totally genuine, because promotion-focused Jasmine would never skip work when the MD was coming to town, without damn good reason.

She settled on the floor in the living room with a vast mound of toxic-looking brown envelopes spread out on the rug in front of her.

It took four and a half hours, three slabs of millionaire's shortbread, five crying breaks, four cups of tea and two cups of coffee to open them. She surveyed the six neat piles before her: statements, final demands, court summons, utility bills, mortgage arrears and one miscellaneous pile.

She felt sick. She'd been leading a life of fantasy, spending money she didn't have, dating other people's men. It was like she'd spent her entire adult life putting on a show, playing the starring role in a tragic play, trying to be someone else, not allowing the real her to 'be'.

She knew why. The real her was a writhing mass of hurt and betrayal. The real her needed love and support, but there was no one to give it, so she'd shut the real her away. And then she fell in love and got pregnant, and that was when the real her could hide no more.

She picked up the scissors and neatly sliced up her credit cards, one by one. She sat, numb, on the floor. There was one thing that would solve all of her financial problems, but she didn't think she could do it.

She looked up at the picture on the wall, at the dark-haired girl leaning her face on her hands, looking so doleful, which had always struck Jasmine as a tragedy for someone so young. It was her prized possession, her last link to her dad. She'd sobbed rivers in the company of that picture. It had been handed down the generations of her dad's family. He'd treasured it when he was alive, said it made him think about what was important in life. Ironically, he always said it wasn't the material things that mattered but the hugs and kisses.

She didn't know exactly how much the picture was worth, but she knew it would fetch at least £50,000. It was an original Millais, and she'd had it valued a few years ago, for insurance purposes. What were her options? There was bankruptcy, but her flat would be repossessed and where would she end up? It felt wrong. There were people struggling to afford to eat or heat their homes, while she'd got into a gigantic heap of debt from buying luxury items and living a life she couldn't afford.

It would be immoral not to pay the debt, and she couldn't bear to lose her home. She was frightened. It was in moments like these that relationships came in handy, someone to share the problems with.

She walked over to her dad's picture and eased it off the wall. It was time to sort her life out. She stood awhile, enjoying being with something her dad had once touched and admired. A torrent of sadness broke loose from her body, tears dropping onto the frame. She kissed her fingers and placed them lightly on the canvas. It was the right thing to do.

'In a while, crocodile,' she whispered.

··········

Jasmine sat at her desk and inched a manicured finger down the internal phone list looking for Angela from Swindon's surname. She was glad to be back in the thick of things. Parting with her dad's painting had been so painful that she'd barely been able to look at the art dealer as he made the significant bank transfer. She didn't speak for two whole days afterwards and didn't go to work for the rest of the week. But the thought of being homeless with no one to turn to petrified her, and when you're that much in debt with only negative equity for company, you have to think of something.

She knew her dad would understand. She wished he'd been able to do something like sell a painting to solve his problems, whatever they were – then maybe he wouldn't have felt compelled to do what he did. There was something cathartic about her dad being the one to help her out of this mess. He was there to protect her, after all. She found a twisted solace in that.

On Saturday, Jasmine had watched her mother marry a man who wasn't her dad on a threadbare carpet in a small town registry office. Despite the unromantic setting, her mum had looked radiant and had laughed more than Jasmine had ever seen her laugh. It was on that day that Jasmine finally resolved to start being true to herself.

She'd no longer do anything with a dubious underlying motive, such as protecting herself from pain and rejection. Pain and suffering were part and parcel of a balanced life. They were healthy and entirely necessary for personal growth. You need germs to protect yourself from germs. It was time to strengthen her emotional immune system. Nor would she ever again do anything, or indeed buy anything, in the unwholesome pursuit of feigning success and happiness. Perhaps if she could let her guard down and live like this, she wouldn't need to pretend she was happy, she just would be.

She finished wrapping her Prada bag in tissue and brown paper and scrawled across the parcel in black marker 'Angela Myers, Swindon Branch' and popped it in the internal post. It was time to stop focusing on herself and think of others a bit more. Angela would appreciate the bag far more than she ever had.

Chapter Fifty-One

Sarah

I had a small fight with some particularly obnoxious ivy and eventually managed to knock on the front door of the Georgian manor house that Jinslet called home, but there was no reply. I got the impression the front entrance wasn't used much, so I walked round the back. It was all a bit too landscaped for my liking with stripy lawns and ornamental yew trees peppering the grounds as far as the eye could see. Beautiful but overdone.

I found Jinslet in what looked like a boot room, full of riding boots, dead rabbits and a breath-taking array of wax hats. I followed her into the house, marvelling at its magnificence, chock-a-block with antique fireplaces, ornate ceilings and terrifyingly thick wallpaper, with numerous open fires throwing heat out from various rooms.

Jinslet's housekeeper appeared with two servings of scrambled eggs, smoked salmon and brioche, and two very large Bloody Marys on a tray.

'Tuck in, sweetness. Don't know about you but I could eat the sautéed saddle of a snotty-nosed stoat right now.' She picked up her fork and winked at me.

As lovely as it was, Jinslet's brunch invitation had been sudden and unexpected. I was suspicious and never one to mince my words.

'Is something up, Lola? Would you like a cut of the profits after all, because it's the least I –'

'Oh darling, absolutely positively not, with a capital A, P and N for that! I'm doing it because you're a friend. But there is something up ... I'm just not sure how to broach it. It's all a bit unsavoury, really.'

My stomach flipped. I had a bad feeling. I waited for her to speak.

She put her cutlery down and I grabbed my vodka.

'OK, I'll level with you. I saw Grant kissing another woman. In The Mockingbird.' She looked instantly relieved, but sad.

'*You can't have!*' I said sharply, expelling my gut reaction.

'I did, sweetness. I'm so sorry.' She perched next to me on the silk-upholstered sofa, rubbing my arm protectively.

'But when? How?' It was invalid input. I didn't understand.

'Wednesday night. I got there about seven. He arrived shortly after me and sat with the girl. He kissed her on arrival, a proper kiss, a snog ... a long one. They kissed again across the table, had dinner, held hands across the table a few times.'

My mind was working furiously, trying to sew snippets of doubt together, and recall any suspicions I'd had over the last few weeks.

'But you've only seen Grant once! How could you possibly know it was him?'

As I spoke I remembered Jinslet's reaction when she saw Grant the other night and him saying he was sure he knew her from somewhere. My whole body jolted with pain at the realisation, like a crash of foul-tempered rhino charging in on my organs.

Jinslet passed me a tissue. 'They caught my eye because they were such an attractive couple. She was sexy but sophisticated.' She stopped. 'Sorry, darling, I wasn't thinking.'

'No, it's important, the details are important. Don't hold back on me now.'

'I asked Kate about them and she said they'd been coming since late last summer, always in the week, and they always asked for the same table. The secluded one in the corner. Kate said they were usually all over each other, snogging and eating off each other's forks and stuff, and he wears a wedding ring and she doesn't, so it was a good bet they were having an affair. Us marrieds don't do stuff like kissing across tables and feeding each other, do we?' She was decrying her own marriage in a bid to temper my misfortune. 'They weren't smooching at the end of the night, though. Quite the opposite.'

'Go on.'

'Kate was short-staffed, so I helped out with front of house – cleared a few tables, poured a few drinks. The woman looked upset, teary, mascara creeping down her face. He looked sheepish. I noticed his eyes when he came to pay, pale-green, deep hazel rings with gold flecks. Beautiful. When I saw Grant in your hall, I thought I recognised his face and then I saw his eyes.'

A freight train of adrenaline coursed through my veins. It was all stacking up too high. Already I couldn't reach to knock down the probability that Jinslet was right, my rope of alibi and explanation simply not long enough to pull down the tower of certainty that rose before me. I was too numb to speak.

'If it's any consolation, I'd say from the look of them that it's probably over now. Something went off at that table, that's for sure, because she was perfectly happy at the beginning of the night.' Jinslet rubbed my back tenderly. 'I didn't know who she was, obviously, but when I recognised Grant I phoned Kate and asked her to check the reservation. It was booked under the name Jasmine Rafferty.'

············

I sat on my doorstep, trying to recall the drive home. I'd reeled between crying ferociously, banging the steering wheel, screaming and zoning out altogether. I couldn't believe it was happening. It was too ridiculous, like some kind of hammy farce. I sat picking moss off the cold step. I didn't want to take the problem into the house, because then it would be real. It would be happening in my world and my life would be altered forever.

A bolt of pain stopped my heart dead as I remembered what Charlotte had told me only days ago. Jasmine was pregnant.

··········

I couldn't sleep, the question mark over the paternity of Jasmine's pregnancy acting like the strongest shot of caffeine into my blood stream. I was desperate to get out of the house. I needed fresh air and perspective.

I buttered sandwiches on autopilot like I was on a factory conveyor belt. I made a flask of coffee, washed three apples, and grabbed some chocolate biscuits, which had crept into the weekly food shop and the boys' diet to boot. I crept upstairs to the boys, which was hilarious considering I was on my way to wake them up. I kissed their faces and nudged them awake. It was 1.00 a.m. They could have the day off tomorrow.

They were excited, their sleepy little faces shining with anticipation as they found their torches and pulled on their hats and scarves. They'd never been on a picnic in the middle of the night before. It was an adventure.

I parked in front of the swings and switched my headlamps on full beam. The park lit up like Wembley Stadium. We chased each other round, jumping out from underneath the slide, and we looked for beasties and bugs outside the remit of the headlights, searching them out with our torches. We ate sandwiches on the roundabout, scaring each other with ghoulish noises. We laughed, and I cried, but not so the boys could see.

What is it about going on a swing that makes you feel better? Is it because it transports you back to that magical state of innocence that belongs only to early childhood? I sat on the swing and watched the boys play, laughing and teasing each other, thrilled with their night-time visit to the park.

Their joy only served to harden my misery. How happy would they be without their daddy? Would they be laughing then? What would life be like without Grant? I'd thought about it a lot recently, but as the grim reality curled its fingers around the corner and peeped at me, it suddenly seemed much harder to contemplate.

When Grant had rung earlier to say goodnight to the boys, I'd kept my cool. I was determined not to blurt it out, and I didn't. Nothing could be solved over the telephone. I'd wait. But when would I confront him? My instinct had been right. Isn't it always?

Tomorrow was Friday, but I couldn't confront him when he got home because Charlie was coming on Saturday and this was bigger than a passing tiff about which shelf the cheese should go on in the fridge. I crunched into my apple and resolved to tell Charlie first, on Saturday, to see what she thought, and take it from there.

·············

The boys were playing nicely together with their Playmobil, lining figures up, trading pieces, and sellotaping bits on to other bits, one of their favourite things to do. I took the opportunity to get out of my pyjamas, into the shower, and then into a fresh pair of pyjamas – it was that kind of day. I was towelling my hair when I heard the door open.

'*Hi, babes, hi, boys! Daddy's home!*' Grant sang from the hall, all open-armed ebullience as he rushed in with spade-loads of Friday feeling.

It was only two in the afternoon. Normally, he didn't get back until about nine. My heart thudded. I didn't know if I could do it. How could I pretend nothing had happened, when the something that had happened was so big and ugly. He'd caught me unawares coming home early. I wasn't ready yet, not fully prepared. I couldn't bring myself to greet him, so I began to brush my hair.

I heard him talking to the boys downstairs.

'*Babes, where are you?*' he then called up the stairs, and jogged up when there was no reply. 'There you are ... in your pyjamas? Rudy tells me he hasn't been to school. Is everything OK? Are you ill?'

He kissed the top of my head and the entire contents of my stomach rose to the back of my throat in one giant, swift wave, quickly followed by a rush of anger surfing across the top of it.

'Why are you home so early?' I finished brushing my hair.

'Yes, well, my baby, you may well ask that question ...' He had a childlike happiness about him. He put both hands on top of my shoulders and massaged my neck. 'And the answer is, because I have news ... exciting news.'

I jumped up, away from his hands and made for the door.

'So don't you want to know what my news is, then?'

I turned to see him putting on a mock hurt face.

'What is it?' I mumbled and set off down the stairs.

'Weeell ... I've just handed my notice in. I cleared my desk and I no longer work in London!' he gushed as he entered the kitchen behind me.

I swung around and gaped at him. 'You've *what*? *Why*? And why the fuck didn't you discuss it with me first?'

'I thought you'd be pleased ...' His face fell and his shoulders slumped.

'*Why the fuck did you think I'd be pleased about us having two little boys to house, clothe and feed and no fucking job to do it with?*'

'Sar! Language! The boys!'

'*How are we going to manage?*'

'We'll be fine. We've got a bit put by and I'll get a job, even if it's just part-time. I don't care what I do. And there's SJ's now, anyway.' He smiled cheerfully, seemingly not wanting to give up hope that I'd be as elated as he was.

'*We can't live off that!* It's a fledgling company. It's not even off the ground yet. It won't pay for months, years even!'

'Let's sell the flat in London, then. We could buy something outright down here with the amount of equity in that flat. We bought well. Come on, Sar, I thought you'd be pleased.'

'*I know, you said. And I'm not.*'

'I'm not spending enough time with you or my boys. You need help, you said so yourself. We can't get this time back, Sar. I did it for us.' He smiled again in one last-ditch attempt to win me round.

I had no more to say.

Grant filled the void.

'OK, so we might have to alter our lifestyle a bit, but our quality of life will be so much better. It's why we came down here. Anyway, it's done now. Tom was furious, after all the time he's invested in me and stuff. I still get paid for the next month, though, so that's something. That should give us enough time to sort ourselves out.'

········•·•····

When the boys were asleep, I got out the guest bedding and set up camp on the sofa in the chill-out room, glad of the excuse his job-quitting antics had given me to spend the night away from him. One thing though: the only reasoning behind Grant giving up a job he adored was that Jinslet was right – the affair was over. He was drawing a line under it, and starting afresh. I had to admire him for that. After all, as Jasmine was given to saying, if I'd fed my man well at home, perhaps he wouldn't have felt the need to dine at another establishment. And what a glamorous establishment he'd picked for his meals out.

Chapter Fifty-Two

Sarah

'*Graaant? We're back!*' Sarah shouted, while Charlie plied a very excited Rudy and Finn with chocolate, Hot Wheels and hugs.

'Daddy's in the kitchen, Mummy,' Rudy said. 'He's got a surprise for you.'

'Hope it's not like yesterday's,' I muttered.

Grant appeared wearing my Cath Kidston apron – my favourite. Couldn't that man get anything right? He took Charlie's coat from her.

'Good to see ya, Charlie. Great tan, babes.' He looked her up and down admiringly.

I tensed. His remark rankled. A line of hairs stood to attention on the back of my neck and a cold shiver ran through me. Grant lavishing attention on another woman, even Charlie, was too close to home today, adding to the vivid pictures already running through my mind on a loop, like a bad home movie.

'Now, girls,' he said, 'I want you two to relax. You don't see each other often, so make yourselves comfy and the boys and I shall attend to your every need. We're at your service.' He bowed regally and smiled wide, lines crinkling round his greeny-brown eyes, Judas eyes, that had condemned him so readily..

'Sounds good to me.' Charlie looked at me for approval.

Grant was trying hard. I had to find it in me to give him a chance.

'Why, thank you.' I smiled back.

Charlie and I sipped our rum cocktails (Grant's surprise, in honour of Charlotte's recent trip) and caught up properly on the last six months of not seeing each other.

'So how did your talk go?'

'I got a standing ovation!' Charlie curled her legs around and snuggled into the sofa. 'A proper, everyone on their feet, everyone clapping, standing ovation. Can you believe it?' She beamed.

'Oh Charlie, that's incredible, and yes, I can believe it, because you're brilliant. I knew you would do an amazing job. You're so much smarter than you realise.'

'Well, like I was saying, it wasn't really me! Bannister wrote it.'

I drifted off in my head for a moment, never far from my troubles. 'So what about your mum then?' I asked, forcing enthusiasm. Poor Charlie, I wasn't the best company this weekend.

'I know! How about that then? You should have seen my face when I opened the door and she was standing there. It was a real moment actually. And she was proud of me up there on the stage, being all lawyery. It felt good.'

'Did you tell her you were upset she wasn't coming then?'

'Yeah, I rang her.' Charlie said. 'I thought it only fair she knew how I felt. It seemed deceitful harbouring bad thoughts and not giving her the opportunity to give me her side of the story.'

'And how did she take it?'

'Really well. I think she kind of knows she's got issues, but that generation aren't like us, are they? They'd never dream of spending money on a therapist. They live in denial and get on with life. Anyway, Rich helped me to see my parents' side of things and I don't blame them anymore. Well, maybe I'm not completely there yet, but I'm getting there.' Charlie took a sip of her cocktail and looked into the fire. 'Mum has always put Rog before me because that's what she'd had to do, from the age of fifteen. It's hard to change such formative behaviour. But she missed Rog's bowls tournament for me, so that's a start.' She smiled.

'I'm so pleased for you. Sounds like you're really working through stuff.'

Charlotte picked at the loose cotton on the scatter cushion she was hugging. 'I've made an appointment with a therapist for next week, so we'll see what happens.'

'That's a great step forward, Charlie.'

'I've got a lot of work to do, but the main thing is I've admitted it now.' She laughed sardonically. 'I've been trying to control boyfriends for years now – those who'd let me, anyway.' She looked ashamed. 'But because I packaged it all up in "it's because I love them so much" gift wrap, my mind fell for it, allowing me to carry on. It's amazing what your mind can let you do, isn't it?'

I nodded, careful not to agree too much in case I upset her. It was OK to wax lyrical about your own faults, but not so nice when someone else did it for you.

A glowing ember spat onto the hearth and disintegrated. Charlotte's face glazed, thick with melancholy.

'No word from Rich yet, then?' I asked, interpreting her wistful look.

'No, nor likely to be, either. I well and truly fucked that one up, didn't I?' She put her hands through her hair. 'I miss him.'

'What about getting in touch with him?'

Grant came in to offer more drinks, tend to the fire, and generally fuss round the room, tidying and collecting glasses.

'I don't have his number, or any details,' Charlie replied. 'I hate that I haven't been able to explain what happened, and say sorry. But if he was interested I think he'd have got in touch with me by now. I told Bannister to give him my number if he asked.' She looked into the fire. 'Nope, it looks like my eggs are all going to die a sad, lonely life, with no one to even notice they've upped and gone off round the world on a SAGA cruise.'

Grant feigned a "dying" face from behind the sofa, theatrically slashing his throat with his hands, taking care that Charlotte couldn't see.

I let out a snort of laughter.

Charlie spun round to see what I was laughing at. 'What are you two up to?' she asked, overtly happy that we were getting on so well, like a proud mother duck watching her ducklings swim off ahead.

'Sorry,' I said. 'Grant's just messing about.'

Charlie grinned. 'Anyway, never mind. Plenty more fish and all that.'

'*Um* ... talking of slippery things, what about Jamie?'

'Don't know, really. And, dare I say it, I don't care. We don't have much cause to see each other at work, but I do know his job's in the balance. They're just waiting for him to put a foot out of line. He won't be making partner, that's for sure.'

'What about the boss? Is he angry with you?'

'*Nah,* any black marks I had against me were all wiped away with Bannister's wonderful speech! Robert was in raptures over it. I'm not bothered, anyway. I've realised Law's not for me. I'm going to follow your lead and do something that makes me happy. I want to bum around the world taking photos of people. Except I can't yet, because I haven't got any cash. But I thought I'd settle for the next best thing and enrol on a photography course. Anyway, anyway, enough about my sad spinster existence, what about you? How crazy your life is right now! Lunch at Larry's!'

I beamed raw happiness. It was the one good thing at the moment. That, and the boys. 'Let's go for a walk, I'll show you the mill.'

··········

It was good to get out of the house. I was worried about telling Charlie about Jasmine and Grant, because I knew the deceit was nearly as much hers as it was mine. Jas was her best friend and it would hurt Charlie badly.

Spring seemed to have arrived barely before winter had time to get its coat off and the hay meadow was awash with show-stopping colour to prove it. We halted at the track that led down to the mill and took in the view. The moody March sea presided over the valley, with verdant young shoots dotted everywhere, the stark black beach holding court to line upon line of white seagulls. We stood a while and watched, marvelling at a buzzard circling serenely overhead, until the crow Mafia arrived to chase it away.

'*Wow!*' Charlie exclaimed, as she drank in the carpet of wild flowers swaying thickly in the Cornish breeze, a patchwork of white, blue and pale yellow. She closed her eyes and took in the smell. 'It's breath-taking. I don't usually take landscapes, but ...' She unhitched her rucksack and got out her camera, altering the lens, framing the view, and taking some photos, a tiny smile pulling at her features.

I pointed out Marion's house and we continued down onto the beach, letting the waves roll over our wellies. I opened my mouth to start the conversation about Jas but thought better of it. I couldn't tell Charlie on the beach – I didn't want my beach tainted. I didn't want to tell her at all. I wanted to shield her from it. She'd been through enough. But I'd only be adding to the hurt if I didn't.

I waited until we were on our way back up the track.

'Grant's been having an affair,' I blurted out, not able to hold it in any longer. 'With Jas.'

Charlie stopped dead. '*What?* What makes you think that?'

I stopped, but didn't look at her. 'It's true.'

'Don't be stupid! Who told you that?'

'Jinslet did. She saw them in The Mockingbird ... kissing.'

'The Mockingbird? That's where Jasmine goes ...' She trailed off. 'Isn't that where your cakes are being ... Oh my God, Sarah, I can't believe this. It can't be true.'

'It is.' I was sanguine – I'd had time to digest it now.

'Oh my God. The baby. Jasmine's pregnancy, was that ...?'

I shrugged. 'I don't know.'

'She had a termination. I know that.' Charlie shook her head. 'I haven't seen her since I've been back, she's been too busy, but we spoke yesterday. She didn't say anything.'

'Well, of course not, why would she? She's not going to tell you, is she?'

'How could she do this? How could Grant do this? Oh, Sarah, honey, I'm so sorry.' She reached out and hugged me hard, then held me at arm's length. 'But you and Grant, back at the house? I don't understand.'

'He doesn't know I know. I only found out two days ago.'

'What? You found out and you haven't told him? Bloody hell, Sarah! Move over, Meryl Streep. I'd never have guessed anything was wrong, let alone something this big. Jesus, I could never do that.'

'You'd be surprised, Charlie. Children change everything. I think it's over between them, anyway.'

'It must be. He can't see her now he's not in London.'

'Exactly. I've come to a decision.' I smiled. I felt in control. 'I want to know what you think.'

'Don't be rash, honey,' Charlie blurted out. 'The trauma's too great at the moment. You can't think straight, you can't be rational right now.'

'Wait, hear me out.' I started walking again. It was nearly dusk. 'I'm going to confront him. But I don't want to know the nitty-gritty.'

Charlotte put her head down and watched her wellies squelching in the mud. Her silence corroborating what we both knew: she'd be the complete opposite.

'Then after I've told him, I'm going to suggest we never mention it again, and wipe the slate clean and start over. It's either that, or leave him. And I can't do that to the boys. Not yet. We have to at least give it a try. Besides, I'm partly responsible.'

'No, Sarah, you can't say that! How?'

'I pushed him away, Charlie. I didn't want sex, I wasn't nice to him anymore, didn't show I cared. It's all been about the boys, ever since they were born. So in a way, I can't blame him. OK, so I'm angry now, but that will pass. If for no other reason than I have to do this for our children.'

'Well, I know this might surprise you, but I agree. What you've had in the past is worth fighting for. The boys are worth fighting for.'

I looked at her, eyebrows raised.

'Just because I couldn't do it doesn't mean I don't think you should,' she said. 'I don't know how you're ever going to trust him again though.'

'Neither do I. We'll have to work it out between us.'

'I don't know about you but I'm not sure I can ever forgive Jas. It's the ultimate deceit.'

'I know. It's a low blow even for her. She's put your thirty-year friendship on the line. And for what?'

'For love, I presume. We've all been guilty of thinking the love of a man is the sole answer to our happiness. But it's not.'

Chapter Fifty-Three

Sarah

Six weeks later ...

'I can't believe how quickly it's gone,' I said, excited the christening had finally arrived.

Charlotte was fidgeting in her seat. 'Got it!'

'What's that?' I asked.

'I don't know, but it was sticking its hand up my arse.'

'You should be so lucky.'

'You're not wrong.'

I glanced at what she was holding.

'Oh, it's a Power Ranger. Yeah, they have a nasty habit of doing that. Throw it in the back.'

'What? Throw it? Just randomly throw it in *your* car?'

'Yeah, I'll sort it out after the weekend.'

'I'm excited,' Charlotte said, hurling the 3-inch Action Hero over her shoulder. 'Wait till you see my new shoes. I splashed out. Russell & Bromley sling-backs. You're gonna love 'em.'

'Those were the days. When I didn't live in a shopless void with only Cornish pasties and fudge for sale.' I gave a wistful sigh. 'My shoes are from Sainsbury's.'

We giggled.

Sarah knew the seven weeks since Charlotte had returned from Barbados had been torturous. Charlotte still hadn't recovered from The Lovely Rachel posting her Filofax entries everywhere, for the world to see her vulnerabilities, and she was still pining for Rich.'

'Have you seen Jas?' I asked Charlotte.

'No, but I've spoken to her.'

'And?'

'I didn't have to say anything. She broke down on the phone, told me everything. Don't worry, I pretended I didn't know.'

'Thanks.'

'She said she feels awful.'

'I bet she does. No one's husband to shag on a cold, wet weeknight any more, the poor love!'

'Think she's having a bad time of it. She even told me stuff about her childhood, stuff I never knew. Apparently, her dad hanged himself and she was the one who found him. She was only eight. They told everyone he'd died from cancer. Says that's why she's got issues with rejection and stuff. That's the reason she's always gone for married men.'

I said nothing. There was nothing I could say in the wake of that news – no one deserved that.

'I feel sorry for her, but I feel bad for you, too,' Charlotte said. 'I still can't bring myself to see her. Told her I needed some time to think about our friendship. How are things, anyway?'

'Good, actually. Really good. Grant's loving being a house husband. He's making a great job of it as well, except he's turned into Annabel bloody Karmel, marinating anything he can get his hands on. What I'd give for a plain and simple spag bol right now.'

'You think it's gonna work, then?'

'What, SJ's or my marriage?'

'Both.'

'SJ's is phenomenal. It's taken off. The cakes and biscuits are going down a storm at Larry's. They loved my strapline – *Happiness From Within.*' I laughed and indicated left. 'It's hard to keep up with demand actually. And Duckpool Mill is the most idyllic base for the business. I didn't think for a minute that Marion would say yes, but it's changed everything. She's amazing. She works really hard. She's dressing differently and everything. She even tells jokes. We gather round every day at coffee break for Marion's joke *du jour*.'

'Who's we? How many have you got working for this empire of yours?'

'There's five of us now. Any more and we couldn't all fit in Marion's kitchen. I've made Big Lass From The North supervisor and she's working it, baby, strutting her stuff. I was worried at first, thought Marion and she might clash, but they're like best buds. I'm like a spare part half the time.'

'I don't believe that for one minute.'

'It's true. As for Grant and me? Yeah, it's OK. But it's too early to tell if we'll make it or not. We do have regular sex now at least. Can't say I enjoy it much, but we're having it, which was more than before.' I pulled into the drive. 'Oh, before I forget, you've got to promise solemnly that when you see Big Lass From The North at the christening, you don't call her that.'

'Jesus, Sarah, what do you take me for?'

·····•·•·····

The service was poignant. It went without a hitch and the boys were notably on their best behaviour, against all the odds, even when the vicar doused them with church-cold water. Reading my poem to my babies had moved me to public tears, not something I was accustomed to. Grant and I felt closer than we had in a long time, and now we were snaking down the track to Duckpool Mill, to celebrate our family.

The marquee we'd hired was spic and span, attached to the side of the Millhouse, a creamy white mirage against the yellows and greens of the gorse on one side, and the patchwork of colour from the spring flowers that carpeted the meadow on the other.

Jinslet appeared with a silver tray full of aperitifs she'd invented, and had named 'The Jinslet' no less, after I'd confessed my nickname for her.

'Oh Sarah, I sobbed the whole way through your poem,' Charlotte said, giving me a big kiss on the cheek.

'Thanks, godmother. Great reading, by the way. Have you ever thought of doing any public speaking?' I laughed and then realised she hadn't been introduced to Jinslet. 'Lola, I'd like you to meet Charlie.'

'Jinslet. Please!' Lola demanded, positively in love with her new moniker.

I left them to it and stepped back to survey the scene. I wanted to drink the occasion in, etch it indelibly into my brain, to be called upon whenever I wanted the company of a soft, warm memory to keep me going. All the children had quickly formed a pack and were running around the room. I watched Rudy roar with laughter at Finn who'd pulled his trousers down to bare his little white bottom to Grant's Great-aunt Joan as she stuffed an artichoke hors d'oeuvre down her gullet, oblivious to what was occurring at knee level.

The room was exactly how I'd envisaged it, all those months ago. Flowers everywhere, quintessentially English flowers, blues, whites and limes, mirroring the wild flowers outside.

The christening cake was built three tiers high from sticky toffee pudding cupcakes, of course, all initialled with an R or an F. Marion had painstakingly iced each and every one of them, and had also been responsible for the pretty LED tea lights dotted everywhere, creating a magical child-friendly candle-filled room. But the best gift from Marion was the sculpture she'd crafted for us. It was a family of four, made from bronze, entwined in one another. Contentment and love radiated out of the metal impression. A lone tear dropped on my face as I looked at it. She'd given it to me yesterday, knowing I wouldn't have the time to appreciate it today, and I'd sobbed. I'd cried for her and I'd cried for me. The sentiment and the hours of love with which it was meticulously crafted were testament to Marion's and my connection. It had been one of the most touching moments of my life.

'What are you doing skulking over here, missy?'

'Oh, you made me jump.' It was Marion with a "Jinslet" in her hand. Marion was teetotal. I wondered quickly whether to tell her about the vodka in the cocktail she was drinking, or just keep quiet. I plumped for the latter.

'That's because you were away with the fairies.'

'Sorry, I was just admiring your gift ... again. I don't know how to thank you. And I don't just mean the sculpture. I mean for everything you've done for me.'

Marion held my gaze. 'You've given me my life back, Sarah. There's no bigger thank-you than that.' She gave my wrist a quick squeeze then wiped a hand deftly across each eye, as I did to mine, public shows of affection something neither of us enjoyed. 'Come on. Jinslet's pouring the champagne ready for the toast and I definitely need to swap this for a glass of that. Have you tasted this thing? How much vodka?'

'*Ladies, gentlemen and kiddies!*' Jinslet announced loudly, balancing on an upturned orange crate in her diamond-encrusted flip-flops, slicing through the noise with her cut-glass tones, commanding silence. 'Does everyone over the age of eighteen have a glass of bubbly in their hand?'

'*Yes!*' came the resounding reply.

'Then pray silence for Sarah and Grant, who'd like to say a few words.'

Bring-bring!

Jinslet's head spun round, incredulous someone could commit such social suicide as leaving their phone on during such an occasion.

'*Shit!*' said Charlie, then burned with embarrassment. 'Some godmother I am!'

Chapter Fifty-Four

Charlotte

Charlotte moved to the back of the marquee to check her phone. She'd never been able to ignore a text:

How you doing, pretty lady?

Bannister! Charlotte glanced down the marquee at Sarah and Grant. She was sure they wouldn't mind if she nipped out. She couldn't risk Jinslet catching her reading a text. She had a feeling the woman might publicly slap her to death with her flip-flops.

She sneaked out, relieved to be in the fresh air. There was something stifling about being at a party on your own ... again. She leaned against a wall to read the message.

Can't find the words to describe how I felt when I opened your present, Charlie. You're one special lady. Missing you, you know. The jetty's not the same without you. Hope to see you soon, though, pretty lady. Thinking of coming back to study. All down to you. Thank you.

Oh, and just to let you know, Rich has been in touch. All sorted with me and him, but he's going to Australia to live. Got himself a big new job over there. He's missing you, Charlie.

```
Hope you're doing well. And remember, you are
master of your own destiny. Grab it while you can.
Rich could be a start to your 'good' Russian doll
collection. He's one of the good ones. And you and
him? It's meant to be. I've never been so sure of
anything. I'll forward you his number.
Love ya. Bannister x
```

Charlie crouched down and put her head on her knees. Her tears dropped one by one. Panic rose inside her at the thought of Rich going to Australia. Every day for the last seven weeks she'd hoped he would ring her or email her, that he'd get in touch somehow, anyhow. She prayed it wouldn't be over before it began – not something as special as they had.

But he hadn't got in touch, and now she knew he wouldn't. Not only did she not have him, but she didn't have the hope that had kept her going now, either. She straightened up and breathed deeply.

Another beep: Rich's number from Bannister.

She had his number now. She could finally ring him to apologise, and tell him how she felt about him. But now he was going to Australia. There was something of the Romeo and Juliet about this. And if he had been missing her, why hadn't he rung her, to give her a chance to explain? He wasn't the shy, retiring type. If he'd cared for her, like she did him, he would have been in touch.

As she turned to go back, her mobile beeped with another text. It wasn't a number from her contacts. What now? More "Mum, I've lost my phone" scams? She read it, anyway:

```
I've left something for you on the stile.
```

She looked around, warily. Was this a joke? Or something more sinister? And there, on the top step of a pretty slate stile, she saw a large bouquet of hand-tied flowers. She walked over and picked them up, nuzzling her face into their centre, the paper-thin petals soft against her skin, stroking away her pain. The flowers were bright, vibrant and if she wasn't mistaken, Caribbean. She gasped as she spotted a Hibiscus, the flower she now loved so much. Who had done this?

She turned over the tag and her heart jumped. The card read simply: *Charlie, holiday thoughts. Rich x*

Rich? But how? Bewildered, she looked around.

Then she saw him, alone on a low wall, his back to her.

She walked over. Took a deep breath.

'Do you mind if I join you, or is somebody sitting there?' she asked, and hopped onto the wall next to him.

'Only Mr Invisible, but I'm sure he won't mind if you sit on his lap.'

He'd remembered.

'I'm going in a minute, so you can have it all to yourself then,' he continued, quoting their first ever conversation word for word, from the cricket pitch in Barbados, taking her lines.

'Oh, right. I'm Charlotte, by the way.' She held out her hand.

'Hi, I'm Rich.' He took her hand in his and gently pulled her off the wall to face him.

'I need to explain, there's so much I want to say,' she began.

'Not now,' he said, and pulled her to him, silencing her with a kiss.

She sank into his arms, revelling in his smell, tasting his sweet mouth with her tongue, running her fingers through his curls. Goosebumps shot up and down her body like rows of falling dominoes, as she immersed herself in the purity of emotion she could feel emanating from him.

They stopped kissing, their foreheads locked.

'How did you know I was here?' she asked.

'You told me in Barbados, don't you remember? This is the weekend I was supposed to be in London.'

'And why aren't you?'

'My life's changed since Barbados. I've got a job in—'

'Australia. I heard.'

'I couldn't leave without knowing if there was a chance you wanted to be with me.'

She looked playfully into his eyes. 'Oh, I wanna be with you all right, mister, but do you wanna be with me?'

'*Hmm*, let me think. I've travelled from Scotland to Cornwall, missed the England match at Twickenham with my mates and haven't eaten since breakfast cos I was too frightened to stop in case I didn't make it here in time. Yeah, I think it's a clear-cut case of the "wanna-be-with-someones".'

'But what about the Bannister stuff? We should talk about it.'

'No need. I was hurt back then, but I understand now.'

'It was Bannister who helped me see. I've spent years looking for someone to make me happy, which has clouded my judgment in the past. I continually compromised on personality traits and incompatibilities, masterminding happiness, because I didn't think anyone would ever love me, not truly. So I thought I had to mould myself to whoever I could get. Kissing Bannister helped me realise I should think more about what was right in the moment, without agenda. Both you and Bannister helped me realise I simply had to love myself first, and the rest would follow. I instigated the kiss with Bannister. I had no desire for a relationship with him, or even sex. I kissed him because I was so fond of him, and because it felt right in that moment.'

Charlotte shuddered in the breeze and Rich peeled off his jumper and handed it to her. She pulled it over her head and wrapped her arms around herself, feeling Rich's warmth spread around her body.

'I finally understood that although I wanted to be loved and thought my hope of happiness lay in that, to be truly happy I have to make myself happy, not rely on someone else to do it for me. Does that sound stupid?'

'It sounds like the most sensible thing you've ever said.'

'It was never about finding Mr Right, like I thought. That was an impossibility if I didn't love myself first.'

Rich nodded, watching the gulls surf the wind..

'We're all the same, you know, Charlie. We've all got issues.' He pulled up the arm of his T-shirt to show her his tattoo, two orange fish in a circle, one swimming up, one swimming down. 'In Ancient Japanese history koi carp symbolise perseverance in adversity, strength of purpose, that sort of thing. If the fish is swimming up, it means you're trying to overcome hardships. If it's swimming down, you've already overcome them. I think that sums up life. We're all battling something. You're no different, Charlie, except perhaps you're brave. You're stoic like the koi. You battle on, trying to sort it, whereas a lot of people channel their energy into ignoring their faults. That doesn't mean I think your behaviour in the past has been right – I don't – but I know the core of you is beautiful.'

All she'd ever wanted was for someone to understand her. For someone to know that she despised being that horrid person. For someone to understand that she was an abuser and a victim all wrapped up in one body. Only she was a reluctant abuser, and she didn't know what to do about it. She had always worried that she was like her dad. A watered-down version maybe, but like him all the same, and that had stopped her loving herself. But she'd realised lately that there was a big distinction between them. She had acknowledged her problems and was going to change. Her dad had done neither.

She thought it was an impossible feat to find someone who'd understand all those things. After all, it was human nature to see bad behaviour and not to look beyond that. Because if you look at the whys, it's like you're justifying the abuse somehow, making it OK, but that's not true.

Rich pulled her tight to him, and she cried, with relief, happiness and the sheer joy of feeling proper love at last.

'I'm not sure I should tell you this,' Rich said, as they made their way into the marquee.

'Go on. I'll show you my knickers if you do.'

'What makes you think I want to see your knickers?'

Charlotte nodded at Lola who was standing by the entrance with a tray of cocktails, extolling the virtues of 'The Jinslet' to anyone passing, and eyeing Rich appreciatively. She gave Charlotte a wink of approval as they meandered past and went inside.

'You can't anyway.' Charlotte smiled. 'Because I'm not wearing –'

Charlotte and Rich swung around.

Everyone turned towards the door from where the unmistakeable crash of breaking glass had come.

Jinslet stood there, empty tray in hand, chards of glass and slices of wet fruit down at her soggy feet.

'*Jas!*' Charlotte cried, her hand flying to her mouth.

Jasmine stood in the doorway, the afternoon light silhouetting her frame, nicely showcasing her burgeoning body and her baby bump.

Charlotte dropped Rich's hand and hurried back to her.

'What are you doing?' she hissed, trying to usher her out of the tent.

But Sarah had already seen her.

She stalked up to Jasmine, with Marion close behind.

'Is it Grant's?' she asked simply, without a hint of malevolence.

Jasmine was visibly shocked, seemingly not realising Sarah knew, but she regained her ice-cool calm quickly enough.

'Where is he? I want to talk to him.'

'No.' Sarah was cold, detached, and resolute. 'I want you out of here. You're not welcome.'

Rudy attached himself to Sarah's side, pushing his head into her tummy, pressing for a cuddle.

'Look, Sarah, can I talk to Grant please? Just one minute ... please?' Jasmine's voice was softer now, her eyes pleading. She brushed a hand through her uncharacteristically messy hair.

Finn was next to race up, grabbing Sarah's leg, seemingly aware something scary was happening. Hot on his heels came Nosey Nora from No. Nine, no less, who looked like she was going to pull up a chair for a ringside view.

'No,' Sarah said flatly, not a quiver in her voice.

'But he doesn't know ... about the baby.'

Rich stepped in. 'Look, why don't we sort this outside, away from the children.' He motioned at the two frightened boys clinging to their mummy.

'And who are you?' Sarah turned on Rich and tipped her head violently in Jasmine's direction. 'Her latest victim? Where's your wife? At home with the children? Pregnant, perhaps? Or maybe you're not married yet. Maybe your girlfriend is off planning your big day, oblivious to the likes of the lovely Jasmine here.'

'I'm Charlotte's boyfriend,' Rich said, calm and gentle. 'Charlie, why don't you take the boys, yeah?' He nodded, eager for her to comply.

They didn't move, clinging tighter to their mummy.

'Yeah, cos you're Mrs Perfect, aren't you?' Jasmine launched back at Sarah. 'I bet Grant doesn't know about your brush with infidelity, does he?'

It was Sarah's turn to look shocked and then she remembered something Charlie had said about sending Jas an email meant for her by mistake.

'He does, actually,' Grant said as he joined them.

He stared coldly into Jasmine's eyes, his chin high, his hands outstretched for Finn and Rudy as he drew level with his family.

Sarah looked at him quizzically.

'I read a text on your phone.' Grant looked at the ground.

'I'm sorry I lied, Grant,' Jasmine blurted out, ignorant of any other predicament but her own. 'About the termination.'

'Please go, Jasmine,' he said.

'But I needed to tell you about the baby. You w-wouldn't take my calls.'

'I understand that, but not here. Not now. Not at my children's christening! I'll ring you. Now please go.'

'But—'

'I've told you before, I love Sarah.'

Chapter Fifty-Five

Sarah

Two weeks later ...

'Are you sure about this, Sarah?' Marion asked as she scrubbed dough off the kitchen table.

'Marion, I've paid for the motorhome, three return tickets to Australia and the first night's accommodation in a hotel, so I think it's a bit late to be asking me that now.' I ran my finger down the list of things I had to do, checking they all had a tick against them.

'Just want you to be sure, that's all. A lot can happen in six months. It's like that song, what's it called? The one where he takes a little time to think things over. And then when he's had his fun and done his thinking and wants to come back to her, it's too late.'

'I didn't know you liked The Beautiful South. I love their songs.'

'Yes, well, anyway, you know what I'm saying.' Marion rinsed her cloth and slammed it on the drainer.

'I do. And thanks for being concerned, but I've got to do this.'

'I don't see what the difference is,' she said, briskly straightening ornaments along the windowsill. 'You were quite happy before that Jasmine turned up all pregnant. The only thing that's changed is that she's pregnant. It wasn't Grant's fault she lied about the termination.' She picked up her cloth again, dunked it in soapy water, wrung it out and attacked one of the worktops.

'I know, it's just that ... well, it changes things, doesn't it? All of a sudden the boys are going to have a half-brother or sister.' I stood up straight and concentrated on my breathing. I'd made a pact with myself that I definitely wouldn't cry any more. 'And Grant's not the sort to ignore a child, not his anyway. He won't be able to, and I wouldn't want him to. So rather than being able to forget what happened, Jasmine's going to be a permanent reminder in our lives.'

Marion stopped what she was doing and looked at me. 'I know ... I'm sorry.'

'I just need some special time with my boys, that's all, to work it all through in my head. Time with no rows, no housework, no baking and no bad moods ... just me and my children having fun. They deserve it after all we've been through.'

'I know you're right. I'm being selfish. Not sure what I'm going to do without you, that's all.' She swiped her cloth across a spotlessly clean work surface. 'You all right for money? I can help you out.'

'You're so lovely, Marion, but I'm all right, thanks. Had an emergency fund tucked away – some shares I've had since my finance days. Besides, with you and Theresa running SJ's, we should all be millionaires by the time I get back.'

'You'd better believe it. That woman runs me ragged.'

'I know, but don't let her know that. We don't want a Big Lass From The North uprising on our hands.'

Marion chuckled. 'Don't you worry. She might have her sights on my job, but I've got her well and truly under control.'

'You can still change your mind, you know?' I said, sneaking a glance at her expression, hoping there might be a flicker of indecision to work with.

'I know, thank you, my darling, but I've a way to go before I do anything as normal as leaving the country.' She looked at me, smiling. 'I said country, not county.'

'I once knew someone who went to that there Devon I did – reckless fool, they was. Didn't see 'em again!'

Marion flung a tea towel at me. 'I hope your Australian accent's better than your Cornish one. Just have a good time and get home safely to me.'

'We will. And if you change your mind, you can always fly out to meet us. I've got a feeling it's going to be quite an adventure.'

Chapter Fifty-Six

Jasmine

'Can't believe I did it, Dad.' Jasmine stripped away the leaves at the bottom of the lily stems and trimmed the ends with her shears. 'But I just had to try one last time, see if he loved me.'

She took out the metal pot and swilled it out with water from her Pepsi Max bottle.

'I thought about you and how unhappy you were. About how I wished we'd known you were desperate enough to kill yourself. So we could have told you that if a person is prepared to take his own life, then he's surely prepared to go to other extremes too. Like run away to the other side of the world and start again. We'd all have preferred that, Dad. We'd have been devastated, sure, but not as much as you denying us your company forever. You made me realise how important happiness is and that I shouldn't be afraid to try for what I want ... what's the worst that can happen?'

She put one of the lilies to her nose and breathed in the fragrance, one of the few smells that didn't make her feel nauseous these days.

'But I was wrong, Dad. I shouldn't have gone. I tried to poach someone else's happiness instead of finding my own. I've been doing that for years now, treading on other people's lives, but I'm not going to do it anymore.'

She put the stems through the holes in the urn, smelling each bloom before she poked it down.

'It was Rudy's face that did it. I know better than anyone what young fear feels like, yet there I was, inflicting it on two unsuspecting little boys who didn't deserve it. That won't happen again.'

She jiggled the lilies around and squeezed one more in.

'But you know what? I think I'm actually quite happy right now. I'm gonna be fine. Me and Elvis here are both gonna be fine.

The wind shook the trees, rattling a noisy crow from its perch.

'Oh, and the best news of all – Mum's moving abroad with her new hubby. Don't worry, he's not a patch on you, Dad, he's got hairy ears.' She pulled a face at the gravestone for her dad's benefit. 'Anyway, the good news bit is that she's sold the house and split the money between us. She said it's what you'd have wanted. Pretty nice of her, hey? She's even going to come and stay for a couple of days before she goes to America, and bring some old family photos, so I can get to know more about you. I think Mum's been possessed. And, wait for it ... I'm going to collect your picture from the art dealer this afternoon. The money from the house sale means I can buy it back, and pay off all my debts too. I'm so excited, I've got butterflies. I've learned my lesson though, Dad. It's not the material things that count – you taught me that. It's the hugs and kisses, and Elvis here will be getting plenty of those all right.' Jas rubbed her tummy protectively. She felt a swift kick below her ribs, right on cue. 'Ow! There you go, that was Elvis saying hello.' She paused for a moment. 'Makes me sad he'll never meet you. But we'll talk about you loads and we'll be strong together. I'll have someone to love again, and I'll never leave him. I don't blame you, Dad, you know that, but I won't put my baby through what I went through, and I think you'll be proud to hear me say that. So that's it, really.'

She sat back on her heels and paused.

'Oh, apart from I finally got my promotion at last – 'bout time. I think they're worried I won't go back after the baby's born, but there's no chance of that. Someone's gotta pay for Elvis's upkeep and I've heard babies are expensive pastimes. So, things are pretty good at the moment, really, apart from the fact I still haven't got anyone to share the sofa with at night ... and I've lost Charlie. Haven't come to terms with that one yet, so I'll keep you posted.'

She dragged herself up unceremoniously and gathered her belongings.

'Well, Dad, that's me.' She kissed her hand and touched it to his headstone. 'I love you, Dad. In a while, crocodile.'

···•••••···

Jasmine put her bags and belongings down while she fumbled to unlock her front door. It wasn't only her body that was taking a bashing from Elvis – her brain cells and coordination were under siege, too.

'Hi there.'

'Oh, hi.' She jumped as 6ft 2 inches of attractive male appeared from the door next to hers, like something out of a coffee advert.

'I'm your new neighbour. I moved in last weekend. Adam.' He thrust his hand out.

'Pleased to meet you, Adam. I'm Jasmine. 'Oh, and this is Elvis.' She pointed to her bump.

'Pleased to meet you, Elvis. Oh, sorry, I've got this for you.' He held out a small parcel. 'It came this morning. The postman asked if I'd sign for it, hope you don't mind.'

'God, no, that's fantastic, thanks. Such a fag if you have to go and collect it.'

'Oh, and I couldn't help noticing your Louis XVI rock crystal chandelier ... you can see it from the street. I wasn't snooping, it's just that you'd got the light on and the curtains open. You'd want to watch that – could be embarrassing.' He smiled an all-encompassing smile, lights dancing in his vivid blue eyes.

Jas smiled coyly.

'I take it it's not a real one,' Adam said.

'What? The bump?'

'No.' He was concentrating hard on not laughing. 'The chandelier.'

'God, no.' Jasmine was relieved. 'But I don't think I've ever met anyone who knows what it's called before.'

'Antique dealer. Listen, I've gotta go – got dinner in the oven – but if you and Elvis ever fancy a coffee sometime, just give me a knock and ...' He stopped speaking and stared at the floor where she'd propped her dad's picture against the wall. 'Jesus, is that a Millais?'

'You know your stuff, don't you?' Jasmine was impressed. 'Yes, it is,' she said like a proud parent.

He walked over and bent down next to the painting. 'Do you mind?'

'Go ahead.'

He peeled away the thin layer of bubble wrap. 'She's beautiful. It's the unnerving mix of innocence and tragedy in her expression ... makes you take stock, look at what really matters in life.'

Jasmine felt tears prickle at her eyes and nose, not sure whether they were tears of sadness or immense joy. 'Couldn't agree more.'

They turned to their respective doors.

'Oh, Adam, before you go ...'

'Yeah?'

'Do you have a wife?'

'No, no wife.'

'Girlfriend?'

'Nope, totally girlfriendless, as of six months ago.'

'So you're single, then?'

'Yep, footloose and fancy-free ... at the moment, anyway.' He smiled and closed his door behind him.

Jasmine unwrapped the parcel he'd handed her.

Inside was a nest of five brightly painted Russian dolls and a note: *Ring Me. Charlie xxx*

She looked up and smiled humbly, thanking someone her dad had never met, the God of Second Chances.

Chapter Fifty-Seven

Charlotte

'Sorry I'm late, babe.'

Rich let himself in and headed straight for Charlotte. He wrapped his arms around her and kissed her, holding her tight to him. He pulled away, gently lifting her hair and kissing her neck.

'I know I said I'd be back for eight, but I got caught up with Professor Jordan, and then the Botley Road was jammed.' He adjusted himself, his enthusiastic hard-on tight against his trousers. He put his briefcase behind the door and loosened his tie.

Charlotte thought for the fiftieth time that week how sexy Rich was and marvelled at how statuesque he looked in her low-ceilinged kitchen, like a Roman Emperor back from a hard day's ruling. It was good to have a proper man around the house at last, even if it was only for a few more days.

'Oh no. I bet you're knackered. I've got a lamb curry on the hob, are you hungry?' she asked, smiling.

'*Mmm*, you bet. Smells great. You don't have to cook for me, you know.'

'I know, but I love it. It's been so good having you here. It feels like we've stepped into domestic bliss. I like it.' She busied herself stirring the curry. Every time she thought about Rich leaving, a mini-Maori punched her hard inside. 'Just a week left now,' she said, stirring faster. 'Have you booked your ticket yet?'

She moved over to the naan bread, arranging it perfectly on the grill pan, anything but watch Rich form the words she'd been dreading for the last two weeks and face the reality of him leaving.

'I booked it today. The clinic have been baying for my blood the last three days – I couldn't put if off any longer. I leave next Friday.'

Charlotte smiled reluctantly, unable to speak for fear of blubbing over the poppadums. No one likes a soggy poppadum.

Rich crossed the room to his briefcase. 'I wasn't going to give you this until later, but I can't wait any longer.'

Charlotte gently unravelled the bow and ripped into the paper. Her eyes lit up. It was a Filofax. No one had ever bought her a Filofax before, apart from her mum all those years ago, of course. It was proof he truly knew her, cared about her enough to think hard about the perfect present.

'It's beautiful.'

She put it to her face to feel the soft hide. It was made from mint-green leather with pearly-white stitching around the edges, and an elegant metal clasp held together by a tiny gold padlock and two tiny gold keys. She'd never seen a Filofax with a lock before. She looked up at Rich.

'Open it,' he urged.

Inside was a list:

Rich Fisher's Short-term To-dos

- *Help Charlotte to love herself as much as I love her*

- *Spend every day for the rest of my life with Charlotte*

- *Have children with Charlotte (two boys, one girl, preferably)*

- *Live in Australia with Charlotte*

- *Marry Charlotte*

- *Own a Bugatti Veyron EB 16.4 in grey-blue metallic with grigio trim (OK, so maybe this one might need to be on the long-term to-dos)*

PTO.

Charlotte swallowed hard as she graciously obeyed and turned the page:

Charlotte, will you marry me?

(If you say no, I'll understand. If it's too soon, I'll understand. If it is too soon, perhaps you'll come to Australia with me. Please? That's categorically not begging, by the way – merely optimism.)

She read the words again, frightened they'd disappear if she didn't. She turned to look at Rich. He was down on one knee, a ring in his hand, smiling nervously.

He took a deep breath. 'Charlotte Bloom. Will you marry me?'

Charlotte blinked. 'Rich Fisher. I most certainly will.'

The End

James Martin's Sticky Toffee Pudding with Toffee Sauce

SERVES 6-8

75g soft butter

175g dark brown demerara sugar

200g self-raising flour, plus extra for dusting

1tbsp golden syrup

2 tbsp black trecle

2 eggs

1 tsp vanilla extract

200g pitted dried dates

1tbsp bicarbonate of soda

FOR THE TOFFEE SAUCE

100g sugar

100g butter

200ml double cream

Preheat the oven to 200°C/400°F/Gas mark 6. Grease a 23cm tin thoroughly with 25g of the butter, then dust the inside of the tin with flour.

Using a food mixer, blend the remaining butter and sugar together. Slowly add the golden syrup, treacle, eggs and vanilla extract to the butter mixture and continue mixing. Turn the mixer down to a slow speed and then add the flour. Once all the ingredients are combined, turn off the mixer.

Place the dates in a saucepan with 300ml water and bring to the boil. Purée the water and date mixture and add the bicarbonate of soda. While it is still hot, quickly add this mixture to the egg mix. Once the mix is combined, pour into the prepared tin and bake for 40-45 minutes until the top is just firm to touch.

Remove the pudding from the oven and allow to cool, then turn out of the tin and cut into squares.

To make the sauce, melt the butter and sugar together in a small pan, add the cream and bring to the boil. Simmer for a few minutes until the sauce reaches a desired consistency.

To serve, reheat the sponge in a microwave or heat for 5 minutes in the oven at 180°C/350°F/Gas mark 4. Place onto a plate with lots of sauce on top and a scoop of vanilla ice cream if you wish.

The sponge and sauce can be made in advance. The sponge can even be frozen and both can be plated up and reheated in the microwave.

Taken from James Martin's *Desserts* published by Quadrille, *2007*.

If you enjoyed this book from Poolbeg why not grab your next page-turner?

www.poolbeg.com

FAST DELIVERY – All books despatched within 24 hours

FREE SHIPPING – on orders over €20 in Rep. of Ireland!*

Whether it's for you or a friend, we've got your next story waiting.

Exclusive offers, new releases – and more from poolbeg.com

FOLLOW US ON SOCIAL MEDIA:

 @PoolbegBooks

 @poolbegbooks

 facebook.com/poolbegpress

*Free delivery on Rep. of Ireland orders over €20 and UK orders over €60.